The Queen's Keeper

Praise for The Queen's Keeper:

"I found this book very interesting. I couldn't put it down. ...action, romance, mystery, suspense...it's all there!!"

"If, like me, fantasy is one of your genres of choice, you'll be delighted by this novel. Highly magical, incredibly creative, and with a couple of deep messages that are particularly important in today's sometimes callous world: be kind to yourself--there is worth and purpose for every individual, and that we choose every day to either follow a path that is light, or to submit to the dark. The best compliment I can give a book is that I didn't want to put it down--and that is definitely true of this one."

"I couldn't put the book down... She has done a beautiful job setting up an intricate and layered story line with characters from the fantasy genre that had me rooting for them, and left me with wanting to know more... True to the fantasy genre, this was a book that allowed me to escape to a world of the unknown."

"I was hooked from the first page. I literally could not put it down. That doesn't happen to me very often. The storyline is very compelling!"

"I read a lot of fantasy books, so I figured I'd like this one - it sounded interesting enough, so I purchased it for a long plane trip. I ended up being so into it that I barely noticed the hours pass! I particularly loved Luvenia's character development because she frustrated me often. Her growth over the course of the book was refreshingly normal (she didn't all of a sudden become this perfect, strong, unwavering heroine) and I felt personally invested in her story."

From The Author:

To subscribe to my mailing list and receive monthly updates, freebies, and exclusive info, sign up on my website jlvampa.com.

I absolutely ADORE chatting with my readers, so feel free to email me at vampajl@gmail.com and follow me on
Instagram : WickedVampa
Goodreads: J.L. Vampa

You can also find TQK merch (and so many other fandoms) at WickedWhimsyBoutique.com

Christa -
May you never
forget your worth.

The Queen's Keeper

Prey, you should've been ready.

J.L. VAMPA

THE QUEEN'S KEEPER

For information contact:
http://www.jlvampa.com
vampajl@gmail.com Attn : Inquiries

Cover design by Isabella Hansen Instagram.com/arrtslave

ISBN: 978-0-578-45147-3

First Edition: September 2018
Second Edition: April 2019
Complete Edition: October 2021

To my Mama—
For showing me what true strength is.

To my husband, Jac—
For never ceasing to believe in me.

To Mr. Tramel—
For fanning the embers of my author heart into flame in the produce aisle of a grocery store eleven years ago.

Many Moons Ago

An ancient woman hobbled along a moonlit path, bent over her cane toward a cottage. She looked cautiously over her shoulder every few paces, for what she'd come to tell the young couple within that summer cottage could not be overheard. The crone reached the veranda and thumped the carved handle of her cane upon the wooden door, adjusting her cowl as she waited for the answer to her knock.

A vibrant young woman opened the door, spilling soft candlelight upon the darkened ground. Confusion knit her brows together as she held the remnant of her waning candle up to better view the visitor. "Might I be of assistance to you, madam?"

The weathered stranger glanced over her shoulder once more and whispered urgently, "You must let me in at once."

The woman followed where her guest's eyes had glanced with concern. "Certainly, come in." She ushered the woman inside, taking a moment to peer into the dark tree line before closing and bolting the door.

"Should I be concerned, madam? Are you in danger?"

"I am being followed. They mustn't know I'm here. No one must know that I'm here," the woman rasped.

"Why have you come? Is it protection you seek? My husband shall return shortly, he's only gone to feed the horses.

The old woman's eyes flashed. "I haven't time to wait for

him. This is urgent." She drew nearer and said with deep conviction in her voice, "You are with child, and you will bear a son. You shall name him Matthias. Only the two of you must know this child is the seed of you and your husband. No one else can know."

The young woman backed away, frightened, until she was pressed firmly against the closed door. "Who are you? How could you say such a thing? I only just discovered I was with child. I've not even told my husband yet." Her hands began to tremble. "Are you a sorceress? An oracle?"

"I am of wind and light, it matters not who I am," the woman began to explain until her attention snapped to the midsummer night beyond the closed cottage door. "I haven't time," she whispered urgently. "They're coming. Here." she took the young lady's hand and dropped a glowing, violet orb into her palm. "This will tell you all you need to know. Hide it. Quickly. I was never here."

The young mother peered at the orb in her hand, speechless, as the woman hobbled quickly away.

Turning back just before the edge of the room the crone warned, "Remember. No one must know," and disappeared out into the darkened forest.

No sooner had she vanished, did a banging sound at the door, shaking the already trembling woman still leaning against it. With a gasp, she hid the orb within the folds of her skirts and unbolted the lock.

Chapter One

The guard standing post outside the throne room of Her Majesty, Queen Lilith Pietro, entered with a swift knock and a low bow.

"Your Majesty, the Chief Collector is here to see you. He claims it is urgent."

"Very well. Send him in." The queen sat perched upon her gold and ebony throne, returning her attention to one of her courtiers, Sebastian Olliander.

The Collector pushed past the guards standing post and entered the throne room briskly. He wore the form-fitting, black leather uniform and matching mask of the queen's Horde, but his mask did not conceal the entirety of his head as the others' did. The Chief Collector was the only Collector permitted to use his mouth to speak. He peered at his queen with unseen eyes, through the mask's thick steel and obsidian goggles while he dragged a struggling man in tow, his strength nearly inhuman.

Queen Lilith lifted a curious brow as she beheld the gagged peasant in front of her. When the captive's eyes met

hers, he began thrashing desperately. The Collector dropped the knife in his hand to the marble floor and reached for the pack upon his back, taking one of the two tentacle tubes attached to it. Putrid green Venom dripped from the needle-pointed end as he thrust it deep into the struggling man's neck, paralyzing him instantly—eyes wide.

Captive subdued, the Collector turned back to his queen and bowed deeply. "Your Majesty."

"Speak," she responded dryly—all edges and petrifying perfection, like a siren luring in prey with her beauty, only to devour it with her fangs.

"This urchin has been on the Watch List for three years." The Chief Collector glanced insidiously at his captive. "He was found today giving bread to those turned away at the Royal Market."

"Dungeon," the queen ordered with a flippant flick of her wrist as she turned back to Sebastian, touching the lapel of his coat sensually.

"Your Majesty," the Collector spoke again.

The grim ruler turned back to him, a snake poised to strike, irritated by an intrusion over such a common infraction. Before she could snap at him for being so insolent, the Chief Collector ripped open the paralyzed man's shirt to reveal the angry red Mark of the Zealots branded on such citizens by the queen's men.

"He failed to don the Mark on his clothing, Your Highness." A savage smile slowly spread across the queen's blood red lips. She looked into the captive's pleading eyes with mock sympathy as she hissed, "In that case, I shall acquire a new head for my collection."

With the sickening slice of a sword, a bloody head rolled to the ground in front of the queen basking in the stench of terror.

Reading on the portico of her family's dilapidated farm cottage, a slight movement caught Luvenia's eye. Startled, she instinctively grabbed the knife she kept tucked into her boot and turned defensively toward the movement. She saw nothing. Not even the wheat in the fields or the grass of the meadow swayed.

Adrenaline pumping, she thought to call for her mother—who was inside obliviously skinning potatoes—to bolt the doors, but she dared not make a sound. She moved swiftly to hide behind the stone pillar she'd just been leaning on and peeked around the side. Still, she saw nothing.

Perhaps it was only my imagination.

She had been irrationally out of sorts lately, with all that had happened in Orford. But how could she not be as people were being taken left and right? The last ten years had been a disaster, but more and more were taken every day.

This is it ...it's finally our turn.

Refusing to go down without a fight, Luvenia ran silently from a pillar to the window, avoiding the loose stones she'd memorized and rehearsed mercilessly with her mother and sister, Ester. They pretended to humor her, but she knew they thought she'd lost her mind. Luvenia had told them countless times that they needed to know their grounds inside and out—every clanging rock step, every hidden alcove, and every inconspicuous weapon.

"You are your first line of defense," she reminded them daily.

She'd known someday she would be proven right concerning her paranoia, and all of the things she'd learned from her father would come in handy, but never had it crossed her mind that it would be this day when she awoke to a bright, windless autumn morning.

I should've been ready.

The window she hunched under, aged knife in both hands, peered directly into their living area. The room had two large windows on the adjacent side, one of which looked straight into the kitchen where she knew her mother was sitting with those blasted potatoes. Her back was most likely to the window, no matter how many times Luvenia told her to never put her back to a passageway out.

If someone were on that side of the house, attempting to watch them, she should be able to see them if she could will herself to raise her eyes above the windowsill. It was how she would spy on them, were it her. With a sudden surge of courage, Luvenia peered into the window, her heart pounding.

She saw nothing out of the ordinary. She hunched back down, believing it all to be in her imagination again, when she heard the sound once more, this time behind her. Luvenia shot up, only to see absolute stillness. Until, just in the distance, she saw the tall grass swaying unnaturally. She began backing toward the front door as quickly as she dared when she saw it.

Bounding out of the grass raced a large family of rabbits.

Luvenia sagged with relief and chuckled at herself for being so foolish. She shoved her knife back into her boot, her heart still dislodging itself from her throat.

"Maybe you truly are unbalanced after all, Veni," she told herself as her pulse slowed. "How did you tiny creatures cause such a large fuss?"

She descended the front steps of the portico, headed to play with the adorable little intruders. Two steps down, she heard a distinctive hoot coming from the stables. The Great Horned Owl had spotted the rabbits where they'd stopped to nibble the bit of lettuce. Silently, majestically, the beast of a bird soared overhead. It wasn't frightened of Luvenia. It had protected their land from crop miscreants since before she could remember, and it knew them well. She shooed the rabbits away and they hopped back toward the tall meadow. The smallest lagged behind and the owl swooped down for the kill.

Luvenia winced.

Well, he must eat, too, she decided as she shrugged.

She began to walk back to the house and stopped abruptly

when a morbid thought struck her. A small, humorless laugh escaped through her nose.

How poetic? I suppose today was someone’s turn.

Prey, you should’ve been ready. The time has come for Collecting. Food for the strong. Death for the weak

Chapter Two

Luvenia had been inside the house for only a few moments, listening to her mother tell of a loose chicken escapade that had occurred earlier that morning in the small market across their village, when the back door slammed shut. She jumped and reached for her boot, but her mother's words stopped her.

"Oh, stop being so excitable, Luvenia, I'm certain it's only Ester. Ester, we're in the kitchen!" she called.

Luvenia shot her mother a glare she instantly knew she would regret and whispered harshly, "Perfect. Announce to the entire village where we are, will you? How many times do I have to explain—"

Mid-sentence she was scooped up from behind, whirled around, and thrown over a big, burly shoulder in half an instant. Wailing and kicking, she caught a glimpse of her mother's face while upside down, beaming with excitement.

Jacob is home.

"Calm down, Veni. It's me! You think I was Collecting you or somethin'?"

"The Collectors are not a joke, Jake. Some of us actually take this seriously." She knew she was beet red from all the blood rushing to her head, "Now put me down!"

Jacob flipped Luvenia all the way around and dropped her onto her feet to face him. Her head spun and she was certain she would have fallen flat on her face if he wasn't such a giant of a man.

A man? When did my taffy haired, reckless elder brother

turn into an adult?

But they had all grown up in recent years, even more so in recent days. Reckless was still an accurate description of her brother, if you asked her. Luvenia knew she should have known it was him. She'd rigged the back door several months ago to make a dragging sound across the floor if you did not hold it up while opening it. Her mother, Jake, and Ester had all obliged and avoided the drag, although Ester struggled with it. The door hadn't made a peep until it slammed shut. She needed to be more alert.

"Where have you been, Jake? It's been four months," she spat at him, leaving her self-berating for the time being. "Last we heard, you were headed to the Miller farm for a few days to help Meredith. Now you've come back four months later all jests and smiles?"

Luvenia realized she was being too accusatory. They'd known he was fine—foolish, but fine—and she'd known where he was. But he did not have to know that at the moment. Jake couldn't get a word out to defend himself before their mother jumped to his defense and gave Luvenia away.

"Luvi, rein in your temper. Is that how you greet your brother after months of complaining about how badly you wish he were home?" She turned to her son, "Jake, we knew where you were or you can be certain I'd have had two missing children with this one," she threw a thumb in Luvenia's direction, "assuming the worst and combing the lands looking for you."

"Miss me that much, Veni?" Jake gave her an impish smile that made her want to punch him in his arm. She did.

Though she couldn't help but half-grin herself. Remembering she was still angry, Luvenia picked at her nails and continued her chastising. "I assumed Meredith's family ended up on the Collection List when you didn't show after several days. I went to their farm and Meredith told me she hadn't seen you in ages. That's when I knew what you'd done. *Fool.*" She spat the last word, shaking her head and dropping into a seat at the kitchen table.

"I went to the Annex and convinced them to look at the Enlist Records for your name, but it wasn't there. I realized you may have been intelligent enough to enlist elsewhere, so I traveled to five towns searching Enlist Records until I found your name on the Elkshire list. Why would you do something so *absurd*, Jake?"

"Absurd? Or are you merely upset you didn't think of it first?" His face was casual, but his eyes were full of regret and something that rivaled fear.

"What do you mean? That's preposterous. I would never Enlist to fight for that she-demon coward." She could feel the heat rising to her ears. Luvenia had never been very good at reining in her temper.

"*Luvenia*!" their mother shouted. "You two cease your squabbling this instant. Luvi, you cannot go around saying things like that or you'll get us all Collected immediately."

Luvenia folded her arms with a huff and gritted her teeth but obeyed in silence.

"Mother, Veni—" Jacob stalled and glanced over his shoulder.

Luvenia followed where his eyes went, wondering at his caution.

He continued in a hushed tone. "Our farm is failing. We have little left to trade with and we *need* the Royal Vouchers. Even so, food and clothing aside, I did this for protection. The last place the Collectors will come to is the farm of one of their own."

Luvenia was stunned and felt like the earth was shifting beneath her chair. She opened her mouth to ask the question, but their mother beat her to it.

"Wait. You're..." she stammered and stood. "You're one of *them*? I thought you merely enlisted in Pietro's infantry!

It's only been four months. How did you advance from Warmonger to Collector so quickly?" She trailed off and dropped back into her chair, horrified.

Jake pinched the bridge of his nose with thumb and forefinger. "I achieved provision and immunity for our family, and *this* is how you thank me?"

He was being far too defensive. Luvenia could see the contrition. He knew what he'd done wasn't right.

She reached past her anger and shock to grasp the calmest tone she could possibly muster. "There is no immunity, Jake. They will come here to ensure you are what you say you are—" She cut herself off. Saying it out loud made it real and she knew panic would soon set in.

Jake's face had gone vicious and stern—a look that she'd never seen cross his usually jovial face. "They won't come here. I gave them the wrong location on my records anyway. I've thought this through, Veni."

But he hadn't. She knew he didn't realize what he'd done. He'd laid them out for slaughter.

Chapter Three

Luvenia woke the next morning later than usual. Typically, she rose before dawn, unable to sleep due to the nightmares that had plagued her for the last nine years. On that particular morning, however, she felt refreshed and could not recall a single bad dream.

She supposed the shock of Jacob's return and his news must have worn her mind out enough for her to sleep soundly for a change. Amusing, considering she purposefully ran herself into exhaustion every single day, attempting to silence the nightmares with deep sleep. It had never worked, though she insisted one day it eventually would.

The freshness she felt from the uninterrupted rest left her in an abnormally pleasant mood and she decided to forego her first run of the day. Luvenia slowly made her way downstairs and into the kitchen of their small cottage, her belly rumbling with hunger. Upon entering the kitchen, she found her sister giggling madly over some silly face Jacob had made. Luvenia smiled. It was wonderful to have him home, even if it was only for a short time and even if he was a traitor. His intentions were noble, she supposed.

Not wanting to think about any of that and ruin her good mood, she joined them at the table.

"Morning Veni." Ester beamed at her.

"Morning, Sunshine." She kissed the top of the young girl's head as she sat, looking up to catch Jacob staring at her. "What?" She made a disgusted face at him.

"You've just grown up so much, Veni." He shook his head

and reached to serve himself more porridge, scooping some into a bowl for Luvenia too.

She looked at her brother quizzically. "Is that *sentiment* I detect in your voice, Jacob Rousseau? I would have thought Pietro would fashion you into a brooding monster, not a sentimental ninny." She smiled at him playfully. Ester giggled, her strawberry curls bouncing.

"Hush and eat your food, you worm," he muttered.

"Ah. That's better." Luvenia was surprised by how content she felt with Jacob home, despite the dread still curling in her belly over what he'd done.

Their mother rushed in the side kitchen door just then, juggling baskets full of items from the village market. Luvenia jumped up to help her. She did not offer so much as a *hello* from her before she lit into all three of her children.

"One of the goats got out. And why exactly has no one fed the horses?" She slammed her baskets on the table, sending a tomato rolling to the ground, and whirled to face them with a fist on her slender hip.

They knew better than to answer. It was best to just let her say her piece. Luvenia wondered inwardly how she could even know the horses hadn't been fed when she'd been to market since dawn.

"Gulliver gnawed a chunk out of his stall door, that's how I know!" Luvenia and Jacob looked at each other, and she tried not to laugh at their mother answering her silent question. Gulliver was Jake's ornery but loyal mount.

"They should have been fed ages ago! One of you get your tail out there right this instant and feed those horses *now* before you have to cut a new stall door instead! The other of you, go find that wandering goat. Ester, start snapping these green beans." Genevieve Rousseau certainly knew how to command a room. She radiated love for her children, but she most assuredly did not lack authority. She couldn't be too lenient, not while raising three children on her own.

With that, she donned her apron and set to chopping vegetables. Her two older children headed outside, barely making it to the back porch before they let their laughter escape.

"Welcome home," Luvenia said chuckling.

"I must say, I truly did miss our mother, fussing and all." Jacob headed toward the stables. "You get that foolish goat. I haven't said hello to Gulliver and the other horses yet."

Luvenia sighed. A goat was always getting out of the fence, usually Puck. They only had three, as Orford was still in famine. The citizens had done their best to revive what they could of their farms and shops, somewhat succeeding as long as the queen kept busy elsewhere.

The best place to begin looking for Puck was always the strawberry patch. Three years ago, there was only one small strawberry plant left in all of Orford. It had grown wild in the Rellum Forest and was found and uprooted by Weiland Cornick. He planted it on his land and soon became a wealthy man, by Orford Commoner standards, anyway. As soon as Queen Pietro found out, Cornick ended up on the Watch List and soon an unfortunate fire broke out, wiping out his entire farm—clearly an *accident.*

The entire Cornick family had since been Collected. Though, before all of that, Luvenia traded for one of those rare strawberries for Ester's sixth birthday. She had wrapped it in a scrap of parchment paper and tied a bow around it with the pink ribbon she'd worn as a child. Ester was beside herself with glee as she'd never tasted a strawberry. She wanted to share it with Luvenia, since she hadn't had one herself since before the war, but Luvenia refused. Ester took one nibble to discover the flavor and promptly ran away. Luvenia followed her to discover she'd planned to plant the strawberry and make her own strawberry patch.

Ester dug a little hole with her shovel, smelled the sweet

aroma of her birthday gift one last time, and put it in the hole, covering it with dirt.

She turned proudly to Luvenia. "Now we'll have many strawberries, and we can have coin like Farmer Cornick. We won't have to trade our freedom for food, like you said Pietro forces people to do."

Luvenia shook her head in surprise. "You never cease to amaze me, my little Sunshine."

"Sometimes something has to die to bring new life. Right, Veni? That's what you taught me." Ester beamed at her elder sister.

And with that memory, the ever-present gaping hole in Luvenia's chest opened wide, threatening to swallow her whole as it brought another memory to the surface.

"Why do we plant seeds, Father?"

Luvenia had awoken early that morning to help her father plant wheat in their field. A curious girl of only four, she wanted to learn everything her father knew.

"So it will grow, of course." He wiped the sweat from his brow, leaving a streak of dirt across his tanned face.

"But seeds aren't wheat. They look different. It doesn't make any sense," she said, quite sure of herself.

Henry Rousseau chuckled at his daughter's self-assurance, as if he were the foolish one and she were the one with it all figured out. "Plants come from seeds, Love." He held one up to her. "The outside of this seed will die, protecting the life within it, which will in turn bring life to the wheat. Sometimes something must die in order to bring new life, Love. Remember that." He ruffled her hair and plopped the seed into her hand.

The memory left Luvenia short of breath and she willed her tears away. The memories of her father that snuck up on her were the most difficult. He'd been dead almost ten years, but the raw pain in her soul never ceased. She had taken it the hardest.

Luvenia thought she would die of grief and guilt until Ester arrived alone at their door a few weeks later, swaddled in a basket, asleep despite the cold. She'd begun helping her mother care for the tiny child that quickly became a very welcome distraction they all fell in love with immediately. Sometimes Luvenia dared to think that maybe, just maybe, Ester had been brought to her family to ease their pain.

Unwilling to think on her father or her despair and guilt any longer, Luvenia pushed off the tree she hadn't realized she'd stopped to lean against and trudged on to find the missing goat. She reached the small strawberry patch to find the escaped goat had opened the white picket gate and was gnawing on the twine, of all things, that held the *Ester's Berries* sign to the fence.

She sighed and repaired the sign Ester had so painstakingly painted. "Strawberries galore and you find twine. You really are an imbecile, Puck. They won't be around much longer with the first frost coming soon."

Luvenia laughed slightly, trying to let the silly goat's antics drive away the familiar dark cloud from her mind to no avail.

"Come on, you." She led Puck back across their land to the goat pen.

Once she had him safely returned, she patted him on the head and ambled to the barn to retrieve the goats' food. As she filled a pail, the familiar Great Horned Owl swooped in and perched on a haystack behind the chicken feed, looking her right in her face.

"Hullo there, Owl. Did you enjoy your little rabbit yesterday? You know his family is missing him now, don't you?" The owl simply blinked at her and turned his head ever so slightly, obviously unconcerned by his choice in meals.

"You know," she mused, "After all these years, I should

give you a proper name."

The owl screeched, offended, and ruffled his feathers.

Luvenia chuckled, "Owl it remains, then." To this, the regal owl gave a soft, satisfied hoot and flew away. She smiled and grabbed her feed pail.

Just then, she heard the scuffle of feet. She opened her mouth to call out to see who was there, then cursed herself for almost being so foolish again. One night of sweet sleep and her brother coming home did not mean it wasn't still Pietro's Orford. There were still Collectors everywhere you turned and the Watch List to stay off of. Their strawberry patch—which they had to be very careful to hide and sell from secretly—already made them a target. Now Jacob had made them an even greater target. She had to be more careful. She set down her pail and silently made her way to peer through a slit in the wood.

Luvenia sighed with relief. It was only Jacob standing in Gulliver's empty stall. But as she was about to go around to greet Jake, she saw him put his hands on his knees and let out a deep, shaky breath. He leaned back against the side of the stall and slowly slid down to the ground, hugging his knees like a child. She watched in mute confusion as her elder brother buried his face in his hands and began sobbing.

Luvenia was at a loss for what to do. Should she go comfort him? He obviously wanted to be alone, or he wouldn't have come to hide in a horse stall. She felt like an intruder. He used to talk to her about everything, from Meredith to the loss of their father. She was certain he would come find her to talk once he'd had some time to collect his thoughts. She decided to leave him alone and finish her duties so she could freely talk with him when he was ready.

The rest of the morning and early afternoon went by quickly while she fed their animals, collected the few eggs the chickens had laid, tilled a small section of land to plant radishes, and helped her mother hang out the washed clothing. Luvenia enjoyed the hard work that came with their small farm. It kept her mind busy and her body in reasonable shape, if even a bit too girlish and thin for lack of enough food.

She used to find her father conditioning his body with sword work even after a hard day on the farm. Luvenia and Jacob would attempt to mimic him with sticks, which inevitably resulted in their father's rumbling laughter, simple lessons in the art of sword-wielding, and playful tumbling in the grass.

That is, until their mother would call them in for supper or threaten to make them wash their own grass stains out of their clothes if they didn't cease their scuffling immediately. They were empty threats Henry Rousseau always met with attacks of kisses that made his wife squeal and swat at him with her kitchen towel as he chased her inside.

Luvenia smiled at the memory. Thankfully they didn't all debilitate her.

Henry and Genevieve Rousseau had certainly loved each other madly. Her mother still wore her wedding band almost ten years after her husband’s death and spoke of him every day. Sometimes Luvenia would hear her mother weeping in the night or talking to the other side of the bed as if he were still lying beside her. Luvenia knew her mother felt the loss just as profoundly as in the first days, no matter how much time had passed. They'd been inseparable since they were children, and one does not carry on easily after a break in a bond that is so deeply rooted.

Everyone had always told Luvenia she was just like her father, but she knew she had a great deal of her mother's heart in her too. That, and their resemblance was uncanny with their chestnut brown hair—a wild mix of waves and curls. Which also meant they both had a mess to contend with every morning. Luvenia usually pinned hers up into a simple twist at the nape of her neck, though one or two stray curls inevitably always came loose, framing her face. Neither Luvenia nor her mother were particularly stunning, but their full lips and emerald eyes with flecks of amber sprinkled in made up for their otherwise fairly plain features.

While Luvenia helped her mother hang the washed clothing, Genevieve had once again encouraged her daughter to go with her on trips to the village market. She insisted Luvenia needed some friends besides goats and an old barn owl. When her suggestion was once again met with eye rolls and sighs, Genevieve left well enough alone.

The last pair of Jacob's pants hung on the line, Luvenia followed her mother into the house for lunch. Rounding the corner into the kitchen, they were both hit with the flying green bean ends Ester had snapped off that morning. Ester ducked behind the table, as if they could not see her, and Jake hid behind the open pantry door. They both snickered, knowing they weren't the slightest bit sneaky.

Their mother lifted one finger to her lips, looking at Luvenia, and motioned toward the bowl of cherry tomatoes on the counter next to her. They each grabbed one and waited silently. Jake and Ester popped their heads out of hiding at almost the same moment and were each met with a tomato square to the forehead. Luvenia and her mother were both very accurate shots. Henry Rousseau had taught his girls well how to aim.

They all laughed and went for the table to sit. "Jake, grab those tomatoes and rinse them off in the basin. We can't waste perfectly good food," Genevieve told him.

Together, they enjoyed their meager midday meal of tomatoes, green beans, stale bread, and a sliver of cheese split four ways—though Luvenia slipped her cheese to Ester under the table. Their stomachs were not always full, but they had each other and that was enough. A plate full of savory meat in somber solitude couldn’t compare to a nibble of cheese shared in love around their old wooden table. If Luvenia had to choose between working hard for a little and having abundance from the hand of Pietro, she would choose the little—every time.

When they finished, Ester asked if she could ride with Luvenia to gather water from the well. She of course told her yes, and invited Jacob to join them.

"Nah. I think I'm going to go see Meredith. I have some explaining to do," he told her, half smiling, half grimacing.

Luvenia and Ester grabbed an apple to share along the way, saddled their horses, and leisurely rode the distance to their well, Ester jabbering the entire way.

"Milly is such a good pony, don't you think, Veni? She does eat all the wildflowers, though, silly pony. There are hardly any to enjoy looking at and she goes and eats them all! Autumn leaves are certainly pretty, but I prefer spring flowers, even if there are only a few. Remember when everything was just rotted and brown? I know I was just little, but I remember. I'm big now, but I still remember. I didn't know what a flower was until I was five! Do you brush Peony's tail every day? Mother says I should brush Milly's every day, but she swings it so much she hits me in the face! I'm so happy Brother is home. Aren't you, Veni?"

Realizing the girl had ceased talking long enough to desire a response, Luvenia answered her sister. "Yes, I remember very well the rot. Yes, I do brush Peony's tail every day. You need to hold Milly's tail while you brush it, so she can't swat you with it. And yes, I'm glad Jake is home. You do know that he has to return back to training soon right, Sunshine? He's just home on leave, which is like a festival break for the Warmongers." She answered the chattering girl's many questions in one fell swoop, quite used to doing so.

The little girl sighed and lifted her freckled face to soak up the sun and feel the crisp breeze on her cheeks. "Yes, I know.

I don't want to him to go."

"I know, neither do I. I'll miss him too."

Ester looked at her sister, "Oh, it's not only that...it's just...he's different, like they changed him. I don't like it."

Luvenia shifted in her saddle and pulled the reins for Peony to stop. Ester noticed and did the same with Milly.

"What do you mean, Ester?" She'd always been so intuitive, sometimes alarmingly so. This particular insight curdled the dread in Luvenia's gut that she'd been suppressing.

The little girl blushed. "I saw him pacing in the meadow earlier. He seemed upset, so I offered him a hug and he snapped at me. He told me to go away." Ester shrugged. "I started to cry and ran to tell Mother, but he ran after me and said he was sorry. He said we'd throw the green beans at you and Mother when you came in for lunch." She kicked Milly's sides and set off toward the well again, evidently wanting to leave that subject of discussion behind.

Luvenia followed, leaves crunching beneath their horses' hooves, though she was still disturbed by what Ester had told her. Jacob had never been harsh with Ester, even when she was pestering him or asking countless questions. Luvenia hadn't always been so patient, but Jake was. Something was definitely awry. Surely, he would talk with her once he returned from visiting Meredith and their mother and Ester had gone to bed. She could wait a few more hours.

The sisters returned to their house with the water containers just in time for Luvenia's evening run before dinner. She kissed Ester's cheek after depositing the water on the porch and went up to her room to change out of her simple work dress into the fitted cotton pants her mother had made for her out of a pair of her father's old trousers. No other woman in their village, or even Alban, wore pants very often, but Luvenia wasn't exactly an average woman, nor had her mother ever forced her to be. She unwound her hair and wove it into a braid as she headed back outside.

She ran the perimeter of their land taking in the wondrous colors of autumn. Luvenia loved this season most, even if it held the hardest memories for her. For some reason, she'd always been drawn to the bittersweet things in life. Maybe it made her feel safe, to always see things with a shred of despair mingled in—something she often thought she was very possibly unbalanced for thinking. Though to her, it meant she could look upon the beautiful, yet remain prepared for the next tragedy without being either blindly joyful or crushed by disaster when it inevitably struck. Her mother always told her that was a mindset capable of leading to self-destruction. She told her repeatedly to either be hot or cold, never lukewarm, and to always find the beauty in things.

"Goodness and beauty are always there, Luvi, *always*. You simply have to find them."

Luvenia never took her mother's comments seriously, knowing full well she should.

She returned from her twilight run to the aroma of baked chicken tickling her nose. Huffing, she made her way inside, heading directly for the kitchen. She plopped down at the table, unwilling to wait until after bathing to enjoy the rarity that was chicken. She ripped off a leg and bit into it, savoring the delicious flavor.

"Manners, Luvi, *please*," her mother chirped as chicken grease dribbled down Luvenia's chin.

"Sorry," she mumbled around a mouth full of chicken, causing Ester to fall into a fit of giggles.

Jacob strode in, whistling a tune their father used to sing to them as young children. He gave each of the girls a kiss on the cheek, grabbed a plate and dug in. If anyone besides Luvenia was confused by his back-and-forth behavior, no one showed it.

After dinner, Genevieve ushered a protesting Ester upstairs for a bath. Luvenia cleared the table as Jacob tended to the fire in the sitting room. The autumn air had chilled considerably with the setting sun. The rest of the evening came and went with simple conversations in front of the fire and the reading of books until sleep claimed them one by one and they padded drowsily to bed—without a single mention of what had been bothering Jacob.

Chapter Four

"How could you do this to me, Luvenia?"

Her father looked up at her with accusing eyes from the ground where he lay. He was almost unrecognizable, his skin charred black and blistering red. He was dying in her arms and there was nothing she could do to save him.

"I'm sorry!" she screamed. She wanted to touch his face, but his skin had melted and frayed to reveal his skull. "I—I didn't know! I didn't intend to!" she stammered, her hands hovering over him, desperate to figure out how to help.

"You should not have been so selfish, Luvenia. This is all your fault," he choked out.

He closed his eyes and gave his last struggling breath.

Luvenia hugged her beloved father close, knowing she could no longer hurt his skin and not caring how burnt and mangled his body was. He was her father.

"I'm sorry," she whispered again as her tears streamed down her cheeks, sizzling onto his blistered face.

Luvenia woke with a choking gasp, sitting straight up in bed. She was soaked with sweat and struggled to remember where she was.

"You're in your bed at home, Veni, calm down," she.whispered to herself in the dark room. "It was just a dream. We do this every night. Calm down."

Once she caught her breath a bit, she climbed out of bed wearing her long nightgown and lit the oil lamp, returning to the safety of her bed with a tattered book in hand. She chased away the monsters the only way she knew how—becoming lost in a story. It never worked for long, but it helped ever so slightly on nights like this one.

Judging by the moon outside her window, she'd only been asleep a short while. The morning would be slow in coming and filled with fatigue, but she'd functioned on less sleep before. Maybe Mother would let her have some of the coffee she kept hidden behind the bread box.

Coffee was extremely hard to come by, but every year on her parents' anniversary, Genevieve Rousseau would wish all her children well, saddle up Vesper—Henry's horse—and ride four towns over to Ambleton to purchase a small bag of coffee. It was her husband's favorite. She would also purchase a thimble-sized bottle of rose perfume—his favorite scent for her to wear.

What else she did every year on that day, her children didn't know. She would return late into the evening, eyes rimmed with red, and her cheeks flushed as if she'd been crying for hours. She would retire to bed early and spend the rest of the year cherishing her coffee and perfume.

On second thought, Luvenia didn't want any of her mother's coffee.

A couple of hours into her novel, she became restless and decided to start her first run of the day a bit early and race the sunrise. She shed her nightgown and slipped back into her running cottons—still a tad damp. She grimaced.

A few short moments later, Luvenia was running down the dirt and rock path that led to the front gate of their farm. She relished the crunch of leaves underfoot and the brisk air in her lungs.

Her mind certainly felt the clearest when she was running. It was when she did all of her best thinking and Jacob's odd behavior came to mind again soon after she began. He had already been home nearly a fortnight, but he was still acting...strange. She couldn't quite put her finger on it. There hadn't been any other mishaps with Ester—or anyone else for that matter—but something had changed in him. She just wished she knew what it was.

The sky was turning a lighter gray as Luvenia reached the front gate and made to turn around and head back toward the house, but she caught sight of two familiar shapes in the morning light, sitting on the fence.

She jogged over to Jacob and Meredith. "What are you two doing up so early...or up so late, perhaps?" She was hardly winded, she noted to herself with a bit of pride.

"Up early," Meredith answered for them both, her caramel skin and hazel eyes as stunning as ever, even in such dim light. Luvenia wasn't prone to jealousy, but Meredith often challenged that trait.

"I couldn't sleep, so I brought some eggs and a bit of ham," she said as she held up a basket. "I wanted to surprise you all with breakfast, but when I got here Jake was out pacing. Now here you are, too."

"We can go back to the house and feign surprise if ya' want, but that breakfast is happening whether you like it or not, now that we all know about it." Jake leaned in and gave her a kiss on her cheek. She shoved him away playfully, sending her abundance of hazelnut curls swaying and almost knocking Jacob off the fence.

"Oh, you're both going to help now." She handed Luvenia the basket and hopped down. "Well, c'mon. I haven't got all day." She swaggered off, swaying her feminine hips as she walked. Jake shrugged and the siblings ambled after her.

They made their way back to the house as the sun contemplated its rise and Luvenia bathed while her brother and Meredith made breakfast. She only got out of helping because Jake had told her she smelled.

"We can't have sweat in the food, Veni," Meredith told her with a wink. Luvenia knew Meredith wanted any excuse to be alone with Jacob, anyway.

After her bath, she combed her wet hair and twisted it into

her normal fashion before it could frizz and become wild curls. She decided to dress in her riding clothes that day, just for the slight joy of doing something different. She donned her supple leather boots—her father's old knife safely inside—and padded toward the stairs, meeting a sleepy-eyed Ester at the top landing.

"Morning, Sunshine. You're up early."

The little girl rubbed her eyes. "I heard giggling and banging on pans. What's happening down there?"

"Meredith came to surprise us with breakfast."

"She's not very sneaky," Ester mumbled irritably.

Luvenia chuckled at her grouchy Sunshine and grabbed her hand. "C'mon, Grumpy."

Genevieve made her way downstairs shortly after Luvenia and Ester, having heard a joyful commotion in her kitchen. She leaned against the door frame, blissfully watching her loved ones for quite some time before they noticed.

Henry had adored moments like these.

"C'mon, Mother! The eggs are getting cold," the smallest little love beckoned to her. She smiled and strode to the table. They didn't have much, and what they did have came with hard work and more sacrifice than they had any knowledge of, but they had each other and that was all that mattered.

After their laughter-filled breakfast, Meredith hugged them all goodbye, needing to hurry and get to market before all the flour was gone. Luvenia began her chores with the washing of her running cottons, then the milking of the three goats and one cow.

They never discovered how, but the young animals on their

farm hadn't died when the famine and disease hit. They had grown up healthy and lived long lives. The rot hadn't wreaked havoc on their farm as badly as other areas, either. The Rousseau family mostly used what they had for quiet trade with the nearest families, ensuring the health of their farm was kept secret. For they were certain the more they amassed, the greater the target they would become.

Orford's capital city of Alban had fared the best when everything was wiped out and left as rot. Luvenia credited that fact to the hard-working citizens who refused to be owned by a ruthless queen. Pietro's men had combed the lands after the famine hit to survey the damage—or so they said—but somehow, they had missed the Rousseau Farm, even though they were located a mere half a day's ride from Alban.

Luvenia carried the milk into the house to her mother and went to help Jake plant the rest of the beets in the area she'd plowed several days prior. Both of them were soon sweaty and covered in dirt.

Luvenia turned to her brother. "What is it like in the infantry—being a Collector? Have you taken anyone?"

Jacob had gone very still at her questioning but didn't turn to face her. "It's not so bad," he said flatly, his lips pursed.

She knew he was lying.

"Well," she prodded, "tell me what it's like. I don't know anything about your new life. Will you get to come home often? Do you have your Collector uniform already?"

He turned to face her, laden with irritation. "No. I get my uniform when I return to Elkshire. And no, I won't get to come home often. This may be the last time you see me for a very long time." He smiled ever so slightly, but it didn't reach his eyes. "That's why I'm asking Meredith for her hand tomorrow."

Luvenia almost threw her shovel at him out of sheer excitement. She was also successfully distracted from his previous statement. "We have to celebrate! Let me help."

He chuckled. "There isn't much to be done. I used some of my saved vouchers to purchase a small ham that Mother said she would prepare, and a small jar of plum wine Healer Merric made. I'm going to move the table outside so we can all enjoy the meal under the stars, and I will ask for her hand after."

Luvenia was beside herself. "Who knew you were so charming."

"I did learn a thing or two being Henry Rousseau's son," he smiled, but it faded quickly. "Mother gave me her wedding band to give to Meredith." He shoved his hands in the pockets of his work trousers.

She thought she *must* have misheard him. "What? Not *her* wedding band; a different one?"

"No. Hers. From Father. She told me she wanted me to have it. I tried to talk her out of it—"

Luvenia didn't even try to school her anger. She tossed her shovel down and went to find her mother.

"How could you, Mother?" she spat by way of greeting when she found her at the stables.

Genevieve's brows rose as she inclined her head toward Granger, the old man from the farm behind theirs. He'd come to help often since her father died and even more frequently since Jake had gone a few months ago.

"Where are your manners, Luvenia?" She narrowed her eyes at her daughter and turned to Granger. "I am so sorry, Grange. If you'll excuse us, I need to remind my daughter how to properly speak to her mother." She smiled sweetly at her old friend, the seething anger toward her daughter visible underneath it.

"No problem at all, my dear." He tipped his hat to them

both. He stopped next to Luvenia on his way out and said in a hushed tone, "Go easy on her, will ya'? She's having a hard day."

Luvenia stiffened but decided not to heed his advice. As soon as he was out of earshot, she accused Genevieve again. "How could you?"

Her mother put her hands on her hips. "How could I *what,* Luvenia Jane? What have I done that has caused you to forget everything I ever taught you about how to speak to me?"

"You gave Jacob your wedding band, that's what!" she shouted.

"Luvenia Jane, you raise your voice at me one more time and I will drag you by your ear to shovel every bit of manure Grange was going to shovel *for* us. I don't care what you think I've done, you will not speak to me like that again. Do you understand me?"

"Fine."

The anger in Geneviève's eyes only grew. "*Excuse* me? Try that again."

"Yes ma'am," Luvenia muttered.

"Better. Now, are you prepared to be a civilized adult and have this conversation, or would you like to remain acting like a child?"

"Yes," Luvenia said, but Genevieve glared at her. "*...ma'am,*" she added. "We can have a civilized conversation."

Her mother's eyes softened, and she sat on a hay bale against the wall, suddenly looking much older and terribly exhausted. She patted next to her for Luvenia to sit. The girl hesitated but conceded.

Genevieve put her arm around her daughter lovingly. "Luvi, your father has been gone a long time and I don't need that band to remember him or my love for him. He hasn't left my heart and he never will. The ring is just a symbol, and your father would have wanted his only son to give it to his wife. Regardless, I still have the amulet he gave me the day you were born. *That* will eventually go to you." She sighed and laid her head on Luvenia's slim shoulder. "I will always miss him. Ring or no ring, Luvi."

They sat silently for some time before Luvenia realized her mother had fallen asleep on her shoulder and a single tear rested on her cheek. She wiped the tear and gently woke her. "Mother, did you not sleep well? It's not even midday yet." She wasn't acting herself.

Genevieve fussed with her hair, "Oh...no. Not really," she stammered nervously and stood, smoothing her dress. "Well, lunch isn't going to prepare itself. See you in a while, dear."

The following day brought about every ounce of femininity Jacob never knew his mother and sisters had. They fussed over his hair, his clothing, his shoes, even how well Gulliver's mane was brushed before he went to meet Meredith. Ester had even tied a ridiculous pink ribbon on Gulliver's tail, which Jake had promptly tried to remove, but she said it was a special ribbon and he needed to leave it.

The three of them had spent the entire day making the back porch and grassy area as beautiful as possible. Luvenia had placed candles absolutely everywhere—he couldn't fathom where she even found so many. Ester had picked half the strawberries—for which Veni scolded her but allowed her to set them on the table—and his mother had made the delicious smelling ham and a stunning bouquet using the last of the few flowers still blooming in the meadow.

They were definitely ruining his element of surprise, but they were so happy. He couldn't take that from them. Not this final night.

With bellies full, laughter abundant, and the stars shining above, Jacob got down on one knee in front of his family and held out his mother's beloved ring to Meredith.

"Meredith Coraline Miller, will you be my wife?"

She held herself like a princess, her vibrant eyes filled with tears. "Of course."

Hugs, tears, the soft hooting of an owl, and laughter filled the candlelit night until Ester fell asleep on the table and Jacob had to carry her to her bed.

Chapter Five

Luvenia sat scarfing down a bit of bread left from the night before as her mother fussed with her hair and picked lint off her riding pants.

"Mother, I'm just going to Market. I don't need my hair to look as if I'm attending a ball."

Genevieve sniffled and wiped her nose with a handkerchief. "Bit of dust in the air today, isn't there? Anyway, there is nothing wrong with looking your best, Luvi."

A gentle *tap tap tap* sounded at the window and they saw their loyal owl perched on the windowsill.

"Right then. You'd better be going, darling. It's a long ride." Genevieve planted a lingering kiss on her daughter's forehead and bustled out of the room as Luvenia rose to go to the stables.

Out of habit, she stopped at Peony's stall and reached for her saddle but decided to saddle Vesper instead. He didn't get to see much riding time now that he was nearing the age of fifteen, as opposed to the other much younger horses. Vesper was still in good health and as quietly fierce as ever. She wasn't exactly sure why they didn't ride him more often. Today was as good a day as any, and the ride to the Alban Market was a long but leisurely one, so she decided to take the black beast.

Luvenia wanted to go to Market to purchase some special items for Jacob's last dinner the following day. She debated doing without, considering she would lose almost an entire day riding to Alban's town square, but she really wanted his last day to be special and the simple village market near their farm didn't have nearly as many options. Not to mention she adored the Alban Market and took advantage of any excuse to go there.

Jacob had tried to give her some of the Royal Vouchers, but she'd refused. He told her they would never do without now that he had joined Pietro and that they would receive vouchers with the post as often as it came—usually once every month or two. Luvenia wanted nothing to do with the vouchers and would continue trading and buying in the Commoner Markets. Their mother had smiled painfully at her son and put the vouchers in a drawer, reminding him that their farm wasn't failing as he seemed to think.

Once Vesper was saddled and stomping his hooves with excitement, Luvenia tied her basket filled with goods for trade to his saddle and mounted. The horse was thrilled. He held his head high and began proudly prancing his way out of the stables when she gently kicked his sides.

As she was leaving the farm to head down the back trail to Alban, a dense fog still hovering over the ground, the Great Horned Owl followed them, hooting with a sense of urgency. Luvenia continually glanced at him, barely visible soaring high above, and a pit began forming in her stomach. There didn't seem to be any apparent danger, though. Eventually, Owl flew back toward the farm, and all was quiet again. They'd never seen any Collectors on the back trail. It was a private—and well concealed—trail her father had forged long before Orford became what it currently was.

"You never know, Love," he said as she rode beside him on her tiny pony. "You never know when you may want a faster trail to and from Alban. The main road could become busy if Orford continues to grow as it has been. King Alestair is a good man, but more citizens mean more problems and your mother and I prefer the quiet life." He winked at her.

Luvenia and Vesper continued meandering through the

dense forest, savoring the solitude. She smiled as she remembered the many afternoons spent in the Rellum Forest with Jacob. Climbing trees, catching fireflies, playing with frogs, attempting to catch trout in the river with their hands like bears...encountering an actual bear once and running back to the farm for dear life…then running from their mother when she threatened to skin them alive for going near the Arichan Mountain caves when she had specifically ordered them not to. They had so many memories of this place. The trees had recovered from the rot quickly. They stood tall, full, and beautiful, but the quietness had taken some getting used to. Few birds even dared to chirp.

After a good while of steady movement, Luvenia veered Vesper just off the path into a small clearing where he grazed on what he could. She found an old well her father dug when the stream dried up and drew some water from it for herself and the horse. The stream itself would be running somewhat steadily after autumn rains, but it ran deeper into the forest on the other side of the trail, too far out of her way.

Luvenia allowed them both a bit of time to rest as she pulled out an apple from her satchel and ate. Vesper smelled the apple immediately and nuzzled her side until she relented and gave him the other half, core and all. "C'mon, you greedy horse."

She climbed into the saddle and onward they rode, at a bit faster pace. The forest remained peaceful and serene as they went. The trail finally reached its end, but Luvenia knew how to navigate the last bit through the trees to the back alleys of Alban. The sun was nearing its zenith when she heard the din of a crowd and smelled the delicious aroma of meats not sold in their local market. The mass of trees broke off ahead to reveal an alley—a mixture of dirt and broken cobblestone—leading directly to the Alban Commoner Market. She rode Vesper through the old, broken iron archway without so much as a blink from any Alban citizens. No one bothered to patrol the back entry as the people had no need to enter the forest on that side.

Vesper's hooves clopped on the cobblestones as they made their way down the alley, passing drunkards still sleeping off the previous evening's revels. The shortage of alcohol after the queen's takeover was brief. It didn't take long for the townspeople—at least in Alban—to learn how to use what they could find to make fermented drinks to drown their sorrows. This resulted in many deaths due to failed attempts, and many an addict. The makers of such poisons still managed to be the wealthiest among the Commoners. The queen's Royal Market continued to supply the finest wines shipped in from Vilora, the continent at Orford's Eastern border.

Luvenia had never been inside a Royal Market, but she had heard talk of the costs and often wondered how the Royal Vouchers could possibly be enough to purchase such items as wine and jewelry. One day she would look into it.

Rubbish filled the alley and the door to a brothel stood open as she rode past. A disheveled man held a broom in one hand and the arm of a sobbing young lady in the other. "How many times do I have to tell you how to sweep properly?" Luvenia heard his thundering voice even after she'd already passed the open door, "Get upstairs! You have a client waiting!" A sharp slapping sound and more sobbing followed his words.

Luvenia shuddered and pushed away the thoughts of that poor girl. So many had sold themselves to brothels to survive when their fathers, husbands, and sons left to join Queen Pietro, or they forfeited their land so their families could receive food. But sometimes the Royal Vouchers ceased arriving, with no explanation at all. Luvenia thought she didn't want to know what the sinister alleys were like at night when they were this grotesque at midday.

Finally reaching the end of the alleyways, she dismounted and led Vesper onto the bustling street of the Alban

Commoner Market. Since the original wooden building had burned nearly ten years earlier, the Alban market was set up daily in the town square under partial cover of the remaining posts and boards and tattered cloths. In the rainy season, makeshift tents were erected and whatever possible was used to fill in the gaps in the rafters. On that particular day, the sky was bright and almost cloudless. No tents, no makeshift cover, just alive with people.

Luvenia smiled and breathed in deeply. She loved Market.

She tied Vesper's reins to the horse post with all the other mounts and strapped her satchel to herself, grabbing her basket. As she did so, she glanced across the square toward the Royal Market and Annex. It stood partially outdoors with brilliant bouquets of bright yellow flowers and an abundance of fruit. The rest was housed in a fine stone building of new construction. The massive oak door swung open just then and she caught sight of rows and rows of carts and baskets filled to the brim with goods. The door shut swiftly, allowing her no more spying.

She made her way to the Commoner side of the market, bustling with people dressed humbly like herself in ratty, old clothes and with unkempt hair. Precisely why she'd told her mother her hair didn't need to be pinned up prettily. Luvenia noted that the people in the Commoner Market grinned more often than those leaving the Royal Market and she smiled to herself.

The queen can't take everything.

The first vendor Luvenia came to was a crippled dress maker with a few dresses hanging about her stand as she sat huddled on her stool.

"Ahh pretty girl," she cooed in an accent Luvenia couldn't quite place, her eyes squinting against the sun. "You need pretty dress for pretty girl."

"No thank you, ma'am. I haven't enough to trade for a new

dress."

The old woman sniffed. "But I smell lavender deary, and—" she sniffed the air once more "And *strawberries*." She raised an eyebrow.

Luvenia clutched her satchel tightly and kept moving, stopping at the only confectioner in the market.

"Hullo there, darlin'. What can I do for ya'?" He was a friendly fellow, well fed by the looks of him, better than most in the square.

"Hello, sir. I just wanted to see what delights you might have for trade today." She smiled at him sweetly.

"Well let's see here. I have some lemon drops here." He pointed to a pail filled with frosted yellow candies. "A wee bit of licorice there, a few chocolate truffles there, and..." he walked to a small cake next to the truffles. "One last vanilla cake. Ran out o' vanilla, I did."

"What will you take for a truffle?" She walked over and pointed to a specific truffle that had a slightly different hue than the others.

"Ah, well that'n'll be traded for somethin' special. That one there's got hazelnut in it. One'a the Royal Market rats dropped it." He winked at her.

She reached into her satchel and pulled out two of the juicy strawberries she'd stolen back from the supper table when Ester wasn't looking. The confectioner's eyes went wide.

"One hazelnut truffle for two of these?"

"Where'd ya' get those, girl? Haven't seen a strawberry in this market in ages!" he whisper-shouted, glancing around nervously.

"Doesn't matter," she said curtly. "Do we have a deal?"

"O' course we do!" He bustled about retrieving a small burlap sack and placing her hazelnut truffle inside.

She gave him the strawberries with a smile. "Thank you, sir. Make something delightful with them. Have a lovely day."

Jake would love the truffle. She continued on with a little more bounce in her step, looking at all the different vendors' stands. None of them had much, but they each had something, and slightly more every year. That meant Orford had a fighting chance yet—if the Collectors would cease taking so many people, that is.

As Luvenia reached a cobbler's stand, she noticed a strange woman in the middle of the square. She wore pants—her head concealed in a scarf of the most vivid blue. As if the woman knew she was being watched, she turned and Luvenia almost choked on her own saliva. She was the most stunning woman Luvenia had ever laid eyes upon. Strangely, no one else in the square seemed to pay her any notice at all, even though she was in very odd and rather sensual foreign clothing. The beautiful woman caught Luvenia's staring eyes before she could look away and suddenly, she had the greatest urge to find an orange. Luvenia didn't even like oranges.

Fully forgetting the woman, she found one of the few fruit stands and traded some basil for one small orange. The odd craving vanished, and she decided to save it for Ester.

Luvenia ambled along, taking in every last vendor and their goods as she went, letting the aroma of cooking chicken pull her toward the meat side of the market.

Rounding the corner to the other row of vendors, Luvenia tripped. A strong, gloved hand caught her arm before she could fall.

"I apologize. My foot was carelessly placed," a deep voice spoke, his gloved hand still holding her arm. As if realizing this fact himself, he quickly dropped it. "Are you alright?"

Luvenia looked up at the tall, hooded man who had been leaning on the corner beam, not watching where his boot stuck out in the way of foot traffic. His face was completely concealed in shadow and his cloak was the darkest of blue, almost black, and of fine make with golden buttons.

"I'm fine, thank you." She brushed off her pants out of nervous habit and swiftly walked away. Once out of range, she checked her satchel and basket to ensure the stranger hadn't been a thief. Everything appeared to be present. She continued, hurriedly passing the first butcher when she realized who it was. She stopped at the second and traded a bit of wheat from her basket for a few slices of bacon. Genevieve already had a chicken to make for Jake's last dinner at home, so she would make him breakfast.

She had one more item to procure before her last errand. She needed soap. The small market near the farm sold soap, but it was oatmeal and didn't smell very good to her. The Alban Market had a soap maker who also had an affinity for growing flowers, allowing her the creative pleasure of producing delightfully aromatic bars of soap.

As Luvenia approached the middle-aged woman's stand, she could already smell the roses and another new scent.

Curious, she asked the woman, "What is that scent? It smells different."

The soap maker looked up and beamed as she beheld who stood in front of her. "Luvenia Rousseau!" She rushed over to give her a hug, gushing. "How are you, dear? How is your mother?"

"Hi, Agnes. I'm well and so is Mother. How are you?"

"Quite well, quite well. You know Edmund is as ornery as ever, as is that son of ours. Would you believe he cannot stop ogling at every young girl that passes by? Especially that ridiculous daughter of Schrute's!" Agnes shook her head. "He's fourteen going on twenty-five, that boy. Oh! The newness you smell is my precious over here."

She led Luvenia to one single, magnificent flower that resembled a star. "This beauty is a lily. It smells divine, doesn't it?" Agnes held it out to Luvenia.

"It certainly does. You must be selling it for a fortune!"

"Oh, heaven's me, not on my life! Took me ten years to grow another lily and I will not be selling it. When I've enjoyed its beauty and it begins to wilt, I'll bury its seeds. Hopefully I can get more that way."

Sometimes something must die to bring new life, Love.

"I hope you grow a field full of them, Agnes." She smiled at her mother's friend. "Will you trade one rose for a strawberry?"

"For Genevieve? Oh darling, just take one. I sure love that sweet mother of yours. Don't tell anybody, though, ya' hear?" She smiled at her.

"Are you certain? Your labor is worth the wages, Agnes."

"My word is my word, Luvenia. Just take it." She put her hands on the girl's shoulders. "Besides, I'd eat that strawberry in the blink of an eye. I just can't seem to savor such things long enough." Agnes kissed Luvenia's cheek and handed her the prettiest rose of the bunch.

"Thank you, Agnes. Mother will be so happy."

"Don't mention it, sweetheart. Is that all you need?" Agnes asked her.

"Oh, no, I almost forgot. I need a bar of soap, please."

"Ah, your lilac soap? I saved one with extra lilac just for you. I thought it had been a while since you last came by." Agnes shuffled around in her things. "Let's see. I know it's here somewhere...aha, here it is." She held up a bar of soap with a slightly purple hue.

"It's even lilac colored!" Luvenia squealed and inhaled the soap's scent deeply. "Perfect. Just perfect. You are a delight, Agnes. Thank you. I have a small dagger Jacob found, will that do for a trade?" She told her, pulling it out of her satchel.

"You know, on second thought, I think I'll take the strawberry for the soap, how's that?"

Luvenia stuck the dagger in her boot and handed the last

strawberry to Agnes. "Thank you again."

Agnes already had the strawberry almost in her mouth. "I'll see you soon, Luvenia. Tell Genevieve hello for me."

One errand left and she could head back to the farm. She passed by nut stands and lackluster jewelry stands. It seemed some women—even in poverty—had to have jewelry, regardless of how hideous it was. Past the last stand in the market, there was a small road with tiny shops still functional. Luvenia stepped inside the Apothecary and took in the many bottles of tonics and elixirs. She didn't know which to choose, so she went to the counter only to find a sleeping old woman.

"Excuse me, ma'am," she spoke softly.

The crumpled woman startled awake, taking a moment to realize where she was. "You didn't have to shout, girl. What are you looking for? Standard contraceptive tonic?" She glanced at Luvenia's stomach, "A conception remedy perhaps?" She gave her a wry smile.

Luvenia had never taken the contraceptive tonic required by law. She never saw the point—considering her distinct lack of a man in her life—and her mother never pushed the matter, nor did she take it herself. And Luvenia had always found the conception *remedy* appalling.

"No, of course not. I need a simple tonic to relieve coughing. My sister has been having coughing fits in the night."

"Right then." The woman hobbled from around the counter wearing a long black robe. Her wild, white hair reached her waist. Luvenia followed her to a shelf near the back of the small shop. Apothecaries across Orford had never closed their doors in the famine, but she wasn't sure why. Perhaps they were kept open to supply the tonics Pietro forced women to take if they already had one or more child and found themselves carrying again. Either way, it was a bit suspicious.

"Here you are. Coughing Tonic." She held up a small bottle

of sickening brown liquid. "Have your sister take a sip before bed each night. She'll sleep like an infant, no coughing. Sure you don't need the contraceptive tonic? You know you could end up on that Watch List for not taking it, don't you?" She peered up at Luvenia, such a tiny woman with accusing eyes.

"I'm fine, thank you very much. Here." She handed the woman a small vial of her mother's lavender oil. "This should do."

The old woman snatched it from her. "Lavender. Good for sleep. And the skin." She patted her own leathery face and hobbled away.

Luvenia took all her trades, strapping them and her satchel to Vesper to make the trek back toward the farm. She decided to retrieve her mother's rose from her satchel and slip it inside her jacket; it seemed less likely to crumple there. As she mounted the saddle, Luvenia caught another sight of that brilliant blue scarf atop the rare beauty's head. She'd all but forgotten her.

"I certainly would like absolutely anything in that color, Ves."

She patted the horse's neck just as a commotion sounded from where the blue scarf woman had been standing. Mystic beauty had swiftly been replaced by horror. The woman had fled, was nowhere to be seen, and a Collector prowled in predatory circles, his black and steel uniform hissing from the Venom tubes. Everyone in the area froze in place. The smell of fear coursed through the air as each and every person wondered if he and his Warmonger Mouthpiece were there for them and if they could outrun him.

No one had ever outrun a Collector.

With everyone's attention, there was no need for the Mouthpiece to require it. Instead, he merely gave the usual Call.

"The time has come for Collecting," he shouted. "It is law and order in this land." But this time it didn't end there. "Food for the strong. Death to the weak."

A tremor went through Luvenia. She'd never witnessed the Death Call. They were rare in recent days. Fear ran too deeply to so truly defy Queen Pietro. Most were given the paralytic Venom and taken to the dungeons to serve their time—or so they were told.

The Mouthpiece's part already played, the silent, masked Collector strode deeper into the crowd and withdrew a screaming woman by her hair. She writhed and clawed at his leather-clad arm, to no avail. He took the Venom tube from his pack and swiftly injected it into her neck. He then dragged her away through the dirt, to the queen—to her death.

Shaken, but relieved it wasn't her turn, Luvenia quickly urged Vesper toward home.

Back in the solitude of the forest, Luvenia's mind wandered once more to her surroundings. Thinking on anything but that Death Call.

It was rare in the last ten years to see many deer or large game any longer. Rabbits were beginning to become more abundant, though they were generally killed quickly for the meat. The forest used to teem with wildlife. Rabbits darted in and out of brush, countless birds chirped overhead, deer frolicked just out of range, and even turkey was easy to find in this forest. Turkey was Luvenia's favorite, but she would never taste it again, even if she was given the chance. With the reminiscent thoughts of turkey, the dark cloud in her mind grew thicker. She tried to push it away, but she was too late.

Her father rode through the front gate of the farm that chilly, late autumn morning, his Market purchases tied to his saddle. He smiled at Luvenia as she approached, tiny Puck following her. He dismounted, rubbed Vesper's nose, and told him he was a good steed, to which Vesper whinnied with quiet glee.

"Hi, Love." He knelt to his young daughter's eye level. "What have you been up to since I left for Alban?"

Luvenia curled her cold hands into the pocket of her father's wool coat as he wrapped his arms around her waist. "Playing with Puck. Mother says I must start doing more chores soon. She says I'm not an infant anymore." She scrunched her face and her father laughed, his grey eyes dancing.

"Is that so? Well, you are almost eight years old now." He pulled her onto his knee. "And why exactly do you not have gloves on, little one? It's becoming rather cold out."

Luvenia sighed. "Puck ate them. I tried to get them back, but ..."

Her father tipped his head back and laughed heartily. "That goat!" He set her back on her feet, "We better go in and find you some new ones. I need to kiss that mother of yours, too." He winked.

They took Vesper to the stables and headed to the house with the baskets from Market.

Jacob came bounding down the stairs as they entered and hugged his father. "You were at Market so long this time!"

Henry ruffled his son's hair. "I had some city business to tend to as well, Son. Next time you can join me, how about that?"

Jacob grinned and began rifling through the baskets. Luvenia wasted no time joining him. Genevieve came through the back door, laundry in hand, and dropped it all when she was swept off her feet by her Henry. She squealed and he kissed his wife long enough that both children gagged. They laughed and he set her down.

"Jake, I have a bag of feed and a bag of seeds to be taken into the stables, they're both the last in this area. We'll have to travel farther next time. Would you go move the bag of seeds for me?" Henry asked.

"Yes, sir," he replied and made for the door.

Genevieve picked up her discarded laundry and turned to Henry. "I need to put these sheets on the bed. Care to help?" Her eyes shone mischievously.

Henry made an expression Luvenia didn't quite understand. "I'll be right up." She sauntered up the stairs, Henry watching her all the way to the top.

"Ick. You two are very strange."

Luvenia's father laughed. "Oh, Love. You'll understand true love someday. Now, let's get this all put away."

They began unpacking the baskets, but Luvenia didn't see her turkey. "Father, is my turkey in the stables too?" She had shot her first turkey the day before her father left to Market with the small bow he had made for her. He'd told her there was a butcher in Alban who would add some of the last remaining rare spices to it and let it marinate so it would be extra special for when her mother cooked it for Luvenia's birthday.

Her father's face fell. "Oh, Love...I'm so sorry." He swooped her up to sit on the table in front of him. "I never picked it up from the butcher. I completely forgot." He ran his hands through his hair. "I'll go back and get it tomorrow, alright?"

Luvenia's lip trembled, and she began to wail. "But you promised! Tomorrow is my birthday! How will Mother have time to cook it?" She jumped off the table and ran to her room, crying.

Henry followed and sat next to her on the small bed. "There is still plenty of light. I'll go back right now and get it, how is that?"

She sniffled and looked at him. "May I come?"

"No, Love. It will be very late when I get home, but I promise we'll get that turkey cooking for your birthday dinner tomorrow, alright? And don't go around snooping. I hid your present where you'll never find it." He kissed his daughter's forehead, his whiskers tickling her nose. He tucked Luvenia in and went to tell his wife where he was going.

When Luvenia rose on her birthday morning, it was not to the silly birthday songs her father sang each year. He had not yet returned.

Her mother had a brave face on, but Luvenia knew something was wrong. Horribly wrong.

"Where is Father?" she asked cautiously.

Her mother opened her mouth to speak but a knock sounded at their front door. Luvenia rushed with her to see who it was. Surely it was her father, but why would he knock? The door opened to reveal Vesper next to the front porch, snorting nervously, and a portly man she did not know stood in front of them.

Genevieve pushed Luvenia behind her skirts. "What is it, Schrute?" Her tone scared Luvenia but she peeked around her anyway.

"Mrs. Rousseau," the man stammered and took off his hat, fiddling with the brim. "Ma'am, there was a fire in the Alban Market...it seems some folks are fighting back against the queen after she killed a woman and her daughter in the caves. The fire—ma'am, there were no survivors. I—I found this horse in the chaos, and I knew it belonged to Henry."

Genevieve Rousseau hit her knees and wailed as her daughter looked on in confused horror.

Luvenia pulled Vesper's reins to an abrupt stop and jumped off. She tied him to the nearest tree in a small clearing and ran to the stream deep in the forest. As soon as she hit the edge, she dropped to scoop the cold water and splash it on her face. Her adrenaline was pumping from reliving the memory she tried so hard to keep out. It must have been because she'd been in Alban and seen the butcher that had come to her door that fateful day. She splashed more water on her face and sat back to look around. Surveying her surroundings, Luvenia realized she wasn't far from her father's grave.

There were no bodies left for families to retrieve after the fire, or the rest of the Purge War that followed that day, but Genevieve said he had always told her he wanted to be buried deep in his beloved forest. So, Granger had fashioned a gravestone out of a large rock, and the four of them had taken it to the forest. She knew she was close because they had purposely put it near the stream and the Arichan Mountainside.

Luvenia decided to go talk to her father. She hadn't been to his gravesite very many times, but now was as good a time as any. She stood, brushed herself off and headed to a shallow spot in the stream to cross over. The trees grew thick again in between the other side of the stream and the clearing in front of the mountains, but she remembered the way.

As she drew closer, she began to hear something—it sounded like voices. She reached for the knife in her boot, but remembered she had the larger dagger Jacob had found in the other boot.

Even better.

She inched closer, as silently as possible, dagger drawn. The voices became louder, but she couldn't quite make out their words. It sounded like two men speaking harshly. She inched as close as she dared and peered around a tree. Looking into the clearing, her father's grave was fully visible. Surrounding the grave stood three gargantuan black horses and one gray. Atop two of the black horses were Collectors, one with his mask not covering his mouth.

Strange.

He was the one speaking. Atop one of the other horses was an Orford Warmonger—his horse had a prison wagon in tow.

The gray horse and its rider were facing the open-mouthed Collector, his back to her. He wore the black uniform of the Warmongers and he pointed toward the northwest as he spoke.

Nothing is northwest for a long way, she thought...except our farm...

Fear crept in with her realization, as the rider atop the gray horse turned slightly and her heart stuttered to a stop.

Jacob.

Three of the riders galloped swiftly toward the Northwest—toward their farm—leaving the prison wagon behind in the clearing, and Luvenia shaking like a leaf.

Chapter Six

Luvenia's mind raced frantically as she stood frozen next to the tree where she had just witnessed—she wasn't sure what she'd just witnessed. There was no time to figure that out. She had to get back to the farm as quickly as possible and warn her mother. She turned and raced through the brush and branches back toward where she'd tied Vesper. It wasn't an incredibly far distance, but she had lost precious seconds standing numb from shock, when she should have already been running back to the horse.

A little over halfway to Vesper, she tripped over a tree root, and it sent her tumbling down a small hill, a bolder stopping her violently at the bottom. Pain lanced through her forearm, and upon swift inspection, she found the sharp stone had torn through her riding jacket and her shirt, slicing her arm, leaving a nasty gash. She discarded her jacket, ripped the already torn sleeve of her shirt, and tied it swiftly around the cut to stop the bleeding. She'd lost her dagger in the leaves, but there was no time to find it. Nor was there sense in wasting time retrieving the now bloody and crumpled rose she'd also dropped. Scrambling to her feet, she ran the rest of the way full speed, throwing on her jacket as she went.

Vesper seemed to sense the urgency as she approached and began snorting and tossing his head, as if that could encourage her trembling hands to untie his reins from the tree any faster. Luvenia fumbled with the knot for what felt like centuries, cursing the shake in her hands. Reins finally untied, she managed a hand on the horn and one foot in the stirrup before Vesper took off toward home as fast as he could in the dense forest. Luvenia held on tightly and managed to swing her right leg over to fit her other foot into the stirrup.

Vesper reached the trail, and she didn't have to encourage him to gallop the last of the distance as fast as he could carry them. Jacob had surely taken the Collectors to the back trail in order to enter the farm unnoticed. That meant they must be in front of her and well ahead, considering the only signs of other horses were fresh hoof prints in the dirt and trodden leaves.

“Faster, Ves," she encouraged him anyway.

The horse threw every ounce of strength into his stride and indeed ran faster. As they approached the farm, Luvenia could see Jacob had closed the back gate, no doubt to stall her if she were to arrive back from Market while he and his comrades were there. She began to pull on Vesper's reins, but the magnificent beast surged forward at lightning speed.

He means to jump the gate.

"C'mon, Ves. You can do this," she whispered.

She wasn't entirely certain that was true anymore, but she'd never seen him run so fast, even in his prime. She closed her eyes as he leapt, but they landed safely with a thud of hooves that kept on galloping. When she opened her eyes, she saw the three horses tied in front of her house, but Vesper ran all the way to the side of the house where the windows peered into the kitchen.

She decided to revisit later how the horse could possibly know that was the best place to take her. She jumped off, not bothering to tie him or to retrieve her satchel and raced for the window. Peering in, she saw her mother and Ester, both tied to kitchen chairs. Nausea roiled in Luvenia's stomach and bile stung her throat. Ester had tears streaming down her face, but her mother was staring down the Collector with half a mask, fury alight in her eyes.

Without another thought, Luvenia had her small knife out

of her boot and was bursting through the side kitchen door. All three men—if they could be called that—took her in.

Her mother and Ester were gagged, but Ester began shouting incoherently from behind hers.

"Jacob. What are you doing?" Luvenia asked him fiercely, surprised at the gravelly tone of her voice.

Jacob opened his mouth to speak, but the Collector with the free mouth held up a hand. "What do we have here, Rousseau? Your lover, perhaps? Meredith, is it?" His voice was arrogant and filled with poisonous amusement.

A shiver went down Luvenia's spine, his darkness tangible. "I'm his sister, you *filth*. What are you doing in our home?"

The Collector positively cooed. "Another sister? Why, Rousseau, you failed to mention *another* sister." His smile was vicious, all the more frightening with his eyes concealed behind the obsidian goggles, reflecting back the terror and fury on her face. She much preferred the fully masked Collectors over this monster.

"And with such fire, this one," he said, turning his attention from Jacob back to Luvenia. "We're here, little girl, to collect your dear mother and sister, but now that you're here as well, you may certainly come along."

"*Never*. We've done nothing to warrant this." Her voice sounded strong, but her heart was faltering.

"Oh, how wrong you are, girl. What is your name?" he hissed, the tone of his voice so low it grated on her bones.

She merely stared at him, so he turned to Jacob, who couldn't meet their eyes.

"What is your secret sister's name, Rousseau?" Before Jacob could answer, the Collector let out a deep, sinister laugh. "*Luvenia*, am I right?" He turned his goggled eyes back to her, both she and Jacob's surprise barely concealed.

"Shouldn't I know all the members of the family I come to Collect? Family Records are easy enough to obtain, hm?" He immensely enjoyed toying with his prey. "Now, shall we discuss the strawberry patch you unlawfully sell from, or just get to business?" No one made a peep and he continued. "The time has come for Collecting. You should have been ready. It's law and order in this land."

Luvenia held her breath, afraid he would continue into the Death Call. Ester began crying again and straining against the ropes binding her. The Collector in charge motioned to his silent, masked comrade. He swiftly crossed the room toward Ester, causing Genevieve to strain forcefully against her own ropes and Luvenia to lunge toward her sister.

Luvenia was met with a heavy backhand to her face and fell to the ground, knife clattering to the floor as her lip began to bleed. She watched in astonishment as the Collector reached behind himself to the tentacle tube protruding from the pack on his back and shoved the needle-sharp end into her little sister's neck. The girl instantly went limp in her chair, unconscious with enough Venom to paralyze a grown man.

Luvenia became a raging bull. She jumped up and charged the Collector, who merely grabbed her and held her arms down while she kicked and screamed every obscenity she could think of at Jacob.

"You filthy traitor! I hope you *die* for this!" She screamed at him as she thrashed in the Collector's grip.

The Collector in charge clicked his tongue at her as if merely dealing with a small child. "Now, now, Luvenia. That isn't very polite. So unlike the loving, doting sister our dear Jacob so conveniently forgot to inform us of."

"You can rot right along with him, maggot." She simply stared him down, as struggling was futile.

The Collector chuckled. "At least I know *you* aren't a Zealot, girl. But this one—" He strode to where Genevieve was breathing rapidly through her nose, defiance still in her eyes. “This one is."

He brushed a loose curl behind her ear tenderly and ran the back of his finger sensually down her cheek and neck slowly.

Stopping at her collar, he violently ripped open her dress to reveal the Mark of the Zealots.

Luvenia gasped. How could she not have known such a thing? All the Zealots bore a Mark, not only branded on them with a cattle iron, but sewn onto their clothing as well. It was required by law. Her mother had never had the Mark on any of her clothing.

The Collector in charge made a motion and Luvenia's captor released her, but she dared not move to retrieve her knife. He pushed her to the side and withdrew his long, sharp sword. The half-masked Collector removed Genevieve's gag.

"Any last words, *Zealot*?" he growled, leaning in close.

Genevieve smiled serenely and promptly spit on him, right on his uncovered mouth.

He backhanded her across her face and whispered, "Food for the strong. *Death to the weak.*" He turned toward his comrade. "Off with her head."

The sword-drawn Collector raised his blade.

Genevieve locked fearless eyes with her trembling daughter. "Luvi, *run*."

The blade swung through the air and sliced through flesh, muscle, sinew, and bone. Genevieve Rousseau's head thudded to the ground and rolled just inches from Luvenia's feet, the sickening sound clawing its way into her soul. A guttural scream filled the room and Luvenia realized it was her own as she launched herself at the half-masked Collector smiling at her.

Something smashed her head, and the world went dark.

Luvenia awoke to the sound of rain in complete darkness. She blinked to clear her headache-laden vision and surveyed her surroundings. Realizing she was in the prison cart she'd seen earlier in the clearing, her pulse quickened, and her stomach roiled with nausea once more. Her mother...*Ester*. She sat up in the hay that filled the bottom of the cart and wrapped her hands around two of the bars. This couldn't be the cart from the clearing. This one was covered in black cloth to conceal the prisoner inside.

Think. Think.

She had lost her knife back at the house—where her mother lay dead, she remembered again with a fresh wave of nausea. She had to get to Ester.

She sat very still and listened closely. The cart was jostling on a trail and the patter of rain drowned out surrounding noise, but she could just make out the sound of voices. Listening carefully, she picked out three distinctly different tones. One was definitely Jacob, and the other two she didn't recognize. If the half-masked Collector was there, he wasn't speaking—she could never forget that bone-grating voice—which led her to assume he had left the traveling party. Someone else must have joined in his place, or the Collector that had killed her mother had removed his mask to speak with the others.

Previously there had been only one cart, so another Warmonger must have joined the group with the tarp covered cart when they discovered there were two girls to be taken instead of one. It made her wonder how long she'd been out cold, but it meant Ester had to be near, in the original prison cart. Luvenia ripped a button off her riding jacket. The back of it protruded slightly and she pushed the back of the button into the tarp until she managed to make a tiny hole. Throwing the button to the side, Luvenia pulled at the small opening, ripping the cloth tarp until she had an opening the size of her eye.

Peering through the hole, she could see the Arichan Mountains to her left, but they were heading away from them, presumably moving south. There was no sign of the other prison cart on that side, so she felt her way to the other back corner and realized she should have kept the button, as it was now lost in the hay. She ripped off another button and worked another hole into the tarp, a bit smaller, just in case. She peered through to see the muddy back wheels of a cart—no tarp.

Pulse quickening again, she angled the tarp at the opening for a better view of the cart. There was Ester lying in the hay, soaked to the bone and still unconscious. She had to get to her.

Her mind spun trying to think of a way out. Her father had taught her to pick the lock to her mother's confection cupboard once, and she'd practiced on many a door since. If she had the right tools, she could pick it, but she didn't have anything, and she hadn't even located the lock yet. She fumbled around at the back of the cart, a bit of grey light streaming in through the two holes she'd made and found the lock. It was a standard lock, nothing special, and she knew she could open it if she could find something to use to pick it.

She had to hurry. There was no way to know when they would reach their destination, though she suspected their stopping place was very far away. She groped her way around in the hay, thinking possibly a previous prisoner left something behind. It was no use. There was far too much hay, and it was still far too dark. She wondered for a moment why they put her in this concealed cart and Ester in an open one. Did they want to keep her a secret? Or did they want paralyzed Ester to be a statement to those who defy Pietro's laws?

Just then, she remembered the jade hair pins her mother had insisted she wear in her hair that morning before leaving for Alban. They'd been a gift from her father on their second anniversary. Luvenia may have rolled her eyes then, but she was eternally grateful now. Even more grateful she had placed them perfectly, concealing the long part of the pin. Luvenia dug her fingers into her hair—now a mess and full of hay—until she found both pins and pulled them out. She bent one side of each pin up and out of the way, successfully creating two lock picking tools. Quickly, she set to opening the lock, finding success in only a few moments.

The tarp covered the door to the cart as well, so she needed to figure out how to get past it, but first she had to get the door open without it squealing on its old hinges. She pushed the unlocked door gently to test it. Mercifully, it hardly made a noise. It swung outward, restricted by the tight tarp, but if she pushed hard enough, she could squeeze through the opening of the door and slide down to the grass below, the rain drowning out her descent.

Suddenly, it occurred to her that there could be a patrol Warmonger behind the cart as well, so she ripped off yet another button and made a third hole—the smallest—to view behind her.

With no one visible at the back of the traveling party, Luvenia took a deep breath, pushed open the door, and slipped through the narrow opening to the wet ground. As soon as her feet hit, she dropped to her stomach in the tall grass to stay concealed for a moment. The horses and carts trudged forward, none the wiser. Luvenia jolted up and ran ahead, as silently as she could, to the cart she'd just been imprisoned in and peered around the side as it went.

Ester's cart was nearly side by side with the one she hid behind. If she was careful, Luvenia could reach the back of it without being noticed. Jade pins in hand, she slipped from behind the tarped prison cart and hopped onto the back of Ester's, nearly slipping.

She needed to move faster. They could see straight through the cart to her if any of them turned around.

Luvenia held onto the jostling cart, her elbow hooked around a bar, with great difficulty as she attempted to pick the lock. It finally clicked open, and she went inside to retrieve Ester. She made to pick her up, but the little girl was completely limp and too heavy as slippery dead weight, so she began dragging her out by her heels, grateful for the rumbling thunder.

They made it to the back of the cart when it suddenly halted, and the door swung open behind her.

"Well, well, well. What do we have here?"

Luvenia dropped Ester's heels and stood protectively in front of her sister. The Orford Warmonger reached in, grabbed Luvenia's ankles, and yanked. She fell back, partially onto Ester, and cracked her head on the bottom of the cart where the hay had been shuffled away by their movements. She kicked and pulled, to no avail, obviously no match for her captor.

The Warmonger had her out of the cart and slammed onto the ground in a matter of seconds. She threw her arms at his face and went for his eyes with her fingers, but he turned, and she missed. He pulled her up, tightly gripping her arms, and she kicked him in the groin. He released his grip for a split second, and she ran. The injured Warmonger yelled for his comrades, who rode after her on their horses, shouting for him to lock Ester's cage.

Luvenia made it to the wooded area opposite the mountains and kept running, back toward their distant farm. The Collector, her brother, and one of the Warmongers dismounted and ran into the forest after her.

"Veni, stop running!" Jacob shouted after her. "This will be so much easier for you if you just cooperate!"

Luvenia ran faster, swallowing every vile word she wanted to stop and throw in her traitor brother's face. She needed to focus on escaping, hiding, and then planning how to go back for Ester once they camped for the night.

But the Collector was fast—too fast. After only a few moments, he'd caught up with her, Venom at the ready. He grabbed her by her sopping hair and yanked her to the ground, shoving the needle deep into her neck. She screamed and arched her back at the pain, but it failed to paralyze her.

Jacob and the other Warmonger caught up to them, unaware of why the girl was writhing on the ground.

"Administer the Venom, Collector," the Warmonger Mouthpiece said.

The Collector held up the dripping needle to show them he already had. Luvenia was thrashing in his grip, the burning sensation in her blood unbearable.

"What?" Jacob spoke. "How is that possible?"

The Warmonger was equally as perplexed. "Do it again."

"It will kill her!" Jacob protested, but the Collector injected her again. The burning filled every part of her body and she whimpered in agonizing pain as the fire spread and intensified.

Still, it did not paralyze her, let alone kill her.

"This is simply not possible!" the Warmonger shouted. "There has only been *one* person found to be immune to the Venom. Drown her, Collector."

He pointed to a small brook up ahead that the rain had brought to rushing life. Jacob protested vehemently, but the Warmonger promptly knocked him out cold and left him in the wet leaves.

The Collector dragged Luvenia to the brook and into the water, just deep enough to hold her head under. The adrenaline pumping through her pushed out a portion of the burning sensation and she began frantically fighting back. He still managed to push her under the gurgling water, and she knew better than to yell in panic under the water, or it would fill her lungs even faster. She writhed and kicked against his immense strength as she looked through the ripples at the pure evil in that mask, reflecting her futile struggle.

Just as she was beginning to black out, she saw what looked like a giant bird begin to attack the Collector. He swatted at it, but it came back with vicious claws and beak. There was no way for it to get through the suit, but it made the Collector just angry enough that he let her go, only for an instant.

It was all she needed.

Luvenia lurched up out of the water, gasping for air as she scrambled to get up, not wasting a second of time. The Warmonger cried out and started toward the water as the giant bird...an owl—a Great Horned Owl—let out a piercing screech and continued to attack the Collector. It cracked the Collector's goggles and the water around his ankles began to freeze, holding him in place long enough for Luvenia to flee.

She didn't wait to see what happened to the owl. She ran for her life, soaking wet and without shoes. She couldn't recall if they'd taken them before she had awoken in the prison cart, or if they'd fallen off in the water. The brush and rocks ripped her skin open, but she couldn't even feel it.

The Warmonger was closing in on her when she reached a steep hill downward. Unable to slow her pace in time, she slipped and somersaulted down the hill. When she finally came to a stop, she risked a glance behind to her to see no one. Taking that opportunity to stand and veer off to the right, she zigzagged through the trees to throw them off. She could hear them behind her, some distance away, when the earth suddenly gave out from underneath her and she began to fall into an abysmal pit of darkness.

Deeper and deeper she fell into the impenetrable black of a forgotten well, so fast her breath caught, not even allowing her a scream. Luvenia landed at the bottom, far below the earth's surface, with a thud that reminded her of the sickening sound her mother's head made hitting the floor of their kitchen.

With that, she lost all consciousness.

Minutes or hours later, Luvenia opened her eyes to see, instead of the opening of a well and a circle of clouded sky, the inside of an enchanting cave. The cave walls stretched high, covered with moss the hue of fresh spring grass and glowing flowers of every shade imaginable.

She heard a waterfall nearby and sat up. Her head throbbed and it made her vision swim. She touched her lip to find it still split and bleeding, and she could still feel the throbbing of the bandaged wound under her jacket.

I didn't think injuries bled over into dreams or unconsciousness.

She rubbed at the back of her skull and groaned. Regardless, this was the most vivid and beautiful dream she'd ever had. Despite her injuries, she felt lighter than air and rather peaceful.

Sensing someone, she pivoted to find a very bird-like man with fire-orange hair. He was clothed in tan trousers and a tunic, perched on a rock, head tilted to one side eyeing her closely.

Chapter Seven

The bird-like man dropped gracefully to the ground and stood in front of Luvenia. She rubbed her eyes and looked up at him as he reached out a hand to help her.

Taking his outstretched hand, she mused, "You look familiar."

The man let out an ever so slight, low chuckle. "The name is Khyan." He flourished a bow. "But I believe you know me as 'Owl'." His smile was so genuine it sent a flood of comforting warmth through her.

She wasn't the least bit surprised her owl friend stood before her as a man. Her dreams were often very creative—albeit gruesome, typically. Luvenia curtsied and returned Khyan's smile, surprised at how serene she felt.

"So, where am I, Khyan? And can you change into an owl in this dream, or are you merely my mind's human depiction of Owl?"

She brushed the mud off her damp clothes as best she could; more or less making it worse.

Khyan took her in, calculating for a moment before answering. "You certainly aren't simple-minded, now are you? Are you ordinarily aware you are dreaming whilst inside a dream, Luvenia?"

"Ah. So, the owl knows my name, and how to divert questions. No, ordinarily I do not. This is definitely an odd one..." She took in her enchanting surroundings once more and still felt as if someone was watching her, but she wasn't afraid. She merely looked back to Khyan, "*Well*?"

"Well, what?" He smirked impishly and she put a hand on her hip, irritated at his deflection.

Khyan feigned surprise, putting an exaggerated hand to his chest. "Oh! You meant *me* diverting questions? I would never." He straightened, keeping the impish grin. "You are in Aureland. Yes, I am able to shift into my owl form whenever I so desire." He began to walk toward the mouth of the stunning cave, looking at her over his shoulder. "And this is not a dream. C'mon, let's get out of this drab cave."

Luvenia looked around, paying no attention to his claim that this was, in fact, reality.

"Drab?" She jogged after him, catching up just before the edge of the cave. "What do you mean *drab*? This is the most beautiful place I've ever seen—" She gasped as she beheld the forest beyond the cave. It truly was drab compared to what lay before them.

Trees, as far as the eye could see towered over them with leaves in every hue of purple conceivable and inconceivable. It was dusk, but the glorious trees exuded a sort of mist made of light. Instead of brush and bramble along the forest floor, there grew beautiful bushes of plum and golden hues, sparkling in the light of the mist. Flowers grew in thick abundance—lilacs, violets, lavender, iris, wisteria, and so many more she couldn't name. Wine-colored ivy climbed the trunks of some trees, and others glittered in the light of the setting sun. She walked toward one and reached out to touch the purple crystals within it, mouth agape.

"What *is* this?" she inquired, transfixed by the wonder of what she was beholding. Khyan leaned against the cave mouth, shoving his hands into his pockets. "Amethyst."

She turned to him, astonished. "What is this place? Aureland, you said?"

Khyan opened his mouth to speak, but a woman sauntered

out from the cave behind him. "Hullo there, Khy."

He took in the woman and nodded. "Glad to see you've decided to join us out in the open, Theralin."

The woman wore a solid black outfit somewhat resembling Luvenia's riding clothes, though both the top and bottom pieces hugged every well-formed curve the woman had. Her riding jacket—if it could be called such—was cinched tightly around her waist with straps, a bit like a corset. Her boots were of fine make and laced all the way to her knees. Her gloves matched her boots, laced to her elbows, and there appeared to be some sort of thin armor shielding her breasts and thighs. The woman wore a quiver of arrows strapped to her back and a hood with a piece of cloth that concealed the lower half of her face.

The mysterious woman handed Khyan her bow and approached Luvenia, removing her hood and the veil over her mouth before she curtsied. "Thera Revencloud. Pleased to meet you."

Her hair fit the surname—raven black—and her eyes were an astonishing cobalt blue. All Luvenia could think was how frightfully beautiful the woman was, and how strangely dark, yet absurdly ravishing she seemed in contrast to the enthralling forest.

"Luvenia Rousseau." She curtsied in return.

She was beginning to feel the slightest bit nervous and as if she'd seen the woman somewhere before. Theralin smiled at her and warmth filled her again, the peace seeping into her bones and all nervousness subsided.

"Yes, Miss Rousseau, you are in Aureland," Theralin answered for Khyan. "But these," she gestured to the glowing forest around them, "are the Amethyst Woodlands." Her soothing voice did not match her fierce beauty. "We want to take you to meet our queen. Would that be alright with you?"

Luvenia felt oddly giddy and clapped her hands together as if she were a child receiving a treat. "That sounds positively splendid! Let's go!"

She turned and practically began skipping along the purple, stone trail. To where, she did not know, nor did she care.

Khyan watched as she frolicked away and raised an eyebrow to Theralin, who shrugged. "She's been through a lot today, Khy."

The pair followed Luvenia, allowing her to stop at every flower she desired to smell, until they reached the waterfall she'd heard while they were in the cave. Foamy white water cascaded onto massive boulders and came to rest in a refreshing pool surrounded by weeping willows and a few stone benches.

She turned to her ambassadors. "May we swim? Please? I don't know how, but pretty please?" She was beaming and bouncing up and down, clasping her hands. "Please, Owl?" She gasped as a thought struck her. "Maybe you should transform for me! That would be divine! Please?"

Before he could even answer her, she saw something alight in the darkening forest flit past Khyan's head and she immediately followed, eyes wide as saucers.

Khyan turned to Theralin, lips pursed. "Lay off a little, Thera. She's prancing around like a crazed child."

Thera rolled her eyes and crossed her arms. "Today, that girl was abducted, her sister was taken from her, and her mother was beheaded, Khy. *Beheaded.*"

Khyan sighed deeply. "Fair enough. But tone it down at least a bit. I don't intend to present a lunatic to Queen Nuria."

Thera huffed but agreed. "As you wish. Now where did she go?"

"We're nearing Sourn, I have no doubt she's found something there to ogle at."

They found her at the southern Sourn Village Gate, hands on her hips, contemplating what she could possibly be looking at. Khyan approached and stood beside her. "This is

Sourn Village."

"Why have the trees gone green again? And why are the houses so tiny? There are so many..." Thera came to Luvenia's other side and her giddiness subsided, but the peace and wonder remained.

There were thousands of small houses built into tree trunks and tree branches alike. There were several within each tree, all glowing with a warm light shining through the tiny windows and doors.

Thera handed her bow to Khyan and began climbing a tree just inside the gate—which she'd also swiftly climbed—to reach a house high at the top.

Khyan explained, "The Amethyst Woodlands end here at the Sourn Village. Our queen requested a friend of ours join us for supper, so Thera has gone to tell him we're here."

Just then, Thera jumped down from the tree, walked through the gate—now somehow mysteriously open—and approached with a creature upon her shoulder. He stood less than a hand tall and bore the resemblance of a tiny man mixed with a hedgehog. His nose and mouth came to a point, twitching as he sniffed the air a bit. His eyes were black and beady, very much like an animal, and his hair was a wild mess of brown and white sticking up all over his head. He was bare-chested and barefoot, wearing only ripped trousers and the tiniest of leather suspenders.

"What is he?" Luvenia asked Thera in amazement.

The tiny creature spoke from Thera's shoulder, nose upturned at Luvenia. "I am most certainly capable of introducing my own self, madam, and that is *not* how you inquire of one's origin."

Luvenia blushed slightly, barely visible in the glow of the Amethyst Woodlands behind them and the two ornate lantern posts on either side of the gate. "Certainly, I am so sorry, sir. My name is Luvenia Rousseau."

The creature eyed her suspiciously for a moment, then must

have decided he approved, for he became a very hospitable host. He bowed atop Thera's shoulder. "Hold out your hand, dear girl."

Luvenia obeyed and the creature leapt into the air, landing in Luvenia's palm. He held out his little, four-fingered hand. "My name is Smithwick. I am a Porter of the Sean'an."

Luvenia gently took hold of Smithwick's tiny hand with her thumb and forefinger, feeling a bit like she was holding a small bug. "Pleased to meet you, sir. May I ask what a Porter is? And a... what was it?"

"Sean'an. Porters are the Aureland Gatekeepers. We live near each of the four Gates into this realm. We Sean'an are a race of small wise creatures. Guides, perhaps, would be a proper term."

Luvenia contemplated the information for a moment, and then asked, "Are there many Sean'an Porters here?"

Smithwick smiled with his petite animal-like mouth. "Certainly."

He reached into his pocket and then held out his hand to reveal a very meager pile of white dust. He turned toward the Village Gate, drew a deep breath, and blew the dust into the air. Immediately, the trees and sky before them were illuminated in a sparkling light, similar to the mist of the Amethyst trees.

Luvenia gasped for what seemed like the hundredth time since arriving in Aureland as she beheld thousands upon thousands of creatures just like Smithwick flitting around, jumping from tree to tree, sitting upon the gate, and hopping along the ground. Some of them had hair like Smithwick's, others had long orange, pink, or other colored hair. Many had almost invisible sets of wings carrying them through the air. They were all utterly silent.

She turned back to the Sean'an in her palm, who was

beaming at her with pride.

"They're all so quiet," she mused.

"Ah, yes, only at night, isn't that right, Prince?" He pointed to her shoulder. "May I?" And she set him there.

"Quite right, Smithwick. You little sneaks know how to cause a ruckus in the light of day," Khyan teased the creature.

Smithwick laughed and peered at Thera. "You're unusually quiet this evening, little Raven. Do we have something to discuss later?"

"I suppose." Thera looked at the ground, and then busied herself with a flower hanging from the vines along the gate. "We'd better be going. Her Majesty will be sorely disappointed if we miss supper," she said and took her bow back from Khyan.

"Yes, yes, let us go." Smithwick clearly intended to commandeer their little travel party.

Khyan shook his head, huffing a laugh. "At your command, Your Highness Smithwick. Watch out, Luvenia, he'll pull your hair."

Smithwick laughed out loud, a strange and joyous sound in Luvenia's ear. "Oh, Prince, I wish not to diminish your leadership of this fine journey, but I am, in fact, a Guide. Luvenia, he does speak the truth. I have to hold on somehow." He shrugged, and with that, grabbed a bit of her horribly messy hair. She hadn't realized the full extent of its state until that moment, though she couldn't find it within herself to much care.

The four of them walked through the inviting foliage and tree house-filled paths of Sourn. Some Sean'an dipped their chins in greeting, some glared, others snickered silently, and still others picked at the travelers' hair and clothing, finding themselves rather comical. After a while, they reached the northern Sourn Gate—which also mysteriously opened of its own accord—and they walked through to what Thera called the Torren Forest.

Luvenia suddenly realized something Smithwick had said. "Khyan? Why does Smithwick call you Prince? Why do you call him Prince, Smithwick? I thought he was an owl."

"Would you like to answer her, *Guide*, or shall I?" Khyan responded dryly.

Smithwick snorted. "You are in quite the mood, Prince." He glanced at Thera who was still silently ambling along. "Feel free, Khy."

"I am ever so grateful to be allowed your permission." Khyan mock bowed at his little friend upon Luvenia's shoulder. She was rather amused by their bickering. Khyan continued as they walked, "I am a Prince who can take the form of an owl. I am Queen Nuria's younger brother. Therefore, the Prince of Aureland."

"Well then, Prince Khyan, I am honored to be in your company," Luvenia told him.

He snorted through his nose. "I appreciate it, but you can just call me Khyan. And keep the flattery. I don't care for it."

Thera punched him in his arm. "Don't be rude, Khy. She's merely trying to respect you." She moved to stand on Luvenia's opposite side. "He doesn't like to be fussed over is all. Don't take it personally."

Luvenia nodded. "I understand. I find that titles rarely indicate the truth of someone's life, anyway. They don't really matter."

"Ah. Well then, we shall get along just perfectly, Rousseau." Khyan clapped her on the back, almost knocking her over and sending Smithwick rocking.

He tightened his grip on her hair and she winced. "She is feeble and carrying precious cargo, Prince!" Smithwick complained.

Khyan rolled his eyes and Thera laughed for the first time during their journey. It was a sound like the tinkling of bells, and it sent a fresh wave of joy and peace through Luvenia.

"I think you're the one who is in a mood, Smith," Thera informed him, chuckling. "Shall we stop off so you can have a lie down?" She snickered silently to Luvenia, where Smithwick couldn't see her.

He grumbled incoherently but decided to curl up on Luvenia's shoulder and have that lie down. "No sense in wasting a perfectly reasonable suggestion," he murmured to himself.

As they walked along, they passed streams, animals, and foliage Luvenia couldn't wait to see in daylight. She had to somehow ensure that she didn't wake up before she met the queen or saw the enchanting land in the light of the sun.

Smithwick's nap lasted only a short while, and when he awoke, Luvenia's companions chatted about many things. What they might be having for supper, how Thera's quest had gone, what Smithwick's new mount had burned in the last week—Luvenia stored that in her mind to inquire about later—and much else.

Thera was beginning to lighten up and turned out to be quite humorous. She seemed close with the prince, but not in the way one would assume. They had a comfortable camaraderie that reminded Luvenia of her and Jacob.

At the thought of him, a pang of sorrow pierced through her and her step faltered ever so slightly. Thera's smile faded in an instant as she drew nearer to Luvenia. Peace flooded her heart again and she could no longer remember what she'd just been thinking of. Thera and Khyan exchanged a worried glance, but Smithwick distracted them all.

"Luvenia, you are going to adore Queen Nuria, right Prince?"

Khyan cleared his throat. "Yes, quite right."

Smithwick continued, "She is the greatest ruler this kingdom has seen in thousands of years. Her beauty of heart is unmatched. I must warn you, however. Like her brother, she despises being fussed over. Though she relishes fussing over everyone else."

Thera smirked. "Don't forget the smothering by hugs and kisses."

Khyan chuckled. "And food. My sister believes everyone to be starving at all times and in need of fattening."

Luvenia thought it so lovely to listen to a queen's subjects speak of her as if she were their precious, loving mother.

"Just over this hill you will see the castle, Luvenia," Thera whispered. "It's unbelievable at night."

They crested the hill and yet another gasp escaped Luvenia's lips. She had to halt in order to take it all in. Before her ran a long path of cobblestone lined with towering trees on either side. The trees were each aglow with hundreds of tiny orbs of light, like fireflies. At the end of the gleaming path there lay a smooth, serene lake, across which stretched a cobblestone and iron bridge, ornate with swirls and whorls.

The real splendor stood on the other side of the bridge, in the middle of the lake. The most magnificent castle Luvenia could have ever fathomed. Solid white—almost iridescent, like snow—its towers and spires all glowing with amber light, much like the Sean'an homes. The castle walls shimmered as if partly a mirage, bits of emerald inlaid within them.

Thera took her by the hand. "C'mon. Just wait until you see the inside."

Chapter Eight

The traveling party made their way down the glimmering path, the many orbs of light dancing in each of their eyes. As they approached the bridge, the two sentries standing guard bowed deeply to their prince and immediately moved to let them pass.

Khyan dipped his chin in acknowledgement to each man, "Good evening, Patel. Sall," and proceeded to lead the way across the bridge to the white stone gatehouse.

Luvenia found herself wondering how the stone could possibly be so pristinely white as they entered through the circular iron gate, opened for them by two more guards armed with swords and bows. They made their way across the courtyard alive with servants bustling about and ascended the stone steps to enter the open castle doors.

The entry hall was beyond any building Luvenia had ever seen, from the white marble floors with golden veins, to the beautifully carved ceilings and pillars. Sheer, golden curtains framed every large window standing open to let in the evening breeze.

"Royalty certainly enjoy lavish things," Thera spoke next to Luvenia, "but I must say, I have never seen a castle quite as magnificent as Nuria's." She smiled kindly at Luvenia and turned to the prince. "We'll see you at supper, Khy. Smith, you go with him. I need to get this girl some clean…and *dry* clothes. She's been wandering around barefoot and filthy."

Luvenia hadn't noticed her clothes were still rather wet and had forgotten quite how dirty she was from the day's events.

She thought there was something significant she was supposed to remember about the day, prior to meeting her new friends, but she couldn't quite put her finger on it. Something about her mother, perhaps.

Thera sensed the wheels turning in Luvenia's mind and promptly looped an arm with hers. Within seconds, the distant thought vanished completely. Thera instructed Smithwick to vacate her shoulder and hurried her new charge up the marble stairs and down the corridor leading to the ladies' wing of the castle, passing several people along the way, each looking more exotic than the next.

"The people here are so different from those in Orford," Luvenia mused.

"The people of Aureland come from many different places," Thera explained as she opened the door to her chambers. "Welcome to my humble abode."

Luvenia followed her in and chuckled. "I wouldn't exactly call this humble."

Thera's chambers were only slightly less ornate than the other parts of the castle she'd seen thus far. They consisted of a small entry, a dining area, a bedroom, a sitting area with a roaring fireplace, and a bathing chamber—all of which made up a space larger than Luvenia's entire house. The walls were painted a feminine powder blue, complimenting the ivory bedspread perfectly situated on the massive canopy bed. Everything else matched the shimmering silver curtains pulled shut over the windows.

"I suppose you're right." Thera smirked at her. "Make yourself at home. Feel free to take a bath. It should already be drawn. Helga knows I love a hot bath after a quest. I will find you some clean clothes to wear." She pointed her in the direction of the bathing room and sauntered off to her bedroom.

The cast iron tub was indeed filled to the brim with steaming hot water and an abundance of soap bubbles. The aroma was magnificent, but Luvenia couldn't quite determine what it was. She caught a glimpse of herself in the looking glass above the wash basin, startling herself. She truly looked dreadful.

Shedding her sodden clothing, she sank into the hot, bubbly bath. The water spilled over the sides, but she hardly noticed. Her baths had been lukewarm at best for her entire life. Her father used to boil some water over the fire to add to her and her mother's baths, but there was never enough to create this kind of divine warmth.

She wasn't sure how much time had passed, but the water was no longer hot when Thera burst through the door.

“Did you drown in here? Supper is beginning!"

Luvenia hadn’t even begun to wash yet, so she hurriedly set to scrubbing and washing her hair. Within a few moments, she was dry and padding into Thera's bedroom in a fluffy, powder blue towel.

Clothes were laid out all over the bed and the floor was covered in crumpled piles of clothing that were not there when they came in. Thera had changed into a cobalt dress that matched her eyes, her hair loose and cascading down her back. She had one hand on her hip and the other held her chin thoughtfully.

The sight of the dress reminded Luvenia where she'd seen the beauty previously.

"Oh! You're the woman from the market. You had a scarf on your head that same color. Now I remember the strange clothing and why you seemed so familiar," she explained enthusiastically.

Thera looked at her, unamused. "You're the girl on that black beast, hm? I wasn't exactly supposed to be seen, so let's keep that between us, shall we?"

Luvenia nodded in agreement.

Thera turned her attention back to the clothing. "I think all the clothes on the bed could fit you. They might be a bit loose in the bust and hips, but we can cinch them up. Goodness, we've got to get some food in you. You're skin and bones! Take any you like and try them on. There is a looking glass in the closet so you can see them."

Luvenia wasn't quite sure what to make of so many different colors and fabrics, nor had she ever cared a great deal about clothing, but the moment seemed wonderfully exciting. Possibly her lack of interest was merely due to never having the opportunity to experience such grand clothing before. She simply couldn't decide which to try.

Thera sighed. "We are already late for supper. Hurry!" She stomped to the bed, grabbed three dresses, and shoved them into Luvenia's arms. "Here. These. *Go*!"

Luvenia hurried into the gargantuan closet and instantly forgot the three dresses in her hands at the sight of the other hundreds of every color and style hanging around her. Thera poked her head in to see which dress the girl had chosen and caught her staring wide-eyed at the racks.

"*Luvenia*! There will be plenty of time to ogle at everything in this castle and I will allow you to try on every last dress if you so desire, but right now we have *got to go*. Put the green one on and let's go!"

She obeyed and dressed quickly. The seafoam gown was elegant and beautiful, though it was indeed too large in the bust and hung limply on her hips and waist. Regardless, she had never worn anything so lovely and felt positively dignified. There was no time for an elaborate hairstyle, so Thera tied Luvenia's hair to one side with a seafoam ribbon, the drying mess of curls falling over her shoulder. She knew as soon as they fully dried that the frizzy curls would tickle her chin relentlessly, but she let it be.

The two young women made their way through the castle to the royal dining hall, shoes clacking on the marble the entire way and Luvenia tripping every other step.

"For goodness' sake, Luvenia, I gave you the simplest

slippers I own. If I'd known you would trip the entire way to supper, I would have given you my lounging slippers to wear instead." Her laugh tinkled like bells. "Tell me you don't always wear boots."

Luvenia blushed, "Not always…How do you walk in these things? Can I just take them off?"

Thera laughed again. "Your dress will be too long. You'll trip over that too. Regardless, a lady does not gallivant around *barefoot*, and you've already managed to do so for a great portion of the day."

Luvenia sighed. "If we're going to get to this supper before sunrise, you want me to take these off."

"Alright, alright. But I will make a lady out of you eventually."

Luvenia rolled her eyes and continued toward the dining hall, shoes in hand and bare feet on the cold marble.

The women entered the lavish dining hall greeted first by the enticing aroma of enough food to feed an infantry and second by a servant who promptly took Luvenia's shoes out of her hand—to her great embarrassment.

A majestic woman in a gown that shone like the stars, rushed toward them, crushing Thera in a long embrace. "Oh, I've missed you so, my sweet Thera. Three days can feel like an eternity even when you're as old as I." She kissed Thera on both cheeks and turned to Luvenia. "And you, lovely girl, must be Luvenia Rousseau." Her smile was endearing as she placed warm hands on Luvenia's shoulders and looked at her adoringly. "I am so very pleased to meet you. My brother has told me a great deal about you. I've longed for years to make your acquaintance." She held a delicate hand to her chest. "I am Nuria."

A tall man with walnut colored skin, clad in riding leathers and a coat the color of midnight, slipped in the door behind them. "I don't think you really need an introduction, Nuria." He smiled crookedly and kissed her on the cheek as he passed, taking a seat next to Khyan at the long table and reaching for the leg of an as-yet-undisturbed chicken.

Nuria caught him out of the corner of her eye. "Hands off that chicken, General. You wait until we are all seated." She turned back to Luvenia. "That would be Darius. He is the general of my armed forces, the Aureland Horde." She glanced back at him, "Table manners are not his strong suit." She winked. "Come, I'm sure you are famished." The queen grasped both women by the hand and led them to the table where they took their seats across from Khyan and Darius.

Luvenia's stomach grumbled loudly, but no one seemed to notice. Nor were they filling their plates with food. It was then that she noticed one last empty chair at the foot of the table.

Thera's mood suddenly soured again, though Luvenia couldn't understand why, the food looked divine. She wasn't sure what most of it was, but was anxious to dig in.

"Ya' smell better, Miss Rousseau," a tiny voice spoke to her from the center of the table.

She hadn't even noticed Smithwick leaning against the candelabra. She smiled. "Oh, the wonders of soap and water."

They all chuckled except for Thera, who was staring at Darius with daggers in her eyes. She wondered what had gotten into her new friend.

Queen Nuria interrupted Luvenia's thought. "Smithwick, Sebastian will be here any moment, please kindly take your seat. We do not need your grubby little feet on our dining table, anyway."

Smithwick made his way across the table, leaping over a dish full of something orange and creamy, and stole a kernel of corn before taking a seat in a tiny chair contraption attached to the table next to Khyan. The queen gave him a stern look and he set the kernel on the table with an apologetic smile.

The general spoke across the table, "Thera, could you

please stop murdering me in your thoughts? I told you I was sorry."

Thera opened her mouth, presumably to say something very unkind judging by the look on her face, but the door opened and in walked another new face.

A long, lean man with slightly almond shaped eyes and steely features. He sauntered in with confidence, but there was something almost tragic about him. Something Luvenia thought he kept well hidden behind the sly smile he wore. Whatever it was, this darkness, it seemed familiar in some way, and it beckoned to her, as if it were calling her name.

Thera interrupted her musings with a gentle whisper. "Sebastian Olliander," she leaned over and explained. She smiled her tranquil smile, her anger apparently subsided for the time being.

Sebastian said nothing to the others. He simply strode to the head of the table, kissed Nuria's hand, and took the empty seat.

The queen looked intently at the new arrival. "We have much to discuss, Sebastian." She turned to Darius and Thera. "As it seems the three of us do as well but let us enjoy this feast before it becomes any colder. Every last one of you was tardy."

Luvenia looked around awkwardly, but no one paid her any mind. They were too busy filling their plates with food, so she began to do the same. Determined to try everything, she quickly became immensely full and so very pleased. The majority of what she ate was entirely new to her, every morsel more delightful than the last. Her dinner companions—with full bellies—had forgotten their issues for the moment and chatted casually well into the night, until servants began clearing the table with them all still sitting there.

Luvenia's eyelids began to droop by the time Khyan suggested they move their conversations to the parlor for a hot cup of coffee. Coffee sounded like a marvelous idea to the tired girl, but so did sleeping for days.

How could I feel this tired within a dream?

Thera looked at Nuria, who nodded almost imperceptibly. Thera placed her hand on Luvenia's shoulder. "It's been quite a long day for you, my friend. Why don't we get you to bed? You can join us in the parlor tomorrow evening, hm?"

Luvenia nodded sleepily. Exhaustion seeping into her bones and dragging her under.

"I had Helga prepare the chambers next to yours for her, Thera, if that is alright," Nuria explained.

"Of course, My Lady," she replied and took Luvenia by the arm, leading her to the door.

Nuria called after her, "Thera, a word before you leave, please."

Thera smiled at a half-awake Luvenia and went to the queen. Nuria whispered to her as she leaned over the queen's chair, "We can move her chambers later if you like. I know you enjoy your space, but she has been through so much. She will need your gift a little longer, please, darling."

"Of course, it's no trouble at all. Shall I lift my gift in the morning once she has rested?" Thera inquired.

"Let us see how she is feeling after a good night's rest, hm?"

"Yes, My Lady."

Thera led her charge back through the castle halls to a door opposite her own. Luvenia was asleep before her head hit the plush pillow, clad in her dress and all. She hadn't noticed anything other than the grandeur of her chambers—lavish, with soft grey walls—and that she had forgotten her shoes in the dining hall.

Chapter Nine

The sun was already high above when Luvenia was awoken by light shining on her face as thick curtains were flung open. She squinted against the brightness streaming in as she sat up to determine who had entered her room, ready to chastise Ester. She was startled to notice she wasn't in her bedroom at home, though even more so by the vacancy of the room. She sat up and looked about, the curtain-opening culprit nowhere to be seen.

She heard the jingling of a bell and a small creature jumped upon her bed, startling her once more. She yelped and pulled the covers up to her chin with wide eyes.

"Mornin' Miss," said the cheerful creature as it grabbed the comforter and attempted to pull it from Luvenia's grip. ""tis actually nearin' afternoon, Miss. Yer missed breakfast'n mornin' tea'n all. Yer were sleepin' like the dead in here!"

The creature resembled a thin, two-feet-tall elderly woman with bushy white hair, and round spectacles perched on a bulbous nose. Poking out from her hair sat rather oversized and very pointy ears. Atop her head she wore what Luvenia assumed was a giant stocking with a bell at the end.

She supposed she must look horrified, for the little wrinkled creature dropped the covers and put a fist on her sassy hip.

“Never seen an Elfe before, have yer?" She sighed and rolled her eyes. "Name's Helga. The queen sent me to get yer dressed." Her rosy, round cheeks pushed her glasses up as she smiled.

Helga was so frightfully adorable and cheery that Luvenia

couldn't help but smile in return. She determined to no longer be surprised by her findings in Aureland—a task she was already certain would end in failure.

Helga helped Luvenia wash up—to which she protested vehemently, but Helga merely stated it was her job, so she let her. A large selection of dresses hung in her new, borrowed closet. It was nowhere near the amount in Thera's, but nonetheless a collection any young woman might dream of. She chose a russet dress patterned with miniature ivory flowers—pleased to find it fit her perfectly—but Helga made her put it back.

"All those colors and yer pick this one? No ma'am, yer put that back! It'll wash yer right out! Yer need a green or a purple." She jingled her way over to a small wooden ladder and climbed up to reach a dress the color of green olives, "This'n'll be divine with yer eyes." She handed the soft dress to Luvenia and hobbled down the ladder.

The dress Helga chose truly did complement Luvenia's eyes, and chestnut hair for that matter. It also fit her perfectly, as if it were tailored just for her. Silver buttons ran from the high collar down to her waist, where Helga cinched a thin white ribbon. "To give yer a shape. Yer need to eat more, by golly."

Out of habit, Luvenia began twisting her hair at the nape of her neck in her normal fashion, but Helga swatted her hands away, informing her that her curls were lovely and needed to be on display. She pinned the sides with small silver clips shaped like flowers and handed her a pair of flat, silver slippers.

"Miss Thera says yer got problems with heeled slippers. She says yer gotta work on that'n, but we'll tackle that 'nother day."

Relieved, Luvenia slipped on the shoes and followed Helga through raincloud and lilac decorated chambers to the door. Thera met them in the hall where Helga bid the women adieu before they made their way through the castle to another dining hall.

At the midday meal, more unfamiliar delicacies were brought to the table, much to Luvenia's delight. Midday meal seemed to be less formal, since Thera began eating immediately and the general was already halfway through his third plate full of food when they arrived.

After one bite, Luvenia decided she favored an unknown vegetable dish and filled her plate to overflowing. "What is this? It's delicious!" she exclaimed to Thera around a mouthful.

The general chuckled kindly at her. "Saffron rice and curried vegetables. Those spices have been outlawed in Orford for seven years, in the Commoner Markets, anyway."

Thera glared at him. "She was speaking to *me*, Darius."

The general set down his utensils—two wooden sticks, Luvenia noted curiously—and crossed his arms. "Theralin, do we really need to have this conversation again? I told you I was sorry, now *let it go*. This is pointless and acting like a spoiled child is only wasting time."

At that, Thera slammed her fork down on the glossy wooden table with a bang. "That's the problem, Darius!" she shouted. "I am *not* a child. Stop treating me like one. I can go on an assignment without your needing to spy on me or *protect* me. I've been training nearly as long as you have and I've been out on my own countless times without any of you."

"You're acting like a child right now, Thera," Darius shot back with a growl. "I'll stop treating you like one when you stop acting like one. I don't care how long you've trained or how many gypsy caravans you've traveled with to avoid us. I needed to ensure this assignment was carried out flawlessly. It's my duty to do so."

Khyan cleared his throat from the door, drawing the attention of the trio. "You're both acting infantile at the present moment. Possibly this can be addressed somewhere other than in front of our guest. Finish your meal and we'll let you spar it out, how about that?"

The two glared at each other and mumbled, "Fine," in unison.

"Very well." Khyan sat and smiled at Luvenia. "Did you sleep well, Veni? I must say, I'm accustomed to checking on you in the middle of the night, it was quite odd not to."

Khyan's familiarity took her by surprise. It was almost as if a pet could suddenly speak his mind after years of mute companionship. She wasn't sure she liked it.

"I did sleep well, thank you. You truly came to check on me in the night in Orford?"

He swallowed a bite of roasted carrots. She noted that she hadn't seen him eat any of the bird meats.

"Of course. I merely wanted to ensure you were safe." The prince shrugged.

"So," Luvenia wondered, "Did you really live in the stables or just fly from Aureland each day?"

"Oh, a little of both," he smiled kindly.

After the conclusion of the meal, the four of them stood in a large, open room deep within the castle. Few lanterns burned and the low-lit room was made of rough stone with weapons hanging from every inch of the walls. The floor was stone as well, a large mat arranged in the middle.

There's nothing royal about this place.

"Alright, normal rules apply. Three would-be hits and you lose," Khyan explained from the middle of the mat as the two opponents stared each other down, wooden sparring swords in hand. "Regardless of who wins, you will still verbally work this out afterward. Understood?"

Darius nodded.

Khyan looked across the mat. "Theralin?"

"Fine," she muttered.

Khyan left the mat. "Spar!"

Wood slammed against wood as Thera rashly swung and

the general blocked her with ease, pushing back against her. With a grunt, she came at him again, her blow deflected once more, and his sword swiftly tapped her shoulder.

"That's one. You're fighting from anger, Thera. Your emotions will mislead you," Khyan instructed from the side as Luvenia watched on in fascination. The fact that a woman was sword fighting a man thrice her size in a glistening gold dress was not lost on her.

Khyan's instruction made Thera angrier, and she lunged for Darius, only to have her sword knocked away as he dodged with a spin maneuver and made contact with her leg.

"Two. You're better than this, Thera," Darius encouraged her. "*Come on.*"

She mistook his encouragement as a taunt and with a yell, ran straight for the general. She made no attempt to guard herself and he made no attempt to move. Darius stood his ground, shoved her sword away, and knocked her feet out from under her with one swift movement of his foot. She landed on her back with a thud, as her wooden weapon clattered to the floor near Luvenia's feet.

Darius stood over her, sword tip at her neck. "You need a handle on those emotions. They're out of hand. You're better than this. I'll be in the Armory when you feel like truly working this out." He threw his sword down and left.

"This isn't the Armory?" Luvenia whispered to Khyan.

"Not even close," he responded and turned to Thera, still on the ground. "Get up, Theralin."

She groaned and sat up, hugging her knees. "Don't even say it, Khy."

"You know I must. Darius is right. You are better than that. I've seen you fight off four men, each twice your size, in those ridiculous heeled shoes without even breaking a sweat, and you just lost to Darius in the blink of an eye. Emotions are a terrible guide, Thera. Anger can motivate, but it cannot lead.

Take a walk and then go to the Armory. We'll talk later."

Thera stood and hung the wooden swords on the wall. "She had better come with me," she said quietly, pointing to Luvenia.

Khyan thought for a moment, conflicted. "No. She can come with me to see Nuria."

His decision appeared to upset Thera slightly, but she simply nodded and strode out. Luvenia turned to the prince. "Would you teach me to use a sword like that? My father taught me a little, but that was incredible!"

He looked at her with pity in his eyes that she didn't quite understand. "That was a terrible match. But yes, I will gladly teach you to wield a sword." The sadness in his voice deepened. "I'm afraid you have a tougher battle to win first, Veni. Come with me."

Rather confused, she followed the prince out into the castle halls. Out of nowhere, a sense of dread began to creep into the back of her mind and a pit formed in her stomach.

Only a few steps down the hallway, she halted and looked at her guide with pleading eyes. "Khyan, I think something's wrong..."

He placed a gentle hand on her shoulder, his concern evident. "Yes, Veni. Something is wrong." He sighed heavily. "I hoped Thera's gift would stay with you long enough to make it to Nuria. I hadn't realized it would fade so quickly." He turned to her fully, looking intently into her frightened eyes. "You're going to remember some things as we walk. Try to just keep moving. We will hurry."

Luvenia had gone pale. "I feel sick..."

Khyan took her by the hand to lead her to the queen's wing of the castle with haste. Nearing the queen's chambers, she stopped cold as realization hit her like a battering ram.

She gasped. "My sister. *Someone took my sister*!" Panic set in as her mind spun, looking for a way out of that truth.

"Yes, Veni, they did. We're going to get her back, alright?

Right now, we need to get to Nuria."

She had gone numb, horror written on her features. Khyan placed an arm around her waist and ushered her along for the rest of the way.

They reached the door to Queen Nuria's study just as the sound of her mother's severed head hitting their kitchen floor reverberated through Luvenia's memory. She went limp and began to tremble uncontrollably. Khyan had no need to knock, for Luvenia's screams alerted Nuria of their presence.

The door flung open and Khyan carried the hysterical girl past the queen. "Put her on the floor in front of the fire," the queen directed as she rushed to pour a cup of steaming tea, to which she added a calming tonic made of lavender and chamomile.

Nuria threw the train of her gown behind her and knelt before the writhing girl on the rug, "Luvenia, you need to drink this." But the girl was sobbing violently and murmuring something about it all being her fault.

The queen turned to her brother urgently. "Where is Thera? This all came back too quickly! Her mind cannot handle this! What happened?" Luvenia began to thrash against Nuria as she attempted to get tea into her mouth.

Khyan's eyes darted between the two of them, helpless. "I didn't realize it would wear off this quickly. I dismissed her."

Luvenia knocked the teacup from the queen's hand, screaming. Nuria cried out as the scalding tea soaked through her dress into her skin.

"Go!" she exclaimed to her brother. "Find Thera *now*!"

Within a blink, Khyan shifted into owl form and swooped into the hall. Several moments later he returned as a man, Thera running close at his heels. Luvenia was still sobbing, though she had ceased thrashing and screaming. Nuria had her arms wrapped around the girl, rocking her back and forth and humming.

The fire had died down to embers and the room had become

chilly. The queen continued rocking the girl as she released one hand to send blue flames sparking into the fireplace. The logs blazed and the chill subsided quickly. She turned her attention to Thera.

"Darling, I need you here for this. Help her, ever so slightly. She experienced far too much trauma to confront it all at once after you blocked it out. She will need to ease into this."

Thera nodded to her queen as the girl's sobbing subsided and she calmed down. She stared blankly into the fire for several moments before looking to Nuria.

"*My mother...*" Her lip trembled. "I thought this was a dream."

Nuria stood and held a small, blue flame in her hand under the teapot to warm it. She prepared another cup with chamomile and lavender tonic, presenting it to Luvenia. This time the girl willingly took a long sip.

"Dearheart, this is not a dream. What happened to your mother is real. Thera has a gift. She is able to...influence certain emotions by altering chemicals within the body. You had gone through so much, we thought it best to let her give you some peace of mind and a good night's rest before facing such trauma. She must be in close proximity in order to influence others. Therefore, when Khyan dismissed her earlier, the influence left as she did. With as much distress as you have endured in such a short span of time, there was no way for your mind to catch up gradually. Essentially, it is the difference between a ship with a slow leak, and a ship with a gaping hole in the hull."

Luvenia took another sip of her tea, the cup rattling on its saucer due to the shaking in her hands. She spoke as she turned dead eyes back to the fire. "I don't know if I should be angry that you dared interfere in my life or grateful that I don't have to face such a gaping hole." Her voice was monotone, but she was coherent.

Nuria knelt in front of the girl once more. "Dearheart, you

mustn't become dependent on Thera. You must face the gaping hole, but we are here to help you face it."

"It's stifling hot in here," was the girl's only reply.

Nuria stood and held out her hand. "Come, we'll go for a walk in the gardens."

Luvenia set her teacup on the ground and took the queen's hand to stand. The three women moved together toward the door as Khyan watched them, his heart breaking for the girl he'd spent so many years silently caring for.

"Brother," his elder sister said pulling him from his thoughts, "Extinguish that fire, would you?"

With a slight flick of his wrist, the prince sent ice and mist into the fireplace, choking out the flames.

Chapter Ten

Sebastian Olliander rode horseback alongside the Queen of Orford, winding through the Arichan Mountains, and surrounded by armed Collectors. One of Queen Lilith Pietro's most trusted advisors, Sebastian made the perfect earpiece—and mouthpiece—for the Queen of Aureland. He was a master in the art of secrets and deception. Pietro had made him that way after all, and she was none the wiser regarding his true intentions.

"Explain to me exactly what I gain from pursuing an alliance with Anjali?" Queen Lilith inquired of Sebastian, rather bored.

"Warriors. You gain warriors. The Anjalian people train their children in combat from the time they take their first step," Sebastian defended his point.

She flipped her hand at him dismissively. "I have no need of warriors, Sebastian. You'll have to do better than that."

"You *do* have need of warriors, Lilith."

The queen glared at him.

“Alright,” he relented. “If you insist. Though, if you do not pursue an alliance, and choose to swoop in and seize their land, you will start a war against Anjali. If they're not on our side, they're against us."

Pietro pulled the reins of her white horse and came to a stop, the entire traveling party following suit. She turned in her saddle to look at Sebastian, dripping with aggravation.

"Have you learned nothing these ten years? There shall *be* no warriors left to contend with when I am through with them." She kicked her mount with her heels, and they continued on. "Anjali aside, we have greater matters to tend to."

"Oh?" Sebastian inquired, curious what she could be referring to.

"The rebel forces have gained momentum."

It was Sebastian's turn to pull his mount to a stop. "Pardon? Gained momentum? We've snuffed out every rebel force for the last ten years before they could advance even a single step. How can this be?"

The surprise and urgency in his voice was sincere, but not for the reason the Orford Queen assumed. She and her silent men did not stop with him.

"Oh, keep moving, will you?" She was vexed, but when was she not? "We should have done this indoors if I knew we were going to halt every few strides. Shiv's spies caught wind of a rebel camp deep within the mountains. One of their own got cold feet and confessed everything he knew, which did not amount to much. No leader of even meager intelligence would let a man like that within his informed circle. Regardless, evidently this band of rebels is composed of survivors from the Alban War. They have been living hidden in the mountains, training in secret for all these years."

"You seem unconcerned..." This was the first time Sebastian had heard any word of such a rebel force. He assumed Nuria must have been in the dark concerning the rebels as well, though he couldn't fathom how.

"I'm merely perturbed. It never should have come this far. They're led by some man they refer to as The Liberator. *Fools*," she spat.

"They are certainly no threat to you, My Queen, only a nuisance to be dealt with." Queen Pietro lifted sensual eyes to Sebastian and nodded her agreement.

Oh, he was so very good at his duplicity. "Did their former member not disclose their location?"

"He didn't know it. According to him, this 'Liberator' fellow led every last one of them into the mountains blindfolded during the night," she fumed.

Sebastian's brow furrowed. "One man? Highly unlikely. Certainly there is more than one person who is aware of their location." He shook his head. "It's no matter. If the informant left this camp and made it to Alban, certainly he could recognize landmarks and point Shiv's men in the correct direction."

Lilith cracked her neck, the cruel obsidian crown atop her head unmoving. "No. The informant was found blindfolded, gagged, and tied to a horse trough."

Sebastian thought for a moment. "A trap, then?"

"No. I believe the man was telling the truth, and I believe he was a weak link for this rebel force, one they needed to be rid of while they could still use him as a pawn. They've successfully captured my interest, which I'm certain was their intention. They are more than likely ready to make their first move and desire that I be waiting for it." She paused for a simmering moment. "Sebastian, this *Liberator* must be found. *And eliminated.*"

Pietro's face had gone rigid with rage. Her advisor's countenance read cool calculation, but a small spark of hope had ignited deep within the tortured caverns of Sebastian Olliander's soul.

Hidden under an abandoned fortress, a little girl in tattered rags shivered in the dark. She huddled in the corner of a cell reeking of vomit, unsure whether the vomit belonged to her or someone else.

She refused to close her eyes. Behind her eyelids lived the ghosts. The violent insect men that beat her. The woman with demons in her eyes. And the rat-man who asked if he could purchase her.

She had no idea how much time had passed, but one thing she did know.

No one came for her.

Luvenia had dismissed Thera after their walk in Queen Nuria's garden. Thera had her life to tend to, and Luvenia knew the time had come for her to face her own—alone.

"I didn't block the memories this time, so it is just the heartache that will seep in. Remembering the events should help you cope better the second time around." Thera had given her a gentle kiss on her cheek and walked away. Luvenia spent the following four days refusing food, baths, and company.

Partially into the fifth day of solitude and misery, Helga jingled in to retrieve the uneaten food trays and informed the girl that her aroma had become "undesirable." Luvenia promptly threw a pillow angrily at the little Elfe, quickly apologized, and soaked in the tub for an hour.

She was drying her hair by the fire, sipping a cup of tea, when a knock sounded at her door. She opened it to find Prince Khyan standing in the hall, dressed in black trousers and a grey tunic.

"I just stopped by to check on you. I'm pleased to see you've left your bed...and bathed," he teased.

"Helga said my aroma was displeasing," Luvenia shrugged.

Khyan smiled slightly. "Helga certainly has a way with words, doesn't she?" He noticed she was in her robe and cleared his throat. "Right. Well, I know you don't really care for visitors right now, so I will leave you be, but I'm glad you're up and about and do hope I'll see you at supper this evening."

He started to walk away, but Luvenia called out into the hall, "Wait! Stay. Please?"

"Of course." The prince nodded, hands in his pockets.

He followed her back in, leaving the door open. As she began walking back toward the sitting area, she finally realized that she was still only wearing her dressing robe. Embarrassed, she told him, "Have a seat, I'll be right back."

After changing into proper clothing, Luvenia took the seat opposite Khyan in front of the fireplace. "Thank you for checking on me."

"My pleasure. I've been checking in on you for many years now. May I have some of your tea?" he asked as he stood and strode to her table.

"Sure, go ahead. I think Helga said it was peach. It's delightful, whatever it is."

Khyan poured a cup for himself and topped Luvenia's off.

"Are you ready to talk about it?" he asked her as he sat and handed her a teacup.

"You certainly don't waste any time, now do you?" she snapped, far too defensively. "I'm sorry." She tried again. "No, I'm not."

"Understandable. There is no need to apologize. Though, when you are ready, you do need to talk to someone. It doesn't need to be me, or even Nuria, but you need to talk with someone..."

"Just leave it alone." she ground out.

Khyan held his hands up in surrender.

They sat in uncomfortable silence for the next several moments. Khyan wasn't certain if he should leave, or just give her time to calm down. After she'd stared into the fire for what seemed like hours to him, he decided to go ahead and leave. As he made to stand up, she finally spoke.

"Did you really eat that rabbit that day on the farm? The

small one?" She looked at him, entirely serious.

He let out a breathy laugh. "That is what you've been pondering all this time just sitting here?"

She shrugged. "Beats the alternative."

"I suppose it does." He sat back down in the armchair. "Yes. I did. My owl form needs food, too."

"I feel as if I've known you forever," she mused. "Isn't that odd?"

"Not really." He shrugged. "You have known me many years now."

"That doesn't count. You couldn't even speak to me. You were a bird."

"An *owl*, thank you. And I could speak, just not to you. Though I have the same personality as an owl as I do as a man," he explained.

Khyan caught a flicker of the girl she used to be—the girl untouched by tragedy and despair—flit across her eyes. He jumped at the opportunity to pull that thread, no matter how slight.

"Ah, I see those questions burning a hole in your mind. What else would you like to know?" he prodded her and took a sip of tea. Maybe she didn't want to discuss recent events, but he could still help her, without her even realizing it—just as he had for many years.

Luvenia pulled her legs up into the plush chair to sit cross-legged. Excitement and interest replaced the numb look of shock that had been on her face in recent days. Maybe it wouldn't last long, but he had to try.

"Really, I have a lot of them. What are you? I may have been in some tonic-induced stupor by whatever strange thing Thera can do to—to my chemicals, was it?" She shook her head in disbelief. "Regardless of that…we'll get to that. I saw Nuria *put* fire in that fireplace. *Blue* fire. And I saw you flick ice at it to snuff it out. Yet, you tell me this is all real. It makes no sense."

Khyan chuckled at how animated the girl could become when she wasn't suppressing who she was. "Slow down, no need to get your knickers in a twist. First things first, I am a Keeper." She stared blankly at him. He continued, "Keepers are sent to protect. To keep order in the realms, you could say. We are here to halt calamity and prepare the way for the End."

"Wonderful," she said, sitting back. "I have officially gone mental. Keepers? Realms? The *End.* That is all madness."

"You truly still believe this is all a dream? Oh, you're in for a rude awakening, madam."

The girl glared at him and answered sarcastically. "Fine. Do continue, *prince.*"

"I shall, thank you very much. Keepers are mortals, born of mortals, but they are chosen and appointed even before birth, often even prior to conception. Keepers are equipped with exceptionally long life, an inner knowing concerning Light and Darkness, and a gifting—more often than not, more than one gifting. Mine are ice and shifting, obviously into an owl. Nuria's are fire and also shifting—"

Luvenia interrupted him. "Hold on. Slow down." Genuine interest etched itself all over her features. "So, how old are you then? Nuria is your sister, correct? What does she transform into? Is Thera a Keeper too, since she can alter my emotions? Why is it you have the coloring of fire and Nuria of ice, but your giftings are opposite?"

Khyan couldn't help but smile at the girl. She sounded just like Ester, prattling on with all of her many questions. He'd flown for two days searching for the little child, to no avail. He shoved that thought away—he would have to address it later or risk losing these precious moments with Veni to despair again.

"May I answer now, or do you have several hundred more

questions to add first?" he teased her.

She spread her hands in invitation. "By all means."

"Nuria and I are siblings, yes. She is one hundred and thirty-three years old. I am ninety-four. Nuria also shifts into an owl, a white one. Thera is a Keeper as well, though she is only twenty…she still has much to learn, that one. I haven't the slightest idea why our appearances differ from our giftings, I'd like to think our creator merely found it clever and creative." Khyan smiled at that thought, as if it were a cherished memory. But dark fog was rolling in behind the girl's eyes.

"My father and mother would have found you so fascinating. So would Ester." She stood, the thick numbness fully returning. "I'm going to lie down."

Khyan knew he should leave, but the sudden dramatic shift in the girl left him off kilter, so he remained seated for a moment as she walked away.

Just outside her bedroom door, Luvenia turned back. "Owl?"

He looked up, surprised to hear her call him by that name. "Yes?"

"Might you shift for me? Just for a moment, please?" Sorrow shrouded her like a heavy blanket—its comfort deceiving and counterfeit—but he could not deny her such a simple request.

His empathy-filled eyes blinked, and an owl hovered in the air, wings pumping. Luvenia gave no response. She merely turned and entered her room, leaving the door open. She climbed under the thick covers, lying on her side to stare out the window at the autumn trees. The owl perched on the foot railing of her bed and softly hooted until the girl fell fast asleep.

And then for some time after.

Across the Aureland castle, Queen Nuria had grown tired of waiting for her brother to arrive for their council meeting and had begun without him. She could fill him in later.

Sebastian had deemed the gathering urgent, but she had given the floor first to Darius, to discuss the matter of Anjali's safety. He'd spent the first of his time going over a well thought out plan to smuggle supplies into Anjali to aid survivors, if Pietro refused alliance as Sebastian feared.

Nuria spoke from her golden throne as Darius took a seat. "Thank you, General Cremeux. That is a fantastic secondary plan. Though, as all of you know, I do not *do* secondary plans. Never mind that the number of survivors will be incredibly minimal if an attack takes place." She locked eyes with her informant. "Sebastian, your task was to convince Pietro she needs the Anjalian people alive and to form a *true* alliance as opposed to her false alliances. As we well know, those end in destruction. Instead, you come back to my castle and inform Darius we need an alternate plan."

Sebastian opened his mouth to speak, but the queen continued. "I am fully aware that a true alliance could potentially result in Anjali strengthening Pietro before we can get to them, but at this moment, our main priority is to keep the civilians of Anjali *alive*. We stand a much greater chance of infiltrating an allied country than a war-torn one."

The general stood again to speak. "Your Majesty, might I suggest convincing Anjali to dupe Pietro before she has the chance to do the same. In turn, giving Anjali the upper hand."

This piqued the interest of the queen and all on the council.

She leaned back on her throne. "Do continue, General."

"It is easier to infiltrate an allied country than a war-torn one, yes, but it is infinitely easier to infiltrate a country allied to no one, as is Anjali's current state. Undoubtedly, the Anjalian Emperor has heard rumors of being presented with an alliance by Pietro. Why not beat her to it? Make it his idea, his stipulations?"

The queen shook her head. "The emperor will not be difficult to turn toward our side once we have secured their safety, but he will not be easily swayed while stuck between death for his countrymen or an alliance with Pietro. I see little success in convincing a man fearing the demise of his country to follow a ploy of trickery against the queen threatening him."

Darius had already considered such an argument. "Ah, yes, but his fear of demise could be the perfect note to play."

Nuria rested her chin on her hands thoughtfully. "Go on."

"Already we assume too much. If Sebastian succeeds, Pietro will still wound Anjali. We cannot assume she will keep her word and continue a true alliance. We also assume Emperor Nakamura is aware of Pietro's true intentions. There is a good chance he is unaware. If this is the case, we inform him. Either way, we infiltrate Anjali's ranks immediately and plant the idea that the alliance is a good plan, but for the purpose of gaining Pietro's trust and access to her supplies, with no intention of aiding her in any way. Instead, convince Anjali to be a leech, sucking Pietro's supply lines dry, little by little. His country will then gain reinforcements, debilitating Pietro and gaining the upper hand. He will be aware of her true plans, and that will leave far less ability for retribution. This could effectively wound Pietro, even slightly, and save Anjali."

Councilman Linden interrupted, "Pietro is far too powerful for such a plan. She would realize what was happening and obliterate the entire country as intended. She doesn't need supplies to destroy a traitor."

The other councilmen murmured in agreement, though their queen remained pensive.

Sebastian cleared his throat. "Linden may have a point, Majesty, but Darius is onto something here. The queen doesn't need supplies, but her men do. In addition, Lilith is distracted, possibly just enough for such a plan to work if we move swiftly and pull at the supply lines gradually, particularly her Venom vaults. We may not need any more time than the amount in which she does keep her word. The business I came to speak of does not only concern Anjali, though this all may go hand in hand. A rebel force has been gathering secretly in the Arichan Mountains since the Purge War. or the Alban War as they call it. They are led by a man referred to as the Liberator."

Murmuring spread through the council, though he continued over the din, "Not much is known, but current information leads me to believe this man is far from foolish. He's outsmarted Lilith for ten years, and he has a plan. I move that our first order of business be to locate this rebel cause, align forces with them, and Anjali may be saved in the process."

The Queen of Aureland smiled as hope spread through her council like wildfire. A beautiful ghost of promise.

Chapter Eleven

After five days of seclusion, Luvenia elected to don a simple blush dress with pearl buttons and venture to breakfast in Queen Nuria's dining hall. She ambled through the castle, eyeing all of the beautiful paintings hanging on the walls, choosing her favorite to be that of a colorful meadow and a quaint, stone cottage. The cottage didn't exactly resemble her house in Orford, but it held the warm feeling of home. She stared at the painting for quite some time, wishing her mother could be present to see it as well.

"Do you like that one?" Luvenia jumped half out of her shoes as Darius spoke. "I'm sorry, I didn't mean to startle you." The general hung back, watching her.

"That's alright. I didn't hear you coming," she told him, her hand on her rapidly beating heart. "I do like it, very much."

"I tend to have a quiet step. Part of my training." He pointed to the painting. "That is my father's home, where I grew up. Well, mostly where I grew up, that is. I spent many a night in this castle as well."

"Oh?" Luvenia gladly welcomed the distraction from her thoughts of home and her mother. "It sounds as if you had a lovely childhood."

Darius breathed a laugh. "That's rather debatable." Luvenia looked at him curiously, but he only smiled, dodging her concern as best he could. "It made me who I am today, we'll just say that."

Sensing his desire to leave the current subject, Luvenia gestured to the long row of artwork. "The paintings here are very realistic, as if you could simply step right into them." They all seemed to be done by the same hand. "Who painted all of these?"

Darius ran his fingers through his messy locks. “That would be yours truly, believe it or not."

Her surprise was far from concealed. "Truthfully? They're wonderful. A general and a master painter,” she mused. “What an interesting combination."

The general laughed heartily, a tinge of embarrassment mingled in. "I would hardly say 'master painter,' but yes, I do enjoy it immensely. It helps me forget all my responsibilities and just...be myself. Create what I want, when I want, how I want it. That is one luxury my position does not allow much of. Many people are under my charge, and I must answer to Khyan and Nuria as well. It doesn't leave much room for leisure."

Luvenia looked back at the painted cottage, pointedly ignoring the general's proximity. "It is quite a gift you have." Her choice in the wording reminded her. "Are you a Keeper as well?"

Darius put a hand to his broad chest. "Me? No, no." He shrugged. "Just an average mortal who appreciates art. If you will excuse me, I have a meeting I must attend.” He bowed to her cordially, to which Luvenia returned a slight curtsy.

The general started past her, but something made him want to turn back, to say something, anything at all, just to look at her once more.

"If you..." he stuttered, having not planned his words before opening his mouth. She gave him her attention again. "...possibly, if you'd like, I could show you around the castle this evening after supper. Of course, I mean, unless Khyan already has..." He'd thoroughly embarrassed himself and sounded like a jealous schoolboy. He shook his head at himself in dismay. "That...I'm sorry. That came out strangely."

Luvenia almost smiled at seeing the disciplined Aureland Horde General stutter himself in circles. She decided, rather, to interrupt his embarrassment. She assumed he merely wasn't used to having guests. "Will there be more paintings to discover?"

"Nuria insists on hanging every one since I was eight. So, yes." His cheeks warmed and he looked down before she might notice, rubbing the back of his neck.

"Then I would be delighted," Luvenia offered, with the best smile she could muster, knowing full well it more than likely resembled a grimace.

Darius, however, looked up and smiled broadly, his eyes twinkling. "Very well." He bowed again. "After supper." He turned and walked toward his meeting, feeling strangely buoyant with a lightness he hadn't felt in several years.

Luvenia continued to dawdle through the castle halls, half wondering if her pace was actually due to the dread growing in the pit of her stomach. She didn't want to eat, or converse with people. It seemed so wrong. Her mother could no longer eat, or enjoy the company of friends, or paintings on a wall, or a beautiful amethyst forest. There was no one to numb her mother or Ester's pain by being near and altering the chemicals in her body.

Withdrawal was so much easier than facing others. She could remain numb and unfeeling while curled in bed asleep, her body and mind weak from lack of nourishment. No part of her wanted to face the perfect queen of this perfect land. Nuria would make her face the thoughts and images ripping her heart to shreds.

Luvenia focused on the gentle swoosh her slippers made on the marble floor as she walked, realizing that some small part of her must want to face the queen and the pain in her heart, or she would have gone back to her rooms by now. She paused for a moment, solitude beckoning to her once more.

She looked over her shoulder, back toward the way she'd come. It would be so much easier to simply go back, to return to her borrowed bed and waste away to nothing.

But she heard a gentle whisper in her ear. “You must continue forward, Luvi. For Ester."

Luvenia snapped her head around, looking in all directions for the source of the whisper. The halls were deserted, save for a servant rounding the corner with a tray of tea. No one called her Luvi except her mother. Unsure of what had just taken place—and frankly quite frightened—Luvenia picked up her pace and made her way swiftly to Queen Nuria's dining hall.

I will leave this place. Today. That is the part of me that drew me out of bed this morning.

She was slightly out of breath upon her arrival, but her breakfast mates paid no mind.

Thera sent her fork clattering to the table as she jumped out of her velvet seat to crush Luvenia in a hug.

"You look positively skeletal!" she exclaimed. "Come." Thera shoved her in the seat next to her own. "*Eat*! Nuria will be beside herself to see you so famished." She began piling food on the silver plate in front of the girl. "Have you eaten none of what Helga brought you?" She didn't let her answer. "You could have starved! What are we going to do with you?"

"There is no need to fuss, Thera. I'm fine. I will eat. Sit down and finish your own breakfast," Luvenia waved her off.

Thera obeyed and returned to her seat, curling one lug under herself in the chair. Luvenia noticed she was wearing a red and gold tunic with simple riding pants and her hair was tied in a braid over her shoulder.

“No elegant dress today?"

Thera answered around a mouth full of fried potatoes, "No evening wear until evening, of course. There is training to be had and work to be done."

"What are your days like, anyway?" Luvenia inquired of

the beauty.

Thera wiped her mouth with a cloth napkin, the Orford Queen's seal embroidered on it. "Each day holds a different adventure around here. Typically, I rise early to train. You know, running and combat, that sort of thing. Then after breakfast," she spread her hands wide, gesturing to the table, "I am either sent out on the queen's business or Darius sends me on an assignment of some sort, usually in Orford."

"What were you doing in the Alban Market that day I saw you?"

"Oh, I was there to gather information on the woman who was Collected that day. You saw her, yes?" Thera answered and took another bite of eggs.

"I did. It was a Death Call." She shuddered inwardly. "Did you learn anything of value?"

Thera nodded. "She was a Zealot who had refused to be branded with the Mark. And I gathered all my information without Darius' help, yet the oaf insisted on spying on me." She rolled her eyes with a shake of her dark head.

Luvenia had many more questions that came to mind, but Khyan and Nuria entered the dining hall, a bit at odds. They hadn't noticed Luvenia yet as they stood just inside the doorway facing each other rather angrily.

"I do not care, Brother!" the queen hissed at Khyan. "You cannot split up. Two of you to Anjali; two of you in search of the Rebels."

Thera and Luvenia both ceased eating and listened intently.

Khyan rubbed his eyes with thumb and forefinger, exasperated. "Nuria, Sebastian needs to be in Orford with Pietro gaining information and staying well out of suspicion. That already eliminates him. Thera cannot infiltrate Anjali, as they have no female warriors, and Darius needs to stay close to both Orford and the Horde. Your plan is simply not possible."

Luvenia noticed Sebastian and an unknown Hordeman

lingering in the hall, also unnoticed by the quarreling royalty. She didn't know much about running a kingdom, but she assumed it was best to keep battle strategies quiet.

They must trust those within these castle walls immensely.

She didn't find that wise. People are rarely what they seem.

"My orders are final, Khyan Karra! Thera and Darius to Anjali, Sebastian and yourself to the Arichan Mountains." She glared at her brother with steely eyes. "You leave tomorrow. This discussion is finished."

Thera turned her head, popping her neck irritably upon hearing this news. Nuria turned toward the table, her shimmering silver-blue gown catching the sunlight streaming through the dining hall's windows. She saw Luvenia and her features instantly softened from regal ruler to loving matron.

"Oh, dear me, Luvenia. I am so pleased you have joined us this morning." Her words were so kind and sincere, despite the argument she'd just turned away from. "Forgive the minor disagreement you have just witnessed. We have much at stake. But you need not worry your beautiful mind about such matters." She kissed the top of the girl's head and took her seat at the end of the table. "Khyan, sit."

The fiery-haired man, who falsely appeared to be no older than his mid-twenties, threw flames at his sister with his eyes, but sat obediently on Luvenia's other side.

"Oh, cease your sulking, Khy. Council matters can wait until we have had a hot meal."

Her brother said nothing in return. He merely gave Luvenia a small, tight smile and began eating a bowl of piping hot porridge. Sebastian entered behind the queen and prince and took a seat as well, shooting her a sly, seductive grin. Luvenia quickly looked away.

Thera and Nuria exchanged light conversation while Khyan ate his porridge angrily and Sebastian interjected bits of playful banter into the ladies' conversation.

Luvenia's mind lulled as she watched them. She had to

admit they were a pleasant distraction, and it was nice to feel cared for. Her thoughts drifted to Darius and his invitation to view the rest of the castle later in the evening. Ester was alone and afraid somewhere and she was making plans to gallivant around with a handsome stranger. Disgusted with herself, she shook the thoughts loose. She had to leave this place immediately and find her sister.

Luvenia cleared her throat and addressed Queen Nuria. "I would like to thank you all for taking me in and allowing me a bit of time to recuperate, but I really must be getting back to my family's farm."

Nuria ceased eating and concern filled her features. "Oh, darling, you mustn't leave so soon. There is much we need to discuss."

Luvenia blinked at her, the beginnings of feeling trapped seeping in. These people seemed to care for her and perhaps they wanted to help, but it all felt a bit too much.

"We have nothing to discuss. I wish to leave," she bit out.

Nuria placed her fork gently on the tabletop. "Dearheart, you are truly in no shape to return to your farm and face all of this alone."

Luvenia only became increasingly angry at the queen's invasion and insistence. "Who are you to tell me what I am or am not? You cannot keep me here." She slammed her hand on the table and stood so forcefully that her chair fell back and clattered to the ground. They all simply stared calmly at her, infuriating her even further. The room began to spin, and her vision went white with rage. "You don't know me, or my family, and you've taken me hostage. You're no better than the monsters who abducted my sister! I *need* to get to my sister!"

Nuria raised her hand gently to the livid, frantic girl, "Please calm down. We have not taken you hostage, nor do we wish to do anything more than help you. You fell into *our* land, remember?" Nuria stood to approach her, but Luvenia backed up, grabbing her butter knife from the table. “One more step and I promise you I will slit your throat wide open."

At her melodramatic outburst, Thera deftly rose, drawing her own knife, and stood defensively next to her queen, as did Sebastian. A small part of Luvenia swelled at the satisfaction of causing at least one of them to finally flinch. Khyan stood slowly and held a gentle hand out to Luvenia—which she promptly swatted away.

"She will not harm me. Lower your weapons," Queen Nuria ordered, unphased. Thera looked at Nuria in silent question. "No. Let her emotions rage, Theralin."

"I am not some experiment or a doll you can toy with," Luvenia screamed, horribly appalled by their ability to intrude within even her emotions.

Guards rushed into the room, but Nuria raised a hand to halt them. The queen's still unruffled, calm demeanor squelched Luvenia’s earlier satisfaction. "I am leaving! *Now*." She shattered her plate against the wall for good measure and stormed out.

Khyan threw his chair back to rush after her, but his sister grabbed his arm to stop him. "No, Brother," she told him with a shake of her white-blonde hair. "Let her go. She cannot leave Aureland without Smithwick knowing."

"You didn't take her portal key from her when she arrived?" Khyan squeezed his eyes shut briefly in nervous frustration.

"Of course not. Staying here must be her decision, or we truly are no better than the monsters who have taken Ester."

"Nuria, what are we going to do if she does leave? She isn't safe in Orford. She can't retrieve that girl on her own." Khyan's face twisted with his own exasperated rage.

"I do not believe she will leave. She needs to confront this savage anger and process it on her own terms. She must *choose* to do what it will take to free her sister. Regardless, I am not certain she even knows she has a Key. Do you have any more information on where they are keeping the little girl?" Nuria asked the question with sincerity, but she also knew that the inquiry would distract the prince from Luvenia for a moment.

Khyan scrubbed a hand down the length of his face. "No. Not a trace. The trail runs cold after Lugen, a great distance south of the Arichan Mountains."

"You have until dusk to discover more, Brother."

Khyan nodded to his sister and left briskly. He opened a window down the hall and a Great Horned Owl flew away.

Luvenia raced through the white and gold castle, dress hoisted up so as not to trip. She glanced behind her every so often, but no one followed her. Servants of all different shapes, sizes, and unfamiliar races jumped out of her way in surprise. Rounding a corner, she ran directly into a very tall, lanky man with pointed ears and skin like tree bark. The timberous man hardly budged, though Luvenia bounced off him landing square on her rear, the man's tray of dishes tumbling onto her lap. The glassware shattered, remnants of food littered the ground, and stains covered the front of Luvenia's pretty blush dress.

She looked up at the man, embarrassed. He scowled back at her with tree-hollow eyes. "Watch where you're going, girl!" He bent down with his long form to begin cleaning the mess as a tinkling Elfe hobbled over to assist.

Luvenia brushed the food and broken glass off of her lap and stood, a small trickle of blood from her arm dripping on the floor and her dress. The gash she received while in Orford must have reopened. She would worry about that later. She glanced up to see Sebastian rounding the corner and headed her way.

"I—I'm sorry. I have to go." And she was off at a run once

more.

"Hey! You're not even going to help? That is very rude!" the tree man shouted after her.

Within moments, she was outside of the castle, racing through the gate and across the cobblestone and iron bridge over the lake. She considered for a moment why none of the Hordemen or guards paid her any mind, but settled on being relieved instead of suspicious.

She made it to the Torren Forest and plunged deep into the tree line, bounding as quickly as she could while fumbling with her voluminous skirts. Still, no one appeared to be following her, but she needed to make it as far as possible toward home before slowing down. Brush and branches ripped at her face and dress, though she hardly noticed.

After running for what seemed to her like hours, Luvenia finally slowed to a breathless halt near a crystal-clear pond. She looked about herself until satisfied that she was indeed alone in the forest. Alone was not the most accurate term—the forest was quite occupied by the sounds of many creatures—but she was free from the watchful eye of Queen Nuria's Hordemen and court. As she knelt beside the pond and scooped up the chilly water in her hands, she marveled at hundreds of multi-colored fish swimming beneath the surface. Every color darted by, and they seemed...happy. They swam about chasing one another gleefully. A particularly vivid yellow one looked her straight in the eye and she could have sworn it smiled at her. Luvenia was torn between feeling unsettled or mystified by such an event.

She stood and surveyed her dress—or rather the dirty rag that remained—and her injured arm. The cut had mostly resealed itself, though she thought it wise to go ahead and wash it and apply a bandage. She reached back into the crisp water and rubbed the dirt and dried blood out of her cut. She'd never been very squeamish with blood, not like Ester. Ester would vomit at the sight of it.

She found herself feeling immensely grateful the little girl had been unconscious while their mother had been killed. Luvenia's chest ached fiercely with the thought. She closed her eyes, inhaled deeply the autumn air, and slid calculated determination in heartache's place. She had to get home.

She ripped the hem of her dress until she had shortened it to just below the knee, for two purposes. She needed it shorter to better manage through the forest, and she wanted to wrap her arm. After feeling the warmth from wrapping one forearm, she realized just how cold she was now that she'd stopped running. Luvenia took off her slip and tore it to wrap around her shoulders like a shawl. It wasn't much, but it would do.

If her calculations were correct, Smithwick's village should be just ahead. Then she only had to make it through the Amethyst Woodlands and into the cave and back to Orford. She was rather unsure how she would make it past the Porter Gatekeepers, and where the cave let out, but she would worry about that when she must.

Luvenia trekked through the forest at a brisk pace, not allowing herself time to marvel at the plethora of interesting creatures she came across. Her sister was in trouble. She had no right to revel in fanciful things while her little sister, a mere child, rotted in some horrifying place Queen Pietro had shoved her in.

If she is even still alive.

Luvenia shook her head abruptly at the thought. She would not even consider such a possibility. She continued on for some time as doubt crept slowly in. She should have been in Sourn Village by now. It hadn't taken so long from the Sean'an Porters to reach the castle.

A few moments later, the towering green trees of the Torren Forest gave way to lush trees abundant with small, pink flowers and tangibly warmer temperatures. Her heart pounded in her chest as she approached the astoundingly beautiful path filled with pink petals. None of it was familiar.

"No." Luvenia spun slowly in a circle, hands on her head in dismay. "*No*...no no no..." She'd gone the wrong direction, with no idea where she was. "No!" she screamed at the top of her lungs and hit her knees in the fluffy flower petals, unable to push back her despair any longer. She hid her face in her hands and sobbed.

She cried in the middle of the pathway and wailed until she had no more tears and had successfully slobbered on her dirty dress. Doing so had relieved none of her sorrow and she proceeded to forcefully throw fistfuls of blossom petals at nothing.

"If only I'd been there! Once again I've failed everyone I love." She sagged in defeat and saw her father's face in her mind. Her heart panged but she stood, hating that anything beautiful could exist while she was in anguish. She cursed the pink trees—their loveliness mocking her.

Just then, a brilliantly indigo and violet bird flit about her head. Instinctively, she swatted at it, never quite making contact, until the bird hovered in front of her. The lovely bird's wings beat up and down to hold itself at eye level as she stared in astonishment at the bird's tiny rider.

Chapter Twelve

"Smithwick?"

The little creature moved his arms as if revealing a grand surprise. "None other, my lady!"

"You're...riding a bird..." She shook her head in disbelief. "I told myself I would no longer be shocked by these things." Luvenia wiped her eyes and sniffed, hoping Smithwick hadn't been present for her melodramatic tantrum.

"Ah, well, possibly someday." He grinned at her. "Lost, are you?"

Luvenia sighed. "Yes. I need to return to Orford immediately."

"That would be the other direction, of course." His little beady eyes sparkled in the sunlight.

"I realize that now, thank you. It will just take me a lot longer to get there now and I need to avoid the castle." She realized she should have omitted that last part.

"Is that so? And why is that?" He eyed her suspiciously, his animal nose twitching.

Luvenia raised her chin defiantly. "That is really none of your concern. Now, you are a Gatekeeper, correct?"

Smithwick nodded wearily. "A Porter, yes..."

"Then you shall accompany me to the Gate and help me get through to Orford. Let's go." She turned toward the direction in which she had come, but the bird flew ahead of her and stopped again in front of her face.

"You hold on one moment, young lady. First of all, you have no right to walk about demanding things of me.

Secondly, what if I have other plans for this fine day? And thirdly, do you even have your Portal Key to get through the Gate into Orford?"

"My what?" She placed both fists on her hips.

Smithwick raised a tiny furry brow at her. "You listen here, girl." He pointed a finger sternly at her. "Your sass will not be tolerated by your present company. Your tantrum and despair are no doing of mine, and you shall not treat me as if it were. Or order me about, for that matter."

Luvenia's face softened and she dropped her hands to her sides.

Smithwick continued, "Now, Aureland is not the place to house prisoners, unless they've warranted a stay in the dungeons. And are you in the dungeons?"

Luvenia shook her head mutely.

"Correct. Anyone else living here will be here of their own volition. If you have your Portal Key, I will gladly guide you to the Gate."

"I don't have a Portal Key. I don't know what that is." She attempted to keep the smidgen of irritation from her voice but failed.

"Certainly you do or you wouldn't be here in the first place. Perhaps you left it at the castle. You did leave in haste, you know." The Porter raised a fuzzy eyebrow knowingly.

"How could you know that? Did you follow me all this way?" She was angry at yet another invasion of her privacy.

"That overly emotional temperament of yours is damaging, dear girl. No. Not the entire way. Khyan was concerned. He found me before flying to Orford and asked that I keep you safe."

She threw hands in the air and growled. "Why do you all insist on treating me like a child?"

"Oh, calm yourself. No one is treating you like a child. They merely care for you, especially Prince Khyan. You have been a part of his life for over ten years. He cherishes you deeply.

Can you not see that? Here you are fretting over mistakes you can no more go back and change than you could go back and change the War. It does not do to dwell amongst your ghosts and miss the land of the living, dear girl."

Luvenia picked at her nails sheepishly. "I didn't realize Khyan cared so much. Thank you for telling me. But I think he just wants to ensure I don't leave Aureland."

"That is simply not true. Certainly he wishes for you to stay, as do the others that have grown fond of you, but the prince wishes more for your happiness and wellbeing than your location. You will not be safe in Orford, Luvenia."

"I don't care about my safety. I care about my *sister's* safety. *I want my sister out of danger.* Perhaps Khyan can empathize with that."

Smithwick sighed. "Quite right. Well, if I cannot persuade you to stay, we must retrieve your Portal Key. Come along." He shifted the reins on the bird and off they went toward the castle.

Luvenia spoke as they ventured back, "I don't know what my Portal Key is. Maybe I don't need one."

"Everyone needs one to enter Aureland. Unless you are a Keeper, which you, my dear, are not," he explained.

"Khyan was there and he's a Keeper, maybe he brought me through?"

"Hmm," the Sean'an considered the possibility for a moment. "No, you came in alone. Quite a tumble you took."

"How do you know that? You weren't there. We had to travel to Sourn to see you."

"Oh, I know all that happens at each Gate. I am the Master Porter, after all. The events at each entrance into Aureland scroll through my memory like moving paintings."

Her curiosity sparked. "That's incredible. What is happening there right now? At the Orford Gate?"

Smithwick smiled. "It was about time for me to check on them anyway, good thinking." He closed his eyes and

Luvenia watched expectantly. "The Orford side is calm. This is good news. Several Collectors have come to investigate the site of your disappearance in the last few days. Hmm… All appears well at the other outer Gates. Let's peek at the Aureland sides." He scrunched up his little face. "Not much is happening on the west side. Just a few bonehound cubs fighting over a piece of meat. This is also good news. A rather questionable gentleman entered the North Gate a couple of days ago. On the east side we have several Hordemen preparing for General Cremeux and Miss Revencloud to enter Anjali tomorrow. Bad idea, that is, but my queen knows what she's doing. Hmm… North side. Oh dear .." Smithwick chuckled.

"What is it?" Luvenia prodded him, feeling a bit more cheerful for the first time since Khyan had come to visit her rooms.

Smithwick opened his eyes to explain. "The West Gate is located beneath the Potame Sea. This particular sea is home to a large population of merpeople—"

"Who people?" Luvenia interrupted.

"Oh! Why of course you wouldn't know what they are. Merpeople. They are half human and half sea creature. Goodness, you positively must meet one before you leave Aureland. Anyway, there is a mermaid...a girl merperson, who takes a great deal of pride in playing tricks on the other merpeople. Morgana is her name. It seems this morning Morgana has successfully convinced a sailor to lend her a large looking glass and she has arranged it to reflect the Portal location. She is currently hidden, watching the mercreatures swim into it, thinking it is the Portal." Smithwick wiped a joyful tear from his eye, laughing. "Oh, that one! Truthfully, I should reprimand her, but it is just so amusing!"

Luvenia smiled and tried to imagine a merperson. A *mermaid*, he'd called her. She thought she would like to see one of those before leaving, but there simply wasn't time.

"And the South Gate?" she asked, back to business.

"Ah, yes." Smithwick closed his eyes once more. "Oh." He sighed and his face dropped. "Darius is there. He seems to be waiting on something. I would venture to say you, my dear." He opened his eyes and looked at her sidelong.

This took her by surprise. "Me? Why would the general wait there for me?"

"He must have learned you were attempting to leave."

"Alright, I suppose. But why wait there? To stop me?"

Smithwick thought for a moment. "Knowing Darius, I would assume he wants to accompany you and help you rescue your sister from harm."

General Darius Cremeux paced back and forth within the cave that housed the southern Gate into Orford. He felt like a blind fool for disrespecting his queen to help a girl he knew nothing about, but he simply could not stop thinking of her, not for one instant since he first laid eyes on her.

He could claim that he abandoned his duties because he wanted to help her find her sister—which he did. He could claim that he wanted justice served for the abduction of a child—which he did.

But it was neither of those things that had led him to the cave, and he knew it. Something within her called to him. He was unsure if it was his desire to comfort a broken soul, or possibly the interest she'd shown in his paintings, or perhaps the heaviness he longed to bare for her. Maybe he had merely found the first girl he thought beautiful since Lydia.

Thera was beautiful, but not like the girl. She had

something beyond physical beauty, and it called his name.

Darius shook the thoughts loose.

Luvenia wasn't certain what to make of what Smithwick had said. Why would Darius help her? They'd only spoken a couple of times, briefly. Wasn't he supposed to go to Anjali in the morning with Thera?

"I don't understand," she finally said.

"General Cremeux has a heart that beats fiercely for justice. He is not a rash man by any means at all. I'm certain he spoke with Nuria and formulated a plan to assist you...or he's become irrational and blinded by a beautiful woman." He winked at her. "Take your pick."

Luvenia blushed. "That is preposterous. He hardly knows me. Nuria probably wants him to keep an eye on me. Khyan sent you, after all. Like brother, like sister, I suppose."

Ignoring her jab at the queen and prince, the Sean'an Porter said, "Do you see how much they care for you now?"

She pursed her lips at him and changed the subject. "About my Portal Key. How does that work? What does it look like?"

"The Keys were originally forged by Keepers and infused with power, allowing the possessor of the key to enter Aureland, or one of the other Keeper realms. The Keepers knew the make and location of each Portal Key at one time, but this has grown increasingly more difficult over the centuries as more travel throughout other continents. The Keys are all quite different. Usually, they are in the form of a piece of jewelry or a trinket—something passed down over many generations. Do you have anything similar?"

She thought out loud, "I have some jade hair pins passed down from my mother, but I think my father bought those and I'm fairly certain they're lost at the bottom of a prison cart. I don't wear any other jewelry and I certainly don't have any trinkets."

"Hm. Do you recall any other pieces of jewelry, maybe a pocket watch or a pendant, that have been in your family for many generations? Possibly something that could have found its way into your pocket, perhaps, or a bag?"

Luvenia thought carefully and shook her head. "No, nothing in my satchel like that. I lost it back on my farm anyway. I left it on my father's horse." The thought of Vesper made her miss him and hope he found his way safely into his stall in the stables to keep warm ...

"The stables!" she shouted.

"Not following, dear."

"A couple of days before everything happened, my mother and I had a conversation in the stables about her wedding band, passed down several generations, and the amulet my father gave her the day I was born." Maybe she was onto something.

"That sounds like a jolly good start! And you have these items?"

"Well, no..." Smithwick looked at her disapprovingly. "Those are the only items passed down that I know of. I had nothing else in my possession, so either I ended up with one of those on accident, or something else I have is the Portal Key. All I have right now is this ridiculous borrowed dress," she fumed.

"A trip back to the castle is inevitable, dear. You, at the very least, need a change of clothing and a cloak or riding jacket. We can't have you running around the realms looking like a fugitive. Though, I suppose that is what you are," he told her with a grin.

She hadn't thought of that. "A fugitive. That's a new life dream attained." She chuckled sarcastically.

Smithwick laughed out loud with his tiny animal mouth.

"Was that a *jest*, Luvenia Rousseau?"

A hint of a smile crossed her lips.

"Sometimes things are so terrible, there is nothing left to do but laugh at how absurd it all is, hm?" He smiled at her. "Would you mind if I showed you around a bit on the way back to the castle? Considering we must head there regardless..."

"I really don't want any detours. I need to get to my sister as quickly as possible."

"Even if we made it to the castle in the next few moments, you wouldn't make it to Orford and through the woods to your farm before dark. You might as well enjoy your last day here, retrieve your Portal Key, get a good night's rest, and venture off tomorrow at dawn. In addition, you should truly leave on better terms than the ones recently established."

Luvenia sighed. "You have a point I suppose. What about Darius?" She certainly didn't want to leave the man waiting around for her if she wasn't going to be there. The idea of him possibly risking his position for her had left its mark.

"Ah, yes." Smithwick closed his eyes to see if Darius was still waiting at the Gate. "Still there." He snickered. "Sword fighting an invisible opponent. He must be rather bored." He opened his eyes. "I'll send Marla to inform him. She's tired of flying me around, anyway."

He pulled out a notebook the size of a thimble and scribbled a note with a tiny quill. He attached the note to a string around Marla's neck and deposited the notebook back into his satchel.

"Coming over!" With that, he jumped off the bird and landed on Luvenia's shoulder with a grin. The bird zipped off at unnatural speed.

"She's a Bluestreak Rapidflyer. They're perfect messenger birds. Most can't tame them for riding—they're such free spirits—but Marla loves me…for a while, anyway." He grabbed a small chunk of Luvenia's hair and made himself comfortable on her shoulder. "Take a left, just up ahead. I think you'll rather like the Viridian Bay."

After meandering through the forest for a good while—stopping every so often to let Luvenia inspect and pet all of the strange animals—and passing a couple of friendly villages, the trees ended abruptly, as did the earth. The air was warm and humid in this area of Aureland— how the temperature could fluctuate so much in only a short distance was beyond her—and the smell of salt filled Luvenia's nose.

She halted to take it all in before advancing to the cliff's edge. The sea protecting the Alban Castle back home in Orford was another half a day's ride from the Alban Market and Luvenia had never been that far. Her father had promised to take her once she turned ten, but he'd never gotten the chance. Every so often, she could catch a hint of the sea salt on the wind at Market, but never anything like the scent hanging in the air now. She'd dreamed of seeing the sea her entire life.

Smithwick seemed to sense her desire to soak up every ounce of the moment, and held his peace, letting her take her time. She carefully submitted to memory the scent and the view of the earth dropping off ahead of her, then made her way to the edge of the cliff overlooking the Viridian Bay.

What she saw took her breath away more than any of the other amazing things she'd seen over the last several days. Just below her, waterfalls cascaded off the cliff rocks, spraying her feet. The warm sun glinted off the calm water below, the only disturbance was the foam developing where the falls crashed into the bay.

Just ahead, the water funneled into a channel, where a bridge connected two pieces of land before the channel opened into a vast body of water, continuing farther than the eye could see. She could make out several boats coming in and out of what she believed her father had said was called a port. A small village sprung up from the port, all the way to where the water ushered into the channel.

Smithwick thoroughly enjoyed the mystified look upon the girl's face and smiled as he said, "Welcome to Viridian Bay. That," he pointed out to sea, "is the Potame Sea."

"The one with the merpeople?" She was hardly able to contain her excitement.

Smithwick chuckled. "Yes, the sea ends here. The North Gate area where they live is much further out and, well, north of here."

Luvenia frowned.

"But." he continued, "a few mermaids tend to find solitude here at times. Ah." He pointed to where a fin broke through the water in the bay. "There is one now." Luvenia looked but didn't see anything more than ripples.

"Just over there is a staircase that will lead us down to the beach and the water's edge. Would you like to go...Oh!" She was already walking toward it, quite hurriedly. She descended the stone steps, anticipation carrying her and Smithwick as fast as her legs could walk. Smithwick swayed back and forth, pulling her hair to stay on her shoulder, "Slow down! The sea is not going anywhere!"

Luvenia indeed slowed her pace, but more out of apprehension than obedience, as her excitement was replaced with wariness of the unknown. "Are the merpeople dangerous?"

"Oh, goodness me, no. Aureland is a safe haven."

"So, no harm can come here?" she wondered aloud.

"I didn't say that, exactly. Harm can come, and creatures can choose to do harm or evil, but our queen and her Hordemen are very good at keeping evil out, and Keepers are very good at inspiring us all toward what is true, right, noble, and pure."

Luvenia snorted a humorless laugh. "Right. Like some sort of slave masters?"

Smithwick shook his head, unphased. "No, not at all. Pure

love can inspire a great deal. Love is strong enough to influence without the fear of punishment, but not afraid to do so for the greater good. The Keepers are guides. Quite like Sean'an Porters and quite like the lighthouse in the port," he pointed toward a tall stone structure near the shore as Luvenia followed his line of sight.

"Ships are tossed about in the sea in the dead of night, nothing to aid them but a compass to point them in the right direction, and the flames of the lighthouse to guide them home. Everyone needs a lantern in the dark to guide their step, why not the ones empowered by Wisdom? Sure give ya' better odds." He winked at her.

She rolled her eyes, unimpressed. "Let's see what all this mermaid fuss is about." She continued walking toward the beach.

Upon reaching the end of the steps, Smithwick suggested she ditch her slippers and feel the sand beneath her bare feet. "You'll love it!"

Luvenia took his suggestion and left her shoes on the bottom stair, proceeding to gingerly step one foot onto the sand and then the other. It felt so soft and warm between her toes, like walking through powdered sunshine. Each step toward the water's edge left her more and more giddy. She could hear the waves crashing against the shore and the moored boats on the other side of the channel, but the water before her lay tranquil and still. She reached the wet sand holding the bay in its place, testing the consistency with one toe before stepping further.

Finding the texture rather delightful beneath her feet, she stood upon her toes and spun gracefully, holding Smithwick steady. She breathed in the sun's rays and walked on, straight into the water that beckoned her. She waded in up to the hem of her dress, Smithwick bouncing on her shoulder. The water exhilarated her. It was the perfect temperature to cool, but not chill, in the humid weather of Viridian.

"Well, keep going, of course," Smithwick urged her, gesturing to the rest of the bay.

"This is quite far enough, my dress will be wet," she responded firmly as a small, red fish nipped at her toe.

"Oh, don't be a ninny. You want to see a mermaid, do you not?"

She took the bait. "You mean to tell me I can't see a mermaid from here? I need to go in further?"

Smithwick grinned at her impishly. "I mean to tell ya' you must go all the way under!"

Luvenia recoiled. "But I haven't any extra clothing and I don't even know how to swim."

He howled with laughter and shouted, "Ya' better learn quickly, then!" before leaping off her shoulder into the clear turquoise water in a perfect tiny swan dive.

Just then, the sand shifted below, and her legs went out from under her as she was pulled into the water with a yelp.

Instinctively, she struggled against the two sets of hands pulling her deep below the surface by her ankles. She thrashed against them, her memory flashing with terror to the Collector who held her beneath the brook attempting to drown her, until she caught sight of two enormous, exquisite fish.

The sight stunned her into passivity, just long enough for her to realize they weren't fish at all. Her eyes traveled up their long fish-like tails to witness two human torsos on either side of her, holding onto her legs with their human arms. Atop their elegant necks were two gleaming, playful faces.

Next to them, a silently laughing Smithwick sat upon a miniature swimming horse. She noticed with great surprise that it, too, had no legs, but a tail that curled up underneath it and it wore a petite saddle and reins.

Luvenia realized she should have drowned by now. Or quite possibly had drowned in that brook and truly was dead, what with all of the madness she'd encountered. She noticed it mattered not how deeply they pulled her under the water, her air never ran out, and her lungs never burned. Resigning to believe she wasn't in immediate danger, she elected to take in her surroundings instead of panicking.

The sea dwellers were more remarkable than she could have dreamed. Every unique shape and size seemed to live in the enchanting, emerald world beneath the surface of the bay. The mermaids hauling her along were somehow even more stunning than Thera—something she never thought possible. The one at her left had long, wavy, auburn hair with pearls dangling here and there as well as inlaid in her shimmering tail. Long lashes drew attention to her vivid green eyes shining with mischief.

The mermaid at her right smiled broadly with her full lips and pink cheeks. She had blonde hair that reached halfway to the end of her long tail. Her caramel eyes glinted jubilantly, as did the pink jewels embedded in her tail and swaying in her hair. They appeared to radiate, as if the sun were always hidden behind them, peaking around its playmates. They each had human ears, but also a fin-like attachment around their ears that fluttered like butterfly wings as they swam backwards, Luvenia in tow.

Finally, the mermaids relinquished her ankles of captivity and let her attempt to swim on her own. They laughed mutely as she frantically kicked and paddled about in circles. Smithwick joined in the amusement, though he dismounted his seahorse and swam about, emphasizing his movements for her to mimic.

A quick learner, and with unlimited air in her lungs, it took only a few moments to get the hang of it and begin propelling herself forward through the water. Once she had, the blonde-haired mermaid beckoned her forward toward a flickering light.

Certain by now that she was in fact dead, she continued

toward the illumination curiously. The light grew closer, yet never brighter as they approached. She saw Smithwick grin and the mischievous mermaids wink before the water went pitch black. She hardly had enough time to consider panic before she was immersed in radiance.

Above, below, on all sides, they were surrounded by thousands of brilliantly glowing creatures, like giant underwater fireflies with fluffy tentacles. Even the mermaids looked on in wonder and astonishment, as if seeing them for the first time, though she knew this couldn't be the case. Satisfied to simply stare at them forever, Luvenia was surprised to see some of the light creatures flicker and some glow off and on in sync with others, as if they were preparing for something.

She looked to her left just in time to see the auburn-haired mermaid open her mouth to sing. Flowing from within her came the sound of an entire magnificent orchestra, far greater than the one that played for the Alban Ballet her father had taken her to a few months before he died. She'd fallen in love with the music and dancing, determined to one day join their ballet company.

Pietro shut them down after their following performance.

But this...*this* music defied the earth. It was extraordinary. As if her song were not enough, the blonde mermaid joined her with a beautiful melody in a foreign tongue. As she began her underwater singing, the glowing creatures swayed, moving about in time with the mermaids' music, blinking their lights in rhythm as they moved fluidly around one other.

They'd been preparing to dance for her. Despite being submerged in water, her eyes filled with tears.

She'd thought it time and time again since arriving in Aureland, but now she was certain—no sight in all the world could be more marvelous.

After several moments that felt like mere seconds, the performance ceased, and the mermaids lured her and

Smithwick further. They must have swum underneath the channel and into the Potame Sea, for the sea dwellers had become massive in size. She'd learned about some of the gentle giants in her studies growing up, but no schoolbook could have captured their magnitude. Just ahead of her, a snow-white whale, double the length of her large castle chambers, let out a long, low note like that of a trombone and coast gracefully toward the distant returning calls.

The path ahead was clear—aside from colorful fish swimming wildly about—and the lovely mermaids led the way to a pod of playful dolphins. They swam quickly by, flipping and rolling and nudging their onlookers sweetly. Each mermaid grabbed hold of a dolphin's dorsal fin, urging Luvenia to do the same. She first looked around to ensure Smithwick's tiny self hadn't been eaten by a whale. Finding him beaming atop his little seahorse once more, she deemed it safe to join the mermaids and their dolphins. A particularly loving one swam a cheerful circle around her, wanting her to select him. No sooner had she done so, the dolphins propelled the underwater excursion party swiftly forward and toward the sunlight.

In no time at all, they burst through the surface of the sea next to a large sailboat, *Lady Seafire* painted on the hull. Luvenia and Smithwick sucked warm, salty air into their lungs, keeping themselves afloat. The waves lapped at the sides of the boat as well as their faces, making it hard for Smithwick to breathe.

In between the water sloshing into his mouth he managed, "Let...me...climb atop...your head!" Luvenia reached out and set him on her head, feeling rather comical. Settled in with two fistfuls of hair, he ordered her, "Swim to Lady Seafire, we're here for her!"

Luvenia obeyed and swam alongside the ship as Smithwick whistled astonishingly loud for such a tiny fellow. Seconds later, a raven-haired head popped over the side, brilliant blue eyes flashing.

"Well, hullo there. What are the two of you doing out here in the middle of the sea?" Thera shouted over the sound of the waves. "I'll pull you up!"

Her head disappeared for a moment and a rope swung over the side, the looped end hitting the water next to them.

"Put your foot in the loop and hang on!" Thera shouted.

Luvenia did just that, and Thera hoisted them up and over into the boat, with the help of a very portly, grimy man with an eye patch. She freed her foot from the rope and reached atop her head to set Smithwick on a stack of crates. He promptly looked over the side and shouted his goodbyes to the mermaids. Luvenia leaned over the side and bid them farewell with him as their new friends waved elegantly back, gleaming in the sunlight. Harmoniously, they both leapt high above the water into the air, showing off their stunning tails once more, and dove into the sea with the slightest of splashes.

Luvenia turned around to find Thera scowling at her. The angry woman placed her hands on her hips moodily, remembering the morning's events. "Thought you were gone. Thought you decided you wanted to *slit my queen's throat*," she snarled, moving swiftly from moody to infuriated...and frightening, quite frankly.

Luvenia looked at her feet, ashamed, and picked at her nails. "That was uncalled for, and I apologize. I don't really wish to do that at all. Nuria has been very kind to me. You all have." Thera softened a slight bit and crossed her arms, listening as Luvenia continued. "This has been an extremely difficult time for me. I don't even want to think about it and everyone wants to lock me in a castle and counsel me. I will have those conversations when I wish to have those conversations and with whom I wish to have them." She crossed her arms defiantly, mirroring Thera—who dropped her arms and sighed.

Only one of them could be ill-tempered at a time, unless they desired that the entirety of Aureland be engulfed in storm—something Thera could already see the two of them had the capability of achieving together, should they join forces.

"You're right. We shouldn't force you. You do understand that you're not being held here against your will, though, correct?" Her blue eyes held only sympathy and concern for the girl.

Luvenia nodded. "I do realize that now that I've calmed down, yes."

"And had a marvelous day with yours truly!" Smithwick piped up from the crates.

"That as well," Luvenia admitted.

Thera smiled gently. "Come now, you're dripping everywhere. Let's get you some fresh clothing. Smithwick, this here's Frank. He'll figure out what to do with you." She slapped the large, unshaven man on the back and put her arm around her stowaway's shoulder to lead her into the cabin below the deck.

Thera rifled around in a trunk, pulling out a pair of old, plain brown riding pants and a simple, darker brown tunic. She handed them to Luvenia with a shrug. "Sorry. I keep a spare pair of clothes on the boat, but I've never needed them. I think they've been tucked away in that trunk for years."

Luvenia took the clothes, grateful to be dry again, even if dust and sand filled the air each time she moved in them.

Back on the deck with Smithwick, Thera pointed inland. "We're headed into the village. I have a couple of things to purchase before we ride back to the castle." She looked pointedly at Luvenia. "You are coming back to the castle, correct?"

The girl nodded. "I don't have much of a choice until

tomorrow."

"Alright. Sunset is not far off, so we'll need to find a horse you can ride. You do know how to ride?" Luvenia nodded once more.

Smithwick had his animal face upturned, soaking in the rays of sun. "My transportation shall be here shortly. I won't be joining you for supper. My sister's birthday celebration is this evening. The entire village is going."

Thera looked at him curiously. "A silent birthday? Why not have the celebration in the day when you can make a ruckus?"

"We make a ruckus every day! Birthday celebrations are quite different for the Sean'an. You will have to join us one day. I'm quite surprised you haven't already. I suppose your nomad blood keeps you away too often, hm? Ah, there is my transportation now! Smart little spitfire, she is."

A lizard creature with wings and a smoking snout approached and hovered in front of them proudly. Thera squealed with delight. "I've been so excited to meet the newest addition to your collection of mounts. May I touch her?"

Smithwick hopped off the crates and into the air, landing on the saddled back of the scaly, winged lizard. "Eh...You can try! She gets a little feisty around the larger folk."

The reptile watched her with sharp yellow eyes as a clear lid flipped down and up before a scaly lid followed suit. Thera reached out gingerly and gently touched her on the forehead between the eyes, much like she would her horse. The creature flew back slightly, and a bit of flame huffed through her nose.

Thera stepped back respectfully and clapped with glee. "I've never seen an infant dragon! What will you do when she grows full size?"

"I do believe Nuria's birthday should be around that time." He winked at Thera, her eyes wide.

This was all very fascinating, but something occurred to

Luvenia, and she was through with being distracted from her mission. "Wait. You can’t go. I need you to help me locate my Portal Key."

"Thera can assist you, I'm sure. Farewell, friends!" Off Smithwick flew on the infant dragon.

Luvenia glanced at Thera, one brow raised in question. Thera shrugged. "Shouldn't be that hard to locate. Oh, here we are." She pointed to the port behind Luvenia. "We'll be in and out in no time."

"What do you do on this boat anyway?" Luvenia wondered.

"It's the fastest way to get to the northside of Aureland. Some of our Hordemen are stationed near there and I deliver the orders when Khyan and Darius are...occupied.”

Luvenia sensed a slight hostility in her voice. "Oh. They're occupied because of me?"

"Yes, partially. The prince has gone out again to try and locate your sister. Darius, however, has lost his mind completely. He claimed you had a right to leave if you wished to and that you will need help rescuing your sister. Why he felt *he* needed to be that help when he is needed here and has orders is beyond me." Thera shook her head.

"Do you think Khyan has found anything concerning Ester's whereabouts?" She did not wish to discuss Darius.

"I suppose we'll find out at supper."

Lady Seafire slid up to the dock and Thera helped Frank tie her up and bring in the sails. They exited the boat and made their way down the dock to the small, bustling port village, Luvenia's sea legs a bit wobbly.

The homes and shops were alive with color. Unlike the bland stone and wood structures of Orford, these buildings were painted in different shades of blues, yellows, oranges, reds, and other vivid colors with terracotta roofs and wide-open doors. Practically every door and window—home or shop—stood wide open to let in the sea breeze. The villagers hauled about goods in large baskets, each person friendlier than the last as the women walked along the pathways.

"Here we are!" Thera announced, chipper, and led Luvenia around a corner into a loud market.

All around, baskets upon baskets overflowed with goods. Fruits and vegetables she'd never seen before and some that she'd heard of but that no longer existed in the Alban Commoner Market. As well as spices of varying scents and fabrics of all different colors and textures.

Thera sauntered down the aisles, returning the jovial smiles of the marketeers and chatting with a few until she stopped at several large baskets filled with purple and green grapes.

Luvenia had only eaten grapes—purple ones—one time when she was four. They were rather an expensive delicacy before the famine and non-existent once it hit.

She supposed the Royal Markets must have some, considering they had wine, but the Commoner Markets most assuredly did not.

She must have been making a face, for when Thera glanced at her she chuckled and said, "Would you like some?"

Luvenia answered her with an emphatic nod.

"Nuria adores grapes, and this market sells the juiciest ones." Thera winked at the seller as she handed her coins and picked up a wicker basket to fill. She then handed Luvenia an entire bushel.

"Thank you so much, I haven't had grapes in a very long time." She hadn't realized quite how hungry she was, but the sight of food in her hands made her stomach rumble. She ate one, wanting to savor them, but they were so delicious, and she was so ravenous they were gone by the time they reached Thera's next stop.

"Corbin here is the best shrimper in Aureland." Thera beamed at the tan, aproned man sitting on a short stool in front of them.

He ceased carving the piece of wood in his hand and looked up as Thera spoke. "Aw shucks, darlin'. Jus' know where ta' find the lil buggers, is all!" He took in Luvenia and gestured to her with the knife in his hand. "Who's ya' friend? Pretty lil' lady, she is." He smiled kindly at her.

"This is Veni. She's new around here, so we need a special deal, how 'bout that?" She winked at Luvenia.

"Now, now, darlin', I already give ya' a deal cause ya' buyin' for muh queen. How's about a trinket?" Corbin reached into a basket behind him and presented Luvenia with a small painted carving of a mermaid.

"Oh, it's lovely. I just met the mermaids, and they were so delightful. What a perfect trinket to remember my visit here. Thank you, sir. You are too kind."

The villager chuckled. "Ya' more than welcome, lil' lady. Glad ta' have met ya'." He turned to Thera as he filled a basket full of shrimp. "Ya' tell Queen Nuria 'tis been too long since we seen her 'round here." He handed her the basket with a broad smile, his teeth stark white against his red-tan skin.

"Will do, Corbin. You're a good man. Tell Linny and the children Aunt Thera said hullo."

"Sure thing, darlin'. Ya' take care'a ya'self, ya' hear?" His voice held a rather fatherly tone that received an eye roll from Thera.

"You know I do." She kissed him on the cheek and handed the shrimp basket to Luvenia to carry.

"Doesn't Queen Nuria have servants to travel and deliver orders and purchase her special items for her?".

"She has servants, yes, but only those that have chosen their position. They aren't typical servants like those Pietro owns. Queen Nuria owns no one. They are free to go if they please and she takes very good care of those in her charge, as well as pays them. They're more like a staff. They do generally handle these matters, but not when shrimp is involved."

They made their way out of the market and up to where Thera's horse was grazing. "Corbin and his wife took me in when I first traveled to Aureland as a child. They very much became my family, so I enjoy coming to market when I need to travel this way. Usually, I would stay for supper and an evening with their sweet children, but we must be getting you back. Not to mention Darius and I leave in the morning...if he's gotten his head on straight again."

"Why is it so bad that he should want to help me?"

"It's not bad. A noble man for a noble cause. Darius despises injustice as the rest of us do and he wanted to help. There is nothing wrong with that. The problem lies in the fact that he is typically an extremely calculated man, and he has duties. He is the general of our Hordemen and the leader of our excursion into Anjali tomorrow. He acted rashly when he discovered you had run away to return to Orford alone to find your sister. He stormed into the queen's study and demanded an explanation of why you'd been treated in such a manner that led you to feel running away was your only option. He declared that he would not be going to Anjali. Instead, he would be going to Orford with you to find Ester, and *then* he would search the Arichan Mountains and leave Anjali to someone else."

Thera shook her head, her dark hair silky in the sun. "He left without so much as a response from Nuria. Never has he treated orders in such a way. He, of course, can get away with that, but he's never attempted to before."

Luvenia was unsure of how to feel about Darius' reaction. She felt her face flush and purposefully focused on the part having nothing to do with her. "Why is it that he can get away with disobeying orders or speaking to the queen in such a manner? Pietro would have him hung if he did that in Orford."

They reached Thera's horse and she began tying the grape basket to the mare. "Nuria is nothing like Pietro. She practically raised Darius and his sister when their father went mad. We've all trained with her and Khyan since we were children, but Darius has always held a special place in her heart."

Luvenia didn't respond. She was realizing there was far more to these people than she first assumed. Thera had come to Aureland as a child and had to be taken in by a strange family, meaning she had come there alone. Darius' father had gone mad when he was a boy and he also had to be taken in by another. It seemed there was a common thread running through the lives of her new friends, one that wove through her as well.

"Come, let's see if anyone has a mount we can purchase for you," Thera said, interrupting her thoughts.

After speaking with several villagers, Thera found a sweet older gentleman with a mare he claimed he'd never be able to ride again. He told them it would be a delight to donate the horse to his beloved queen. Thera thanked him profusely and bowed courteously. When he turned to go back inside his house, she slipped several coins in his empty soup bowl sitting on the porch, covering it with the hat lying next to it for him to find later.

She shrugged. "Such a sweet man. There is no way I can take such a generous sacrifice."

The women mounted their horses and set off along the trails toward the castle and what Luvenia hoped would be a long bath, a hot meal, and a chance to locate her Portal Key.

Halfway into their journey, they heard sounds of a struggle in the brush. A feminine voice whimpered and Luvenia looked in alarm at Thera, who halted her horse and appeared uneasy yet focused on locating the source of the sound. She put one finger to her lips to ensure Luvenia knew to keep silent. She held out a hand, instructing her to stay put, and slid off of her horse onto the ground, silent as a cat. She snuck into the trees and brush, her dagger at the ready. Soon she was no longer visible from where Luvenia sat.

She squirmed on her horse as she waited for Thera to return. She hated feeling helpless and being left out in the open.

Aureland was supposed to be safe, Smithwick had said as much, but that fact made the sense of dread spreading through her stomach deepen all the more.

Unable to handle the suspense any longer, Luvenia dismounted and tied the two mares to a nearby tree. She proceeded to follow what she could of Thera's path through the brush, the tracking instincts her father had instilled in her coming to the surface. She tried desperately to move silently, though her borrowed boots were a bit too large, leaving her clumsier than normal. Just ahead she heard a rustling of brush and turned to follow the sound. Seconds later, a woman screeched in fearful alarm followed immediately by a surprised curse from a gruff male.

Luvenia abandoned all stealth and raced toward the noise, arriving just in time to see a bloody woman slump against an oak tree, trembling in fear. The bodice of her dress and underclothes torn clean off, she clutched the hem of her skirts to her chest, shielding herself as best she could.

Several feet from the battered woman, Thera stood at the ready, her dagger poised to strike as she took in her opponent—a vile sort of man with a rotted smile and an innocent woman's blood caked on his shirt. Courage and compassion flooded Luvenia's chest, crashing into one another and urging her to act.

At the same instant, as if it had been planned, Thera advanced toward the filthy man while Luvenia raced for the woman, stripping off her outer tunic as she went. Luvenia crouched to the ground, wrapping her tunic around the shaking woman and holding her close as they both waited for what would happen next.

The perpetrator licked his raw lips and showed his rotted teeth once more as Thera slunk toward him. Within the blink of an eye, Thera's dagger sunk into a tree, a hair from missing the man's face.

He looked at the knife and snickered. "You missed."

But Thera was already bounding the last few steps toward him and leaping into the air.

His eyes went wide just before she threw her weight into him, her elbow jamming into his throat while she kicked his legs out from under him. In the same swift, graceful movement, she pulled her dagger out of the tree. The man hit the ground with a thud and cloud of dirt as she stomped her boot onto his chest and held her dagger to his throat.

"I *never* miss," she purred with feline ferocity.

The man coughed, the air knocked out of him. "Theralin Revencloud, eh?"

She smiled a vicious, beautiful smile. "My reputation precedes me."

The victim woman had gone into hysterics, but Luvenia was frozen, her eyes bulging out of her skull, shocked by what she had just witnessed. The man was twice Thera's size, if not more, and she'd disabled him in one move, looking like some dark, glorious wraith as she did it.

He struggled against her peculiar strength, and she slammed him back down, digging the tip of the dagger into his skin, just enough to draw a trickle of blood.

"Your name," she growled, glancing at an inky mark upon the inside of his forearm.

He smiled at her. "You wish you knew, *Theralin*." He uttered her name with such lust. She slammed her boot down on his esophagus so hard he gagged.

Thera leaned into his face and whispered, "If I hear my name on your tongue again, I'll cut it out. Understood?" The man sputtered and nodded his head. "I think I'll let Darius deal with you, *pig*." His eyes went wide again, and she knocked him out, one clean blow to his temple with the pommel of her dagger.

She turned to Luvenia and smiled sweetly. "Veni, please be

a dear and retrieve some rope from my mare." Luvenia detangled herself from the bloodied woman and rose, still in shock, and nodded. "Quickly, please." She glanced back at the woman and Thera reassured her. "He's out cold, Veni. I'll keep an eye on her."

Luvenia ran as fast as she could, paying no mind to how exposed she was in just her underclothes for a blouse. She retrieved the rope and arrived back at the scene to find the man still unconscious and the woman sipping from Thera's small water pouch that had been strapped to her belt.

"Thank you," Thera told her as she took the rope. "We'll tie and gag him, but I had to send a messenger sparrow to some of the Hordemen to come retrieve him."

Luvenia watched as she tied the man's feet and hands, then tied him to the tree she'd thrown her dagger into. She ripped the hem of his shirt to make a gag that she fit into his mouth. Once he was entirely secured, she inspected the mark on the man's forearm with great concern before dropping his arm limply back to the ground and approaching the woman once more. She gently helped her put the tunic on and used the last of the water and a ripped piece of cloth to clean the woman's wounds.

She gestured toward the horses. "She can ride with us. The Hordemen will be here shortly to retrieve him. He won't be awake for a while."

They made their way slowly back to the mares and mounted. The woman sat behind Thera and soon fell asleep against her back, her arms wrapped tightly around Thera's middle.

Once she knew the woman was sleeping, Thera spoke to Luvenia. "Good thinking back there, Veni. You have a good heart in you."

Luvenia looked at her strangely and answered with a bit of a bite. "That was you. I felt the urge to help her come upon me like the other times you altered my emotions."

Thera looked confused, if not a bit offended. "I did no such thing. I haven't influenced your emotions since that day in the garden and I never will again unless you ask me to do so, or I must in order to save your life or the life of someone else. That was completely your doing and entirely your choice."

Luvenia thought hard about what Thera had said for the rest of the journey back to the castle. She thought about her heart, not believing it to be good at all. Only pain, hatred, and loss lived there.

She thought about the courage that had surged through her to help someone who needed it. She thought of how something so terrible could have happened in Aureland when Smithwick said it was safe. She thought of the grace and power Thera held. But most of all she thought of rescuing her sister and what she would need to be in order to do so.

Thera rode on in silence, acutely aware of her new friend's emotional turmoil. The girl would ask her questions later, and Thera would answer them.

Upon arriving at the castle stables, Luvenia said nothing to Thera or their rescued victim, knowing she would be taken care of. Instead, she dismounted and stormed directly to the castle, Thera shouting after her—something about needing a proper blouse. Luvenia didn't hear her and took the fastest route to Queen Nuria's study. She barged in without so much as a knock and not a single guard stopped her. Nuria certainly deemed her no threat. The queen and Darius both looked up as she entered and stomped her way to stand in front of them.

Fists clenched at her sides, fury alight in her eyes, and the roaring fire at her back she demanded, "*Teach me to fight.*"

Part Two

Chapter Thirteen

The stars twinkled high above in the velvet sky as Darius led Luvenia to a gazebo in Queen Nuria's garden, the last stop of the castle tour he'd promised her that morning—a time that felt like ages ago.

The queen hadn't been the slightest bit shocked by Luvenia's demanding intrusion prior to supper. She had merely smiled proudly at the girl and told her that her training would begin the following morning.

Upon Nuria's command that Darius arrange for said training, he had promptly informed Luvenia that they would train her only if she ceased running away fitfully and if she would promise not to rescue Ester by herself. She agreed, though she wasn't certain she was truly being honest and left to bathe and pretend she hadn't just stood in front of a queen and a handsome general in only her filthy under blouse.

The evening had mostly been filled with her new friends' joy at her return—especially Helga, who hugged her legs tightly for several moments—followed by more arguments at supper over the Anjali and Rebel missions. Luvenia had said nothing, but her mind was far from silent.

Darius had shown her about the castle over the course of the evening, only squirming slightly when she wanted to stop at each and every one of his paintings. She'd claimed a new favorite—his first—an extremely rough depiction of Smithwick he'd painted as an eight-year-old boy passing time in a large castle he'd explored countless times already. Luvenia smiled gleefully at the stick-like little creature with crude, wild brown lines for hair. Darius had been slightly embarrassed, but he'd hardly seen her half-smile, so he didn't mind. In fact, he rather enjoyed it.

He found himself wanting to spend as much time as possible with her before he left for Anjali, regardless of how little sleep it caused, though he couldn't quite pinpoint why. He hadn't felt that way since his childhood sweetheart had taken her own life when they were sixteen. Shoving those thoughts away once more, he'd decided to take Luvenia to Nuria's garden.

Luvenia couldn't recall much of what she'd seen the day she'd walked in the garden with Nuria and Thera, but she was certain it was much different in the daylight. At night the flowers seemed to sleep, but golden lights danced in between the blooms as fountains here and there splashed lullabies for them.

Her life had been a mass of chaos as of late and the angry, vengeful pain remained simmering below the surface threatening to erupt, but she had to admit the day had been exciting and delightful—for the most part.

Darius interrupted her thoughts after realizing he'd been staring at her for a moment. “I'm sorry we didn't locate your Portal Key.” He'd helped her look for it when they reached her wing of the castle during their exploration.

“I'm sure I'll find it soon. Perhaps Nuria can help me in the morning.”

"She has a good sense for such things." He ran a hand through his close-cropped beard and changed the subject, anxious to soak up every detail he could about the girl he was trying—and failing miserably—to not care about. "Tell me about your family."

She looked at him with a disapproving smile, but a smile no less. "Ah, so this was all just a ploy to counsel me like the rest of them?" she questioned him, brows raised.

He laughed. "No, I have no intentions of counseling

anyone. I merely wanted to learn about you. No hidden intentions." He placed a hand over his heart. "On my honor."

She looked at him and smiled again genuinely. "You first." She nudged his shoulder with hers, sending sparks through him.

Darius huffed a laugh. "Fair is fair. I am actually from Orford as well. My father is from Toulona and my mother is from Vilora. I was born near Alban and raised there with my younger sister until my father went mad.

My mother died when my sister was born. I was only five at the time. My father was alright for a while, but he slowly began to lose his mind with grief, and I began to have to care for my sister, though I was but a boy. It's simply not possible for a child of seven to care for a toddler and a madman." He shook his head, both at the memories and at the abnormal openness the girl drew from him.

"Soon," he continued, "Khyan showed up at my father's house and convinced him to move us to Aureland. This wasn't difficult in the slightest, considering my father couldn't tell the difference between reality and a dream anyway. My sister and I took to Khyan instantly. I think—I think we were desperate for a real father. He brought us here with nothing more than the clothes on our backs and settled us in the small cottage you saw in the painting this morning.

He would come every day and bring me and my sister to the castle to explore and have lessons with Nuria. Eventually he taught me to fight and trained me to be General of the Aureland Horde in place of my father. He'd been the general until he married my mother. Khyan acted in his place, though he hated it immensely. Everything I am I owe to Khyan and Nuria…and Imogene of course. She is the Elfe who cares for my father."

"What of your sister? Will I meet her as well?"

Darius' mood dampened. "No. My sister decided to leave

several years ago to live with a family in Orford."

Luvenia waited a few heartbeats before responding, to ensure he was finished speaking. He obviously wished not to discuss his sister, though she wondered what her name was.

When he offered no more information she simply said, "I'm so sorry for the loss of your mother…and your father. I lost my father when I was seven as well, but it somehow seems worse to see your father every day, and not be able to get to him—the *real* him."

Darius was taken back by how insightful she was. "Yes. I don't think anyone has ever quite understood that truth before. Nuria taught me to mourn my father like a death." He shook his head. "But it's so much more than that. It's like looking at a ghost of him or a reflection but never the real thing. It's like—"

"Being taunted?" she interrupted.

"Yes. Quite like being taunted. I don't remember that much about him, but I know he was a good father."

"I have no doubt he was, Darius. After all, he raised a young boy to have a heart of bravery and a regard for others. So much so, that you tried your best to care for your family when most children would have simply shattered into pieces."

Her words brought great comfort to wounds he thought were healed, but he was discovering they were still easily opened, even after so many years.

"Thank you," was all he could manage.

She sensed his desire to move on, so she asked, "What about Thera and Sebastian? What are their stories?"

"Ah. I'm somewhat surprised Thera hasn't told you all of our life stories by now." Darius laughed.

"She told me tidbits. You know, enough to make a girl curious."

"Of course she did. Well, one thing Thera will always leave out is the fact that she is a princess."

Luvenia let out a small gasp. "She is? Of Aureland? So she's

Nuria's daughter? No, she said that shrimper in the Viridian Bay took her in..."

Darius laughed again, realizing he quite liked when Luvenia talked herself in circles. "No, not Nuria's daughter. She is Princess Theralin Revencloud of Vilora. She has four elder brothers and an elder sister, so she will likely never take the throne. When her parents learned they would give birth to an appointed Keeper, they made plans to send her to Aureland for training when she reached seven. They planned for her to travel all over the world to become well learned in all things regarding other countries. Their intention was to gain a diplomatic tool.

When they sent Thera through to Aureland, they sent her through the North Gate, which is a lake on the Viloran side, not realizing she wouldn't end up on dry land here. The North Gate is in the Potame Sea on our side. Some of the merpeople saw her floundering and took her to the surface where the shrimper you're referring to, Corbin, happened to be sailing at the time. He took her in and alerted Nuria. She showed up to retrieve her almost immediately. She let Thera go back often and stay with Corbin and his family since Thera loved them so much and Nuria knew they could be trusted.

I was eight when she came and had only been training with Khyan for a short while, but she saw us one day while on a break from her studies and threw a colossal fit—you've surely learned already how Thera can be—until Nuria allowed her to join us.

It didn't take Nuria long to unravel the Viloran King and Queen's true intentions for their daughter, and when Thera grew old enough to make wiser choices on her own, Nuria explained the situation and presented her with the choice to follow their wishes or stay in Aureland.

Thera chose to travel the world as her mother and father wished for her to, but she has never returned to see her family. She's rather notorious around the continent for being a nomad princess and she doesn't stay in one place long. What they don't know is what she *does* when she's traveling. That is Thera's own story to tell. This time she's stayed in Aureland nearly a year. That's a good, long stretch for her."

Luvenia hadn't noticed she'd leaned in closer, engrossed in the story. She sat back quickly and asked, "Do you think she ever will? See her family again, I mean."

Darius ran a hand through his curly mess of hair. "I'm not sure. I think if she does it won't be pleasant."

"Hmm," was Luvenia's only response. "What about Sebastian? I feel awful for treating you all with such contempt when I didn't even take a moment to learn who you truly are."

"It's alright, Veni. We all understand. Oh," he caught himself, embarrassed. "I apologize. I shouldn't have called you that."

She smirked in the sweet way that made his cheeks feel warm and waved her hand dismissively. "Most everyone calls me Veni, actually. My mother calls me Luvi." Her heart dropped a bit with the thought. "*Called*, I suppose." Life without her mother was going to be difficult to get used to.

The general took her hand briefly. "I'm so sorry for your loss. Perhaps in her honor I should call you Luvi." He wasn't sure if his suggestion was crossing a line and was foolish, or a welcome tribute, but Luvenia smiled sadly.

"Thank you. That is very thoughtful." She squeezed his hand once before letting go.

"Sebastian," Darius changed the subject, chewing on his lip. "He is a bit more of a mystery to us all. He and I don't always get along, but I think I would dread life without him. We're like two infernos trying to burn our own path yet stay brothers, but he will always mean the world to me.

None of us know his past, though. We know he was found by Pietro when he was twelve in an orphan house. She left him there, only calling on him for visits until he turned eighteen. He's been with her ever since. I'm not sure what she's done to him, but he loathes her. I suppose the rest of us do too, but he despises her enough that Nuria never questions his loyalty to our cause, even with no details about his life. Frankly, neither do I. I worry at times—something is definitely hidden under all that bravado—but at the end of the day I believe I can trust him."

"How did he come to work for Queen Nuria, if he has been with Pietro for so long?"

"That was an interesting event, quite honestly. Khyan had been watching Pietro the day she first issued her new decrees in the square a decade ago and noticed there was one amongst her new courtiers that was hardly old enough to be considered a man. He saw the hatred in Sebastian's eyes and followed him back to Pietro's castle and waited. When Sebastian ran to the stables later that day visibly upset, Khyan pretended to be a stable hand and offered him a way out. Sebastian initially claimed Pietro was his only family, but his curiosity and hatred eventually got the best of him. Now here we are."

Luvenia twirled the ends of her hair—that Helga had insisted she wear down again—considering all Darius had told her. "You know, it's not lost on me that you are all orphans. Like I am," she said quietly.

"Right you are. We're just a misplaced family, the lot of us." he nudged her playfully. "Ya' fit right in."

The sadness left her eyes once more and she laughed. "It's nice to fit in for once, I will admit."

The air was bitingly cold, and their breath became increasingly more visible with each word, but Darius and Veni shivered and spoke late into the night as she wore the general's coat and told him all about her father, her mother,

her brother, and her sweet Ester.

High above the garden in a tree, a pristine white owl sat perched next to an earthy brown one.

"She is *smiling* with him, Brother! Oh, there is hope yet," Queen Nuria whispered before flying off toward her castle.

Khyan's heart danced between comfort in knowing Luvenia was coping and pain in knowing it wasn't because of help he'd offered her.

Hours later, Darius lay staring at his dark ceiling, fingers laced on his chest.

I should not be thinking of her. If I don't have my honor and loyalty, I have nothing. Years I've spent… my entire life I've spent disciplining myself into a man of principle. It cannot be undone by a girl.

I'm not training her. I'll tell Khyan in the morning. I can't. This Anjali mission is what I need to focus on. Sebastian and Khy need to locate the Rebels and ensure that Emperor Nakamura does what he must to keep Anjali safe. That is my main concern. Not the delicate girl who flits about my mind like an elegant bird. Oh, Maker. Now I'm being poetic. never in my life...

This is pathetic. I'm done with this. Right now. I am not her protector, I am not her lover, I am not even her friend, not really. I hardly know her.

Alive or dead, Lydia deserves more respect than this. My honor deserves more respect than infatuation.

Darius drifted off to dreams of a pure, white bird locked in a cage, waiting to be freed to flight.

Luvenia couldn't manage a wink of sleep. The day's events played over and over in her mind, the many emotions creating a storm in her chest. From the raging sadness over her family and the exhilaration of meeting mermaids, to seeing Thera wallop a man twice her size and the nervous anticipation of learning to fight and rescuing Ester.

Not to mention the jittery butterflies in her stomach when she thought of Darius. All such emotions were too much to consider. Instead, she contemplated the conversation at dinner, concerning the Anjali and Rebel missions preparing to take place.

It had become obvious that Queen Nuria wanted Darius nowhere near Pietro, which Luvenia found rather curious, though no one questioned Nuria on it. Therefore, Darius was being sent to the Anjalian Emperor instead of to Orford in search of the Rebels.

This resulted in Thera or Khyan needing to accompany him, considering Sebastian must remain close to Pietro. Nuria had insisted Thera accompany Darius only to be the communication line between him and Nuria, since Anjali did not employ female warriors.

Luvenia found this to be a gross misuse of someone so gifted as Thera, both naturally and supernaturally. She also pondered the idea that if *Darius* were the communication line, he would return to the castle a great deal more and could assist Khyan and the Hordemen in training her more often.

The butterflies in her stomach fluttered once more and she flushed, pushing that thought away when another hit her.

She gasped and jumped out of bed, grabbing her dressing robe and lounging slippers. She hastily threw on the robe over her silk nightgown as she ran down the halls and into the wing of the castle occupied by Khyan and Darius—and Sebastian on the rare occasion he stayed there. She knocked frantically on both the prince and the general's doors simultaneously, pacing back and forth between them until both men emerged, groggy but ready for battle at almost the same instant.

"I've had an idea!" Luvenia shouted at them.

Darius sagged with relief and set down his sword upon seeing it was only the girl, not a guard reporting an emergency.

Khyan, however, hushed her. "It's the middle of the night, Veni."

"I'm sorry! But it's almost dawn anyway," she whisper-shouted. "This couldn't wait. I wasn't sure when you were leaving this morning and I had to tell you both my idea."

Khyan sighed, perturbed. Luvenia threw her hands on her hips sassily. "Well, aren't you a chipper bird this morning."

"It's not morning," he growled back.

Darius smirked at her quiet strength. All his efforts spent trying to untangle his emotions from her and return to solitude melted away. That realization wiped the smile instantly off his face as he became angry at himself. "What is this idea that just couldn't wait to be shared?" he interrupted Khyan and Luvenia's staring contest.

Veni turned to him. "I was thinking quite a lot about the missions commencing this morning and I think that using Thera as a communication runner is a poor decision." Both men chuckled and she scowled.

"Poor decision or not, we don't question our queen, Veni," Khyan told her gently. "Nuria could choose any one of our well-trained Hordemen to enter Anjali or act as messenger, but she chose Thera and there is a reason, vocalized or not."

"That's fine," she said. "I don't really care. I still think it's a poor choice and I have an idea. You may reject it if you wish and so may the queen, but I personally think it's brilliant."

"Let's hear it then," Darius urged her, crossing his toned arms across his chest. She faltered slightly, realizing he was in his sleeping clothes, and they did little to hide his muscular build.

She cleared her throat, back on track. "Thera should enter Anjali as Princess Theralin Revencloud of Vilora. She can infiltrate Emperor Nakamura's court and I have no doubt her beauty and abilities will win her favor with the emperor, who, if I recall, is still a young man, correct?"

Darius chewed on his lip, pensive, as Khyan cocked his head to the side, thinking as well. Luvenia watched them anxiously for a few moments as they contemplated her plan.

Finally, Darius looked at Khyan and shrugged with eyebrows raised and a surprised smile. "I think it's a really good plan, Khy..."

Khyan shook his head in disbelief. "It is. Why didn't we think of it?"

"Because you know she's a Keeper, but you forget she's a Princess," Luvenia answered for them. "I just learned these facts last night and I assume no one outside of her parents or the people of Aureland know that she isn't just still traveling around the world as a nomad studying different cultures. Which, by the way, gives her an upper hand in Anjali—knowing their customs. Also, she's of marrying age now, so why wouldn't her family send her to find a diplomatically sound husband? It's the perfect cover."

Darius huffed a laugh and ran a hand through his hair, pleasantly surprised by her clever mind. "Where did you say you're from again?"

She smiled proudly and shrugged.

The men dressed quickly and walked with Luvenia to Queen Nuria's study. Confused, she asked, "Isn't Nuria sleeping?"

Khyan shook his head. "No. My sister rarely sleeps."

Warm, flickering light filtered into the hallway from the open door of the study and Khyan led them in with one unnecessary but courteous knock.

The white-haired queen looked up from her desk. "Why, good morning my darlings." She glanced at the grandfather clock in the corner by the fireplace. "It is only the wee hours of the morning. Whatever are you three doing awake so early? And prancing around in a *dressing gown*, Miss Rousseau?" She raised an eyebrow at the girl disapprovingly.

Luvenia's cheeks reddened. She'd completely forgotten.

Darius spoke, "Luvenia came to us with an idea. It's truly a rather brilliant plan concerning Anjali."

Queen Nuria turned her attention back to the blushing girl, her entire plan suddenly forgotten. "Um—" Was all that came forth.

Darius jumped to her aid. "She states that Thera should infiltrate the Anjalian court as Princess Theralin Revencloud of Vilora. Thera already knows the language and the customs, and she is of marrying age, as is the young emperor. It is a perfect reasoning for her appearance there. The Viloran King and Queen are well known for sending away their youngest daughter to acquire cultural knowledge and a diplomatic union would likely be the next item on their agenda. Her beauty is unmatched, and her gifting can easily gain her an audience with the emperor, leaving him in the palm of our hand and Thera as a great influence in his ear."

Veni was relieved she didn't have to speak, though she felt a little irritated by the general's 'beauty unmatched' comment. It seemed uncalled for.

Queen Nuria looked at her with calculation before finally responding. "You are a very intelligent young woman, Luvenia Jane."

Veni wondered how the queen knew her middle name, but

she knew everything else, so why not know that as well?

She continued, speaking to Darius and Khyan, "I considered this very plan long ago. It is both simple and advantageous. However, I am not certain Theralin is ready for such a task on her own."

"I will still accompany her," Darius said.

"You would become nothing more than a guard and my communication line, General, and that is preposterous. If you're not on the front lines there, we need you here."

Khyan interrupted, "Sister, if I may, Thera is more than capable of this. She can be rash and emotional, yes, but I believe what holds her back from being a mature leader is the mere fact that *we* hold her back. It's time we instilled confidence in the girl and trusted her. She can do this."

Nuria thought for a drawn-out moment, tapping a long nail on her desk. Finally, she sighed. "Very well. Khyan, you will accompany her. We need you here more than there, but you can reach her the quickest."

The queen seemed uncharacteristically uneasy as she went on. "Darius, you will go to the Arichan Mountains with Sebastian. You will both remain entirely concealed. *Entirely.*" Her tone was fierce with the last word. "Inform Thera and Sebastian and the members of your convoys immediately. You depart at half past dawn, precisely."

Both men bowed with a, "Yes, Your Majesty."

Luvenia bowed a bit late, horrified that she curtsied holding her dressing robe like some evening gown. The men left and she turned to follow, but Nuria beckoned her. "Come here, Veni."

Nervous, she approached the queen's wooden desk.

The tender queen returned once more, through with giving orders. "You truly are a wise young woman." She smiled at her. "Your parents raised you so very well, dearheart."

A lump formed in her throat, but Luvenia managed a small

nod.

"I know you feel as if this journey has lasted a lifetime and that you have a lifetime yet to survive, which is partially true, but you have grown leaps and bounds in the last week alone. From the moment you stepped foot in my castle until now, there has been a dramatic change in you. That being said, I also know you are hiding deep anger and a ravaging desire for revenge against your brother. A desire that only grows deeper with each passing day, no matter how well you believe you're suppressing it."

Luvenia's heart raced, bewildered how the queen could know such a thing when she hadn't completely admitted it to herself yet.

"You know it is there, dearheart. You feel it pulling you in like quicksand. Do you not?"

She managed another small nod, tears threatening to leak from her eyes.

"Anger is natural, Veni. Fury at injustice is a gift, if you ask me. But revenge is *not* the answer. We need that particular fire extinguished immediately. There is a right way to fight injustice. You have taken the first step in beginning training later today, but you need to face the truth. The most fury you hold is toward yourself."

Nuria let that sink in a moment. "You must let that go, dearheart. Do not let the anger rule you. *You* rule the anger. Use it to drive you, not lord over you. My people know the difference between justice and revenge. And you shall as well." She smiled sympathetically. "Run along and dress in some proper clothes, hm?" She winked. "I shall see you at breakfast."

Before Veni could contemplate what Queen Nuria had told her, or make it to breakfast, a knock sounded at the door of her chambers. Helga opened it to find Khyan standing there in full riding gear and armed to the teeth.

Helga curtsied. "Prince." She hardly came to his mid-thigh

in height.

"Good morning, Helga. You look ravishing as always." She blushed and he bent down to kiss her hand.

"Yer such a schmoozer, Prince. Are yer here fer Veni? She's a still gettin' dressed. I'll accompany her ter breakfast if yer want."

"That's quite alright. I actually came to speak with her in a hurry," he told the Elfe.

"Girl!" Helga yelled unceremoniously over her shoulder from the doorway. "Prince Khyan's here ta' see yer!" She turned back and smiled impishly at the prince before hobbling off to tend the fire.

Veni came out of her bedroom in a sky-blue dress, twisting her curly hair into her usual style.

"Hi there. Haven't seen you in a while," she told him sarcastically around the hair clips sticking out of her mouth.

"It's been ages," he humored her. "Listen...I thought you might like to accompany Thera and myself to Anjali."

Luvenia ceased twisting her hair and stared at the prince.

He continued, "I'm merely accompanying her to the castle, ensuring her safety, and then returning to Aureland. I will fly in each day to check with her, or as often as I can at least. We are sending correspondence ahead of her to the Anjalian Emperor, so we have an opportunity to slowly travel there. I thought you might like to join us and begin your training with me and Thera instead of just one of the Hordemen while you wait for Darius and I to return."

"Yes!" she nearly shouted. "Yes. Anything to get Ester back faster. What do I need to wear? To bring?"

"Certainly not that frilly thing," he pointed to her dress. "You'll need riding clothes and boots and a water pouch. Helga—"

"On it, Yer Highness." She hobbled quickly out of the room to retrieve what Veni needed.

"This is exciting," Luvenia said. "What did Thera think of

the plan?"

"I think it opened a few wounds that haven't completely sealed, but she is thrilled to play the frou-frou princess card and woo a poor sap. This is her first large-scale, lone mission. She's even more thrilled that it was your idea."

Helga returned with riding clothes for Luvenia, and she quickly dressed. By the time she was finished, it was time for the traveling parties to depart to Anjali and Orford. Helga had asked the kitchen to pack some food for the journey, requesting a little extra for Luvenia since she missed breakfast and "needed ter fatten up a bit."

Darius bid them farewell with haste—pointedly ignoring Luvenia—claiming he needed to meet Sebastian as quickly as possible. The girl was taken aback by how deeply it hurt her feelings but shook it off.

The Anjali party, five strong, mounted their horses to head east toward the portal into Anjali. Before departing, Nuria approached Veni's horse and held out her gentle hand. In her palm sat a necklace. Luvenia's heart lurched as she realized it was her mother's amulet—the one her father had given her the day their daughter was born.

The sun glinted off the honey topaz in her hand, its ornate, golden filigree encasing the violet opal center. "This is your Portal Key. Helga found it sewn into the pocket lining of the riding jacket you arrived here in."

Luvenia's mouth hung open, speechless. After an astonished moment, she reached down and took the amulet from the queen and fastened it carefully around her neck with trembling hands. She was rather afraid to move wearing something so precious.

"Thank you," she whispered as she touched it delicately with her fingers.

The queen merely nodded and strode away, the perfect depiction of elegance in her black trumpet sleeve gown and furs.

Prepared to leave, one of Darius' most trusted Hordemen led the way, followed by Khyan, Thera, Luvenia, and another Hordeman bringing up the rear. They all had much to contemplate and spent the first several minutes in near silence.

Luvenia held the amulet at her neck, considering the strangeness of it being sewn into her riding jacket. Why would her mother do such a thing? Did she know the Collectors were coming? How could she know that? If it wasn't her, then who could have done it? Jacob? He did know she was away when he led the Collectors to the farm. Did he want her to make it out? Did he know about Aureland? Her mother had the Mark of the Zealots—those who follow the spirit ways of old. She'd never seen her mother take part in their practices. What else was her family hiding? She was no closer to having any answers when the path widened, and Thera held back a moment to ride next to her.

"The East Gate is just a short way up ahead. We'll need to camp soon after we arrive. It will be nearing sunset in Anjali. They're almost half a day ahead of our time. Regardless, we need to send Ruben well ahead of us with the correspondence from my parents. Well, the correspondence from me, *signed* as my parents."

Luvenia nodded. "Are you ready for this? You certainly look the part." She gestured toward Thera's clothing. She looked quite regal in her decorative riding clothes and black hooded cape with gold embroidery. Meanwhile, the rest of them looked rather plain indeed.

"Ah, yes. News travels quite quickly, especially regarding the Viloran royalty. My family is fairly well known for their lavish parties and for throwing them wheresoever we please."

Thera shook her head. "I'm ready for my first mission on my own, but I am not ready to pretend I'm anything like my family. Don't misunderstand me, I *adore* a grand party, but I have never attended one in Vilora. I did, however, attend one my eldest brother put on while he visited Toulona, and I happened to be living there at the time. It was really a lot of fun. Especially considering my brother begged me to dance a thousand times, having no idea I was his sister!" She laughed in that bell-chiming way of hers. "He would have just *died* if he knew!"

Her laughter was contagious and Luvenia couldn't help but join in and imagine the Viloran Prince's surprise if he found out he'd pined after his own sister.

"I suppose you don't look alike, then?" she asked Thera.

"No, no, not at all. My great grandmother was from Anjali, and I have her black hair and slightly almond eyes, the rest of my family has light brown hair and round, brown eyes. I'm not sure where my blue eyes came from." She shrugged.

Onward they rode, gradually letting their new bond take root.

As the Anjali party continued east, Darius made it through the Orford Gate and arrived at the designated meeting spot where Sebastian was already pacing. "What took you so long?" he accused Darius.

"I'm early, Sebastian, steady yourself," he answered him sternly. "What is the matter with you?"

Sebastian continued his anxious walking, a clear path already marked in his wake. "She's gone completely mad!" He ran a nervous hand through his hair.

"Who? Stop your pacing and tell me what's going," the general ordered.

Sebastian stilled and shoved his hands into his pockets. "Pietro. She held a public execution in Alban this morning. In the damn *town square*, Darius. Five innocents. Just...sliced their heads clean off. Two of them were women. All of them bore the Mark of the Zealots. Lilith claimed they'd all committed treason. She also had this *filth* hung all over the city." He held out a wrinkled piece of parchment and Darius took it.

Queen Lilith Pietro's seal, inked in red at the top, towered over a faded and dripping Mark of the Zealots, as if washing them away. Below, in harsh red script, was scrawled:

"However the enemy may threaten or attack us, it is no worse than it once was. Our ancestors often had to endure the same treatment from such zealots. We must recall the statement of my late father: 'Were the World full of monsters, we must still succeed!' We shall not allow another civil war in this great country because of our enemy. No more lives shall we let them steal with their lunacy!"

Darius crumpled the paper, jaw tightly clenched.

Sebastian went back to his pacing. "People are going to believe this, Darius."

"You need to remain steady. Your panic is not going to help us now. Yes, people will believe this refuse. She's already planted it in their minds for a decade that the Zealots are unbalanced and solely responsible for the Purge War." Darius thought out loud, "Does she think this will inspire the citizens to kill the Zealots for her out of fear, or scare the Rebels into inaction?"

Sebastian rubbed his face. "I think perhaps both. But that will be chaos. She can't control chaos. She must assume the Liberator and his band of rebels *are* Zealots as you previously suggested and she wants to stop them from entering the city. I don't see why else she would do this."

"They most likely are Zealots. It makes sense..." Darius responded, wheels turning. "The informant said survivors of the war fled to the mountains."

"That could mean those who fought or those who didn't, we

don't know either way."

The general chewed on his bottom lip, contemplating before he spoke. "This Liberator must be stationed in his position already. And he *must* have been recruiting new members all these years. The survivors, were they those who fought, would be at least in their fourth decade now. Possibly they had children in the mountains, but then we're looking at ten-year-olds and middle-aged men and women. He's been recruiting, Sebastian." He was gaining confidence with a look inside the Liberator's mind. "I'll bet you anything, anything at all, that his men are in position and have been for some time. Pietro has figured that out and now she's moving her pawn in order to flush them out. This is just a game of chess, Sebastian. And I am *very* good at chess."

Sebastian snorted a laugh. "Trust me, I know, General."

"What does Pietro claim these traitors did to deserve death. A public one?"

Sebastian shook his head. "All she claimed was that they were plotting her assassination."

"It's a fear tactic and manipulation to make the people hate the Zealots as well as fear standing up to her."

Sebastian nodded thoughtfully.

General Cremeux stood a bit straighter. "First things first, we put our spies in place. You have yours ready, yes?"

Sebastian nodded once more.

"Good. My two are close on my heels, I left before them. Get yours in the castle as close to Pietro as possible. I'm willing to say there is a Zealot or a Rebel already in the castle, and more than likely they are one and the same. Do *not* trust the Rebel informant. He's a weasel playing both sides and Pietro knows it. The Liberator most likely knows this as well. Plant your men with care, Sebastian. I'll plant mine in the city to see if they can get a whiff of the Rebel movement and who is recruiting. We meet at our location in the Arichan

Mountains the day after tomorrow."

"Yes sir," Sebastian said and mounted his horse.

Something within him tugged at Darius as Sebastian turned to ride away, "Sebastian."

He turned his horse back to face his general.

"You've done well. Don't fail me now." There was deep warning in his voice, and he wasn't quite sure himself why.

"Yes sir," Sebastian responded and rode off in the direction of the Alban Castle.

The Anjali party reached the East Gate and dismounted their horses, unable to take them through without Sean'an Porter permission. Each one of them passed into Anjali with their Portal Key and Luvenia closed her eyes as she went.

When Thera told her they were safely through, she opened her eyes to see the lush, autumn foliage in the wilderness of Anjali. It quite resembled a more vibrant Orford, though the trees were not straight. Their trunks twisted and turned, as did their branches.

In the distance, there rose a vast mountain range with snow-covered caps, unlike the Arichan Mountains already blanketed with snow by mid-season. The leaves were the bright shades of autumn as well, but the temperature was more like that of springtime in Orford—not too hot, not too cold—though the air was rather sticky in Anjali. Along the horizon, the sun was beginning to set, lighting the trees on fire in its decline.

Night swiftly approaching, Khyan led them just a bit further into the woods to camp. Before starting a campfire, he sent the Hordeman—Ruben—ahead of them with the forged Viloran correspondence announcing Princess Theralin Revencloud's arrival.

The second Hordeman that Darius had insisted lead them

into Anjali and remain for additional protection—a statement both Thera and Khyan had laughed at— gathered firewood and arranged it for Khyan to kindle. He did so very quickly with two rocks and a stick, much to Veni's surprise.

Thera passed around portions of the bread and cheese the castle kitchens had sent and the four of them gathered around the warm fire and ate. They chatted about the journey, what might be happening in Orford, and the perpetrator that awaited in the Aureland dungeons for Darius' return.

Veni asked about the woman they'd helped, and Thera informed her that she was currently in their wing of the castle until Nuria felt she had gathered all the information she needed and that the woman was ready to return to her village in the Monarbre Forest.

With full bellies and night wrapping them in her comforting embrace, the conversation fell silent, only crickets to be heard. That is, until Thera began to sing, the fire crackling and the sparks alight against the darkened sky.

Lift your eyes, oh Little One,
Now can't you see?
My love is a fire,
Consuming every broken piece.

I whisper your name on the wind,
In the waters at your feet.
Lean into my embrace,
All your tears I wish to keep.

I long to store them in a bottle,
I'll release them in the sea.
I only yearn to make you whole,
I desire you forever here with me.

Lift your eyes, oh Little One,

Now can't you see?
My love is a fire,
Consuming every broken piece.

The silence ushered in by her last, perfect note felt wrong in Luvenia's ears. Something about the song felt familiar. It felt like home, though she knew she'd never heard it before. She looked to Thera with misty eyes, unable to speak. Thera merely smiled in return, her eyes clouded with a deep, unidentifiable emotion.

They all lay upon their bedrolls and slept under the starry sky. All except for Luvenia, who was haunted by the song late into the night.

She finally drifted off to dreams of a man she somehow knew. She couldn't make out his face, though his familiar voice told her it must be her father. He beckoned to her from a ship with sails the purest of white. She looked down, expecting to see the sandy shore, but only raging waters moved beneath her feet.

"Keep coming," he called to her, "Keep coming."

Chapter Fourteen

The following morning, after very little sleep, Veni awoke to the delightful song of a redbird. The aroma of coffee tickled her nose, pulling her the rest of the way out of sleep. She tied her bedroll to the pack Helga had given her and sat next to the fire over which Khyan was brewing the coffee.

"Morning," he told her by way of greeting and handed her a full, hot cup. "Not much sleep, hm?"

She breathed a small laugh. "Look that poorly, do I?"

He smirked at her and shrugged. "A bit. Thought you might like some coffee. I know you enjoy it immensely and are seldom able to have any."

Veni looked at him strangely, head cocked to one side. "How often did you watch us, Khy? You know an unsettling amount about me."

"No more than necessary. I merely notice a great deal," he explained.

Veni smirked at him. "It's still strange." She looked around, noticing the other Hordeman's absence. "Where is Rovak?"

The prince waved a hand dismissively. "He's of more use in Aureland. I sent him back. Thera has gone to bathe in the lake and prepare to look like a princess," he rolled his eyes, "which will take her ages. Would you prefer to join her or start some training before we head further?"

She sipped her coffee, savoring the warmth and flavor. "Train. Definitely."

Khyan stood from the fire, brushing the dirt off his riding

pants. "Wonderful. Let's get to it, then."

"What about my coffee?" she asked, sipping faster.

"Warriors don't wait until their coffee is finished to go to battle, Veni. Come on." He tied his long red hair back with a piece of twine and strode to the open area next to their camp.

Luvenia guzzled as much of the hot coffee as she could manage and set the tin cup on a rock hastily before jogging to where Khyan waited.

"I'm ready. Let's do this," she told him, rocking from side to side on her feet with excitement.

Unamused, her trainer crossed his toned arms. "That coffee affected your nerves awfully quickly, now didn't it? You need to be focused and centered. Understand?"

She ceased rocking but shook her head. "No. Not at all."

Khyan explained, "The first thing you need to know is that every fight is first won or lost here," he held two fingers to his temple, "and here." He placed two fingers on his heart. "Now, do you believe you can beat me?"

Veni shook her head nervously. "I don't even know how to fight."

"I don't care. Do you believe you can beat me?" he asked her again sternly.

Her palms began to sweat, and she stuttered. "Perhaps later...with some training—"

Khyan interrupted her. "That isn't what I asked you, if you could beat me *later*. I asked if you *believe* you can beat me."

"Then no!" she shouted, feeling a bit like a caged animal. "*No*. Alright? Are you pleased?"

Khyan eyed his protégé closely as she grew more and more uncomfortable. "Then the answer is, in fact, no. How many battles have you won, Veni?"

"None," she spat.

Khyan looked her in her eyes, and said with fierce calm,

"*Wrong.*"

She stared at him, confused.

"You have won thousands of battles." He continued, "You have looked tragedy, fear, doubt, uncertainty, *Collectors*, death, hunger, failure, and countless other obstacles square in the face *thousands* of times. Yet, here you stand. How did you win those battles, both mental and physical?"

"I—I don't know. I never thought of any of those things as a battle," she stammered, her mind racing to follow him.

"You refused to give up and you refused to surrender. Am I correct?"

She shrugged. "I suppose. I—"

"Fighting is definitive, Veni," he interrupted her again. "You cannot be indecisive."

Frustrated, she threw her hands up. "Then yes! I refused to give up."

"You also cannot be tossed by every wave and merely believe everything you're told or everything you think. Do you truly believe you've survived this long because you refused to give up, or do you believe it was all by chance?" She opened her mouth to answer, but he held up a halting finger. "*Think.*"

She contemplated for several moments what she'd just been told and the events of her life leading to the current moment. Images of her family flashed before her. Consoling her mother as a little girl when her father died, the meager suppers—some evenings going to bed with rumblings in her stomach because she gave most of her meal to Ester when her mother wasn't looking—working each day to ensure their home was safe—that her family was safe—and the fury that consumed her when she saw Collectors standing in her kitchen—when she saw her *brother* standing as one of them.

Finally, she spoke. "Both. I had a sister...*have* a sister," she corrected herself with a wavering breath, "to protect. I couldn't let starvation be an option. I couldn't let my father's death kill me or my family because we needed each other."

Tears welled in her eyes, but she continued, "I can't allow my mother's death or my brother's betrayal to paralyze me, because my sister *needs* me. In that, I do believe I made up my mind to never surrender and never give up. I wanted to waste away into nothing when the memory of my mother's death came flooding in, though I knew I couldn't. I heard her voice in the hallway when I decided to leave, reminding me I can't give up. I have to get to Ester.

But...I did give up under the water with that Collector holding me down." She shook her head, remembering the moment vividly. "I fought back for as long as I could, but I was far too weak. There was simply no way. It was only by chance—" Luvenia gasped, remembering the owl that attacked the Collector, leading to her escape. "That was you! *You* saved me." She marveled at her trainer for a heartbeat before continuing. "You see, that was pure chance. I wouldn't have survived that one if you hadn't been there."

"Ah, but it was *not* chance. I followed you. Was I not also weaker than the Collector? Was I not even weaker than *you*? Yet I won. Defeat was not an option. I had you to protect."

He let that sink in for a moment. "That need you have, to protect, let it be a driving force in you. However, do not let it be the *only* driving force. You must look after yourself as well. Were Ester dead along with your parents, you would still need to determine that you will never give up. That you will not waste away to nothing."

She twirled the ends of her hair, considering his words. "If Ester is dead, there is no more reason for me to be alive."

Khyan's brow furrowed. "You really believe this to be true?"

Veni shrugged. "I do."

"Then we cease training right here. You will never win a fight."

She looked at Khyan blankly as his words sliced through

her like hot metal. He made to walk away but the hurt in her eyes stalled him.

He slid his hands into his pockets and explained. "That was not my assessment, Veni. It was yours. You don't believe you can win. Therefore, you've already lost. You don't value *yourself*. Therefore, you've already lost. You do not deem yourself valuable enough to even *eat* correctly. Tragedy aside, you still find your value solely based on others and you see no reason to live if your sister or mother or father is dead.

You cannot be a victor for another unless you can first be a victor for yourself. Laying one's life down for another is valiant, yes, hold onto that with all you have, but you must realize that the value of anything is known by the value used to purchase it."

He closed the distance between them and placed his hands on her shoulders tenderly. "What I mean is this...if you intend to lay down your life for your sister, not even unto death, but just laying your entire life aside *for her*… It is worthless if *you* are worthless."

Anger and rejection stormed through Luvenia, and she pushed Khyan away. "It is not worthless because *Ester* is not worthless! If a *rat* can die so a princess may live, then so be it!"

Khyan's deep voice rose in anger. "And you are the rat in this scenario? *You* are worthless? The princess' life is only worth a *rat*? A *king* would die for the life of a princess. A *king*, Luvenia. Can't you see? *You* are infinitely valuable."

Thera arrived back at their camp just then, the tension thick. She noticed the angry standoff and began taking purposefully loud steps so they would know she was coming.

Khyan looked in Thera's direction and turned back to Luvenia. "We're done here until you can realize that." He put out the fire with misty ice and they loaded their packs to continue.

A while later, the trio approached a village where Thera

insisted they purchase horses, as her feet were aching due to her decision to not wear riding boots and the mere fact that 'a princess does not arrive on foot.'

Khyan agreed but told the pair of them to stay in the forest. News that the Viloran princess was arriving soon would travel quickly, but her last known whereabouts were in Toulona and she didn't need to be seen coming in from the opposite direction if at all possible, though she had dressed the princess part just in case.

Khyan ventured onto the stone street leading into the village ahead with its strange roofs that sloped dramatically and came to a rising point in each corner and a point in the center. He'd hardly gotten a few paces away before Thera pressed Veni for details about their disagreement.

Veni sighed and sat in the dirt and grass against one of the twisted trees. "He said he was going to train me to fight, but he mostly insulted me."

Thera bunched up her grey dress and sat delicately on a rock across from her friend. "I could pretend I didn't hear the last shouting bit, but I did. That being said, it didn't exactly sound as though he were *insulting* you. More like he's infuriated you don't see what he sees in you."

Veni picked at the still green sprigs of grass, hugging her knees with her other arm. "He says my training is over until I can grasp that I'm *valuable*. It's ridiculous. What does that have to do with fighting?"

"Everything," Thera told her. "You must be confident to be a skilled fighter. You must value your own life and you must believe in who you are. Otherwise, you will be beaten to a bloody mess each and every time, *if* you don't die in your first battle. A warrior is quite the opposite of a self-loathing coward."

"Can we just…not?" She looked at Thera with exasperation and rested her chin on her knees. "Please?"

Thera smiled sweetly. "The first lesson is always the most

difficult, especially with Khyan. My first lesson—I was only seven, mind you—Khy informed me that I could never win a battle because I was, and this is a direct quote, *'too emotional'*. Can you believe that? I was *seven*!" Thera laughed. "I can still, at times, be too easily led by my emotions and he is always right there to remind me it's destructive. His methods do not include coddling, but he is surprisingly insightful, pinpointing the weakest areas and eradicating them. He has trained the fiercest warriors in Aureland, including Darius. Don't give up, Veni."

A short time later, Khyan returned leading three mares and carrying a burlap sack he claimed contained treats—a peace offering. He handed each of the women a warm, rounded bun of sweet bread, much to their delight. All three of them devoured their bread, savoring the modestly sweet plum filling. Momentarily, Luvenia forgot why she was so angry at the prince.

General Darius Cremeux hid in the shadows, crouched atop a thatched roof across the street from a rundown Alban tavern, The Dead Horse. The sun had set hours ago, just before Cremeux's men took their positions.

He watched as townsfolk stumbled into the tavern where Lydigen had taken a bar hand position. He would pull as much information out of the town drunks as possible. There was nothing left for Darius to do there except wait, so he rose and noiselessly ran across the roof. He leapt into the air between buildings, landing like a stealthy lion on the next roof, continuing until he had travelled the span of two blocks. The night concealed him well—considering the street lanterns did little to provide much light—as did his inky armor, cloak, and the hood that hid his face.

In the house below Darius' boots, his man Sillow attended

a dinner party put on by a butcher Darius had caught wind of earlier that day in the market. Queen Lilith's notices hung along every surface of every building and had been nailed to every city dweller's door. It hadn't taken long to hear the whispers of fear and dissension. Most ambled through the market, determined to keep their mouths shut and their families safe, but the brave few dared to murmur. Darius suspected none of those few belonged to the opposition, as none of the Rebels would be so foolish. Though he decided if he could spot those displeased and willing to admit it, then so could the Liberator and they would eventually follow the murmuring in order to recruit.

One such vexed townsperson was the old butcher who had let slip to a long-time customer that he felt the country was doomed and he feared Pietro to be far more malevolent than anticipated. A few patrons later, old Schrute mentioned a dinner party his wife was putting on that evening in celebration of the healthiest livestock they'd had since before the war. Darius gave Sillow orders to obtain an invitation to said dinner party. He had, with ease. Schrute's daughter—a rather aggravating and obnoxious young woman—had made her way to her father's stand just before Sillow, two dead chickens in tow. The general watched with no small amount of amusement as the girl fawned over Sillow, who claimed to be in search of vegetables. Moments later, he had the girl's arm looped through his as he was dragged to a nearby stand. He emerged triumphant with the location of the party, an admirer, and a basket of beets.

Darius chuckled to himself on the roof, wondering if Roberta had gotten under Sillow's skin yet. He'd met her the day he followed Thera to Alban. The day he'd accidentally tripped a different girl, a beautiful girl he had no idea would enter his life like a battering ram later that evening.

Pushing thoughts of Luvi away, he again imagined Sillow's awkward evening with Schrute's daughter. He couldn't say he had necessarily *planned* for Roberta to bother Sillow when he discovered the butcher would be a good lead, but he had to admit he'd certainly hoped as much.

He checked his pocket watch. Lydigen would need until sunrise when the tavern closed, though he'd told Sillow to meet him at midnight at their safe house. It would take Darius a good while to arrive there and ensure the area was secure. He slunk to the back edge of the two-story house and jumped into the air, flipping twice, landing silently in a crouch. With a quick glance around, he determined no one was in the vicinity and snuck into the alleyways, taking the lesser traveled path to the safe house.

A block from his destination, Darius sensed an unwelcome presence behind him and changed direction, unsheathing his talon-contoured dagger. Picking up his pace, he turned several corners attempting to lose the nuisance and slipped into a shadowed alcove. His pursuer approached soon after, cloaked in black, looking up and down the dark alley. Deeming the alley clear, he turned to look for Darius elsewhere. As he did, Darius lunged from his alcove, grabbing the intruder from behind and holding his talon dagger to the man's neck.

"Why are you following me?" he growled with deadly calm.

The man raised both hands, breathing heavily. "I have information you want to hear."

The general spun the man around and shoved his back against the stone wall hard enough to knock the breath out of him. He held him there, his forearm digging into the man's chest as he said, "And why should I trust you?"

The stranger struggled to breathe against Darius' weight, but managed a choked, "Olliander."

Darius shoved off him, keeping his dagger at the ready. "You have one chance. Begin with your name."

The man cleared his throat and pulled off his hood, hardly

older than a boy. "Name's Beck, General Cremeux. Sebastian Olliander sent me from the castle. He wasn't certain where your safe house was, but he thought the slums were a good place to start. Been lookin' for ya' since dark. Saw a man lurking in the shadows, thought it might be you—"

"You're wasting time, Beck. Get on with it," he ordered the babbling young man, reminding himself to speak with Sebastian about his choice in spies.

"Right..." Beck stuttered. "Olliander needed you to know the mountains aren't safe. Pietro's Warmongers are everywhere. You can't meet there tomorrow. He is sending word to your people to take over. Somethin' about flying."

Darius nodded at the young man, thankful Sebastian wasn't foolish enough to disclose *everything*. Beck continued, "He said to meet him behind The Dead Horse at dawn."

"Very well. What is your position?" Darius asked him, dagger still out. He wasn't the trusting type.

"Queen's kitchen." Beck shrugged. "Pietro killed my mother nearly ten years ago."

Darius sheathed his dagger. "Now you're a man and you want revenge?"

Beck shook his head forlornly. "Just liberty."

Darius nodded once. "Wise choice. What do you know about the Liberator, then?"

"Very little. Queen's doin' a swell job of keeping the Rebel news quiet. Sebastian's looked out for me for years, ever since he found out the dead Head of Kitchen was my mother. We thought she died of fever, but Sebastian says Pietro killed her. Poison 'r somethin'. He said he needed my help. I'd do anything for Sebastian. Pietro plucked him outta the same orphan house they sent me to."

"You did well, kid. We're happy to have your help. Be very careful, though, Beck. This is an extremely dangerous game we're playing and you're on the front lines in that castle. Trust no one until you can be certain. Do you understand?"

Beck straightened. "Yes, General."

Darius nodded and the young man walked swiftly away, setting his hood back in place. The general made his way to the safe house, finding it void of lurking intruders, and knocked softly in the pattern predetermined by him and his Hordemen. He expected to hear silence in return but instead received a low, two-note whistle. He opened the door to find Sillow already inside, sharpening his knife.

"General," Sillow greeted him plainly.

"Well?" Darius asked, taking off his cloak.

"I learned no new information, sir."

He was clearly ill-tempered.

Darius hid his smirk. "You're in a bit of a *mood*, now aren't you? Did you make any new friends?"

"I most certainly did not." Sillow was beginning to squirm in his seat, annoyed. "I was not attending a celebration for *celebratory* reasons, sir."

"Quite right, Sillow. But *no* new friends? Not even one? Not even that *darling* Roberta?" He successfully contained his laughter as he said it, though barely.

Sillow eyed him, furious. "You knew about her? You sent me there on purpose, didn't you?"

He could no longer contain it. The general laughed heartily at the expense of his Hordeman, shaking his head.

"This is not a laughing matter! We are on assignment from our queen, and we do not have time for your games, Darius!"

Darius clamped down on his laughter. "We are still on assignment, *Hordeman*."

Embarrassed, Sillow corrected himself. "Yes, sir. *General*. I apologize."

Darius laughed again and clapped Sillow on the back. "Relax. I'm merely giving you a hard time. Lighten up. Now, you truly learned nothing of importance?"

Sillow sighed. "No. Most guests were all rather content.

They hardly mentioned the notices except to say what a nuisance they had been tacked up everywhere."

"None of them appeared to be anyone the Rebels might target to recruit?"

"There was an older gentleman, a quiet fellow, he seemed pensive the entire night and perturbed when Pietro's notices were mentioned briefly." That certainly grabbed Darius' attention. "He wasn't interested in conversing with me, though. For all I know, he was just in a foul mood."

Darius thought for a moment while he took off his boots. "Better than no lead at all. Did you catch his name?"

Sillow nodded as he stood. "Yes. Man by the name of Kinnick. I'm going to make some tea. Would you like some?"

Darius nodded and Sillow continued, making his way to the hearth to start a fire and a pot of tea. "He grows cotton a short ride outside of Alban."

"How does he know our good Butcher Schrute?"

"Wasn't mentioned, but I gather they've been friends for some time. He knew his way around the butcher's place and seemed comfortable enough there to sulk in public. Did hear him mention he would be bringing a load of cotton in to a tailor in the morning."

Darius leaned back in his chair, feeling fatigue begin to seep in. "Then I suppose it's about time we acquired a few new tunics, now isn't it?"

The pair of them drank their tea and slept for a few hours before dressing in plain riding clothes and heading to meet Sebastian and Lydigen at the tavern. The sun hadn't quite begun to rise as they arrived and entered through the front door to inform Lydigen why they were there. He was forcefully nudging a very inebriated gentleman passed out on a soggy table as they entered.

"It's time t'go, fella!" Lydigen said as he nudged him and heard the entry bell jingle. "We're closed! It's *dawn* for goodness' sake." His tone was irritable as he turned to see who had entered to consume alcohol at the first light of day. "Oh. Thought you were another drunkard. Aren't we meeting later?" The general looked pointedly at the drunk man on the table and Lydigen jumped to explain. "It's safe. Fella's passed clean out and I'm the only other one here, sir."

"Good." Darius glanced at the drunken man with mistrust. "Meet us out back when you're done here."

Sebastian arrived in the alley moments after Lydigen, dark circles under his eyes.

"What is the situation, Sebastian?" the general asked.

"Lilith's men are combing the mountains. They have yet to find evidence of a camp, but they can't be far from it now. I sent word to Nuria yesterday. I received a letter from her in the night stating that Khyan is still accompanying Thera and won't be back for several more days. She said she will fly over the mountains herself and will leave first thing tomorrow morning. I don't like that plan in the slightest."

"Nor do I," Darius said, becoming extremely uneasy. "I expect I'll receive post from her shortly. Hold your positions and await my orders until then. Lydigen, what do you have for us?"

He wiped liquor off his hands as he spoke. "Didn't hear much of anything about a rebel force. Nothing of the sort. I did, however, hear talk of a shipment leaving in a few weeks." Lydigen's downturned mouth told Darius that he wasn't going to enjoy what was about to be said.

"Shipment? What sort of shipment?"

Lydigen's face was grave. "People." The other three men ceased breathing as he continued. "Children. Pietro's dungeons are full and she's having them transported to labor in Toulona."

"Where did she get *children*?" Darius growled, his fists so tight his dark knuckles had gone white.

Lydigen looked down. "As the dungeons fill, so do the orphanages. She takes them and has some hidden fortress where she keeps them until the shipment time."

Fury turned Sebastian crimson. "Where did she take them from?"

"Mostly from Greer's," Lydigen answered. The orphan house Pietro had taken Sebastian from all those years ago. Where Beck had grown up. Darius closed his eyes, the truth heavy on his shoulders.

Sebastian ran his hands through his short dark hair and began pacing. "Then they aren't laborers. She's selling them," he snarled.

Realization brought nausea roiling through Darius' stomach. "We must stop this. Tell me everything you know, Lydigen."

Khyan had been training Luvenia over the last few days as they trekked across Anjali. They needed to take a wide route around the capitol so that Thera could enter from the direction of Toulona. This provided a fair amount of time for Khyan to push Luvenia farther than she'd ever pushed herself physically or mentally. She was used to running long distances and lifting heavy things, but she had never run so far so quickly or challenged her muscles so intensely as Khyan required of her.

"C'mon, Veni! You can do this!" Thera huffed, encouraging her friend as she ran backwards next to her.

Khyan had ordered her to strap on both her pack and his—to which he'd added an obscene number of rocks—and run alongside the walking horses until he said to stop. That had begun a great distance ago. It hadn't taken long for her entire body to begin to burn and scream for her to stop. Each step felt like it would surely be her last, but Khyan's words rose up within her as she drew in each breath.

'Never surrender. Never give up.'

She clenched her teeth and ran harder. He'd told her that her body was a temple to take great care of and she would be no help to Ester or anyone else as a weakling. Everyday she'd awoken with aching muscles and an insatiable hunger. They'd stopped in every village they came near to purchase more food because Veni continually ate it all. Khyan merely encouraged her, stating it meant she was doing something right.

Her legs felt more leaden with each and every step. Her breathing grew shallower and shallower as sweat dripped to the ground. Still, she continued on, but her pace slowed over the next humid distance as doubt crept in, telling her there was no way she could do this.

You will never be strong enough. You will never get Ester back. You will never win.

Luvenia refused to listen. If she could just place one foot in front of the other, she was one step closer. She was hardly more than walking, but she kept going. Just as she was beginning to believe she could succeed, she tripped over a rock and almost fell.

Managing to steady herself and stay upright, Veni willed strength into her legs and pushed on, but her pace slowed further as she saw a large hill looming before them. Doubt whispered lies in her ear once more. Her body screamed obscenities at her.

But Khyan had also taught her over the last several days that *she* was in control. Not her mind. Not her body. *She* could decide what to think. *She* could decide what she could conquer.

From atop one of the horses, her trainer opened his mouth to push her, but stopped as he watched his protégé stare down the hill as if it were her greatest enemy. Proudly, he watched as she set her face like stone and launched herself—heavy laden with packs full of rocks—up the hill faster than he'd ever seen her run. Khyan kicked his horse into a trot and Thera sprinted up the hill to keep up with her.

As Luvenia crested the top of the hill, her legs gave out, unable to take another step, and she hit the dirt and rocks, squished painfully between the pack on her back and the one on her front. Khyan looked down at her from his horse to find her smiling from ear to ear as she breathed heavily.

"I did it."

Thera jumped and cheered as Khyan dismounted to help her up and take off the packs. "You won. You *obliterated* that hill," he told her, flooded with pride. "Come, you can't lie down, you need to walk until your heart slows. I'll help you."

They made it two wobbling steps before Veni lost all the food she'd eaten for days.

Once she was again able to hobble on her own, Khyan led the pair of them, and the horses Thera had insisted he purchase—though they continually didn't use them—to a small hot spring just outside the area where they would camp for their final night before reaching the Anjalian castle.

"Pushing your body to new levels of strength is essential," Khyan explained. "Though, just as importantly, you must rest your body. You've done well and exceeded my expectations, and I believe your own as well. Take your time, I'll be gone awhile. I'm going to hunt for some food for tonight. I've had just about enough strange Anjalian food." He grabbed his bow and turned to Thera. "Keep the pair of you safe, Theralin. I'm certain word of your journey has spread. We're a day's ride from the castle and looters will be awaiting the arrival of royalty." She nodded in agreement and Khyan mounted his horse and rode away to hunt.

"I wondered why he hadn't hunted thus far," Luvenia thought out loud. "I assumed maybe he was just used to royal food or something."

Thera chuckled. "Khy? Hardly. He's a prince in name only.

He has no interest in anything to do with royalty. I think he was uneasy leaving you for long enough to hunt." She shrugged. "I suppose he trusts me all of a sudden or the game is now abundant closer by. Come on, this hot spring will be divine."

Thera shimmied out of her riding clothes and gracefully descended into the steaming water, the ever-beautiful depiction of perfection. Luvenia tried not to be intimidated, but she couldn't help it. She would never look like Thera...but she wanted to be okay with that. She could tell her body was changing the more she trained with Khyan and decided to appreciate herself in the transformation process.

Maybe I am learning some things about my value after all.

Putting her thoughts of comparison away, she discarded her sweaty clothes and stepped into the water. Divine was an understatement. The water felt so soothing on her aching legs that she wanted to be submerged instantly. She awkwardly slid the rest of the way into the water with an ungraceful plop and stifled a groan.

"Feels wonderful on aching muscles, hm?" Thera beamed at her.

"So very," Veni responded as she closed her eyes.

Thera laughed, reminiscent. "This reminds me of an occasion whilst traveling in a gypsy caravan through Toulona."

Veni watched her intently, prepared for a typically intriguing Thera tale.

"This barkeep I met at a chariot race put my adventurous spirit to shame."

Oh, this is going to be good...

Thera continued, obviously immensely fond of the mentioned barkeep. "There I was, quietly enjoying the race…" She snickered. "We both know I wasn't quiet. Anyway, this dashing young man catches my attention and I begin to watch him closely because he has this horribly mischievous look in his eye and he's all by himself. I watch him as he sneaks up to the next pair of chariot horses, the ones waiting to race. The lunatic crept past the talking chariot drivers and *unhooked* one of the horses from its chariot!

He was sneaking to the other horse when the drivers ceased talking and one began to approach. I panicked! He didn't see him coming and I was fairly close by, so I did the first thing I could think of." She laughed genuinely as Veni listened, enthralled. "I ripped off my head scarf and dashed to the chariot drivers. They turned to me *just* in time to miss the little fiend. I gave the least handsome one my scarf and told him to win for me, effectively making the other rather jealous."

She laughed again and shook her head. "The chariot villain watched me save his hide from in between the wagons with a wicked grin. He completed his sabotage and strode off *whistling*! He found me in the crowd just before the next race began, snuck up right behind me and whispered, 'watch this.' If I hadn't known it was him by the mischievous tone, he would have gained a dagger in his gullet. We watched those drivers whip their horses at the start of the race and nearly *died* of laughter as the horses took off full speed without their chariots, those drivers just standing in them bewildered."

Thera shook with laughter, Veni joining in. "Oh my, that man. He is a riot. Anyway, it reminds me of this spring because after the races, he took my hand and declared I *must* see something else. We ended up sneaking past guards and servants into the Captain of the Guard's private oasis out in the desert." She laughed again. "We were nearly inseparable after that day..." She trailed off with a smile still upon her lips, lost in her own thoughts.

Veni could see a trickle of sadness in the woman's countenance as they sat quietly. She wondered what happened to the barkeep and how they could have let go of one another if they reveled in such joy side by side.

A long time and wrinkled toes later, the women were clean, dried, and dressed, collecting firewood.

Khyan arrived with an abundance of blood on his tunic and several skinned rabbits. He gave them to Thera to prepare and cleaned himself up in the spring. They'd chosen to camp against a rock face that opened into a partial cave in case looters were in search of a royal caravan—the exact reason Khyan had chosen to forego one. They could protect themselves.

Luvenia was relieved Khyan had found so many rabbits, for she ate an entire two all on her own. She most likely could have eaten more, but her eyes were beginning to droop once her belly was full.

Khyan nudged her. "You're going to fall into the fire, sleepy." He laughed. "It's hardly dusk. Ready to train some more before bed?"

Veni glared at her trainer as if she wanted to maim him and Thera snickered, choking on her food.

"Training isn't for the weak of heart, *princess*," he told Veni, provoking her.

His teasing left her fully awake and scoffing. "Excuse me, *prince*? I'm the only one here that *isn't* fancy royalty, thank you very much."

Khyan laughed and stood, quite pleased with himself for getting a rise out of her. "Come on then." She followed him out into the open, Thera trailing along for her own amusement.

Well past sunset, Khyan rehearsed self-defensive moves with Veni, over and over. He taught her the weakest points of an enemy to aim for, how to escape from certain holds, and how to shove an assailant's nasal bone up into their brain—that one was her favorite, along with a jumping maneuver that used her body weight against the attacker to break their grip.

Satisfied that her memory was beginning to retain what he

was teaching her, Khyan had just begun to show Veni an aggressive attack maneuver when Thera declared the girl needed a water break. He conceded and told her they would continue in the morning.

They joined Thera upon the rock cluster she'd viewed their training session from, and the trio sat under the cover of the forest and an abundance of concealed stars, discussing Thera's assignment within the Anjalian castle. As Luvenia had suggested, Thera would enter the castle as a guest of the emperor's court, with the goal to win the emperor's favor and convince him to form a false alliance with Pietro. Nuria's plans would soon be in motion, so long as Sebastian played his part correctly.

"Why do you not save time by merely influencing the emotions of the emperor to do what it is you wish him to?" Luvenia asked Thera sincerely.

"I will use my gift with the court and castle servants in order to obtain a fairly constant access to the emperor, but I will not alter *his* emotions, simply because that results in feelings and decisions that are not genuine and therefore unstable," Thera explained. "My natural charms will have to suffice with him." She batted her eyelashes dramatically.

Luvenia smiled at her. "That makes sense. Though, what is so important about a false alliance with Orford? Pietro has made many alliances with countries, as did her father before her, even on other continents. That's how she's obtained food to sustain Orford after the famine. I don't understand what is so bad about Anjali having the Collectors on their side. It beats the alternative. Not to mention it gives Orford more resources. If Sebastian can convince Pietro to take the alliance instead of wiping out a potential enemy, why not just let that alliance happen?"

Thera and Khyan exchanged a glance and the prince

answered her. "None of those alliances are real, Veni."

"What do you mean?" she asked with caution.

Khyan explained soberly, "King Alestair forged very strong alliances across the known world, yes. But when the famine hit, Pietro did not strengthen them to obtain resources. She sent her infantry in to seize each country. It took time, but she managed it, along with many new countries."

Luvenia couldn't even begin to try and conceal her shock. "So, she just rules all these countries, and we had no idea?"

Khyan shook his head. "Not exactly. She doesn't rule them, per say. She dominates them. She sends her Warmongers in to kill the vast majority of citizens, leaving only enough to work as slaves in order to provide the goods she desires be shipped into the Orford Royal Markets."

Luvenia's mouth hung open, appalled. Thera looked at her feet somberly as Khyan continued. "That is how she has been so successful. There is no one left to inform the surrounding areas—to warn them. Except for us."

"What about importing and exporting with other countries? Hasn't anyone noticed something awry?"

"Her men run each and every port. I'm sure some word has traveled, she isn't invincible, but she is quick, and her men are very good at what they do. If word spreads, that is most likely the next area she takes. Perhaps that is why Anjali is her next target. The more powerful countries on this continent—Anjali, Toulona, and Vilora—she has left alone until her forces gain enough momentum to take on such a battle. She must be in dire straits to take on Anjali. That is why we believe Sebastian will succeed in convincing her. That, or she has gained a great deal more power than we yet realize."

"Where does she get enough Warmongers to conquer even a small country? Not all the men from Orford joined the infantry, and even fewer are Collectors. Don't the other countries find it suspicious that a bunch of Orford men run the ports of foreign nations?" Veni once again surprised him with her astute mind.

"She keeps the physically strongest, but weakest minded of each country. She breaks them and puts them to work."

Luvenia's hope of ever seeing Pietro pay for what she'd done diminished to barely glowing embers. She was certainly glad this wasn't her fight. "You truly think you can win this? It's useless. I'm not even certain why you're trying to take her on in the first place—"

Thera held up a hand, interrupting her. "Wait one moment. What are *we* fighting for in the first place? What about *you*? What are you even training for if not this?"

"What do you mean what am I training for? I'm training to get my sister back."

"That's it?" Thera spat.

"*Theralin*—" Khyan tried to stop her, but she wouldn't let him.

"No, Khy. I want to know. *That's it*?" She was waving her hands, fuming. "You hear that Pietro is conquering the world...*killing* innocent people, making others *slaves*, and all you care about is your sister? What about everyone else?"

Luvenia stood, completely beside herself. "I think my sister is *plenty* enough reason and *plenty* worth caring about!" She raised her voice at them both. "You're *fools* to think you can win this when they couldn't even beat Pietro in the Purge War! You're idealistic, the whole lot of you!"

Thera stood and faced her, outrage in her eyes. "You're the fool, *little girl*. That war was peasants battling a *witch*. Of course they lost!" She swatted the air. "Forget it. It's late, I'm going to bed. Fight for whatever you want. We don't need you anyway."

Thera headed toward the mouth of the cave opening and turned back. "I think you were wrong, Khy. She isn't self-loathing. All she cares about *is* herself." She spat the last word and Khyan closed his eyes against the impact, knowing her words had just torn down everything they'd built.

Chapter Fifteen

A snow-white owl swooped gracefully into the second story window of an abandoned storehouse in the Alban slums. She let out a two-note call announcing her arrival and shifted into the elegant Queen of Aureland.

"Are you well?" Darius asked his queen as he entered the room.

"I knew you would worry that I took up the search. I can handle myself, General." She took him by the shoulders and kissed each cheek. "I am safe, darling. However, I have yet to decide if I am well. Where are Lydigen and Sillow?"

"Lydigen secured the bar hand position. He is on his way there now for his third shift. I left Sillow this afternoon. He's tailing a disgruntled cotton farmer to see if the opposition seeks him out for recruitment. Why are you unsure if you're well? What happened in the mountains?" He was anxious to get to the important information.

Nuria sat next to the cold hearth and ignited the logs with a flick of her wrist. "Ah. That is so much better. It is cold in those mountains."

"Would you like some tea? I can make a fresh pot."

"Do you have coffee? I would just adore a steaming cup of coffee."

Darius looked around the small cupboard where they'd stored some goods. "Here is a bit. Lydigen can't leave home without it."

"Wonderful. Thank you, darling."

Nuria spoke as Darius set to brewing the coffee for her. "I knew you and Sebastian would be beside yourselves at my being alone in the mountains, but time is not on our side and I can only estimate so much from the castle. It is vital we find the Rebels swiftly. I considered where I would hide my men from Pietro, were I the Liberator. I decided I would have hidden my Hordemen with our backs to the sea. So, I flew along the coast of the Alban Sea for an entire day…" She paused. "I found the camp."

Darius ceased what he was doing immediately and gave her his undivided attention, full of hopeful anticipation.

She continued, "It was abandoned."

Darius' heart sank.

"They lived within the caves, their backs wisely to the sea as I would have done. However, it is very peculiar…"

"Peculiar? Peculiar how?"

"They *wanted* it to be found, Darius."

"What do you mean?" His hope surged once more. Perhaps he and Sebastian were right, and they were stationed in their attack position already.

"They left signs of their camp on the beach, outside the caves. Upon further investigation, I discovered the fire pits at the mouths of the caves were freshly dug, hardly constructed a fortnight ago. The detail and pure intelligence that established the camp within those caves was not accomplished by a group who would leave *any* sign of their station visible, let alone one so deliberate. They are in the city, I am sure of it, and they want Pietro to know. I have yet to reason what this Liberator's plans are, but he is one step ahead of us all at every turn." The queen drummed her nails on the table. "Pietro's men were swift on my heels. They had already made it to the shoreline when I flew here. It will not be long until they discover the abandoned camp for themselves."

Darius stood, having completely forgotten his task of making coffee.

"The Rebels are in the city..." he thought aloud as he paced and Nuria picked up the brewing where he'd left off. "I hoped as much, but how do that many new people show up at random without being noticed? Immigration has been outlawed for ten years." He scrubbed at the side of his beard. "I suppose citizens do migrate throughout Orford itself fairly unencumbered… It's doubtful the Rebels are stationed within only Alban, anyway. I would fan out wide and surround the city, were I their leader." He ceased talking to himself and turned to Nuria. "Are they a smaller force than we first thought?"

The queen shook her head, her silky, white hair falling over her shoulders. "No. I do not believe they are a small force. The fortress within the caves is vast, with plenty of room for hundreds of people. I cannot understand why they would leave such a fortress to be found and not used for their own gain.

You were correct in assuming they have ways of recruiting. They must have been doing so for all these years. I cannot fathom how they did so in silence, not a whisper has made it to us or Pietro. It is rather intriguing, if not unsettling. I want to believe the opposition is on our side, but until we can be certain of their intentions—and origin—tread lightly, General."

Darius nodded his agreement. "There is something else we must discuss, Majesty."

Queen Nuria's lips pursed. "It is never a good sign when you address me formally. What is it?"

"Neither Lydigen nor Sillow have gained viable information regarding the opposition or encountered any Zealots willing to open their mouths. However, Lydigen caught wind of a shipment leaving Orford and going into

Toulona in the next several weeks."

"A shipment?" she asked warily.

"Of people. Children. As the dungeons and orphanages fill, she takes the excess and sells them for profit in the underground markets." Nausea filled his stomach once more.

Nuria took in the information and promptly shot fire into the hearth until the flames grew so vast, they lapped at the ends of her dress, threatening to overtake her. She eventually gathered her composure and rested her head in her hand. "Just when I think we have reached the end of her darkness, the depths grow more endless." The queen sighed heavily. "When Khyan returns, leave Lydigen and Sillow in Alban and the pair of you do what you can to find that fortress before she ships those innocent children." Nuria looked at the pot of coffee. "I must be going, darling. I should not have made so much. I am so sorry. Could you drink it for me?" She kissed Darius on his cheek and away flew a lily-white owl.

Darius poured himself the coffee, not wanting it to go to waste, and sat before the fire, his mind an intricate web of thought. He found himself struggling to keep his head above the waves. He hadn't the slightest idea how they would get to those children in time. It felt like hope was dashed at every turn and every time they advanced toward freedom, that monster of a queen bared a new set of fangs.

Revolting realization struck him.

Luvenia's sister could be in that shipment.

Darius threw his coffee into the flames and grabbed his cloak.

Princess Theralin Avarochelle Revencloud of Vilora emerged from the forest where she'd been primping herself since dawn. Her golden dress gleamed with the light of a thousand suns, the unique material flowing majestically along the curves of her body and trailing along behind her. The gown cinched at her waist with beading that made its way up and over her full bosom, clasping around her graceful neck.

Dark kohl lined her shimmering eyes, extending in whorls to the edge of her defined brows, flecks of gold strategically placed about her temples. Her luscious lips had been painted crimson and a dainty golden chain fell over her onyx hair, ending in a cobalt jewel that rested upon her forehead. Her arms were lined with gold bracelets almost to her elbows—she even wore one encircled around her taut bicep. Twelve rings glittered on her fingers.

Khyan cleared his throat, covering his prideful emotion for how lovely this girl was that he'd helped raise, and how much she'd grown into an incredible woman. "It's about time. We should have left ages ago."

Thera glared at him. "This," she gestured to her face and dress, "takes time, Prince."

"Why did you choose Toulonan dress rather than Viloran?" he asked her.

Thera rolled her eyes. "If I've supposedly been in Toulona for the last couple of years, do you not think they would have influenced my dress by now?"

Khyan chose to say nothing and leave her mood as it was.

The uncomfortable bitterness between Luvenia and Thera was tangible after their argument the evening prior. Neither one of them so much as acknowledged the other as they loaded their packs and mounted their horses. The trio headed out on their last day's journey to the Anjalian castle in near silence, meeting up with two Aureland Hordemen that had been stationed in Vilora—their home country as well. They would accompany Thera into the palace as her guards—mostly for appearances, as they all knew Thera had no need of guards.

Approaching nightfall, Khyan said his goodbyes to Thera,

letting her know he would fly in every day, if possible, but at least periodically to check with her and deliver messages. She nodded her agreement to Khyan and scowled at Luvenia with piercing disgust before turning her horse and galloping out of the forest toward the castle gates, her royalty mask firmly in place and guards by her side.

Turned back toward Aureland, Luvenia hardly noticed a thing as she rode numbly atop her mount, lost in her own thoughts. She felt relieved to have a break from torturing her body into submission, though it left her mind free to roam whichever way it pleased—which was always a dangerous venture. She hated leaving things with Thera the way they had ended, but she also thought Thera must have been right. Khyan had told her time and again that she was valuable and needed to recognize her own worth, but the person Thera saw was only a selfish coward.

The thoughts taunted her, telling her that Thera was correct. That Khyan only saw what he wanted to see in her, not what she really was. Darkness swelled around her, familiar and unhinged. If she hadn't been so self-absorbed, her father wouldn't have died. If she hadn't been so self-absorbed, her sister would not have been taken. If she hadn't been so self-absorbed, her mother and father would both still be alive. Her father would have been there to protect them—to stop Jacob.

I should have stopped Jacob myself. I should have killed him when I had the chance. If it weren't for me, my family would still be whole.

The vicious, dark clouds she deemed friends rolled in and made their home once again in her heart.

Not long into their trek back to Aureland, Khyan stopped them to camp for the night. He prodded Luvenia to talk with him, but she refused. She also refused supper. Irritated,

Khyan finally lost his temper. "You may sulk the rest of this night, Luvenia Rousseau, but tomorrow morning we resume training, and you will drag yourself out of this mood you're in."

"It's not a *mood*, Khyan. And you can't tell me what to do," she ground out.

"That's how you want to handle this? Like a rebellious child?" He splayed his hands, his face twisted with sarcasm. "By all means, close the entire world off again and handle this all on your own—and *fail*—merely because someone you just met misinterpreted you and challenged you."

He stomped off without waiting for a response and unfurled his bedroll. Thera and Darius may both have stubborn blood, but they couldn't hold a candle to that girl and he could only take so much—nearly a hundred years old or not. If she wanted to forego armor and wrap doubt and fear around herself like a blanket, thinking it could protect her, so be it.

Luvenia lay on her mat waiting for quite some time before Khyan eventually fell asleep. She spent that time chasing away thoughts of what Thera had said, followed by those that unwillingly drifted to Darius—which only frustrated her further. Once Khyan had fallen asleep, she quietly gathered her pack, adding a bit of extra bread, and untied her mare. She led the horse as silently as possible past the dying fire and her sleeping trainer.

Hardly a few paces away, a deep voice startled her. "Going somewhere?" She sighed and turned to face the bare-chested prince, his arms crossed, and one eyebrow raised. "You cannot continue to run from your problems, Veni. Go to sleep. We will leave *together* in the morning."

Fighting him was useless. She simply handed him the reins of the horse with ire and laid out her bed roll again. She slept fitfully as Khyan abandoned sleep altogether to ensure she wouldn't run away and get herself killed.

When she awoke, it was before dawn and thrashing from a

nightmare. Khyan rushed to comfort her, to tell her it was only a bad dream. He had great difficulty staying angry with her when she had the nightmares. All he could see in those moments was the broken girl he'd give anything to make whole.

Once she'd calmed, she took a deep breath and informed him how things were going to go for the rest of their journey back to Aureland. "We are going to train. You are going to teach me everything you know and without all of that invasive counsel. At the very *least* until we return to Aureland. Am I clear?"

He peered at her impassively. "Are you quite finished? Who is the teacher here and who is the pupil? I will grant you this request at the very *most* until we reach Aureland. But in turn, you will respect me, and my methods, and you will do as I say without complaint or argument." She opened her mouth, undoubtedly to complain, but he held up a finger to stop her. "No. Not a word. You don't want to discuss these issues and train in such a manner, then train in silence you shall. Not a word until I say so. Understood?"

She nodded reluctantly, knowing full well her plan had recoiled on her and he continued to have the upper hand...and would somehow still find a way to counsel her.

"Very well. Load our packs to the brim with rocks and strap them on. You will run until we reach the next village, and we can sell these horses."

A little while later, they indeed arrived at a village where Khyan sold both horses, claiming they had no need of them. This made Veni rather uneasy, as they had a grand distance to cover, and she had a sickening feeling she wouldn't be moving at a slow pace—and that she would continue to carry both packs.

The next three days were grueling and very quiet. Khyan continually pushed her harder and faster, giving simple commands and showing little grace. Out of anger or some training tactic, Veni wasn't sure, though she knew deep down it was what she needed.

He showed her attack moves, defensive moves, and sword fighting. He made her run until she threw up every ounce of Anjalian food he gave her and worked every muscle she never knew she had. The more he pushed, the more resolved Veni became. She knew he could see it in her eyes and he pressed harder. The greatest reprieve was the harder she worked, the less her mind thought.

The fourth morning, just two days' walk from Aureland, she began to relish the ever-present ache and soreness in her very bones. She had grown quite comfortable not speaking and was ready for whatever madness Khyan had in store for her.

He led her into the woods, where he handed her a tree branch. "Spear or bow?" She looked at him with questioning eyes. "*Spear or bow*? Which do you prefer?" he asked again.

She made the motion of shooting a bow—it was what she was used to using, even if it had been a good, long while.

"Good. Then make a spear." He handed her a knife and left her behind silently fuming.

Of course.

She wobble-jogged—still quite sore and heavy laden with the packs—to catch up and pointed dramatically to the oversized pack on her front and holding up the tools she'd been given to show him the impossibility of what he'd asked.

He looked at her, feigning confusion. "I apologize, I just have no idea what you're trying to tell me." Khyan snickered and kept walking. She positively growled and stomped her foot in the dirt.

At least I'm not running.

Veni carved at the wood—the best she could manage around the pack—as they walked.

I feel like a bulging fat man with little, tiny arms. That image made her laugh out loud, pushing the dark clouds aside, which in turn drew a smirk and an eyebrow raise from

Khyan.

"Do share what is so amusing. Oh wait...you can't. You've become mute." He laughed heartily at his own jest. She bit her lip to keep from giving him the satisfaction of a smile.

He thinks he's so amusing.

She pushed the prince playfully and went off in a huff, feigning anger. In the midst of stomping about, she lost her balance and the weight of the pack on her back made her fall over in a heap. Khyan roared with laughter as Veni squirmed to right herself and couldn't. He had to lean on a nearby tree to keep his balance and clutched his stomach. Veni wanted to be angry at him for laughing at her expense and for not helping her up, but his laughter was too contagious. She simply couldn't help but join in. He tried to help her up but neither of them could stop laughing.

You can't allow yourself joy, Veni.

The thought came out of nowhere and sunk deep into her marrow, halting her laughter at once. Somberly, she took off the packs, not caring what Khyan might say, and walked into the woods alone with her knife and spear. She knew Khyan was jolted by her sudden mood shift and had followed her. He lingered behind her watching, but she found a rock to sit on and carved at her stick. As long as she kept moving the dread wouldn't seep in. Her task became much easier without the restriction of the packs. When her spear had taken on a decent shape, Khyan finally approached a bit warily.

"You've managed to make yourself a proper spear. And without a single verbal complaint. Well done." When she continued to stare off into the distance ignoring his attempt to rile her out of her mood, he sat next to her.

"Veni, I know you wish for me to say nothing, and I agreed to those stipulations for a time, but I care for you far too much to leave you like this. I need you to know that what you're searching for cannot be found in physical training alone. It won't be found in punishing yourself, either." He paused for his words to sink in and then rose. "Come, we're going on a hunt. I've had about enough rice to last a lifetime. And I'm certain you're famished."

They spent the rest of the afternoon tracking small game and listening to their stomachs grumble as Veni threw her spear time and time again, never hitting their lunch. Trembling from hunger, she was determined this would be the last hare getting past her. She snuck silently through the brush, just as both Khyan and her father had taught her. Unsuspecting, the hare sat and nibbled on whatever bit of its own food it had found. Veni lifted her self-made spear and launched it at the animal. It landed about two strides from the hare, which took off bounding deeper into the forest. Veni stomped over to retrieve her spear, grunting angrily, and launched it at a nearby tree. The weapon hit its mark and sunk deep within the bark.

"You can hit a tree no thicker than my arm, but you can't hit a hare?" Khyan questioned her.

She bared her teeth in response, and he yanked the spear out of the tree. "Here, aim for the tree again."

She steadied herself, willing her limbs to cease their trembling.

You will eat eventually, don't be so weak.

She held the wooden spear so that the weight was balanced and lifted it behind her, ready to launch it once more toward the tree. Using her left arm as her guide, she pointed to where she wanted the spear to hit, just like Khyan had taught her. She exhaled and hurled her weapon at the tree. It stuck in the trunk long enough for her face to break into surprise and turn to Khyan before it fell to the ground.

She frowned, but Khyan beamed. "I do believe we're getting somewhere Rousseau! Here..." He retrieved the fallen spear and handed her the double-edged knife she'd used to whittle the spear as well. "Use the twine in your pack to tie the knife onto the end. A wooden spear most likely won't kill more than a mouse, anyway."

She took the knife, rather excited until she realized what he'd just said. Appalled, she smacked him in the arm with as much force as her sore, shaky arm could muster. "You mean to tell me—"

Khyan interrupted her. "I didn't say you could speak yet. Are you ready to discuss the deeper issues?" She glared at him. "Didn't think so."

Defiantly, Veni took the spear and snapped it over her leg, then threw the two pieces of wood at her instructor, ignoring the pain that throbbed in her thigh.

He shrugged at her. "I suppose you'll become hungry enough eventually."

With that, Khyan spun, dislodging his dagger, and threw it at a deer that had been silently standing several paces behind him. The knife lodged deep in the animal's neck. He turned back to Veni—who hadn't even noticed the deer and stood stunned. "I, for one, shall be enjoying a lovely meal." He picked up the pointed half of Veni's spear and handed it to her.

She snatched it and set to tying the knife he'd given her onto the tip as Khyan dragged away his kill to skin and prepare.

Instead of immediately searching for animals with her new and improved weapon, she decided to practice on the tree until she could figure out what she was doing right and what she was doing wrong.

By the time she came to a place where she had found a stance, motion, and distance that had a decent success rate, she could smell Khyan's meal roasting over a fire. Her stomach had gone from grumbling to painfully hollow and her head swam, but she was determined to make her own kill for her meal. The shorter spear seemed to suit her far better than the long one had.

Veni touched the sharp edges of the knife at the end of her spear, toying with an idea. She decided to try it. She could always tie the knife back to the wood, even if it had taken her ages to stabilize it the first time. She unwound the twine and discarded it along with the sharpened branch. She held the knife from the hilt, pointing the tip forward, though it didn't feel quite right. She weighed the knife in her hand, staring down the tree.

I can do this. I can be as good as them. I can get Ester back. I don't care if it's selfish. Once I have her back, everything will be okay.

Without thinking, she took the knife from the tip instinctually and hurled it at the tree. It sank deep into the trunk—right where she'd aimed it. She let out a celebratory yelp and jumped in the air.

Again and again her knife sunk into the tree with precision. After a while of practicing, a bush rustled nearby. She crouched to retrieve her knife and find the animal that would surely be her supper. She slunk over, knife ready. But her heart sank when a turkey wandered out of the brush, completely oblivious to her presence.

Memories flooded her mind. The taste of turkey. The last time she saw her father's face. The look on her mother's face when that butcher said her father wouldn't be coming home. The sound of her mother's cries. Her gut roiled with nausea and hunger, and she felt a war inside her begin to rage. She could decide to face this fear, or she could starve watching Khyan eat his deer meat.

Maybe he'll let me trade...but he doesn't even eat birds. No. You're going to kill that turkey, Veni, and you're going to eat it. You're going to save Ester. No one else in this family is dying because of you.

Without another thought, she launched her knife at the turkey, sinking it directly into the bird's heart. The clouds in her mind instantly vanished, replaced with triumph. She yanked the knife out—a poor, bloody choice—and threw the dead turkey over her shoulder to find Khyan. Covered in blood, she approached Khyan's fire to find he had yet to eat. She looked at him quizzically.

"What kind of man eats whilst a lady starves? Moreover, what kind of friend?" he shrugged. "Quite a kill you made. Well done." He took the bird from her and began showing her how to properly pluck and skin it.

As the turkey roasted tauntingly, Khyan handed her some deer meat. "You deserve it. Your silence may be lifted as well."

"Thank you," she told him, her voice raspy with disuse.

She began practically inhaling her food when Khyan laughed and took it out of her hand. "Slow down! You'll throw it up. Your stomach will reject it." He handed it back and she took small bites, using every ounce of self-control left in her.

Maybe it was the deer, followed by the nostalgic, sorrowful taste of the turkey, or maybe it was the blanket of stars above them as they laid on their bedrolls next to the fire. Or, perhaps, it was the trust that Khyan had built, but she found herself asking him, "Can you teach me to silence my thoughts?"

The prince had been drifting peacefully to sleep, but her question left him fully awake. He looked over at her, hands behind his head. "Why must they be silenced?"

She glanced at him, then back at the sparks flying off the fire. "They scream at me. I don't know what is real and what isn't sometimes. It seems like they come from outside me at times, like something I wouldn't think. But then again, I suppose I do think it. It's so confusing. You tell me I'm worth something but I've only left pain in my wake. Not to mention the things Thera said… It's all just so much."

"As far as thoughts are concerned, you must learn what comes from your heart and what comes from imaginations. Not every thought originates from your heart. You mustn't believe everything you think. Such thoughts often need to be dismissed, which takes a lot of practice and discipline. Other thoughts do come from your heart and need to be dealt with. As I mentioned before, *you* have the final say concerning your thinking. Some thoughts do need to be silenced, others do not. Any thought with an improper or fearful foundation must be silenced. This can be managed by knowing the truth versus a lie.

I could whisper in your ear all day long that you are a thief, but you would silence me, for you know it simply isn't true and you would move on without another second of consideration. Though, if I were to tell you that you are worthless, you wouldn't silence me for you've already believed that lie. If you believe a lie, you give power to the liar. You cannot merely know when a thought is a lie or false imagination, you must know the truth to combat it. Your mind is a battleground as fierce as any other war ground. Now, as far as what Thera and I say, what do *you* say?"

She thought for a moment, attempting to sort through all he'd said as she twirled her hair. "I don't know. I feel so torn. All the time. For example, I don't want to laugh. It seems so wrong. But I *do* want to laugh. Why do I want to be happy when I shouldn't be?"

Khyan's heart stung, and he sat up on one elbow to peer at her.

"Who told you that you shouldn't be happy?" he managed around a lump in his throat.

Tears snuck down Veni's cheeks, concealed by the dim light. "I've caused so much destruction. My family is destroyed because of me." Admitting the words out loud that held her in such bondage opened the floodgates within her.

"Veni..." Khyan reached over and tipped her chin with gentle fingers. "Look at me."

She lifted blurry eyes to his, her lip wobbling.

"Veni, none of this is your fault. That is a lie you have

believed. It is *not your fault*. None of it. Do you understand?"

She covered her face with her hands. Khyan sat on the edge of her bedroll. "When I was a boy, my father took me to choose my own horse and he let me ride the whole way home by myself. My mare was so small, and I insisted on riding with my satchel loaded full of goods. That satchel was twice my size," he mused, remembering the moment fondly, "but I insisted.

I almost fell off that horse a hundred times, but I kept riding. The poor horse was so tired, and I could barely hold myself upright. Do you know what my father said?" Veni shook her head. "He told me to give him my satchel. He said it was burdening me. He said he would carry it for me so I wouldn't fall off the horse. But I didn't believe him. I told him I was afraid I'd fall off *without* the satchel.

You see, I thought it was the weight of the satchel that was holding me on the horse. But my father told me it wasn't true. He said if I let him take that satchel I would only ride faster. Do you know what happened when I finally gave my father the heavy satchel?"

Luvenia choked through her tears, "You rode faster."

"Yes. Neither the mare nor I were burdened any longer. Take the satchel off, Veni. These things are weighing you down. They don't help you. They hinder you. *Ride hard and don't look back*."

Khyan wiped a tear from her cheek, and she turned her back to the prince, pondering everything he'd told her.

He rested his hand tenderly on her head, stroking her hair for a few moments before he returned to his own bedroll and another sleepless night of watching helplessly as Veni tossed and turned in her nightmares.

A rotted man shrouded like a cloak in darkness loomed over

Luvenia, his hands at her throat, and fangs in her face.

"You'll never rescue her like this," the ghoul told her.

He sounded like a twisted version of her father, like a counterfeit.

"These people can't help you. They're going to use you and spit you out. To save your sister you must use them instead. Don't let them in. They're lying to you for their own gain. They just want to manipulate you into a weak-hearted follower."

She tried to pull away from his reeking breath.

Something wasn't right. But he made sense.

"You're evil through and through and that darkness is what feeds you and makes you stronger. Take their training, take their weapons, and take revenge on Ester. It's the only way to pay for what you've done."

Something within her wanted to combat what the monster said. But that something was far too small.

She believed him.

Chapter Sixteen

The light of hope and freedom Khyan had seen blossom in the girl the night before had vanished as soon as her eyes opened the following morning.

He attempted to ignore the shroud of death covering her, to no avail. She once again refused more than bare minimum food—she refused her turkey altogether. She continued in near silence the last day of travel and became reclusive and surly upon entry back into Aureland.

Every day since, Veni had awoken before dawn to run herself into the ground and spent the rest of the morning training with Khyan between his trips to Anjali and Alban—training with Darius or his men in Khyan's absence. As soon as the trainer released her, she disappeared into the mysteries of Aureland, often training alone until well past sunset, when she would return to the castle and lock herself in her chambers.

Darius watched, leaning on the training room's door frame as Luvenia swung her sword at no one, rehearsing what she'd been taught over and over, time and again.

The girl was caging herself further and further as each day passed. Caging herself with counterfeit protection made of fear and isolation. The general crossed his arms and watched her for some time. She didn't even notice him. Something his warrior mind stored to discuss with her later. She needed to be more aware of her surroundings.

"I know you're there, General," she spoke without turning,

catching him off guard.

He was always so pleasantly surprised by Luvi, even with the dark cloud that had shrouded her since her arrival back in Aureland. He'd gone to her rooms every night since her return to see her. She'd turned him away every time until two nights ago.

When he didn't speak, she turned to face him, "You've been there for ages. Come over here and let me use you as target practice." Her eyes flashed wickedly, and lightning shot through him.

Thera sauntered down the long corridors of the Anjali castle in a marvelous gown the color of a cloudless sky, her abundant Toulonan jewelry clinking as she walked.

She'd successfully ditched her guards—they both knew she didn't need them anyway—and she was supposed to be meeting the emperor shortly for tea in his private parlor. She'd been hinting at the Anjali-Orford alliance for weeks and it was time to discuss it more overtly.

Moments prior, she learned Khyan had just flown in to also meet with her. Aware that Khyan was not one to speak briefly, she decided to pick up her pace, so as not to be late for tea. The prince would scold her later for avoiding him, but Thera needed to make it to this teatime. Rushing around a corner, she ran full force into a man coming around it from the other side.

"Ouff!" he let out, the force behind her speed knocking the wind out of him.

"I am so sorry, sir!" Thera exclaimed in the native tongue of Anjali, reaching for his shoulder apologetically.

Looking at each other's faces, they both spoke at the same

time.

"Amelia?"

"Dax?"

Recognition confirmed, they both exclaimed excitedly and embraced.

"What are you doing here?" Thera asked the tanned man in front of her in the common Toulonan dialect of his home.

"Me?" He smiled broadly. "What are *you* doing here?"

Thera grinned radiantly in return. "You first, *barkeep*."

Dax laughed. "You've caught me. I am no barkeep. I work for the Toulonan Roah. I am here as his ambassador. I took a position in that bar as his lookout all those years ago." He spread his hands. "Now here I am, a Toulonan Ambassador."

"Who would have thought the ever-captivating and mischievous Dax Abayomi was really working for a *royal*?" She eyed him merrily.

Dax leaned his head to the side. "Who would have thought. And you, Amelia? What are you doing in Anjali?"

She batted her eyelashes impishly. "I suppose neither of us are what we seemed on those Toulonan nights, hm?"

Dax's eyes widened as confusion was replaced with realization. "*No*... tell me you're not the Viloran Princess here to woo the emperor into marriage? *You* are Theralin?"

Thera preened and Dax's suspicions were confirmed.

"No!" He laughed out loud, his head tipped back. "Sneaky one, you are. That poor man has no idea what lies beneath that beautiful surface does he? He is in for a very rude awakening after his wedding day."

Thera smacked him on the arm, but Dax continued to laugh.

"Listen, I have somewhere to be, but will you meet me this evening? I have a couple of meetings and then I would adore catching up, if you have the time?".

"I'm here for a few more days. Absolutely, I would be delighted, Amelia. Oh, *my apologies*, *Theralin*." Dax snickered. “Where shall I meet you?"

"Be a good man and meet me outside Akio's parlor in two hours. Make him jealous for me, hm?" She winked.

Dax laughed once more. "I think you're far more *Amelia* than some Viloran royal girl." He nodded. "As you wish, old friend. Let's make him squirm."

Dax did, in fact, meet Thera outside the emperor's parlor, though he took it a pompous step further and went inside to retrieve her, claiming it was of utmost importance that she meet with him right away. Thera stifled a snort and excused herself as Akio grew visibly jealous. When they reached the door, Emperor Akio Nakamura reached for Thera's hand, an extremely open gesture for such a reserved man.

"We are still meeting for our little sparring match in the morning?" he asked her with a quiet smile, obviously trying to ruffle Dax's feathers and claim his territory.

"Spar?" Dax interrupted mockingly in the Viloran tongue rather than Anjalian. "With Theralin? Oh...all due respect, Emperor, but you do not wish to do that."

Thera glared at him.

"And why is that, Ambassador?" Akio eyed him carefully.

"No one beats this princess," he taunted.

"Do you insult me?" Akio grumbled. "I am more than capable of sparring with a woman."

Thera put a mock-offended hand to her chest and scoffed. "Are you insulting *me*, Emperor?"

"No... Princess, I..." the mighty emperor stuttered.

"Let us go, Ambassador Abayomi." She took Dax's arm, and they fled the parlor, hardly making it around the next corner before they burst into fits of laughter.

"Oh, I missed you and your wild schemes," she cooed.

Queen Nuria sat before her most trusted council, appearing

calm and collected as they awaited the arrival of her brother. Though truthfully, she felt more anxious than ever before in all her years.

An owl flew in the window, interrupting her thoughts. In the blink of an eye, her brother stood before her. "I'm sorry I'm late." He bowed and took a seat.

"Very well. We shall begin. General, is there any news concerning the Rebel movement or the shipment departure location?"

General Cremeux stood. "Sillow has determined over the last few weeks that the cotton farmer he has been watching is being watched by another. There is no further information from him. Lydigen has learned of a small band of Zealots that meet secretly once a week. He will tail one of them to learn more. There is no new information regarding the opposition or the shipment's departure since discovering it will take place earlier than anticipated. Pietro wants to transport before heavy snowfall."

The queen drummed her long nails on the arm of her throne. "We have not the slightest idea where this shipment leaves from?"

"No, Your Majesty, we do not. They were taken weeks ago from Greer's and a select few other orphanages, then transported to an unknown location. Only the top-ranking Collectors know the whereabouts."

"Then *bring* me one of these top-ranking Collectors, General," she commanded. "Sebastian?" Darius nodded and gave the floor to Sebastian. "What have your men in the castle learned?" the queen asked.

"Beck has discovered a rather suspicious woman working in Lilith's alchemy chamber. He is learning what he can. He suspects her to be an unadorned Zealot hiding her Mark. Mariah, who is attending Lilith, informed me that she plans to increase the famine even further in hopes of forcing the

Rebels to reveal their hand more quickly.

She still plans to go ahead with presenting the alliance in Anjali. She desires the backing of their warriors now that she is getting nervous. I cannot say how long she will stand by her word, though."

"Very well. Tell Beck and Mariah to keep up the fine work and inform us of any news as quickly as possible. I do not see how Pietro could increase the famine further without her own men dying off. She already sent the land reeling back into desolation when her men discovered the empty Rebel camp." She turned to address Linden. "We may need some relief factions ready if they are needed." Linden nodded. "Prince?"

Khyan cleared his throat. "Good news from Anjali. Thera is gaining ground quickly. Emperor Nakamura has taken to her quite swiftly and is even beginning to allow her in council meetings. She has planted the idea of a false alliance and will begin more direct approaches shortly. I informed her of the increase in Orford's famine, letting her know there is no dire need to pull at hardly available supply lines. A better plan of action is to infiltrate their warriors and attack from within, as General Cremeux suggested. That is a much greater risk, but Thera believes Emperor Nakamura to be a man of principle and someone we can trust."

"This is wonderful news, Brother. Simply wonderful. Sebastian, Prince Khyan, and General Cremeux, stay. Everyone else, you are dismissed."

"Thera is not using less than ethical matters, I presume?" Nuria inquired when the rest of the council cleared the room.

"No, she has not used her gift on the emperor. I do, however, suspect this is becoming more than a mission for her. She speaks very highly of him."

"Hm. I shall accompany you the next time you go, then." The three gentlemen approached their queen with trepidation, for her face read fire and dismay. Her royal authority melted into familiarity, losing none of the spark. "Darius, you have something you wish to say, do you not?"

Darius nodded, jaw clenched, and turned to Sebastian. "I met with Mariah this afternoon. She informed me of some...concerning sensitive matters. Beck has mentioned your relationship with Lilith might not be quite as professional as we thought." He let his words sink in. "Sebastian, are you warming Pietro's bed?"

An imperceptible emotion flitted across the informant's face as the question hit Khyan in the stomach—he'd had no idea.

"And if I am?" Sebastian responded defensively.

Nuria put a hand to her chest. "Sebastian. Please tell me this is not true."

Sebastian snarled at them all, "You think you're all so perfect and righteous. I'll get my information however I damn well please." He stormed out, leaving the other three utterly speechless. Never had they suspected such a travesty of his loyalty.

Tears filled Nuria's eyes, though she blinked them away. "I will decide what to do with him. Let him be for now. Darius, I see the vengeance in your eyes. We will have none of that. Clear your head before you do something foolish. I must think on this."

Seething, Darius bowed and swiftly left to find someone to spar with before he crushed Sebastian's traitorous face with his bare hands. Their professional ventures aside, he took it as a personal insult to their relationship.

Khyan shoved his hands in his pockets. "Sister, I'm afraid we have more to discuss."

Nuria sighed deeply and rose from her throne, linking arms with her brother. "Our sweet Luvenia, hm? Come, let us talk in the garden."

The setting sun cast the beautiful garden in oranges and reds as the siblings walked arm in arm. "You look so forlorn, Brother. Remember you are not required to carry her burdens on your shoulders."

Khyan sighed. "I know. Such murky darkness surrounds her, Nuria. It's tangible now. It's been *weeks* and she still hardly says a word to me, even in training. The only one who can bring out a semblance of the real Luvenia is Darius. The resolve in her eyes is full of hatred. I fear..." He paused. "I fear I'm creating a monster."

Nuria placed a comforting hand on Khyan's arm. "You are keeping your word, Khy. That is all. If Darius can chip away at the dark, let him. I believe he cares a great deal more for that girl than he will let on. I see the way he sends others to go in his place to complete tasks, just so he can be here to train her when you are in Anjali. Do not think you are fooling me, either, Brother. I also see the way it hurts you. Why does it hurt you so?"

"It doesn't matter if it hurts me. Or why. If what she needs is him, so be it. Perhaps I should extend my stays in Anjali and let Darius train her in my place." Khyan looked at his boots.

Nuria smiled and gripped her brother's arm. "Perhaps. It would do you all some good."

Having found no one in the training room after the confrontation with Sebastian, Darius wrapped his hands in cloth and beat the hanging burlap sack of sand until he dripped sweat and had to discard his uniform jacket and eventually the tunic underneath.

He couldn't fathom how Sebastian could be so foolish. He knew something had been off when they met up in Alban weeks ago. In fact, he'd always had reservations about Sebastian, regardless of how close they were.

The training room door opened and, to his delight, Veni walked in. He couldn't help but notice how all her training had formed her body into that of a woman instead of a girl. She was beginning to have curves in all the right places. He promptly splashed some water on his face to halt those thoughts as she closed the door and turned, just noticing him.

"I'm sorry," she said quietly, looking quickly away, acutely aware of the general's bare chest. She began backing up toward the door. "I—I didn't know anyone was in here. I'll come back later."

"No, no, it's fine. Join me. Please." He retrieved his sweaty tunic and put it back on.

"Alright. If you insist." She issued him the slightest of smirks and strode across the long room. He gave her his signature crooked smile in return.

"Looks like you've already had quite a session, Darius," she said.

Oh, he loved the way she said his name.

"That was actually more of a raging fit."

"Is that so? And why are you raging, sir?" she teased.

Sometimes he couldn't handle the way she spoke to him, it sent shivers up his spine, but then again, he couldn't get enough. He would never understand how the girl could put him at such ease that he felt like he could tell her anything yet made him so nervous he couldn't remember his own name. Khyan mentioned a darkness surrounding her, but all he saw was a broken girl with the potential to move mountains.

"It turns out our lovely informant is Pietro's whore," he told her, instantly regretting his choice in words.

Veni balked. "*Sebastian*?" She gasped and her eyes went wide. "Wait a moment. Didn't Pietro take him out of an orphan house when he was twelve?"

"No, she found him there at twelve, she only visited until he was eighteen, then she took him in. What does that have to do with anything?" He didn't intend to be rude, but his blood was still boiling over the entire thing.

"Darius, that orphan house is where she took all those

children from...to be sold as child slaves. Why do you think she picked them all from there? And why do you think Sebastian knew they weren't going to just be sold as house servants. I guarantee the orphanage owner struck a deal with Pietro long ago and she kept Sebastian as her prize." Veni wanted to throw up with the realization, but it all made sense now and she couldn't let Sebastian take that sort of fall for being a slave to Pietro.

Darius sat hard on a bench. "*Maker…*" He ran a hand through his hair. "No wonder he loathes her so much. I must find him. Now. Please find Nuria and tell her what you told me."

Darius shot up and stormed out of the room. Luvenia grabbed the coat he'd left behind and ran for Nuria's study.

Chapter Seventeen

Princess Theralin strode through Emperor Nakamura's castle, trailed by one of her Viloran-Aureland guards. It hadn't taken long for her to truly draw the emperor's attention—she was an eye-catching woman after all—though he was not a foolish man moved so easily by a beautiful woman. This much she had expected, and it took weeks for him to speak with her past pleasantries, but she now had quite a position in his ear and had begun to gain his trust.

In addition, her scheme with Dax to make the emperor jealous once his defenses were down had worked like a charm. Not to mention she indeed walloped him during their sparring session. The hunger in his eyes was growing evident.

On this evening, she'd chosen to wear a simple white dress she'd had made upon her arrival. The attendant assigned to her had been appalled that a princess would travel such a great distance with only riding clothes and two dresses shoved in a pack. Thera informed the dear woman that she was a nomad princess unused to heavy baggage. This was, of course, partially false. A nomad princess she was, though a light traveler she was not. She and Darius had argued relentlessly over the trunk she'd insisted on bringing along. He claimed it would slow her and her party down and the assignment was of utmost importance.

She, however, insisted that the majority of her assignment relied heavily upon her appearance and therefore relied upon her trunk full of clothing and cosmetics. The argument had ended with Khyan intervening—as always—and a hefty coin purse was given to Thera to purchase whatever necessary to accomplish her task. She'd found this to be a winning solution and much enjoyed obtaining an entirely new wardrobe, particularly the bronze headpiece she'd sent for from Vilora.

The piece encircled the crown of her head and her forehead in swirls and small sapphire jewels, with two delicate chains cascading down the back of her long hair. She'd chosen to have the piece made in lieu of a crown and take the chance that her family might hear of her whereabouts—if they hadn't already. She half expected her brothers to show up any day now.

She glided down the corridors to Emperor Akio Nakamura's private parlor, acutely aware that her queen would disapprove of the dress she wore. It was a little too low cut for Nuria's liking and the silk ran along her curves in an alluring fashion the queen would surely chastise her for, were she there.

Thera knew the lines were blurring between assignment and recreation. She hadn't expected to be more than someone for the emperor to enjoy looking at and eventually confide in. She hadn't foreseen a true bond taking root. Deep down she knew a conflict of interest had formed and that Nuria had thought her stronger than crossing lines almost forbidden to Keepers… But she merely couldn't find it within herself to care most of the time, especially after the aching joy of seeing Dax again.

Quick footsteps sounded behind her, and she turned to find her previously absent guard breathing heavily, post in his hand.

"The queen is coming. Tonight. The location is disclosed here." He handed her the letter as guilt trickled into her chest.

Darius strode briskly into the training area where Veni sat

sprawled on the mat, stretching.

"Morning, Luvi." He smiled in that sideways grin of his.

He'd told her in their session several days prior that she reminded him of a bird, and she'd spent the next few days determining what animal he might resemble. She smirked, quite proud of herself. "Morning, General. I've finally got it. You resemble a bat."

Darius laughed heartily. "Finally figured it out, did you? A bat? Hm. I think I like that. Though, I feel as if maybe I should be offended. Bats are rather hideous creatures."

Luvenia scoffed. "Not so! I find bats fascinating. They have a fierce elegance about them."

Darius eyed her. "Well then, bat it is, Little Bird." He tied his curls into a knot on top of his head. "Let's get to it, shall we?"

The two of them fought with wooden swords, true swords, fists, and knives until late into the morning. He beat her easily, every time, though he told her continually she was improving.

She was beginning to gain a handle on combat, though her favorite part of training each day consisted of sinking the throwing knives deep into her target, beating Darius a great majority of the time. This was his least favorite part of their sessions, for he was an atrocious loser, and she was a horribly immodest winner. He'd told her on multiple occasions that she should cease training for combat and take up a position as a professional gloater.

Out of breath, Darius lowered his ever-present, engraved sword—lovingly named Nahaliel many wielders ago. He'd told her previously that the sword was passed down from his father, but he hadn't explained the strange, ancient markings engraved upon its blade.

He squeezed her shoulder. "Come on, let's take a break."

Veni put her free hand on her hip. "What? The mighty

General Cremeux of the great Aureland Horde is *tired*?"

He glared at her and took a long pull from his water skin. "I was out the entire night with Sebastian learning the routes of some Head Collectors, thank you very much. How was your nice, plush bed?" he teased. He could never get enough of the vivacious girl she was showing him more of each day before she snatched it back up and shut him out again.

"Very cozy indeed," she told him. "How is Sebastian? I haven't seen him since the incident the other night."

Darius wiped his face with a cloth. "Nuria and I spoke with him. He's fairly closed off still, but I think he's on the road toward healing. His spirit has taken a horrific beating for years and years—really his entire life. I told him he can't continue to let her hold him hostage, but he feels trapped.

In all honesty, I don't think he knows who he is without her. To think, all these years of friendship and I thought he was just pompous and a seducer. He's really just a broken boy trapped within a man. There was always something...*off* about him and now I know what it was. I wish he would have let me in ages ago." He shook his head sadly and ran a hand through his close-cropped beard. "Anyone can love a person's light. It is another thing entirely to love a person in their darkness as well."

Luvenia chewed on her lip for a moment before responding. "You're a truly good friend. I hope you are aware of that. You lead so well, and you give up everything for other people. There aren't many like you in the world, Darius. At least Sebastian knows he doesn't have to fight alone."

Darius frowned at her. "Nor do you. You know that, right? You know that none of us are oblivious to the storm that rages behind your eyes. You don't plan to stay here a second longer than you deem necessary. As soon as Khyan locates Ester and you feel you've trained enough, you're going to leave, aren't you?"

Luvenia merely stared at the general and debated walking

out.

"You are," he went on. "I also know you want to run from this conversation. Please don't."

The pleading look in his eyes held her feet in place, barely.

"Luvi, I know your intention is to avoid letting anyone in so they don't end up hurt like your family and so *you* don't end up hurt again, either. You think you're responsible for all that has happened to you and if you get close to someone, they'll end up hurt or they'll hurt you. But the truth is you're going to hurt all of us more by leaving, and you'll hurt yourself more by remaining isolated.

You're not protecting anyone by being distant or trying to keep your relationships surface-level. If no one else would be hurt," he put a hand to his broad chest, "*I* would be hurt. *Me*. The second you walk out those doors and into the darkness that beckons you, you'll be gone for good. Not just physically, I mean *you*. Luvenia Rousseau."

He shook his head, frustrated to be admitting so much. "Look...I—I don't know why I'm saying all this. This whole Sebastian thing has me being sentimental. I suppose it's just my backwards way of letting you know I care, even if no one else does, which is not true. But even if they don't, *I* do."

Veni fidgeted and mumbled, "Thank you." It was all she could manage.

Awkward silence fell between them—for the first time ever, Veni noted sadly. Desperate to both fill the silence and not allow a gaping hole to form between them, she said the first thing that popped into her mind. "Is Pietro a witch?"

"What? Where did you hear that?" Darius was taken aback by the random question.

"Thera. When we got in our argument, she said *of course the Purge War was lost by the citizens. It was a load of peasants against a witch*. What does that mean? Is she truly a witch?"

"Witches are what common mortals call anyone with gifts

that they don't understand. By those standards, all Keepers are deemed witches if discovered."

"Pietro is a Keeper, then?"

"A fallen Keeper, yes. Her mother refused to move to Aureland and have Lilith properly trained. Left to her own devices, Lilith gained a grave thirst for power once she discovered her gifts. She was intended to be a Keeper with the gift of healing and a very rare, special gift. The Touch of Life or Touch of Death, only to be used in dire circumstances.

The Touch costs her many years of life when used, so she developed a way to utilize her gifts in conjunction with alchemy to form harmful potions, such as the Collector Venom and a particularly potent fear toxin used to break her Warmongers into submission. She also managed to formulate a powerful vapor that killed the crops and livestock. You refer to this as The Famine, or rot, though it was her all along."

Luvenia was stunned. "And the second wave was Pietro's doing as well? Does she know of Aureland, even though her mother never brought her here?"

Darius nodded. "The second wave was indeed her doing. And yes, she knows of Aureland, though she does not know the location or how to enter. She is extremely powerful and does not lack intelligence. She will eventually learn our location and how to get in, I fear. We could always use another skilled warrior on our side," he said with a smile, desiring to lighten the mood and desperate for another taste of the girl beneath the mask.

"You're plum out of luck then, General," she teased him, giving him precisely what he wanted.

"Oh, am I? You're too good for us?"

Veni laughed softly. "I've got a long way to go to be as good as the likes of you and your men…and women."

"You're too hard on yourself, Little Bird. You certainly had me working up a sweat to keep up with you today. You move as if you've been training for years."

She shrugged. "I still lose most of the time."

"Yes, but you hold your own for far longer than most can manage to do so. I have an idea. Grab your water skin and follow me."

He took his water and she followed him out of the training room and across the castle into a very masculine parlor in the men's wing of the castle. The walls were velvety black and thick, steel-grey curtains framed the windows. A fire dimly burned in the oversized hearth, ornate with iron leaf work.

"If I hadn't already decided a bat was the animal fitting for you, I would have in this exact moment," Luvenia told him, still rather proud of her assessment.

He laughed and told her to wait there while he found Chester, his and Khyan's attending Elfe. Such a sweet old fellow, short in stature like Helga—wrinkled as well—and huge in heart. She'd been very pleased to discover Chester was Helga's husband. So precious they were, both in their spectacles. Though Chester's were tiny, and they perched on the tip of his long, pointed nose.

In Darius' absence, Veni trailed her finger along the spines of books lining a shelf that made up the entire eastern wall of the parlor. There must have been thousands there.

Which one of these gallant gentlemen loves to read?

She lifted a particularly worn book off the shelf and beheld the title. She flipped it open to discover what it was about—an orphan vigilante with the powers of a phoenix, a creature she instantly needed to know more about. As she closed the book, she caught a scribbled name on the inside of the cover and took a peek.

Darius Thatcher Cremeux. Her heart fluttered.

Darius Thatcher. When will the layers of your charm cease to amaze me?

She deposited the book back in its place just before Darius returned with Chester, who cordially nodded hello to Luvenia and climbed onto the piano bench to play a beautiful melody.

"We shall train a bit differently for the rest of our session." Darius held out a hand. "M'lady..."

Reluctantly, Luvenia took his hand, and he pulled her closer, placing her left arm on his shoulder, and resting his right hand on her lower back. His proximity made her knees wobble a bit and her mind turned into a web of anxious chaos.

Holding their position, Darius' eyes locked with her panicked gaze. "The factor you're missing when you fight is foresight. Combat, especially one on one, is much like a dance. Any opponent's next move can be predicted with the right discernment. You want to let your opponent lead the fight, knowing that this gives you the upper hand in the end. Do you know how to dance the foxtrot?"

Luvenia shook her head in mute terror.

"Don't look so frightened," he chuckled, inwardly relishing the very fact that he made her so adorably nervous. "I'll teach you. We're going to move in a counterclockwise fashion around the line of the room. Follow my lead." He began leading her slowly. "Right foot first, we're going to move backward...slow, slow, side, together. Forward...slow, slow, side, together. Good."

After many a squashed toe and several fits of joint laughter, she had the basics down and Darius taught her what he called the promenade and added an underarm turn. He urged her, having learned the gist, to follow his lead, predicting where he would go next and when he would switch to the promenade or add a turn without warning.

"The correlation is beginning to make sense," she told him excitedly as they walked to the lunch hall when they'd finished.

She hadn't taken any meals corporately for weeks. Precisely why he chose not to draw attention to where they were headed. "They're quite similar. You're doing a fantastic job.

You'll be a force to be reckoned with in no time."

Crouched behind a mound of discarded barrels, Sebastian snapped his fingers in Darius' face to get his attention. "Darius! Are you listening to me?" he whispered sharply.

"Sorry," Darius mumbled.

He hadn't realized he'd been thinking about her again. He had to get a handle on this madness. He was the general of the mighty Aureland Horde and currently on an incredibly crucial assignment. There were lives at stake—the lives of *children*—and he was daydreaming about a pretty face. She was far more than just a pretty face, but regardless, he needed to stay focused.

"Sorry," he repeated. "Say that again."

Sebastian clenched his jaw. "Please tell me a *woman* isn't going to be your downfall, Darius. I truly thought you'd go down in bloody glory, not from a blow to the head while you're daydreaming about some girl."

"Watch your tongue, Olliander. Repeat yourself," Darius snapped at him.

Sebastian rolled his eyes. “Don’t pull rank with me just because you don’t like what I said.” He pointed to a nearby stand. "Shiv's right-hand man passes by that flower stand every afternoon—unaccompanied by his Mouthpiece—just before dusk to watch that pretty blonde. See, ya' buffoon, a *woman* will be his downfall."

"Alright, alright. I get your point, Sebastian. You're the decoy. Dusk is swiftly approaching. Let's move."

Sebastian donned his hood and took his post, pretending to browse the Royal Market fruit stand until he spotted the Collector in question, identifiable by the two red stripes lining the shoulder of his black uniform, signifying his high rank.

As Shiv's man approached, Sebastian slipped into the skin of a trained seducer and sauntered up to the blonde at the flower stand. The woman blushed and instantly soaked up the attention. The Collector stiffened. His face remained concealed, but his body gave away his distaste for the cloaked gentleman holding the attention of his girl.

Darius strolled behind the Collector, his thief-like hands dislodging the Venom tube from the pack without so much as a hitch in his step. Distracted, Pietro's puppet failed to notice the Venom leaking to the ground. Sebastian caught Darius' signal from an alleyway to proceed and he became a little physically forthright with the all-too-willing girl. He placed his hands around her waist intimately and the Collector's blood boiled. He ran over to them, reaching for his Venom tube as he went.

He shoved Sebastian off the girl, gaining the attention of everyone in the vicinity—shocked by the scene considering they'd not heard a Collecting Call. Realizing something had gone wrong with his tube, the Collector elbowed Sebastian in the temple, nearly knocking him unconscious. He then shoved his boot into the back of Sebastian's knee to drop him to the ground. The Collector yanked his prey up and held his hands behind his back as he shoved Sebastian toward the alley and reached to pull back his hood.

The target never saw Darius' ambush coming. He dropped onto the Collector from a balcony where he'd been waiting for them to pass. All three of them crashed in a mercifully muffled heap. Darius was incredibly thankful the Collectors' masks restricted their speaking ability, as they were still only a single street over from an area packed with people—they needed to hurry.

Darius held the Collector down with great effort as Sebastian removed the Venom pack and weapons and tied his hands behind him. They needed to get the man to the forest where two Aureland Hordemen waited, one of which had a very convenient gift of vision cloaking. He would conceal the prisoner from the eyes of others as they traveled back to Aureland.

"Someone's coming! We have to go *now*!" Sebastian whispered.

Darius shoved the struggling prisoner into a nearby alcove seconds before two women strolled past. Sebastian smiled and tipped his head charmingly and they giggled as they walked on. Sebastian made sure the way was clear before they pulled the man quickly into an empty alley and made their way carefully through the maze of backstreets toward the forest.

The Queen of Aureland strode into her castle's training hall like an ancient warrior comprised of bone crushing strength and the breathless wonder of snow-capped mountain air.

Rarely did she wear riding pants and a tunic—for she believed one's attire should reflect one's character and *she* was a leader of others into excellence and virtue—but today her leading required a different sort of approach and a gown would not do. Granted, her tunic glistened with fine jewels—there was no need to look like a *peasant*.

Her protégé thought she'd seen fierce opponents in her training, but she hadn't seen Nuria. The queen's most guarded secret may be of an entirely different nature, but her hundred years of honed battle skills came in at a close second.

"Hello, Luvenia," she said to get the girl's attention, her voice silken. "No need to look so shocked, darling. I will be conducting your training this fine morning. Darius needed to sleep. Though achieving his agreement on that fact was a battle in and of itself." She rolled her eyes and smoothed her bejeweled tunic, then clapped both hands together. "Right, then, let us get to it. You are weakest in hand-to-hand combat, yes?"

Veni nodded mutely, feeling as though she were about to discover the queen's beauty and gentle spirit had merely been the adorned scabbard sheathing a powerful blade.

"Very well." The queen eyed the girl. "I will not hold back. Your training will not be complete until you are capable of disarming and defeating *me*. That will not happen today. There is no need for unrealistic expectations. Though you, my dear, *will* beat me one day. Recognize your potential without masking it in obscured reality."

Veni's mind spun. She's going to run me into the ground, physically and mentally.

"Use your words, dear. Are you prepared or not?" Veni smirked and sighed a breathy laugh. "Ready as I'll ever be, I suppose."

Nuria's beauty turned lethal as she lunged for the wide-eyed girl. Before Veni could even get her hands up to defend herself, the queen nicked her chin with her bare knuckles, enough to stun her. In an instant, she had Veni's own arm twisted behind her and forced her to her knees.

The queen released her captive and Veni stood as her vision swam a bit from the blow to her chin.

Nuria wiped the blood from her split knuckle on her pants. "My Hordemen go easy on you and spar with you." She shook her head. "You have had enough of that. Sparring is unrealistic and you have grown used to how it works."

The queen put a finger to her temple. "Your mind is quick, dearheart, but wits alone will not win a battle. A sparring session, perhaps, but not a battle. Darius has taught you well how to predict your opponent's next move, this is wise. However, most of the people you come across in a fight will not be calculated. They will be *ruthless*.

There is a fine line between noble ferocity and ruthless ferocity. The truth of it is you will need to dance on the edge of that line in order to get your sister back. We will help you stay on the noble side, but you must embrace the ferocity. You can spar and train all day long, learning all the perfect maneuvers and defenses, but until you can take a true blow and get back up, you are not learning what you will need to succeed in bringing Ester home. Do you understand?"

Veni's jaw stung, and her heart pounded, but she knew Nuria was right. It was time to cease pretending that she was learning to fight and to truly take hold of it. "Yes," she told the queen. "Again. Let's go."

Fast as lightning, Nuria came at her with no mercy over and over. The girl's blood was splattered on the queen's sparkling tunic and Nuria's knuckles continued to bleed. Veni forgot everything she'd learned in routine sparring sessions and had little success discerning Nuria's next move. That is, for the first half of their session. Once she'd taken several hits and tasted self-preservation as well as a sense of wildness, her training came back to her in a new way. She ended up on her back or rear or face countless times, but it would only take one hit.

Luvenia had to hit that beautiful queen *one* time and she would be satisfied for the day.

"Are you certain you would like to continue? Your eye is beginning to swell." Nuria watched her protégé struggle to stand, yet again.

"I'm sure," she said through gritted teeth. "Again."

Her eye was indeed swelling shut and her mouth was thick with blood and saliva, but she was going to hit that perfect face.

Just once.

Nuria smiled at the look in Veni's eye. She knew in her bones the girl was going to become everything they'd hoped. She motioned for Veni to come at her.

Veni lunged toward the queen and dodged the blow meant for her chin, pushing away the next fist meant for her ribs. They danced around each other for a second before Nuria swung again and narrowly missed Veni's face. She ducked under the blow and nearly landed a punch to Nuria's abdomen, but the queen was too swift. Nuria grabbed her wrist, but Veni thought quickly and threw that arm wide, forcing Nuria to release her grasp as she deflected the next blow as well.

Veni watched carefully as Nuria threw another fist at her. Timing it just right, she spun around the queen's fist and threw her own at Nuria's unguarded cheek, landing one solid, satisfying blow. Nuria instantly halted and froze sternly in place. She reached up to touch her cheek and looked at the little dab of blood on her finger from where her skin had split open over her high cheekbone.

Veni was torn completely in half between an irrational sense of victory and sheer terror from the look in the queen's eyes. Nuria's ruby lips turned up on one side in a smirk before she smiled broadly and started laughing.

"I am certain I have never been prouder of you. Well done, dearheart."

Veni beamed.

Just then, Khyan walked in and gaped at the bloody sight before him. "*What* is happening in here?" he shouted.

Nuria rolled her eyes and turned back to Veni. "My men will no longer spar with you. I will tell Darius myself. You will fight like a real woman, and you will win." Veni stood a little straighter. "Khyan," Nuria said as she turned to her brother, "Ice her down and send for Healer Collins. Her uncomplicated beauty is a weapon, as well. Battle scars are an honor to keep, but a broken jaw is not."

With that, the Queen of Aureland strode from the room like the lethal ruler she was. Khyan watched her go, shaking his head. He sighed and began forming ice pockets encased in bubbles of water over each of Veni's many wounds.

Darius and his men had successfully imprisoned the Collector in the dungeons of the Aureland Castle and stripped him of his mask. Having deprived him of food and water for three days to weaken his resolve, General Darius Cremeux and Sebastian Olliander entered the man's cell to interrogate him.

Sebastian set a chair in the middle of the cell with barely restrained fury and instructed the prison guard to lock the door, him and Darius inside. Darius strode over to where the prisoner crouched in the corner, taunting them with a grotesque smile.

The general stooped down in front of the man and said with deadly calm, "Wipe that repulsive grin off your face before I smash it in."

The prisoner laughed—a dark, hollow sound that grated on Darius' bones. Swift as a cobra, Darius grabbed the prisoner by the collar, lifting him up, and slammed him into the chair. The wood groaned beneath the man as his interrogator shoved the occupied chair up against the wall with his foot and withdrew his talon dagger, holding it in the prisoner's face. The Collectors might be strong by some sinister potion, but if there was one thing the general did not lack, it was his own immense strength.

"I may work for a peaceful queen, you filth," he snarled through gritted teeth, "but I will not be toyed with. They didn't make me General for nothing. Now," he inched the tip of his blade closer, "we can do this in a civilized fashion or in a barbaric one. Which shall it be?"

Sebastian crossed his arms, smug. He loved this side of his friend and general. He believed every man to be like a moon—with a dark side he kept well hidden from the world and a side illuminated by light. He also believed you couldn't trust a man until he trusted *you* with his dark side. Sebastian had to admit he was immensely relieved Darius now knew fully of his. They had their differences with one another, but

Sebastian knew he could trust Darius with his life. He would follow no other general as long as Darius Cremeux drew breath.

The Collector said nothing. He only stared at the general.

"Where is the shipment of children leaving from?" Darius thundered.

A trace of surprise crossed the prisoner's eyes, hardly perceptible, but Darius was *very* good at his position.

"Ah. Didn't know anyone knew a thing about that shipment, now did you? Sparked your interest, did we?" He smiled humorlessly at the man.

"Who are you people?" the prisoner asked, his voice cracking. "Aren't you the queen's whore?" he spat at Sebastian.

In two strides, Sebastian made it to the man's throat and growled, "We're your worst nightmare unless you give us what we want. And if anyone is that witch's whore it's *you*."

With that, he unsheathed his own dagger and plunged it into the man's hand, all the way through flesh and bone and into the arm of the chair.

The prisoner howled in pain and Darius yanked Sebastian to the side of the cell and spoke, his voice low and deadly, "That is *enough*, Sebastian. Get a grip or we'll never get information from the man." Still grasping Sebastian's shirt, he leaned around him and roared at the still howling prisoner, "*Enough*!"

The prisoner did so, realizing that his interrogators were just unbalanced enough to maim him further.

He turned back to Sebastian. "Chain him up. *Without killing him.* I'm going to send for a meal."

Darius returned with a steaming plate of chicken and rice to find the prisoner indeed chained to two walls of the dungeon, arms wide in his shackles. The man was slumped over, presumably unconscious from blood loss and hunger. The dagger still protruded from his hand and Sebastian had left a note with the guard.

Darius,
Do not offer release. He knows who I am.
-Sebastian

Did he think Darius a fool? Annoyed, he crumpled the note and shoved it in his coat pocket before walking over to hold the plate of hot food under the prisoner's nose to wake him. He indeed woke rather quickly, and his stomach grumbled audibly. He looked at Darius but said nothing. This wasn't his first go at an interrogation, most likely, and he would naturally know the food was a bribe.

The general, however, knew how few men could truly manage to keep their physical needs in submission after more than a couple of days. He let the man smell the aroma of the food before he strode to a chair and a small table in the corner. He set the food down and dropped into the seat.

Placing his feet on the table and reclining back in the chair, he let several moments of silence pass before he finally spoke. "This delicious chicken and rice is all yours when you tell us the location the shipment is leaving from, and when."

"I'm not telling you anything. You'll have to let me starve," the bloody man spat as he twitched strangely.

Darius locked his hands casually behind his head. "Oh, and *that* I have no qualms with doing. You think because I reprimanded my man in front of you that I'm the soft one around here. You are *severely* mistaken. He is the rash one, I'll give you that, but I... Oh, *I* am the calculated one. The one you should fear. I know every point on your body that I can torture without *quite* killing you. I also know how to permanently maim you, far worse than that little dagger did."

The prisoner grinned, a vicious smile. "Do you think me a fool? I've interrogated men myself, *General*. I didn't make my way to the top by being a coddler." His words choked off in a violent twitch.

"What I'm hearing is that you are willing to die...alone...in a dungeon, at the hands of a kingdom you know nothing about, never to be found again. All in order to help a sadistic ruler sell *innocent* lives to *other* sadistic rulers." He focused on keeping his concentration as the prisoner continued to twitch unnervingly. Maybe the man was ill.

"I do whatever my queen desires," the Collector stated simply.

Darius dropped his feet to the ground and sat forward, elbows on his knees. "Tell ya' what, you tell me every detail about your time in the training process to become a Collector and I'll give you this meal. A hot bath and a healer, too. What d'ya say?"

The prisoner weighed his options for several moments. It was almost as if he was struggling against some unseen force. "That is *all* I will tell you. Deal."

"The floor is yours, sir." Darius spread his hands in invitation.

The prisoner began—in a surprisingly less vicious tone, "Training started as grueling physical and mental sessions, far more grueling than infantry training. After a couple of weeks, we were all given a tonic just as we were when we went into the infantry, though this tonic blocks out portions of our memory for weeks at a time. It was administered every two weeks, just as our minds would begin to clear. I have no recollection of anything else. Now give me my chicken." By the last sentence his voice had returned to its former savage tone.

Darius stood, disconcerted by the man's conflicting personality. "And how do I know you're not lying?"

The man looked at him with pleading eyes—just for a second. A look that struck the general in his gut. "I know your informant will never let me leave here alive now that I know who he is." He struggled against that unseen force again as he continued, "I can also tell you I have not had my memory inhibitor in several days." At this the twitching became overpowering.

The general knew the man was telling the truth. He also knew some part of him was screaming for help and giving Darius a way to retrieve his answers. If he waited a few more days, the serum would wear off completely. He instructed the guard to unchain the man and place him in his cell with his food, and to send for a healer for his hand.

Darius spoke, so close his breath mingled with the prisoner's, "You may have your food and your bath. I will return in three days. If I find you are lying to me, I will kill you myself."

As Darius turned to walk away, the chains holding the Collector rattled violently and he choked out, "...leaves...in... three... fr...m..." The man fell limp and unconscious before he could finish, foaming at the mouth.

Something warred within the Collectors, keeping them hostage—Darius was now certain of it. The man beneath the monster was warning him the shipment was leaving before the serum would wear off. But from where?

He rushed out of the dungeon to instruct the nearest Hordeman to send urgent notices informing all the spies, Khyan, and Nuria that they must meet the following evening in Alban.

Chapter Eighteen

After another exhausting night of little sleep, Darius waited in the training room for Luvi to arrive. His mind was splattered all over the place.

He hadn't been lying when he told that prisoner he was a calculated man. He always had been, even as a boy. But he continually found himself making decisions based on Luvenia and he couldn't understand why. He wanted to make sure she was safe and happy and accomplishing what she set out to do. He hardly knew the girl, really, it hadn't been more than a couple of months, but she had him tightly in her clutches. He doubted she knew that, though it was true.

When Lydia took her own life by drowning herself in the sea, he vowed to never love another woman. Now that he was a grown man, he realized that vow had been made by a foolish boy, yet he still wished to keep it. He'd mastered his body physically and he'd learned to filter his thoughts and emotions. He could do this. He could care about a woman without falling in love with her. He could also go through with his and Khyan's idea for her birthday approaching soon...

"Get it together, Cremeux," he chastised himself for focusing on his personal life when he needed to remain focused on the plan to intercept the shipment and the concerning Collector below the castle.

Seconds later, in she walked. "Morning, General." She

smiled and all of his resolve melted to the floor.

Veni had come to enjoy training even more than before. It was the only place she felt any hint of freedom, however fleeting it might be. Beating her body into submission and distracting her mind lifted the heaviness that settled on her as soon as she left training.

She had begun to notice, though, that the heaviness never settled quite as firmly as long as Darius was around. She felt at ease with him—accepted. She knew Khyan and everyone else cared very deeply for her, but it wasn't quite the same as it was with Darius. She supposed she'd never had a true friend before.

Their session didn't go quite so well this morning, though.

On the way to meet the general, she ran into Khyan and snapped at him when he inquired how she was. Veni had apologized and let him know she knew he was trying and appreciated it, but for the rest of the morning somberness stuck closely by. Even in training she'd been bitter and Darius had been agitated.

She told herself everyone has bad days as she returned to her chambers to bathe. When she opened the door, Queen Nuria sat next to her fireplace.

Nuria smiled in her loving way. "Hello, dearheart. I have come to inquire if you would like to meet with me for midday meals after your training sessions. Do not fret, I know you do not enjoy crowds. It would be only you and I."

Luvenia thought for a moment, willing her heart to not grow affectionate toward the woman and failing miserably.

"Yes," she said quietly. "I think that would be lovely."

The queen's warmth was tangible. She reminded Veni so very much of her mother. Nuria practically imploded with genuine glee. "Splendid! Shall I call for lunch now?"

Lunch—consisting of thin sliced meats, fruit, and lovely

cheeses—arrived shortly after Luvenia had bathed. The two of them spoke mostly of unimportant things as the queen nibbled and Luvenia gobbled.

Little did Luvenia know, Nuria had chosen to meet with her over lunchtime because she had observed the specific times of day that the girl let her walls down. She'd determined those times to be during training—interestingly enough, only with Darius present—and when she was shoving her mouth full of food so quickly that her mind went silent, as was the case currently.

To the queen's immense surprise and delight, Veni prattled on about how wonderful she found the merpeople and Smithwick, inquiring where the little fellow had been as she flung crumbs all through the air while talking with her hands. Nuria smiled to herself as she watched her, realizing *this* was the girl Khyan had grown to love so fiercely over the years. He'd come to her when he officially had Darius take over her training, distraught that he couldn't be the one to help her. She'd reassured her brother that her battles were not his to win. The girl would let him back in whenever she chose to do so.

It was obvious how deeply Veni loved when she let someone in. She already trusted the general implicitly, even if she didn't realize that yet. Though Nuria knew she had a special place in her heart for Khyan as well. She merely blocked him out because he continuously challenged her to rise above—a fact that made the queen so immensely proud to call Khyan her brother.

"Dearheart," she said when the girl had ceased speaking in order to fill her mouth with more cheese. "What are you passionate about?" Best to start small, Nuria decided.

Veni stopped chewing and spoke around her mouthful, "Passionate?"

Nuria nodded simply.

"Erm...I've never thought about that before." Veni

swallowed her cheese.

"Think on it now, then. What causes your heart to soar above the clouds?"

"I can't think of anything. I suppose I never had much time for passions and niceties."

"I am not talking about frivolous past times, dearheart. I mean to learn what makes you tick. What makes you angry, then? That's a good place to start."

The girl's face fell. "What makes me angry? Injustice. Tyranny. Pietro and her Collectors. That my helpless little sister is trapped somewhere because of me, while I sit here shoving my face full of food and she starves." Veni set her food down, walls securely back in place.

The shift in her mood was so swift that it should've taken Nuria by surprise, but it did not. "Veni, torturing yourself does not bring Ester to safety any faster," the queen told her.

Veni shook her head. "It's simply not right for me to roam about some mystical land meeting mermaids and making friends and enjoying myself. Khyan tells me I'm valuable and I think somewhere in me I want to believe that but I would much rather give my happiness and my life to Ester so *she* can be happy and safe."

"Oh, dearheart, your intentions are noble and pure, but that is not how life works. You forfeiting your happiness does not mean it will be stored up for her. Her happiness does not negate your own. I am not suggesting you merely gallivant around having a grand time whilst Ester is in danger, but I am telling you that you cannot forfeit your life for her potential safety.

If you will allow, and let us in, we shall wage *war* to achieve safety for your sister and for *you*. But you must trust us, and you must trust yourself. *Let go* of the guilt, Veni. You are not responsible for Ester's capture. What haunts you is only what you've allowed to do so."

"If only I'd been there instead of the market. If only I'd

confronted Jacob about his strange behavior earlier. If only I could make him give me answers..." She was beginning to hyperventilate and Nuria halted her.

"Stop there. If you are not careful, you will lose your life to '*if only*'. You cannot go back and change a single moment. As you sit here abusing yourself over things you have done or not done—things now out of your control—and shoving who you are down into a deep, dark cave, you are halting the very process that shall liberate you *and* prepare you to free Ester as well.

We have discussed previously this desire to confront your brother. You and I both know it flows much deeper than that and you believe vengeance will assuage your guilt. You must remember that there is a price to pay for an unrighteous kill."

Veni fidgeted with her nails—broken and torn from training. "I do not wish to discuss my brother," she told her sternly. "And you're trying to tell me that this process you and Khyan continually push me toward will help me get my sister back faster?" She raised a skeptical brow.

"It will assist you in becoming who you need to be, alongside who you need to be joined with in order to get her back."

The memory of the ghoul with her father's twisted voice played in Veni's mind. These people can't help you. They're going to use you and spit you out. To save your sister you must use them instead. Don't let them in. They want to manipulate you into a weak-hearted follower.

"How do I know you aren't just saying all of this to manipulate me and use me to fight your war?" she murmured accusingly.

"It is not *our* war, Luvenia. It is humanity's war. Humanity's quest for *freedom*. Pietro is a monster that will stop at nothing to rule mankind. Yet, you truly believe that of us—that we merely want to *use* you?"

The hurt in the queen's eyes softened Luvenia slightly. "I

don't know what to believe."

Nuria licked her ruby lips. "Luvenia, I do not wish to push you, nor does Khyan. We wish only to help, and we shall all be here when you decide to not wander this path alone. Though, before I go, I want to leave you with something to ponder." She looked deep into Luvenia's soul as she said, "You, dearheart, are a rare and precious gem. If only you knew the treasure that awaits within your scars." She let her words sink in as she gracefully rose. "Do not dismiss what I have said, Veni. Ponder it."

As Nuria walked to the entryway, a knock sounded at the door. Veni rose to answer it, but Nuria did so for her. "Oh! Why hello, General," Nuria smirked knowingly at Darius. "What a lovely surprise."

He fidgeted, having not expected Nuria to be there. Something about her presence as he sought out Luvenia made him nervous. "Majesty." He bowed awkwardly.

The queen rolled her eyes and whispered in his ear as she passed by, "You are fooling no one, General, least of all yourself." Off she strode down the hall, her heels clicking on the marble as she went.

Darius ran a nervous hand through his beard, attempting to unruffle his feathers. "Hi," he finally said.

"Hello." Veni was curious what the queen had just whispered.

"I wanted to apologize for this morning," Darius began. "I haven't been sleeping and there has been much on my mind with the shipment location and the prisoner in the dungeons..." He shook his head. "Regardless, none of that is an excuse to be cold toward you and I am sorry."

Veni nodded. "I forgive you. I was far from nice to you, either. Truce?" She held out her hand.

He gave her a small smile and shook her hand, hating such a formal gesture from her. "Truce."

"Good...because did you say *prisoner?* In the *dungeon*?"

she prodded him, genuinely enthralled and relishing a distraction from what Nuria had spoken to her. It was a chance to finally meet her enemy.

Darius sighed. "I'd hoped you missed that. I'm supposed to be a man with many secrets of war and you cause me to drop all semblance of professionalism."

His statement warmed Veni's heart greatly and made her wonder if maybe, just maybe Nuria was right.

Darius reluctantly continued, "Yes, there is a high-ranking Collector chained in the dungeon. We interrogated him to find out the location of the shipment departure and the timing."

"Did you succeed?"

"Somewhat. I convinced him to tell me about his training to become a Collector. We knew little about the process...still do, really. Evidently, Pietro issues a memory inhibitor periodically, so they don't know what is happening to them in the areas she wishes to conceal from them."

"That is horrifying..." Veni thought of Jacob with sympathy for a change.

"Yes, it is. We knew about the fear toxin she administers to break the Warmongers into submission, but we had no knowledge of a memory inhibitor. It's as if there is a *war* going on inside that man. He was repulsive and defiant then he would begin to twitch and try to tell me where the shipment is leaving from. He also told me his inhibitor would wear off soon and I'm fairly certain he told me the shipment is leaving in three days. Two, now. But he began foaming at the mouth and went unconscious. It's all rather strange. I was on my way to check with him again before heading to our meeting in Alban, but I thought I should come by and see you before I leave."

"Thank you for that. Do you think maybe I could go to the

dungeon with you?" she asked sheepishly.

"Absolutely not," Darius barked without thinking.

"You're training me to *face* the Collectors, Darius. The least you can do is let me confront a *chained* one to gather my bearings," she fired back.

She had a valid argument and he reminded himself he was not her protector...yet. He shoved the 'yet' away and said, "You have a point. Alright." She bounced with excitement, and he held a finger up, his trainer position firmly in place. "Now you wait one moment. This is not a *treat*. This is a very dangerous man who works for Pietro and very likely has some sort of twisted sorcery controlling him. You will not say a word, you will remain ready for anything, and you will follow my every order. Do you understand?" Veni nodded.

The pair of them entered the dank dungeons, both believing they were prepared. They had never been so wrong.

The creature that raised its head to look upon its guests through the bars of the cell was a feral beast. Nothing human remained beneath the skin as his head twisted disturbingly from side to side. "Hello, General," the creature purred, sending shivers up Veni's spine.

Darius said nothing as he contemplated what exactly he was looking at. Something like recognition flitted across the creature's human mask. In an inhuman instant he slammed himself against the bars of his cell, reaching for Luvenia.

"YOU!" he roared as Darius jumped in front of the girl. "*You* are the one that got away." The creature laughed—a most hideous sound. "Oh, how my master would love to get her claws on you."

Veni's hands began to tremble, and Darius cursed the beast, pushing Luvenia behind him. Suddenly, the man's human skin began to split, tearing down the middle with abundant gore to reveal the terrifying monster beneath.

An obsidian demon of solid muscle and sinew slid out of the flesh and roared, its mouth full of razor-sharp teeth. It clawed at the cell bars with talons longer than Darius' forearms and horns protruded from its extremities like spikes. Luvenia, who had been peeking from behind the general, shrieked and Darius instinctively threw her back, reaching for his sword. The guard standing by drew his sword as well, while Darius shouted for him to open the cell door so he could enter, and to lock it behind him.

Luvenia screamed over the roaring for Darius not to go in. Ignoring her, the two armed Hordemen moved for the cell when, as if the dungeon collapsed in on itself, everything went black.

Luvenia blinked. Before her kneeled a long line of people. They wore the faces of everyone she cared about. Her parents, her brother, Ester, Meredith, Darius, Khyan...even Nuria and Thera.

She looked on in confusion. She tried to step toward them, but her feet melted into the floor, rendering her immobile. As she struggled, a young girl skipped in wearing a pretty pink dress and a familiar matching ribbon. Her wild hair ran down her back and in her hand she carried a rusted axe. As she swung it back and forth playfully, she strolled up and down the row of Luvenia's loved ones.

Veni's heart beat like a drum. She had to help them.

She struggled with all her might to detach herself from the floor, but she could not. She shouted at her family and friends, "Get up! She's going to kill you! *Get up! Run!*"

They couldn't hear her.

One by one, the girl hacked Luvenia's loved ones to pieces, blood spraying her as she screamed, forced to watch in helpless agony. The deadly girl reached Ester last of all. The little child stood numbly in a vast pool of blood, staring at her elder sister.

As the murderer lifted her gory axe, Luvenia lunged, her feet at last released. She ran as fast as she could toward Ester, but it was as if she were running against a mighty wind. When she managed to make it a few paces away, the axe sliced through Ester's neck.

Luvenia screamed as her young sister's head rolled along the floor, hit her foot, and stopped with innocent eyes staring up at her. She roared with anguish and fury, flinging herself at the murderous girl. She reached her shoulder and spun her around.

Instantly, Luvenia halted. For she stared into the eyes of herself. Wild, murderous, and wicked.

Darius shielded his eyes against the bright sun on a familiar beach, a vapor of black sludge dancing along the edges of his vision. He could hear a song, but he couldn't quite make out the words. The voice was so familiar… Then he saw her.

Lydia.

He stood benumbed, watching her as the song on the wind became clear.

The sea salted wind blew idly by, as on any other day,
and the waves ceased their crashing for no one.
A jovial passerby paid no mind at all,
nor did the gulls above,
to the silent woman in red.

She sat in her flowing dress, just out of water's reach,
scooping and pouring the powdery sands.
The sea beckoned her home,
to the family that would never return.

"Follow me," the waves sang, "I'll show you the way."

Their allure pulled her in,
as it did each day.
Their embrace held her close,
until her death drew near.
Her family she could almost touch,
their voices she could almost hear.
They reached out for her, to take her hand.
Though, in an instant, she was again on dry land.

The sea salted wind blew idly by, as on any other day,
and the waves ceased their crashing for no one.
A jovial passerby paid no mind at all,
nor did the gulls above,
to the silent woman in red.

The song repeated countless times. Darius watched on in horror as the ghost of his first love drowned herself over and over and over. No movement would come to his limbs. He could only watch helplessly. Just as he thought his heart could bear no more, the song ceased, and Lydia halted at the water's edge. Hope sprang up in Darius, until Lydia's dress became white, and she turned to look at him.

He lifted his eyes to meet hers. But the face of Luvenia stared back.

His heart pounded in his chest as he tried desperately to move toward her. "No..." he managed when she turned to face the sea once more. "*No*."

Luvenia's white dress fluttered in the wind as she walked into the water. Darius willed every ounce of strength into his legs, but they would not move. He bellowed her name so fiercely he thought he would burst. He screamed at her to stop but she continued. She turned to the shore to see his face one last time before the waves crashed over her head and she surrendered to the deep.

A deafening lament built up from the depths of his soul, shattering the sunny beach before the shroud of blackness caved in on him.

Gasping, Darius regained consciousness to find himself prostrated on the dungeon floor and the massive creature still roaring. It had two of the cell bars in its clutches, pulling them apart to escape. The guard lay next to him whimpering and Luvenia lay thrashing and screaming behind him.

Darius had to stop this demon. It had somehow gotten in their minds. He snatched Nahaliel from where it had clattered to the floor when the darkness hit and ran full force toward the cell where the monster attempted to escape. He gritted his teeth as fury filled him with hatred that left no mercy in its wake. The monster's roar turned deafening as it struggled to free itself more quickly, but Darius was already there, aiming for the opening it had made in the cell. He plunged his sword deep into the creature's abdomen. The monster shrieked as warm blood poured from the wound onto Darius' hand. It hit the ground, defeated, but the black vapor from Darius' nightmare began to seep out of the creature's mouth and its laceration.

With no time to consider his options, he left his sword in the monster's body and ran to where Luvenia still screamed. He lifted her up into his bloodied arms and carried her as fast as his legs would take him, up the stairs and out of the dungeon. When they reached the hall, he slammed the heavy wooden door, hoping the vapor would dissipate before it could kill the guard or come up into the castle. Just in case, Darius continued to run, cradling the petrified girl. He ran until they reached a hall with windows open wide, letting in the fresh air.

He dropped to his knees and held her close to his chest, murmuring again and again, "Shh...you're okay, Little Bird. You're okay. I've got you. It's going to be okay."

Some time later, Luvenia regained consciousness, finding herself safely in her rooms with the general pacing at the foot of her bed.

"What happened?" she asked him, still trembling.

He rushed over at the sound of her voice and took her hand. "I don’t know. That...*thing* had some sort of vapor coming out of it. My guess is the fear toxin Pietro injects them with has been weaponized.”

"I was trapped in a nightmare or something..." she whispered numbly.

"So was I." He took her hand. "So was I."

Chapter Nineteen

Darius, Sebastian, and Veni raced through the dark woods atop their steeds, headed for the outskirts of Alban. Time was running out to rescue those children. They needed to get to their meeting and develop the next plan of action as quickly as possible—at dawn, only a day would remain.

The sun was nearly asleep when Darius and Veni had passed through the portal into Orford and snuck to the meeting place where Sebastian waited with horses. Luvenia's horse had been meant for Nuria, but the queen had refused to leave her castle with the dead monster still below it. Veni requested to take her place and Darius hated the thought of leaving her behind after such a traumatic afternoon.

When they'd nearly arrived at the meeting location, Darius led them to a dense portion of the Rellum Forest where they tied their horses and trekked the rest of the way on foot. They came to an old, broken-down shack and Sebastian knocked on the door in a precise sequence.

"This is where I lived before my father went mad," Darius whispered to Luvenia.

The door opened and warm candlelight spilled out. "Hurry," a gruff looking man told them. The trio entered into a small living space, joining the five others squashed around the hearth.

"General," most of them mumbled by way of greeting. Darius tipped his head to them and turned to Luvenia.

"Luvi, this is Lydigen, Sillow, Mariah, Beck, and of course you know the prince. All, this is Luvenia. You can trust her," he added when he saw the gruff man—Sillow—squirm.

They all nodded to her in acknowledgement, except for Khyan.

"Prince, do you have anything before we begin?" Darius asked Khyan.

"The floor is yours, General."

Darius cleared his throat and jumped directly into important matters, his general demeanor firmly in place. "I want to hear from each one of you. We have little time. I need as much information as possible without all of the unnecessary details." Veni noted he'd looked pointedly at the one called Beck as he'd said the last part. "Sillow, you first."

"Yes, sir. I've tailed the cotton farmer for weeks and found nothing of significance. However, Roberta Schrute has let slip that her father had an interesting band of friends before the war that used to meet secretly to discuss Pietro. I'd like to follow that lead, sir."

Darius stood tall, his hands clasped behind his back as the candlelight danced on his bronze skin. Luvenia found herself thinking the way he commanded the room was rather appealing. Before her stood a man willing to sacrifice every day for those he loved, even those he'd never met. A man who could lead the entire Aureland Horde into triumph on a battlefield yet love a woman with loyal tenderness.

"Good." Darius said firmly, pulling Luvenia from her reverie. "Find out all you can. Lydigen?"

"Sir, I've successfully gained an entrance into the band of Zealots I caught wind of. I've grown close with one of the men and gained his trust. I believe soon he will put me to some kind of test, and upon my passing it, he will allow me to join their meetings."

"This is good news, Lydigen. Well done. Do you have any knowledge of what this test might entail?"

"No, sir. The Zealots are not what I expected. They are good men and women. They're not sorcerers, but they are not weak hearted or trusting people. I would venture to say you are right when you say the opposition and the Zealots are intertwined" Lydigen's eyes sparked.

That spark caught fire in them all. Hope seemed almost tangible. They could nearly taste it.

Luvenia found herself being drawn to the charged atmosphere swelling in the room.

Hope. They have hope. And they have passion for their cause.

And with that, a seed planted itself in her heart.

"Well done, my friend, well done," Darius told him. "Make haste to Aureland tonight. You will need to be branded with the Mark before this test of theirs." Lydigen nodded and Darius turned. "Beck." The boy opened his mouth and Darius said, "Swiftly please."

"Yes, sir." Beck squirmed. "The suspicious woman in Queen Lilith's alchemy chamber was indeed a Zealot. She has been beheaded. So has her entire family."

"*Maker*," Darius muttered, closing his eyes for a moment. "You may still discover why she was there, Beck. She obviously was not there merely to earn coin. Find out *how* she got there as well. Pietro is not foolish enough to let a Zealot in her alchemy chamber. Find out what you can. Mariah, what do you have?"

The sheepish, rather beautiful young woman spoke quietly, "Her Highness' policies shall change once more, very soon. She wishes to execute more frequently and in public, for even small offenses. She tells Shiv it will either draw the Rebels out to protect the citizens or scare them away."

Darius shifted on his feet, storing Mariah's information. "Khy and Sebastian, anything?"

Khyan had already spoken in depth with Darius before leaving Aureland and Sebastian had given all his information on the way to the shack. Both men shook their heads sternly.

"Very well." The general held the floor. "As most of you

know, we have yet to gain the location of the shipment. However, we interrogated a high-ranking Collector and have reason to believe the shipment will leave late tomorrow or early the following morning. Beck and Mariah, you will hold your posts. Lydigen, you have your orders already. You will escort Luvenia back to Aureland as you go, then leave after you receive your Mark and be ready in Alban for your test.

Sillow and Khyan, I need you in Mulberry as swiftly as you can. It is possible the holding place is near there or Morrec. Sebastian, you and I will enter Morrec. Millbren is another possible location, though I find it would make little sense. If any of you find nothing in Morrec or Mulberry, head to Millbren. If you are well rested, leave now. Maker be with you all."

Without another word, the general gently took Veni's hand and led her out the back door. Once outside in private he told her, "It's imperative Sebastian and I leave immediately. Lydigen will keep you safe. I shouldn't have let you come if I wasn't taking you back, I'm sorry."

"I appreciate your chivalry, General, but I'm quite capable of protecting myself now. Unless a Collector peels open again, I suppose." Darius frowned at her grim humor. "Why didn't you tell them? They need to know what they're dealing with." She still clasped his hand, releasing it upon that realization.

"We need to learn more before we let everyone in on that information. If they could peel open and spread fear in Orford, they probably would have done so by now. Either she is still formulating the weaponization of that toxin and they don't all have it, or it happened only because he'd come in contact with a realm where powers aren't limited," Darius explained.

That was too much for her mind to digest at the moment, so she changed the subject. "Please be careful, Darius."

Her concern warmed his heart. "I can't promise I'll be

careful, Little Bird, but I can promise I'll come back. Hopefully with a load of safe little ones in tow."

He'd decided not to tell her that he suspected Ester would be in the shipment. He was too afraid to hope or end up dashing hers. He held her chin gently for a split second and smiled before walking away to find Sebastian.

Until Lydigen came to retrieve her, she pondered Darius' words, sitting on the back steps of the house where he'd lived as a little boy. These people were risking their lives for helpless children, just as she was. Perhaps this was her fight after all.

The seed of hope in her heart contemplated sprouting.

Veni spent the next several days anxiously awaiting the return of the rescue parties, hoping with all her might that they were successful and possibly found Ester along the way. She spent her time training vigorously in the mornings with one of Darius' Hordemen, Felix— whom she'd developed a nice camaraderie with, as he was always in a chipper mood, unlike during their trip into Anjali. Once training was over, she spent long afternoons with Queen Nuria. The queen mentioned little about her thoughts regarding the hopeful rescue, though Veni could tell her nerves were fraying further and further the more days that passed.

The first few afternoons were spent in either Veni's chambers or Nuria's, discussing matters of little importance. The queen had told Luvenia she would no longer push her and she'd kept her word. Veni continued to keep Nuria at a distance the best she could, but her resolve was slowly being chipped away as she unwillingly began to trust the queen.

On this particular day, Nuria had suggested they go for a ride after their lunch—accompanied by Felix and three guards. Nuria had given her Darius' mount, Jaq, claiming the feisty horse didn't fare well without his master and needed to be ridden. Veni had no complaints. The steed was a handsome mount indeed. He was the color of storm clouds with bits of white dappled all throughout. Incredibly vast in size and spirit, with an untamed mane, he perfectly matched his master.

"Do you know how Thera is faring in Anjali?" Veni asked as they rode through the Torren Forest.

Nuria, ravishing as always, sat elegantly atop her snow-white mare, clad herself in pristine white riding gear. The daytime climate near the castle was beginning to reach the frigid temperatures of typical autumn in Orford.

Nuria's breath clouded in front of her as she spoke, "I visited her recently. She is well, and her mission is going smoothly."

Partially an untrue statement if personal matters were included. Nuria did not approve of the princess' developing feelings for Emperor Nakamura. Though a just emperor, Akio was a mere mortal who would live only a few more decades, while Thera would remain young for hundreds more years. The conversation between her and her protégé had not gone well ...

"Nuria, I care very deeply for you, and you are my queen—you will forever be my queen—but this is a decision I choose to make myself. You have always encouraged me to follow my heart and be who I am. That is what I'm doing," Thera told her on the warm night Nuria flew into Anjali.

"Theralin, I have always encouraged you to be the you that you were created to be. Not the one that thinks only of herself and her own desires. Our kind are not to be intimate with simple mortals. Your desires matter, my sweet, but you have a high call upon your life. You are a Keeper. You are called to protect, not harm."

"Oh, I'm selfish now for desiring love? And who am I harming? You? Because I want to pursue something for myself?"

"Theralin Avarochelle," Nuria censured her. "Cease this foolishness immediately. You will not spit accusations at me. Think." She threw a pointed finger at the opulent castle in the distance with its ornate, sloped roofing. "Morality aside, that man in there will die of old age before you look a day over twenty-three. He could have a few good years with you and then it will all be over. You cannot be his empress, Theralin."

Tears pooled in Thera's eyes. "We could make it work ..."

Nuria took her hand. "No, my sweet, not without heartache. Have you forgotten Dax?"

Thera could no longer contain the tears as they spilled down her cheeks.

Nuria put a hand on the girl's shoulder tenderly. "Not only will he give his life up for something that cannot last for him, but you will have defied our kind and will have to watch him grow old and die." Her face softened and her eyes misted as she recalled times past. "I made this mistake, Thera."

The young Keeper looked at her queen, shocked. "You did? I had no idea..."

Nuria shook her head to dislodge the memories. "It was the most foolish and heartbreaking thing I have ever done. I am asking you as your friend, not as your queen, to reconsider this."

"I mean no disrespect," Veni said, her words jolting Nuria, "but your facial expression says otherwise."

The queen smiled briefly, realizing she must be gaining some ground with the girl, for she never would have intruded before. "You are an astute young lady, Luvenia Rousseau. I am certain I have told you as much on many occasions." She sighed. "Theralin has fallen into a deep trap common to Keepers. One that I fell headlong into myself once. It dredges up a plethora of unpleasant memories and throws me into a very protective, if not overbearing state." She smiled at the girl. "Worry not, we shall both be just fine. Her task, at least, is going well."

Luvenia frowned, piecing together all the information she'd been given over the last few weeks. "She's fallen for the emperor, hasn't she? And she cannot marry him because he'll die far before her?"

Nuria looked at her, a bit stunned.

Veni continued, "This is my fault, isn't it? I suggested the entire plan..."

"Now, now. Stop right there, dearheart. None of this is your doing. First of all, I concocted the plan long before you arrived. I dismissed it for fear that Thera had not gained a tight enough rein on her emotions, though Khyan convinced me she had when you suggested the same idea. Second of all, I made the final decision. Third, the plan was for her to gain a trusted audience with the emperor, not his heart."

Veni nodded and changed the subject, feeling the cloud of guilt seeping in and wanting to push it away. "Do you think the rescue parties will arrive back soon? Do you think they were successful?"

Nuria's lips pursed before answering. "Do you prefer the honest answer, or the hopeful one?"

Veni winced. "The honest one, please."

The queen's face grew rather grave, a disheartening contrast against the purity of her white hair and fair beauty. "I fear they were not successful. They should have arrived a couple of days ago if they had been. As far as if they shall arrive soon, I certainly hope so." She noticed Veni squirm uncomfortably and continued. "However, I do believe they are safe. You certainly do not have to worry about Darius...or Khyan. Darius is an incredibly formidable opponent, as is

Khyan. In addition, their wits alone could defeat a great infantry, those two." She smiled at the girl reassuringly.

The queen's statement calmed Veni remotely. "What about the children? What will happen to them? Will it be what we feared? The honest answer, not the hopeful, please."

Nuria took a deep, shuddering breath. "If they do not get to them in time, they will be sold into slavery, probably into brothels, through the Underground Market."

Veni's stomach clenched. "Like Sebastian. What is the Underground Market?" she asked.

"It is a vile market system, ironically named Marche d' Blanc—the White Market. The dealers there buy and sell goods and services that are illegal, immoral, or simply filthy. It stretches throughout the entire continent, and I fear even farther. Emperor Nakamura, the Anjalian Emperor, desires to stop the market. However, he is the only royalty on the continent to feel this way. They all benefit so very much from it, Thera's parents included. King Alestair worked tirelessly to halt their dealings in Orford, almost succeeding. Lilith has undone all of his hard work and amplified the entire market, apparently with the selling of innocent lives."

The vast knot in Veni's stomach twisted, though she asked the question anyway. "Do you think that's what happened to Ester?" She was petrified of the answer but had to know.

"I truly do not know, dearheart. I had begun to fear such was the case, as Khyan has flown relentlessly searching for her and the other children. Though, Darius informed me that the beast below the castle called you 'the one that got away.' This leads me to believe they would keep Ester." Nuria had decided the girl was clever enough to discover most of the information she was giving on her own, and if they wanted her to be a successful warrior—even merely to survive her own quest—then she needed the facts.

"Why? Something about that sounds worse."

"Indeed. They would only keep her in order to lure you in—

or to examine her," the queen stated reluctantly.

"Examine her? What does that mean?" Her hands had begun to tremble as she held Jaq's reins.

Nuria halted her horse, partially expecting the girl to become hysterical with the next bit of information. "Pietro may have no idea that Ester is not blood related to you. I would not put it past her to subject the poor child to blood examination and all kinds of other alchemical practices in order to try and decipher how you are immune to her Venom. We have heard much chatter concerning such examination processes, though no one is certain where it takes place."

Nuria had been partially correct. Luvenia leaned over the side of Darius' horse and vomited into the dead leaves and dusting of snow. Once she'd regained her composure, Nuria led her back to the castle, their escorts in tow.

"How do you do it?" Veni asked as they left the royal stables to seek warmth.

"Do what exactly, dearheart?" Nuria gave her a loving smile.

"That. *Smile*. Amidst so much destruction and so many wicked people—how do you smile? How do you lead a country? How do you see any good left in the world?"

"Oh, darling," she took Veni's hand. "Every person is wooed by both darkness and light. It is that which they choose to fall in love with that matters. Not one of us is inherently good. We each must choose, every single day, to follow the beckoning of the light and to leave behind the moments we courted the dark.

Keepers are merely protectors, doing our best to shield the innocent, the broken, and to ensure the lanterns in the dead of night continue to shine. Those such as Ester, Darius, your mother's friend Agnes," she winked at the girl, who was surprised Nuria knew of her, "*you*...You all are the lanterns in the dead of night. Lights shining out into the darkness. Those precious few are how I can continue to fight, continue to smile, continue to lead. You give me hope. Without hope, we shall all perish."

Veni said nothing until they'd almost reached her chambers, when she finally asked the queen, "Lanterns. Is that something for me to ponder like the precious gem statement?"

Nuria chuckled. "Who would I be if I did not leave you something to ponder?"

"I just cannot understand why you would say I am a gem, or a lantern in the dark, or that there is treasure in my scars… I haven't done anything special or *been* anyone special."

"Did you find the gems in the Amethyst Woodlands to lack value or worth because they did not sing and dance for you? A gem's worth comes not from what it can or cannot do. It is treasure merely for what it innately *is*. It is found at great cost and purchased at great cost for simply *being* what it is—a gem. In addition, you found the amethyst to be hidden within the scars and hollowed out bits of the trees, did you not?" She kissed the girl on the cheek and left her at her door without another word.

She hardly made it to the end of the short hall before Darius rounded the corner in search of Luvenia, a shadowy phantom of the man inside.

"General!" Nuria exclaimed, apprehensive. "What happened?"

He was fury and rage—a storm no enemy could survive. "We missed them," he thundered. "They held them in Morrec, but they'd left there days before we arrived. We lost their trail to the second holding place." His jaw flexed with hatred. "I found this in an empty prison cart."

He bolted the last few steps to Luvi, smelling of sweat and steel. He held out a filthy hand to her, meeting her eyes with sorrow and rage as she trembled in fear—fear of what would be in his hand when he opened it. He splayed his fingers to reveal the tiny object in his palm. A bent and broken jade hairpin. The one she'd left in the bottom of her sister's prison cart all those weeks ago.

"Khy said this is yours," he whispered, his storm of fury swelling with her tempest of grief.

Every ounce of strength and hope in the girl cracked the sky in thunderous destruction as realization flooded her and the ravaging waters held her under.

This time, instead of a recluse, her despair indeed created the monster Khyan had so feared.

Nuria had tried to calm her and Khyan had attempted to speak reason, claiming the prison cart could have merely been reused after Ester was transported in it. She knew this most likely was not the case, though Darius had sent five men out with bonehounds—which turned out to be very large wolves, only their skeletons visible in the light of the moon, and capable of smelling down to the bones within a man. They continued the search, along with two other search parties tracking the shipment of children, though no news had returned.

Veni appreciated their effort, but she didn't see the point. She'd come to terms with never seeing her sister again. But her brother...oh, her brother was going to pay. She trained and sparred and ran endlessly, hardly ceasing in order to eat or sleep or bathe. Nothing deterred her, not even the snow flurries that soon began to fall regularly. She had become incredibly strong and capable, defeating most of her opponents in both hand-to-hand combat and with weapons. She favored throwing knives and her bow, though she was becoming rather skilled with a sword as well.

The only person she would speak to was the general. Long talks and laughter were not present, but when they were not training together and she'd exhausted herself, they somehow always managed to find each other and just quietly *be*. He had no need for her to speak and that brought her the only comfort she could find.

Khyan's demeanor had gone sullen, and his eyes were constantly sunken, his cheeks hollow. His sister chastised him relentlessly for not resting. Every day he left before sunup and flew into Orford, spending the entire day in search of Ester—he refused to believe the girl had been in that shipment. He returned at dusk, when the world went quiet, and spent his nights with Darius completing Luvenia's birthday gift, both desperate to bring a bit of good into her life. Her birthday was swiftly approaching, though the prince doubted she even knew or wanted to remember.

Chapter Twenty

The snow mingled with the bright autumn leaves and the sun had not yet risen when Darius nudged the girl asleep on his shoulder.

"Oh," she started, rather embarrassed. Luvenia had finally ceased her conditioning in the wee hours of the morning. Exhausted, she had trudged toward her chambers to bathe and found Darius leaving the kitchens ripping a bite out of a large turkey leg. She found herself smirking at the sight and feeling thankful she was racking up good associations with turkeys instead of depressing ones. He'd looked at her like a child caught stealing sweets and smiled in his charming way. They'd sat on a bench in the hall until she unknowingly fell asleep on his shoulder.

Darius chuckled. "Rise and shine, Little Bird."

"It's not even daylight," she said groggily as she glanced out the window down the hall.

"Like you sleep so much these days anyway. Regardless, it's your birthday and we need an early start."

That woke her up. "What? My birthday? Is it? How would you even know...ah, Khyan," she answered herself and then groaned. "I've been awful to him and here he is remembering my birthday and informing everyone."

"Now don't go and get all morose. We've got things to do!" He jumped up excitedly, despite his lack of sleep. "Helga should be in your chambers already to begin the festivities, and I will meet you in your hall in one hour." She opened her mouth to object, but he stopped her. "No! No objections. No training. No walloping my men and making them look like untrained buffoons. Not today. One hour!" he shouted over his shoulder as he strode toward his rooms.

As Veni walked to her own chambers, she had trouble sorting through the knot of emotions twisting within her chest. She'd forgotten about her birthday entirely and would have been delighted to not be reminded. Memories of her eighth birthday swirled around her head, but they were distinctly contrasted by a small flicker of joy that sprang up when Darius insisted upon celebrating.

Her mother had always sweetly made every birthday after her eighth a very special day, baking her a tiny cake each year and taking her to Alban. Such bittersweet days. She knew her mother would never forget that was the day she'd found out her beloved husband would never come home again, but not one birthday did she ever let Veni see it. The memories made her heart ache fiercely.

Quite possibly this day is destined to contain misery.

But the flicker of joy remained glowing and grew brighter when she entered her chambers to find Helga waiting with a stunning new riding cloak—a gift from Nuria.

The hooded cloak was a magnificent forest green, with intricate gold and green thread woven along the front and shining golden buttons fitting it around her waist, framing her hips. The back laced like a corset along the small of her back and the entire cloak cascaded down to her ankles. It fit her perfectly, showing off her new curves and complimenting her brown riding boots as well as her evergreen eyes.

Helga convinced her to leave her wild curls be once she'd dried them by the fire. "Sir General likes yer with yer hair down, Miss." She winked at the girl.

"Why would you say such a thing?" Veni blushed.

Helga laughed. "Yer two aren't foolin' nobody, Miss. That burly young man looks at yer like yer put that moon up in the sky, he does."

A knock sounded at the door and Helga winked again,

knowing full well who stood on the other side of it. Darius wore a deep gray coat with two lines of bright silver buttons and polished black riding boots. He smiled and handed her one soft pink peony. "M'lady."

Veni smiled at the choice in flower, vaguely wondering how the farm fared. "I take it we're going somewhere on horseback, hm?"

"No need to piece together clues, Luvi. You shall see in time."

Hearing him say the name only her mother used always caused her heart to pang, but especially today. She took his arm as he led her to the stables.

Jaq whinnied and stomped excitedly when they approached his stall. Darius laughed and opened the stall door.

"I missed you too, Jaq, but it's only been a few hours..." The horse walked right past him and nuzzled Veni lovingly. "Oh, thanks, Jaq. A beautiful woman walks in and you forget all about me? Some friend you are." he chuckled and patted him on the rear.

Veni giggled as the horse tickled her neck with his muzzle. Darius beamed at the sight. Jaq was generally a very stubborn and picky horse, giving very few people anything less than a haughty glance.

"Alright, alright, I'll let you be her mount. I'll ride Pomme."

The pair of them set off on their horses into the forest, chattering lightly about the critters scurrying through the trees and flitting about the air. Darius knew the day was not only her birthday, but also the anniversary of her father's death—Khyan had told him as much—and it was also her first birthday without her mother and siblings. He considered skirting around the subject, but he didn't want to avoid or replace the memories, he just wanted to make the day a happy occasion as well.

When the conversation lulled, he approached the subject cautiously. "Tell me about your birthdays as a child." He smiled outwardly, but his heart was nervous. He didn't want to upset her.

To his immense delight, she smiled. "My father used to make the biggest deal out of our birthdays. He would wake us up by singing all of our favorite songs in a horrendous voice." She chuckled. "Then he and my mother would make us breakfast. Breakfast is my favorite, and he always had some gift he'd found that he was incredibly proud of. He died the night before my eighth birthday." Her smile faded, but the darkness thankfully remained at bay.

"After he died, my mother tried her hardest to keep my birthdays special. She would still wake me up with silly songs, bake me a small cake, and take me to Alban to search out a new book to trade for. Usually all we could find were tattered books with pages missing, but it was our tradition and we loved making up stories to fill in the lost pages."

She paused for a moment before saying, "I'm really glad you're here. I didn't even realize my birthday had come, but eventually I would have remembered, and I think it would have been unpleasant. I'm thankful you brought some brightness into this day."

Darius reached across the gap between their horses and squeezed her hand. "Happy Birthday, Little Bird." She smiled sweetly and he changed the subject. "So, you enjoy reading, hm? I have yet to see you even pick up a book."

"Well, I have been rather busy, General," she told him sassily. "I adore reading but I haven't had the time and I didn't exactly have a chance to grab my books before I left the farm."

"Would you like to go get them?"

His question startled her. "I—Yes. I think I would like that very much. I was thinking earlier when you gave me my flower that I wanted to know how the animals are faring.

Peony is the name of my horse."

"They're faring well," he told her with a sneaky smile.

"How do you know? I feel like all of you know everything about me that I don't. It's disconcerting, you know."

"Khyan checks on them frequently. You might know that if you would speak to him," Darius teased her.

"He does?" She sighed. "I really have been awful to him. He just tells me all these things that are completely true, but I don't want to hear them."

"He's been quite difficult to handle with you shutting him out. You'll work it out, not to worry. The animals are fine. Though, they don't live on your farm any longer. Khy went back to Orford the day after you arrived here and left word for a neighbor, some man your mother trusted… I can't recall his name."

"Granger?" she asked, hopeful.

"Yes. That's it. Granger took all of the animals he could to his farm before the Collectors showed back up and burned the crops. They left the house. I'm not certain why. I think they want to know all they can about the immune girl that disappeared. Khy says they don't go there very often, though, so I think we can certainly go and retrieve a few items without their knowledge. Which book is your favorite?"

They ambled on as she told him about her favorite book—one about a pirate that could speak to whales. She added in the details she and her mother had made up for the missing pages—including a pink whale they named Puff. Eventually, they reached a snow-covered meadow with a quaint little house, smoke rising invitingly from the chimney.

"This looks oddly familiar..." Luvenia mused.

"This is my father's home." Darius dismounted. "Come on, I thought you might like to meet him on the way to your surprise."

They tied their horses to a post and Veni followed Darius inside. The warmth from the fire felt delightful as it spread throughout the small house and thawed her frozen hands.

"Imogene?" Darius called as they walked toward the sound of pots clanging.

A short, round Elfe came waddling to meet them as soon as they entered the kitchen. "Ohhhhh!!!!" she exclaimed. "Hullo darlin'! Come down here let meh get a look at yer!" He knelt down and the Elfe placed her child-like hands on his cheeks. "Handsome as ever, Darius. Trim that beard though!" She smacked his cheek. "And whooooo is this?" she squeaked, noticing Veni.

Darius stood. "This is Luvenia. She is from Orford. She's training in the castle for a while."

Veni smiled and held out her hand. "Pleasure to meet you, ma'am."

The Elfe swatted her hand away. "We hug in this family." She opened her arms wide and Veni leaned down to hug her awkwardly.

"Where is Father?" Darius asked Imogene.

"He's havin' a good day, he is. He's up ther stairs just a lookin' out the winder. Talkin' bout some flyin' creature he wants to see." She made a dismissive motion. "Don't know, don't care s'long as he's content. Go up 'n' see 'im. I'm cookin' some food. Off ter a late start terday. Lucky fer yer. Yer two'll stay fer breakfast." She waddled back to her little ladder and climbed up.

Darius took Veni's hand. "Come on. You'll love him on his good days."

Luvi pulled back and looked at him strangely. "I should like to think I would love him even on his bad days. Anyone can love a person's light, right? Besides, he's your father."

Darius drank her in, swallowing the emotion at the back of his throat. He realized for the first time in that moment that he truly was falling in love with her and there was nothing he could do about it, no matter how hard he tried.

She simply smiled, having no idea what had gone through

his mind. "Come on," she said, pulling at his hand. "I truly am excited to meet him."

Darius led her up the creaky stairs and into one of the two small bedrooms on the second floor.

"Father..." Darius led Luvi to where the frail man sat in an old rocking chair, indeed staring out the window. "Father, it's Darius."

Upon hearing his son's name, the dark-skinned man with salt and pepper hair turned with great effort.

"My son..." he uttered lovingly and held out a hand. Darius took it with his free hand, still holding Luvi's.

"How are you feeling, Father?" he asked.

"Oh, quite alright. I'm waiting for my love to come. She's visiting today. Imogene says it is not true, but she told me so in a dream last night." He was so very excited, almost giddy.

"What a lovely dream I'm sure it was, Father. I brought someone I wanted you to meet." He ushered Luvi in front of him, leaving his hand on the small of her back. "This is Luvenia."

His father positively gasped. "A Keeper?"

"Oh, no sir...just an ordinary mortal" She shrugged and gave the man a timid smile.

"But I see it in your eyes! You were born for greatness!" His shouting startled her.

Darius gently pulled her back, placing himself between the two of them. "Yes, she was, Father. But she is not a Keeper, and you need to lower your voice. You're inside the house, alright?"

He spoke to him like a little child and it both warmed and broke Luvenia's heart. No man should have to father his own parent for his entire life. She felt such gratitude for what Nuria and Khyan had done, bringing Darius and his sister in so they could be allowed to be children. Though it seemed that never really did happen for Darius.

"She's just a girl? Like Lila?" he asked his son, confused.

"Yes, Father, like Lila." Darius' voice was uncharacteristically sad.

Is Lila his sister? His mother?

His father's bottom lip trembled, and he wailed like a child having a tantrum, shouting in between sobs, "I miss Lila! I want to see Lila!"

Darius pulled his father up out of the rocking chair and held him in a tight embrace, reassuring him it would be okay. "I know, Father, I know. I miss her too. I'll ensure that she comes to visit, alright?"

He rocked his father gently from side to side while patting his back. Once the man had calmed, he led him to the bed against the wall and helped him get settled. He was asleep within a short while.

Darius turned to Luvenia with an apologetic smile and whispered, "I am so sorry. His moods fluctuate so quickly." He shook his head. "It's incredibly hard to predict."

She held out her hand for him to take it. "It's no bother at all. I'm sure Imogene has breakfast almost ready, anyway. We should let him sleep, hm?"

Darius nodded, her patient understanding pulling at his heart once again. They made their way back to the kitchen where Imogene had indeed begun setting plates on the table that overflowed with breakfast items. Eggs, potatoes, sausage, bacon, biscuits, sweet bread...the list went on.

Veni beamed with excitement and squealed. "These are all my favorites! You make all of this for just the two of you?" she asked Imogene.

"Goodness me no, Miss. Haven't yer seen the size a that boy there?" She pointed at Darius. "Eats enough fer thirty people, he does."

Darius shrugged and laughed.

"He walks in ther door and I got'ta be makin' a lot more.

Keep a good lot 'round just in case he's gon' stop in." She whacked him lovingly with her serving spoon on his thigh. "Love this'n I do!"

"Well, you've a funny way of showing it," he told her, rubbing his leg. "Father is asleep now. We will just need to save him some food."

He and Veni sat with Imogene, stuffing their faces and talking about his father's state since the last time Darius had been there a few days prior. When Veni filled her third plate of food—to Darius' great delight, since she'd hardly eaten in recent days—Imogene cackled.

"Yer eat as much as the boy does! Got'ta cook fer an army ter feed the two a yer." She howled again, her jolly belly bouncing. "Found yer perfect match, Darius, yer did."

"Real women know how to eat," Darius said without thinking and promptly cleared his throat to cover his embarrassment. "So... did you hear all that racket about Lila?"

"A course I heard that. Man howls louder'n a bonehound. No, yer sister hadn' been here in months. Yer haven' seen 'er either?"

Darius set his fork down, obviously agitated. "No. I'll find her." He looked at Veni. "We should be on our way when you're finished."

"Erm finished," she mumbled around a mouth full of potatoes, which successfully put the smile back on Darius' face and sent Imogene into fits of cackling.

"Yer two peas in a lil' ol' pod, yer are!"

They bid Imogene farewell and Darius told her he would return within a couple of days to spend more time with his father. The pair mounted their horses and trudged on through the snow and leaves.

"Where exactly are we going, General?" she asked him,

shivering atop his horse.

"We're almost there. Just over that hill." He smirked.

"Will it be warm?"

Darius laughed. "Toasty warm."

They crested the hill and the climate instantly changed to that of a spring afternoon. The sun was warm and inviting, and the breeze had the slightest chill left over from winter, just enough to cool. No snow was to be seen or even autumn leaves, only lush, green grass and an abundance of flowers and trees.

They both discarded their cloaks and riding jackets while Veni breathed in the warmth. "I will never get used to those shifts. It's a wonder you all don't fall ill!"

Darius laughed once more and kicked his horse into a gallop. "Come on!"

She followed him through the colorful meadow and into the trees until he stopped abruptly in front of a massive, enchanting tree with a door carved into it and twinkling lights hung all throughout the branches.

"Wh—What is this place?" she stammered, completely in awe.

"It's yours," he told her simply. "Khyan and I made it for you. I know how much you like to be alone and that is rather difficult in a busy castle. There is a training area behind the tree as well." He suddenly felt rather nervous. "Do you like it?"

"It's absolutely perfect," she told him with tears in her eyes.

"Happy Birthday, Little Bird." Her returning smile made him weak in the knees. "Come on, let's have a look inside."

They had no need to tie the horses, for the pair of them could happily graze on the thick grass for hours. Darius unlocked the little door and opened it to reveal a carved staircase leading up and up.

"You carved all of this?"

"Mostly. Khyan helped and we may have had some Sean'an

help as well," he told her as they ascended the steps.

The staircase opened at the top to reveal a surprisingly large room—for being within a tree. A stone fireplace was built into one side of the room, bookshelves surrounding it, with two plush chairs on either side.

"One of the Sean'an put a protection charm around the fireplace, just in case. It is in a tree after all," he explained. "I didn't know you liked to read until today, but aside from painting, reading is my favorite pastime, so I suppose I was being hopeful that you might like it as well when I built these..." He was beginning to ramble, afraid there was something she wouldn't like.

"It's perfect, Darius. Even if I didn't love books, it would still be perfect. I cannot believe you did this for me. When did you have the time?"

"We've been working on it for weeks, mostly at night. It's nice the Sean'an are silent little sneaks at night. They were very helpful."

She realized then that she'd only glanced to one side, captivated by all the space to hide her favorite books from the world. She turned to take in the rest of her new escape. Where the shelves ended, a window began, situated in a quaint little nook with a padded bench. The area on the other side of the window gave way to a small cast iron stove, its ventilation leading out the side of the trunk.

"The stove has a protective charm as well. You know, I should have him come back and just charm the entire tree. I don't know why I hadn't thought of that...it would keep you safer..."

Veni laughed and squeezed Darius' arm. "No fires in this tree, hm? I'm certain I will be just fine."

A table for two stood before the stove and a small pantry hung next to it, followed by a wash basin and a small, curtained tub. The curtain was white lace, as were the window curtains.

That was when the tears truly came.

"Lace is my favorite," she told him quietly, tears streaming down her cheeks. "I've never been able to have any. I've dreamed my whole life of having something lace. I don't even know why… That's a foolish dream. I just think it's so pretty."

She turned to look at him and he crushed her in an embrace—hating anything that made her cry, yet cherishing the fact that he had made even the smallest of her dreams come true. They stood there as he held her for a good, long while before she finally spoke again.

"Thank you, Darius. You will never know how much this means to me."

He rested his cheek against the top of her head and spoke softly, "I think your reaction was better than I could have ever hoped for."

She breathed in his scent of soap and wind. She closed her eyes as he continued talking, relishing the rumble in his chest against her cheek as he spoke and the thundering of his heartbeat.

"I wanted you to have a place that's yours—untainted by the world or surrounded by people. I've brought a few books and a bit of food. I placed it in your cupboard and Helga packed some clothing for you in that pack over there. The bench under the window folds out into a bed and of course you see the wash basin. I wanted you to be able to stay here for as long at a time as you wish. Would you like to see the training area Khy built?"

She finally pulled back and looked up at him. It took every ounce of strength within him to not kiss her right there.

"So the inside was your doing and the outside was Khy's? All work and no fun, that one," she said and stepped back.

Darius laughed out loud. "Says the girl who never stops training. Come on." He took her hand and led her back down the stairs and around to the other side of the massive tree.

"Here you have it."

She was utterly astonished. Khyan had built a large, wooden contraption for her to climb, pull up on, jump over, maneuver through, throw knives at, shoot her arrows into… He'd thought of everything. She had no words.

"You haven't even seen the best part yet. Our collaboration." Darius led her to a locked wooden box the size of a horse trough. He pulled out the set of keys once more and unlocked it. "Go ahead," he told her.

Slowly, she leaned down to open the box and gasped. Weapons galore rested inside. Three sets of throwing knives, a jewel encrusted sword, three daggers—one that matched Darius' talon dagger—and the most beautiful bow she'd ever laid eyes upon.

"It's made of rosewood from the blossom trees on the other side of this forest," he explained as she picked it up.

The curved wood was intricately hand carved with an elegant, flowing design, inlaid with gold. The leather quiver matched.

"It was made by one of Aureland's finest carpenters," he explained further. "I know you favor the bow, so I wanted you to have one, but throwing knives are most certainly your strength. You should open the wrapped set."

"*Four* sets of throwing knives? I have my own armory now."

She handed Darius the bow and quiver and opened the small, wrapped package to find that it indeed contained another set of throwing knives. They were nothing short of extraordinary. Perfectly pointed, pristine steel, with jewel encrusted handles—three juniper jewels with splashes of red in them. Underneath the stunning knives lay two letters. Curious, she handed Darius the knives to hold with her bow—receiving a laugh and a comment about him not being her pack mule—and opened the first letter.

Luvenia,
I'm sorry for the way we left things. I hope that you will accept my gift and the peace offering sealed in the second envelope.
Happy Birthday.
Stab something for me.
Yours,
Thera

Veni couldn't help but smile and feel a heavy burden lift from her shoulders. Thera didn't hate her after all.

"Hm," Darius grunted, reading over her shoulder. "She *does* know how to apologize. Who knew?"

"That is private!" Veni mocked offense as she clutched the letter to her chest.

Darius snatched it out of her hand playfully and read it out of reach as she jumped trying to get it back.

"*She kissed it*?" he exclaimed, laughing at the lip imprint upon the letter. "Did she spray it with perfume too?" He sniffed it and howled. "*She did!*"

Veni punched him in his shoulder and seized her letter. "You be kind, Darius Cremeux!"

She folded the crinkled letter and placed it in the pocket of her riding pants for safekeeping before opening the second envelope. It contained a grand invitation to a Viloran party being put on by Anjalian Emperor Akio Nakamura, in honor of his special guest, Princess Theralin Avarochelle Revencloud of Vilora. Attached was a scribbled note.

Please come. Bring the oaf that is undoubtedly reading

my notes over your shoulder and mocking me.
-Thera

Veni giggled and looked at the man who was, in fact, still hovering over her shoulder. The pair of them spent the rest of the morning and afternoon using the training structure as a means to create ridiculous competitions for their own enjoyment, as well as sharing a picnic of the food Helga packed, and discussing their favorite books. Late into the afternoon, they sat upon the window seat in her tree in comfortable silence until Luvenia spoke softly, twirling her hair.

"Lydigen says the Zealots are good men. Do you think that's true?" she asked him as they looked out the window.

"I haven't told anyone this," his voice rumbled in her ears, "but I met one of the Zealots once. I used to hear a voice in my dreams when I was a boy and it filled with me with such peace, despite what was happening in my family with my father's madness." Darius ran a hand through his hair, leaving it disheveled. "When I grew up, I heard once in passing that the Zealots follow a set of beliefs that honor love and peace above all else."

"And you believe this?" she inquired genuinely.

Darius discarded his surcoat and turned to her, unhooking two of the brown buttons on his tunic. He pulled it open to reveal, upon the hollow of his shoulder, a small Mark of the Zealots.

"I do."

She hadn't even noticed it that day in the training room. "You have the Mark. Pietro did this to you?" she demanded, indignant.

"No. I forged a replica of the Mark several years ago and branded myself. One day after Lydia died, I met a Zealot in the Alban Market. He reminded me so very much of the voice that had called to me in the night. Everything about him. He spoke like—like rivers of living water. He knew so much about me, as if he could see past all my walls, all my masks. He told me to keep fighting, that one day I would stand at the end of my life and be told I'd done well."

He closed his eyes for a moment, willing tears away. "He told me I just needed to keep going. He told me I had a lion heart and to never lose sight of that. He reminded me of who I am. Who I *really* am. He told me all the sorrow I've faced in my life will be made into something beautiful." He shook his head and continued with misty eyes. "I never saw that man again, but I came back to Aureland and branded myself with the Mark. I bear it as a badge of honor. And as a reminder of who I really am. A lionheart."

Veni sat speechless, remembering her father calling to her in her dreams. No wonder Darius had insisted to his men that the Zealots were not the enemy.

After a moment, he smiled crookedly and nudged her. "Come on, we need to be back at the castle before supper."

He handed her the keys to her new escape and armory, and they rode together back to the castle.

Darius and Luvenia returned to the castle just before the sun's descent. Barely having made it on the grounds, Khyan swooped down as an owl and instantly shifted into his lithe human form.

"Her Majesty requests to see you both immediately."

"Is something the matter?" Darius asked.

A sly grin was Khyan's only reply before an owl flew away.

"I didn't even get to thank him," Veni muttered as they walked a bit faster.

The pair arrived at Queen Nuria's study where she was looking over hundreds of papers on her desk.

"Oh! There you are. Come in, come in." She rushed over to meet them, her elegant sapphire gown whispering as she moved. "Well, dearheart, how did you enjoy your day?" The queen beamed.

The sincerest of smiles crossed Luvenia's lips, reaching her eyes, to the queen's immense delight. "I love it. I don't think I could have asked for a better birthday. Thank you all so much, from the bottom of my heart. Why the urgency in meeting with you?"

The queen smiled even broader and swooped in gracefully for a hug. "I merely wished to learn how your special day fared, dearheart." Luvenia flinched slightly, but reluctantly returned her affection.

When Nuria pulled back and held Luvenia's hands, the panic concerning the intimacy of the moment began to sink in. She was discovering her comfort with Darius did not extend past him.

Uncomfortable, she dropped the queen's hands with a glance at Darius. "Would it be alright if I took a bath?" she asked Nuria.

"Of course, my dear. We will see you at dinner." She kissed Luvenia's cheek.

"See you in a while, Darius," Luvenia said over her shoulder. "Thank you again." He gave her a crooked smile and she left.

Darius turned to see his queen smirking at him with wide-eyed delight. He furrowed his brow at her and crossed the rug to his favorite spot in her study—the plush, old loveseat. *His* loveseat, as Nuria kept the ratty thing only because Darius had loved it since he was a child. He still sat in it the same way, sprawled out—head on one arm of the seat and legs on the other. Now his legs hung well over the side and his hulking form took up every inch of the seat.

Nuria's smirk remained firmly in place as she poured them each a steaming cup of tea. "Chester was not feeling quite well this afternoon. I made an extra pot of tea for myself when I made his."

As he watched her prepare him a cup, Darius couldn't help

but feel proud warmth for his queen who had never become too proud to be a servant to her people.

Nuria handed Darius his teacup and sat down with hers on a floor cushion, legs curled to one side. She inhaled deeply the soothing aroma of her tea. "I have never seen you like this, General." She smirked gleefully again behind her cup and hid her amusement with a sip of tea.

Darius huffed a small laugh, took a sip, and sighed heavily. "I don't think I've ever felt like this." He took another sip and shook his dark, messy locks. "I'm not certain I enjoy it. We had a wonderful day and I care for her more than I can admit, but sometimes I feel guilty."

"Oh?" The queen's concern was evident as she set her tea down and leaned toward Darius. She took his hand. "This is hard for you, isn't it? Opening your heart after the loss of Lydia?" She didn't let him answer— she knew he wouldn't. "Lydia will always have a place in your heart, darling, and that is okay." She squeezed his hand. "I must say… I meant what I said. I have never seen you like this. You look at Luvenia in a way I never once saw you look at Lydia."

He didn't like where this was going. "I was going to marry her, Nuria. *Marry* her. I can't do Lydia the injustice of falling for the first girl who grabs my attention, no matter how much I want to."

"Always the honorable general," she breathed. "It has been four years, Darius, and the two of you were *children.* You do not like how you feel for Luvenia because it means you have found some happiness for yourself, and you cannot accept that. Since Lydia's life is gone, you cannot justify living yours in joy. *Let her go.* No one is holding you to the naïve promises of a boy except yourself. Lydia would wish you unending happiness were it her speaking to you now instead of me."

The look Darius gave her in return was that of an

exasperated, perturbed child. "Can we talk about this later?"
Queen Nuria raised her hands in defeat.

Veni practically skipped to her chambers. Maybe she wasn't comfortable letting everyone in entirely, but she was comfortable with Darius and all of her friends had made her birthday so special. Thera was no longer feuding with her and the others had not yet given up on her.

She entered her rooms to find a large box tied with a ribbon and a note:

One more for good measure.
Happy Birthday, Dearheart.
Unending Love,
Nuria

Excited, she untied the ribbon and lifted the lid to discover an indigo gown fit for a princess. She gasped and pulled it out gently. Rushing to the looking glass, she held it up and squealed. She immediately ran for the bath Helga was already drawing for her and proceeded to prepare herself for her first dinner with her friends in a long while.

The delicacies the kitchen prepared in Veni's honor came from all over the world's different regions. By the time they had all laughed and talked and eaten late into the night, Veni thought she would burst out of her new dress.

The warm candlelight glinted off the crystal chandeliers as she looked around the table at her friends. Even Smithwick had joined them. Nuria glowed radiantly with joy the entire evening and Khyan laughed freely for the first time she'd seen since Anjali. Darius gave a beautiful toast in her honor, and Sebastian thanked her for seeing the best in him when even

Darius couldn't.

Just as she was about to dismiss herself and go sleep like the dead, Khyan declared he would return momentarily and commanded she stay put. He came back into the dining hall moments later with a small velvet pouch and presented it to her.

"The training apparatus is from me, yes, but this—this is your true gift. I had a little help..." Khyan said as he handed it to her.

For some unknown reason her heart drummed in her chest as she opened it. She dumped the contents of the pouch into her hand—a silver necklace slipped into her palm. She spread it out to better inspect it. A small moonstone hung from filigree at the end of the chain.

Vibrant, violet, and radiant—the twin stone to the one in her mother's amulet.

It shone in the light, and she opened her mouth to thank Khyan but nothing would come out. She couldn't fathom why they would all do so much for her. She noticed tears in Khyan's eyes then, and her heart drummed faster as he explained.

"It's from your father." Her heart stopped altogether as he continued. "It is the gift he hid the night he died, Veni. I watched him hide it in the stables. I've waited ten years to give you this."

She hid her face in her hands and sobbed for several moments. Khyan wrapped his hands around hers as she clutched the moonstone necklace tightly. She hadn't the slightest idea how her father managed to purchase such a necklace, but she would never take it off.

When she finally calmed and whispered her tearful thanks, Khyan pried her fingers open and took the necklace. He smiled gently and clasped it around her neck. The precious necklace lay sparkling atop the chain holding her mother's amulet—her Portal Key. A symbol of her old home and a symbol of her new. She looked up to see everyone else had misty eyes as well.

Smithwick cleared his tiny throat and spoke up. "I hate to follow *that*... but you have one more gift awaiting you outside."

The entire dinner party gathered and made their way to the royal stables. Veni could only imagine what was in store after the surprising day she'd had. They rounded the corner and Smithwick—atop her shoulder—pointed his little furry finger in the direction of the stall next to Jaq.

"There," he said.

She handed Smithwick to Darius and walked slowly up to the stall, her heart pounding yet again. She looked over the door to find Vesper curled up in the corner.

She screamed.

The horse stood and snorted anxiously as he pounded the ground with his hoof. She fumbled with the latch, but she was so excited to get to him, her fingers wouldn't function. Darius chuckled and finally opened it for her. She raced to the horse and threw her arms around his neck. His black mane tickled her nose as he nuzzled into her and nipped at her new dress playfully, whinnying with delight.

"*How?*" she screeched at Smithwick.

"I'm a Gatekeeper, of course. Khyan mentioned your father's horse and its brilliance, and I decided you needed him. Khy retrieved Vesper and I brought him through. I broke several Sean'an Porter laws to do so, mind you. We had to hide the feisty horse until you and Darius had left the stables after bringing your mounts in this evening. He certainly is a magnificent beast. He'll look rather dashing riding alongside Jaq, I must say."

Veni gave her thanks to all of her friends once more as they one by one wished her happy birthday and split off to go to sleep. She and Darius stayed with Vesper for a while, simply enjoying what was left of the night. Eventually, the general could no longer stand upright and walked her to her rooms.

"Goodnight, Little Bird." He kissed her swiftly on her cheek and wandered sleepily to his rooms, hands shoved in his pockets.

Despite being exhausted, Luvenia couldn’t sleep. She lay awake in her bed cherishing her necklaces and recounting the events of the day.

I've never had a more wonderful day. I wish Mother had been here. Ester would have loved all of this.

Her heart panged, but her smile faded not. She was beginning to believe her life could go on and maybe, just maybe, she could be happy.

Regardless, she vowed she would not give up on finding Ester.

Chapter Twenty-One

A little girl twitched uncontrollably in the corner of her filthy cell. The insect man had thrown her into the pile of her own refuse after the latest session of misery.

Her arms had so many puncture wounds she could no longer count them all. For a very long time she'd tried to. It kept her mind from the horrors within. Now the terrors repeated endlessly, and the twitching never ceased. She'd long since forgotten her name or even what she was. The talking insect had called her *girl*. She couldn't remember what that meant.

Foam leaked from her mouth again and the twitching became violent. She repeated within her mind to the only word she could remember, in a voice that wasn't hers.

Sunshine.

Luvenia sat upon the window seat in her tree, distracting her mind with one of the books she and Darius had retrieved from her home.

Someone had mercifully cleaned her mother's blood off the kitchen floor and buried her broken body—presumably Khyan. She'd laid in the snow next to her grave with Darius comforting her for a very long while. Eventually, he pleaded with her to get up, claiming she would freeze to death. The visit had been emotional and trying, but she had gathered a few precious belongings—some books, one of her father's old shirts, the burnt remains of *Ester's Berry Patch* sign, and her mother's rose perfume—then pulled herself back up again.

It had been many weeks since her birthday, many weeks of intense training, unsuccessful trips to Orford, and countless council meetings.

Luvenia insisted on being involved with anything that might lead her to Ester's possible rescue—a hope that she'd decided on her birthday she would refuse to give up. She also insisted on being involved in anything that might lead her to Jacob. That, however, she kept to herself. Aiding in any other missions, she had continued to vehemently refuse. Selfish or not, she had her own battles to fight, and they knew it. They could take it or leave it and she'd told them all as much.

Nuria still joined her for lunch on most days and Veni had let her in to an extent. She trusted the queen for the most part but keeping people at arm's length made her much more comfortable. Khyan, however, had a distinct gift for worming his way past her defenses.

She and Darius had grown significantly closer as time passed. Veni hadn't decided exactly what their relationship meant. She merely knew their lives were intertwined and she never wanted there to be a day without him. He'd told her that his first love, Lydia, had drowned herself when they were sixteen, after her family died in a shipwreck. He told Veni that love had been tainted for him until he met her.

She felt as if he were everything she was not. He was so wonderfully gifted in the art of balance, something she was impeccably terrible at. He knew how to push her limits in training, remain steady and decisive in important matters, and also how to simply let go and enjoy life.

The previous day flashed through her mind.

While eating a simple breakfast of bread and grapes before

the sun had even risen, a harsh banging sounded at Veni's door. She jumped up and opened it frantically, only to be met with a general, grinning from ear to ear.

She smacked him on the arm. "Quite proud of yourself for giving me a fright, aren't you?"

Darius shook with laughter, indeed amused by his own antics. He nicked her nose playfully. "Nothing like a scare to wake you up. Come on, we're going on an adventure for training today." He grabbed her hand and began pulling her out the door, radiating excitement. He knew how desperately she needed an escape. How desperately they both needed one.

Veni laughed and dug in her heels. "Wait! I haven't any boots on yet."

He let go reluctantly so she could get her boots on. "Hurry!" he urged her.

Veni giggled at his childish antics. "Patience, General, patience."

As soon as she'd slipped her last boot on, Darius took her by the hand and yanked her down the hall, Veni laughing the entire way. The few servants awake and, in the halls, hushed them, which merely resulted in more fits of laughter from them both.

"Where are we going?" she asked as they ran through the castle corridors.

"Stables!" was his only response.

They saddled and mounted Jaq and Vesper, dashing through the snow into the frosty forest. Halfway to their destination, Veni discovered where they were headed.

"We're going to Viridian," she shouted as they raced through the trees, Vesper a nose ahead of Jaq.

"Right you are, Little Bird. To Viridian!" Darius shouted back.

A short time later, they slowed their horses, deciding Vesper had won as always. They dismounted to let the horses amble on through the lush grass, free of their burdens. With

Viridian Bay just ahead of them, they discarded their cloaks and the horses followed obediently as the pair walked the rest of the way, hand in hand, enjoying the warm air of east Aureland.

"Will we return in time for my lunch with Nuria?" Veni asked, noticing the sun's ascent.

"No lunch with Nuria today, she had business elsewhere." He grinned, his hair wild and untamed. "You're stuck with me all day."

Once they reached the cliffs overlooking the bay, Darius informed Veni that the day's training would soon commence and not to discard her boots quite yet. The two of them descended the stone steps—horses grazing peacefully in a clearing—and Veni continued onto the soft sand, but Darius spun her around as he finished tying his hair in a knot on top of his head.

"Up we go! Stay with me."

He shot up the stairs like lightning, while Veni scrambled to process what he'd said and catch up—which she did. Close on his heels, she skipped steps and ended up in front of him just before the top.

Taking the opportunity to gloat, she bowed dramatically before he pushed her playfully and shook his head, darting back down the stairs. Scrambling again, she followed him back down. Reaching the bottom, she was ready for the pivot and another ascent. She managed to stay with him, if not slightly ahead, for the remaining countless times they ascended and descended. Finally, Darius held up a hand to signal their resting point. Huffing, they both discarded their boots and walked to the water's edge.

"Your speed is most definitely one of your greatest physical strengths," Darius told her between deep breaths and gulps of water from his pouch. "Most of your opponents will greatly outsize you, but what you lack in stature you can make up for in swift movements. The more hulking the opponent, generally the slower they are."

She grinned slyly. "That's how I just beat you then, hm?"

Darius blinked. "I'm not certain if that was an insult or a compliment…"

Veni laughed. "It was both, General."

He promptly pushed her into the water, his strict, trainer demeanor vanishing. She shouted and splashed him, creating quite a war until a ravishing mermaid poked her head up out of the water and drew their attention.

"General," she spoke with a musical voice, as serene as the waves. She smiled. "Are the pair of you ready?"

Veni looked at Darius, confused.

"We certainly are. Luvi, our next task is to swim out to sea." Her eyes went wide, and he chuckled. "This is Morgana, she is here to guide us and help if you grow too tired. There will be no breathing charm today…why have your eyes gone somehow even wider?" he asked, not catching the transition from shock to excitement.

Veni ignored him and turned to the mermaid. "You're Morgana?" she breathed, beside herself.

The stunning mermaid laughed sweetly. "My reputation has made it all the way to you?"

A tiny voice from atop a tiny dragon answered the question before Veni could. "It most certainly has, you mischievous mercreature!" Smithwick beamed and Morgana beamed right back.

"Is that an infant dragon?" Darius gasped at the little intruder. "What's her name?"

"It is indeed, my fine friend! I haven't named her yet. Growing like a weed, she is. I plan to gift her to Nuria for her birthday next spring. Mum's the word on that now, all three of you. Well, swim along, I'll meet you on the seafront. Go on!" Smithwick shooed them away.

Veni was not ready, especially without being able to breathe inhumanly under the water. Though she was certain

Darius had his reasons—probably something to do with facing one's fears and the unknown, or some other Horde gibberish.

The two warriors and one glimmering mermaid plunged under the Viridian Bay and swam for the Potame Sea. Far more quickly than Veni presumed, her lungs began to burn, and she soon had to dart for the top to draw air. Darius and Morgana swam backwards, allowing her time to catch up. She dove under once more—rather ungracefully—and swam on. The general and mermaid encouraged her mutely, regardless of how many times she floundered or had to rise to the surface for breath, but the watery images of the Collector hovering over her flooded her mind relentlessly. The bay was becoming a fearsome place the farther she swam.

Sensing what was happening behind the girl's scared eyes, Darius motioned for her to rise to the surface.

Popping up and drawing breath, he praised her. "You are doing a wonderful job, Luvi. This is one of the most difficult training tasks you will face. Your muscles are working extremely hard, as are your lungs. Push past the exhaustion and fear. There are no Collectors here."

They kicked and swung their arms to stay afloat, but he continued quickly, "Fear only holds as much power as you allow it. When you go under, and the image of that Collector comes, stare him in his face. Do not cower. Swim straight toward him and know that you will not fall at his hand. You *didn't* fall at his hand." Darius ducked back under, Veni and Morgana following suit.

She didn't know how long they swam, or how her body could possibly continue to pull itself forward. Exhaustion whispered lies in her ear and the Collector continually mocked her. She repeated Darius' words over and over with each stroke, still lagging behind.

You will not fall at his hand. You didn't fall at his hand.

She began to swim farther and farther with each breath, staring down her enemy. After a great distance, something decisively shifted in her mind.

I survived you once. I will survive you again. My sister will survive you. You cannot stop me.

The next time the phantom face of a Collector appeared in the water, her stare bore through the obsidian goggles, past the human eyes, right down to the likely beast within.

I. Will. Crush. You.

She propelled herself at the illusory beast with every last ounce of strength left within her. She gritted her teeth and swam so hard she passed Morgana and Darius, and the image before her burst into a cloud of black, dissolving from her memory. The sea surrounding her was again a serene place of unmatched enchantment. Her body unable to handle any more, she went limp—a smile plastered on her face. Darius swam to the surface, dragging her in tow.

She sucked in precious air and announced between gulps, "I did it!"

Darius chuckled. "Yes, you did. Now let's get you to shore before you drown yourself." His heart panged with the thoughtless words and the image of Veni on the beach in her white dress flitted through his memory. He supposed he still had his own fears to face as well.

Safely on dry land, Veni sprawled out in the sand on her back, utterly exhausted. Darius sat down beside her as Morgana flipped her fin about in the shallow water near them.

"I'm famished!" Veni declared. "We swam for ages.

Morgana chuckled. "Corbin shall bring lunch shortly. You are a delightful girl. Darius said as much, though I like to judge a person for myself." She smiled and swam away to do a few flips.

"Is that so?" Veni asked her trainer, flattered.

"It is." Darius smiled crookedly before a little animal ran through the sand, yelling.

"Why, you could have said you were here! I have been baking in this hot sun for ages and you're over here having a lie down!" Smithwick shouted.

Veni stifled a giggle. "We just got here, Smithwick, calm down."

"Calm down? *Calm down*? It is well past my noon meal hour and we Sean'an rather enjoy morsels in between! Here I am being polite, waiting for you two, and you're just relaxing while I starve!"

Darius laughed at the creature's expense. "Smithwick, you Sean'an are horribly mean when you're hungry. No wonder you desire morsels in between meals. So does this one." He pointed to Luvenia, who scoffed.

Corbin arrived moments later with perfectly pink shrimp and fresh cobs of corn. They ate their fill, laughing with the extension of Thera's family. Veni could see where a great portion of Thera's spicy personality came from, even if they weren't blood relation.

Once they'd eaten and rested a bit, as well as stretched a good deal to prevent soreness in their tired muscles, Darius announced the rest of training would be taking place shortly. Veni groaned, and Smithwick—with renewed vigor—made rude comments about how rough it must be to be human.

Corbin and Smithwick perched themselves atop a large rock, quite ready for a good show. Morgana delicately picked at the remnants of her kelp and seaweed lunch as she readied herself as well.

For what, Veni wasn't sure.

Warily, she looked at Darius, who explained, "Morgana is going to play her music." He pointed far down the coast. "I want you to run in that direction, keeping time with her song.

As the rhythm speeds up or slows down, so do you. Let the music pull you and push you to new strengths." She looked at him as if he'd gone mad. "Just trust me. Ready?" She nodded reluctantly. "Go."

Morgana opened her mouth, ushering forth a song that nearly knocked Veni off her feet. She could hear strings and drums and voices and instruments galore.

She jogged at first, attempting to understand what Darius could have meant. Soon, her feet naturally hit the ground with the pounding of each drum, keeping time. Morgana swam along the shoreline, her song growing louder and faster. Veni picked up her pace involuntarily. The music fed her. It pushed and pulled her and bent her to its will. Surrendering, her movements and the song became one. Running through the thick sand proved difficult, but she hardly noticed for sheer joy.

Far down the seacoast, Darius ran up beside her. "Do you hear it?"

"What?" she shouted over the music.

"*Adventure*." he exclaimed and threw his arms wide as they ran. "It's calling your name."

He ran ahead of her, backwards, basking in the pure freedom that radiated from him. She wasn't certain she would ever understand his freedom, but she most assuredly wanted to. He slowed and turned to run alongside her once more, smiling broadly. The music enveloped them both, wrapping around them like an embrace.

Darius motioned for her to turn around and he challenged her, "Run to where Smith and Corbin sit. You have five paces until I begin as well. He smiled wickedly. "Don't let me catch you."

Adrenaline and confidence coursed through her veins and Veni shot like an arrow down the coast, the music pumping in her blood. She could feel Darius closing in on her, but she refused to lose. She pushed her legs harder, pumped her arms faster—determined to win. The closer the tiny specs of onlookers came to real size, the louder Morgana's music became and the faster the mermaid had to swim to keep up with her. Veni could hear Corbin and Smithwick shouting for her to run faster, having gathered a race was afoot. Darius growled behind her in between heavy breaths. They both hated to lose.

Too bad it will be you, General.

She smiled wickedly to herself and launched forward even faster across the warm sand like a gazelle. Darius lagged behind and she propelled herself the last few steps toward her cheering section. She reached the rock where her admirers shouted her praises and promptly jumped on top of it, arms raised above her head in triumph.

Darius continued to run full speed to the rock a few steps behind her and slapped it, unwilling to simply give up.

"Proud, are you?" he huffed, his face torn between a grin and defeat.

Veni smiled wholeheartedly and flourished a showy bow, Morgana's moving song as her triumphant ballad.

Veni closed her book, smiling at the memory. Her body ached as usual, but she didn't mind it. She got up and gathered her pack. The last meeting before she and Darius left on their trip to Anjali for Thera's ball was beginning near the South Gate at sundown. That didn't give her and Vesper any extra time to ride a rather grand distance.

Veni felt as if she and Vesper shared a unique connection. They were bound by loss and bloodshed in a way that she shared with no human, and she was okay with that. Vesper understood her, human or not. She rubbed his nose and mounted the horse. He carried her swiftly through the warm forest of her tree house—the Monarbre Forest—through the dense and frozen Torren Forest, around Sourn Village, into the Amethyst Woodlands, and safely into the cave in which the South Gate was housed. Remarkably, the powerful beast had gotten her there with daylight to spare.

Lydigen had arrived first, and he ceased his pacing when she dismounted.

"Veni." He nodded to her.

"Looking a little anxious, Lydigen," she said, noting the black Mark sewn onto his tunic. All of his clothing had the Mark since he'd been branded prior to his entry into the Zealot clan he'd discovered.

Veni had never been certain about the Zealots practices, though she knew if Darius branded himself in honor of one and Pietro hated them, they had to be something good.

Lydigen's inside look and the information he relayed about them had given Veni an immense respect for them. She may not be convinced of all their spirit ways of old, but she believed in what they stood for—hope, freedom, and the care of the innocent and broken. Veni thought many times she could stand behind something like that. No wonder Pietro wanted to be rid of them.

"Want to spar?" she asked, thinking he might like a distraction and she could use any practice she could get.

Aside from Darius and Khyan, Lydigen and Sillow were the only opponents she had yet to beat—had yet to be able to hold her own against even, unless they were incredibly exhausted beforehand. Darius certainly knew how to choose his most trusted men wisely.

Lydigen gave her a small, breathy laugh, obviously uneasy. "Not today, Rousseau. Isn't the general with you?"

"No, he had matters to tend to. I'm certain he will be here shortly. What's wrong, Lydigen?"

His uneasiness was tangible and becoming contagious. They'd all begun to respect and include her, though she knew they still viewed her as the weakest link. She would change that.

He began pacing once more. "There is another shipment of children scheduled to leave as soon as the snow melts."

The knot forming in her stomach turned swiftly into nausea.

Just then, trotting hooves echoed through the cave announcing Darius' arrival. Seconds later, an owl flew in. Darius instantly knew something was wrong when he saw Veni's expression.

"What is it?" he asked them both, Khyan shifting to stand next to him.

"Another shipment, sirs," Lydigen told them. "Leaving as soon as the snow melts."

Darius chewed on his bottom lip. "This could be viewed as good news. We're close. With another shipment out there, we *will* find these monsters and stop them once and for all. Don't be dismayed, any of you. Khyan and I will case Greer's tonight. That's the orphan house they were taken from again?"

Lydigen shrugged. "I assume so, but I'm not certain."

Darius nodded and turned to his prince silently seeking agreement. Khyan nodded sternly.

"Alright." Darius turned to Veni "We'll leave for Anjali around mid-morning instead of dawn, alright Luvi?" She nodded. "Any other news on the Zealots?" He asked, turning back to Lydigen.

He shook his head. "No, sir. They are true to their beliefs, as we hoped. Mostly they worship in the old ways and set about secretly helping those in need. Though, many of them continue to exhibit a disciplined strength of heart that leads me to believe they are far more than what they seem. In a good way, sir."

Sebastian and Sillow entered through the Gate then.

Sebastian jumped right to it. "Did Lydigen tell you?" he asked Darius and Khyan, who both nodded their heads to confirm.

Veni could tell Sebastian was having a hard time reining in

his fiery temper. She still couldn't fathom how he looked at Pietro every day without killing her. Let alone how he did the other horrific things she made him do.

"Beck and Mariah were in too deep to leave. I believe Pietro may be on to Mariah, though she certainly has no inkling of who she could be working with. I'm sure she will assume the Liberator." Sebastian scrubbed a hand down his face and continued, "No word of any more Collectors splitting open, but Beck has gathered some interesting notes on the alchemy chamber."

He handed some papers to Darius. "It appears only the high-ranking Collectors are given the specific toxin like that of the man in the dungeon. The fear toxin is given to every Warmonger in order to break them into submission, but it is not weaponized. Collectors do indeed receive a memory inhibitor, though most are only given more fear toxin and an injection that seems to serve the only purpose of making them one-track minded, somehow.

However, the high-ranking Collectors receive the inhibitor, the fear toxin, the injection, *and* another injection that has what Beck has dubbed the Kiss of Death. He says Pietro comes into the alchemy chamber herself and *breathes* into each batch of the potion. A barely visible grey mist goes into the potion, and it boils." He pointed to the notes. "The fancy stuff is all there, but that's the simple man's gist."

Darius nodded and tucked the notes into his cloak. "Has he discovered how the Zealot made it into the alchemy chambers?"

Sebastian shook his head. "No. His theory is she just snuck in one day and never left."

"What have you got, Sillow?" Darius asked.

"I found a stash of well-cared-for weapons hidden in Schrute's barn. I've yet to see him with them, but he is either very good at hiding, or they don't belong to him.

Also discovered the band of friends he had prior to the war

included the Chief Well Builder whose wife and daughter were killed by Pietro's men in the mountains. He had another child, a baby, that was taken the night before the war broke out in the Alban square."

"Well done, Sillow. Stick close to Schrute," Darius ordered.

"Wait. The well builder's child?" Sebastian asked rhetorically. "Pietro has been searching for that child for a decade. Pietro's men took her, but she disappeared from the castle a few weeks later. No one knows what became of her."

Veni's mind spun. A baby taken from Pietro's clutches. Ester had ended up at their door as a baby mere weeks after the war broke out. Alone.

It can't be…

"I—I could be wrong," she spoke up, "but...we never knew where my sister came from. She isn't blood relation…" They all looked at her, taken aback. "The timeline fits …"

Darius looked at Khyan—he'd been on the farm since long before Ester arrived. "I never saw who brought Ester. I was not there much in those days. Alban was a disaster..."

"How did you keep her a secret, then?" Lydigen asked.

"We didn't," Veni answered. Pietro's men never inspected our farm like they did the others and she sort of favors my brother's looks." She shook her head, curious herself how her mother had deterred the other villagers. "I suppose my mother told them she simply hid her pregnancy well… I'm not sure. My mother was very well liked, maybe they just wanted to believe her and didn't want to turn her in. I truly don't know what she told them all. Everyone just loved Ester and accepted her as a Rousseau..."

"What about the family records?" Darius pointed out. He hadn't realized Ester showed up alone in the middle of the night. He and everyone else assumed a family friend was Collected, leaving a baby behind.

"She was always on them." Her mind continued to spin. She'd never considered any of these things, she was only a child herself when Ester arrived, and once she became part of the family, Veni never questioned it. Her mother was a secret Zealot—branded and all— her sister showed up in the middle of the night, and her name had been added to the family records list with no issues.

Who was my mother ...?

Khyan cleared his throat. "If Ester is this child and Pietro has figured it out, she's alive and in her custody. I don't know how she would have figured it out, so at this point, we assume she's kept the girl alive because she believes her to be related to you, Veni—the immune girl that got away. Either way, the child is alive and in Orford. I can feel it. That well builder's child is the reason the war began in the first place. She defies the queen by her very existence if the well builder already had a daughter and did not report his wife was with child. Sebastian, why did Pietro seize the baby instead of eliminating her?"

"I'm not certain. I was still in Greer's when the baby was born. I have only heard Lilith send countless men in search of the child and voice her hatred for her."

Darius turned to Veni, who had gone very still with cold calculation. "This is good news, Luvi. Either way you look at it, Ester is alive and near. Pietro would never let such an important pawn fall away from her grasp once she had it."

Chapter Twenty-Two

Darius and Khyan entered Orford to investigate Greer's Orphanage, only to find it completely abandoned and gutted. Both men had returned to the castle seething and sparred in the training room until just before dawn, attempting to relieve some of their anger and frustration.

The general slept what little he could until mid-morning when he met Veni as he'd promised. He determined in his heart to push all of his general duties out of his mind on their trip, for there was nothing he could do while away. He'd delegated to men he trusted, and Veni needed him to remain steady.

He caught himself still being taken off guard by her beauty as he watched her pat Vesper while he walked toward the stables. She already had the horse out in the grass grazing while she waited for him. He knew she'd been looking forward to Thera's ball for weeks—she'd never been to one before. She smiled as he approached, and his heart leapt in its newly typical fashion where she was concerned. He hadn't kissed her yet, he wanted to wait for the proper time. Such moments were not to be handed out flippantly.

"Morning, Little Bird. You can put old Vesper back in his stall. We have faster mode of transportation."

"We do? Faster than Vesper?" she asked, both skeptical and intrigued.

He nodded with a sly smile, and she led Vesper back to his stall, increasingly curious. When she returned, she was surprised to find Khyan had joined Darius outside the stables.

"Oh! Are you coming as well?" She hoped he was. Their relationship may not be what it once was, but if she could just allow herself to let it happen, she knew it could be mended.

"I am." He smiled and handed her a small vial of amber liquid. "Drink up, Rousseau."

"What is this?"

"I'll show you," Darius smiled wickedly.

He uncorked his vial and drained it. Her eyes went wide when he transformed right in front of her into an oversized bat. She could hardly even breathe from shock.

Khyan laughed heartily. "I will never tire of that flabbergasted look you possess. Drink up. The ball begins in mere hours." And to think she thought they would make it in time on horseback.

"What is this going to turn me into?" she asked Khyan, glancing at the bat—who winked at her. A wink that told her all she needed to know. "A *bird*?" Without another thought, she poured the contents of the bottle into her mouth and instantly turned into an agile, scissor tailed flycatcher.

Khyan beamed at them from the ground as she and Darius flew about. Veni flitted around Khyan's head and nipped at his nose with her beak, completely overjoyed.

Khyan chuckled and swatted her gently away, "We need to get going. Don't worry about our packs. Thera has clothing for us and we'll be there in no time."

In an instant, an owl joined them in the air and the odd trio flew to Anjali, savoring the wind beneath their wings, and the irreplaceable views of the scenery below. Veni's favorite part was easily flying through the clouds. She expected it to feel like cotton, though it was more like floating through a foggy puff of almost imperceptible mist. She flipped and twirled through the air, soaring high above and plummeting until just before the earth's surface. She'd never experienced such a thrilling glimpse at freedom and wished it to never end, though it must.

The transformation potion wore off only a short distance from the castle. Khyan had shifted back into himself to instruct his companions to land, for he knew they would change back shortly, and no one needed to see two humans fall from the sky.

"That was unbelievable!" Veni shouted, human again.

Darius whooped excitedly. "I normally opt for a lion, but that was phenomenal!"

Veni glanced at Darius, her stomach fluttering.

Lionheart.

"Do I dare even ask how that was possible, Prince?" she asked Khyan as they walked the rest of the way.

Khyan chuckled. "In the Monarbre Forest, near the West Gate into Vilora, there is a village of Papiens. One of them is an extremely gifted Keeper with the ability to transform into any non-human creature he desires. He is also gifted with superior intelligence that has made him quite the alchemist."

"I should rather like to meet this fellow. What is his name?" Veni asked.

"You're in luck then, Little Bird," Darius answered for him. "Khy gave him Beck's notes on Pietro's toxins and potions so he can go over them. I will need to meet with him when we return. His name is Hugo."

They continued, the ivory and jade Anjali castle growing ever closer. As they drew nearer, Anjalian warriors could be heard moving in formation, their armor and weapons scraping as they moved, all grunting in unison. As they approached the front gate, Darius handed the guard their invitations granting them entrance, while Veni looked around him, entranced by the warriors.

They were as fluid as water—lifting their long swords above their heads, twisting and gliding as they moved. Some wore leather armor and metal helmets. Others wore plain tunic garments wrapped around them to remain in place.

Aside from their uniform grunts, a peaceful hush permeated the entire area. She wondered briefly if Khyan had spent time training with the graceful warriors, for a quiet ferocity permeated from them just as it did from the Aureland Crown Prince.

Entrance approved, the three visitors were ushered past the training warriors and through a sliding wall with a dragon painted on it. "I thought those creatures were only in Aureland," she whispered to Darius.

She didn't hear his answer, for she had become far too distracted the moment they entered a long wooden corridor with papered lanterns dangling from the ceiling. Soft music greeted them—unlike any she had ever heard. Something about it made her want to keep silent and meditate on pure and peaceful things.

A lovely woman with the same almond eyes as the majority of Anjalian citizens led them to Thera's chambers where they were all greeted with piercing screams—quite contrasting the silence—and neck-breaking hugs. Thera welcomed them all into her rooms, looking as flawless as ever in her Anjalian clothing—a blue silk gown with pink flowers that wrapped around her almost like a bathing robe.

"Oh, my!" Thera exclaimed when she stepped back to truly take in the state of her friends. "What did you do? Cross a desert in a windstorm? You three look awful and smell even worse. It's a good thing you arrived early enough to fix all of...*this*..." She motioned to them, disgusted.

"Aren't you just a delightful little peach," Khyan muttered.

Darius laughed. "Glad to see Anjali hasn't changed your sass, Theralin. Where can Khy and I bathe?"

"I've placed clothing in your chambers. You will share a room three doors down on your left. You each have a sword as well. I know you probably weren't fond of leaving your precious Nahaliel, Darius, though I believe you'll find the sword to your liking. Veni, you and I shall share my room. I have so very much to tell you."

Veni couldn't believe she'd been so nervous to see Thera. She'd apologized and invited her to Anjali. She supposed the girl had truly left the past behind. As soon as Darius and Khyan left for their rooms, Thera grabbed Veni's hands and pulled her to the steaming bathtub. It wasn't exactly in a bathing chamber. It was situated behind a thin, white paper partition that was not attached to the other walls.

"Get in! You stink!" Thera commanded, pulling up a chair on the other side of the screen.

Surely, she isn't going to sit there while I bathe...I guess she is ...

Veni began to discard her dirty clothing and Thera babbled on and on about her days in the castle while Veni bathed. She could see the shadowy outline of Thera's spirited and over-dramatic motions. Surprisingly enough, her friend mentioned very little of her actual mission, opting for the juicer details of life within a royal court. Several of the emperor's admirers despised the foreign girl and Thera had great difficulty holding her tongue in their presence.

"They are so calm and quiet here," she rambled on. "I simply cannot remain that silent. One day I thought I would pull all my hair out, it seemed like torture! I couldn't take it anymore, so I spread a little cheer throughout the court." She laughed in her tinkling of bells way. "Akio thought they'd all had too much wine. Oh, it was marvelous. They're coming around, though. I'll break them out of their constriction with this ball. It's a Viloran ball, after all, and I've been working tirelessly on it. We Vilorans know how to have a grand time."

"I can hardly wait," Veni told her as she climbed out of the tub and wrapped a thin, silk bathing robe around herself.

Thera hopped up and led her to a large armoire. "I had a Viloran dress made for you, I hope you like it. Here, put this on first." She handed her a delicate silken slip to go under her dress.

"Oh my, just the robe and under clothes are beautiful," Vani said, slipping it on and letting her robe fall.

Thera turned to hand her the dress and paused, staring. "Goodness. I hope this dress fits you. I had no idea the girl had become a woman. Training and delicious food do a body good, now don't they? You look ravishing." She winked and handed Veni the powder blue dress.

Veni blushed. "Thank you. How do I get in this thing?" She was attempting to locate the bottom of the dress to put it over her head, but there was such an abundance of fabric.

Thera laughed. "Vilorans make extravagant ball gowns." She rifled through the folds of fabric and ruffles, finally locating the bottom. "And to think, I had yours and mine downsized!"

They eventually got the gargantuan dress over her head, but when they stuffed her in, Thera couldn't fasten the buttons along the back. Yanking on the dress to the point Veni couldn't breathe, Thera said through gritted teeth, "When you left me here you were skin and bones! What is Nuria feeding you? I need to get back to her kitchens! There." She fastened the last button and turned Veni around. She grimaced.

"What?" she asked, rushing to the looking glass. "Oh..."

The dress was awful. It was a terrible shade for her complexion, her upper half was hardly even contained, there was so much fabric she thought she may drown in it, and the bodice was so tight she felt lightheaded.

"You cannot wear that. It's hideous. You look like squished bread dough." Veni laughed out loud, though Thera was entirely serious. She shook her head. "Just hideous. Come, you should be able to fit properly in my dresses now, let's try another. I have a few that are a nice mixture of Viloran and Toulonan. Ah, this one matches your necklace! Where did you get that divine necklace anyway?"

"Khyan gave it to me for my birthday, though it was my

father who picked it out for me before he died. He never got to give it to me, so Khyan did so for him." Her heart constricted.

"That is beautiful. When Khyan loves, he loves with a force of a thousand seas. I know the pair of you are a bit out of sorts still, but Khy would go to the ends of the earth for you. Just so you know that."

Her heart swelled. "I'm beginning to believe that. Why has Khyan never married? Aren't there any lovely Keeper women he could be with?"

"Khy was married at one time, many, many years ago. I believe he was twenty-eight when they married and sixty-seven when she died. I think that's why he loves so fiercely. He is afraid of losing those he cares about like he lost Mai. He doesn't speak of her much."

A short time later, Veni stood again in front of the looking glass, though this time in a dress that indeed matched the necklace from her father perfectly. The gown hugged the curves of her upper body, swirling around her hips in deep violet waterfalls, lightly brushing the floor. There was still an abundance of fabric, though it was elegant and refined. Veni felt like absolute royalty.

Thera had also braided her hair, starting from her temple and traveling across the back of her head, the braid falling over her opposite shoulder. She then fluffed the braid and twisted and folded it into an elegant coil just behind her ear. She added a lavish hair accessory above the braid, reaching almost from ear to ear, comprised of small, bronze leaves. The style looked stunning from the front, though Veni couldn't see the back, or the leaf piece once it was pinned in. Thera gave her a small looking glass to see into the larger one and Veni decided very swiftly that she never wanted to take the leaf piece out of her hair.

Darius will love it.

"You look radiant, Veni." Thera hugged her. "I'm so sorry

for my outburst that night. The truth is I admire you and I simply want you on our side. I do believe your cause is worthwhile, I really do. But I also believe we are better together. Unity brings about victory. I can't tell you the joy that day will bring to my heart. You are a mighty ally to have, whether you know it or not." She gave Veni no chance to respond—much to the girl's relief. "Come, let's add a little kohl to brighten those eyes."

She indeed lined Veni's eyes with a small amount of kohl and added a dab of color to her cheeks and lips. "Darius is going to keel over when he sees you," Thera teased.

"Oh, you heard about that, did you?" Veni asked, blushing.

Thera threw her hands on her hips. "You can’t be serious. We all saw that before it ever even happened, which says a lot. That buffoon has never given a woman the time of day after Lydia. He takes after Khyan, that one. I used to try to seduce him just to see if I could! That man is like a steel armory. Nobody gets in there. Except for you.”

Darius and Khyan arrived then to escort the ladies to the ballroom. Both men looked dashing in their Viloran ball attire. Darius did not keel over upon seeing Veni as predicted, though he and Khyan each worked themselves into a frenzy attempting to get compliments out.

"Oh, *gentlemen*!" Thera chastised. "Do we need a lesson on how to handle a beautiful woman? My goodness, Khy, you're nearly a hundred years old. I should think at least *you* could use your words." She shook her dark locks and swished past them into the hall, turning back exasperated when they failed to follow. "Well, *come along*!"

Thera had opted for a Viloran/Orford style black gown made of alluring fabric and covered in sparkling onyx gemstones. Upon her head she wore a jeweled headpiece in lieu of a crown. She linked arms with Khyan, pulling him along and leaving Darius and Veni behind.

Alone in the doorway, the general soaked up every ounce

of the moment as he beheld the woman in front of him. His heart. His Little Bird. His greatest treasure. She fidgeted beneath his gaze. She knew his heart was intertwining with hers further and further.

He broke the silence first. “I can truthfully say I have never laid my eyes upon a more beautiful sight than you.” Veni blushed and looked away. “I mean that,” he assured her. He held out his arm for her to take and the four friends made their way down the uncharacteristically bustling hall, Darius sneaking glances at Veni the entire way.

Eventually, they reached a ballroom fit for a queen. The room looked absolutely nothing like the rest of the Anjali castle with its muted pink and gold walls, marble flooring, and lush bouquets of pink and white flowers on every surface visible. Round tables sat throughout the large room with gold plates atop them and exquisitely dressed guests around them. A piano filled the already vivid air with songs fit for dancing.

"Ah," Thera sighed. "This is more like it. I've had them working to decorate this room for weeks."

Couples spun and danced in the open space between the tables and guests laughed, while others sipped their bubbling drinks and nibbled their food. Darius instantly eyed a table along the far wall overflowing with sweet delicacies and promptly grabbed Veni's hand to drag her over.

Darius took a chocolate truffle and shoved one into Veni's mouth as well. She couldn't even chew it for laughing so hard as the general popped three more truffles into his own mouth and smiled at her like a chipmunk. The two of them sampled every sweet treat they could until they both effectively gave themselves stomach aches.

"Would you do me the honor of allowing me to dance with a beautiful woman?" He smirked and held out his hand. She returned his smile and took his hand as he led her onto the dance floor.

The charge in the air was intoxicating. The friends and

guests laughed, sang, danced, ate, and simply *lived* for hours upon hours. Emperor Akio made a toast in Thera's honor upon his arrival to the ball and had not left her side since. Veni found him to be a very handsome and delightful companion for Thera but decided they would discuss the less appealing details later and the fact that she never once smiled at him like she had during her tales of Dax.

Darius and Veni became lost in their own world countless times as they danced and laughed. Veni simply forgot anyone else was even on earth as he held her tight and spun her around and around, whispering in her ear from time to time. When she managed to come back into reality, she wondered on several occasions if Thera had anything to do with the joy in the room, but when she asked, Thera had laughed and said no, she just knew how to throw a good ball.

Flushed, Darius pulled a giggling Veni outside. "It is stifling in there."

The Anjali night air was only slightly cooler, though it was something. They stood quietly on a balcony overlooking a mountain range, a blanket of stars sprinkled overhead.

They breathed in the fresh air for some time and looked into the ballroom, playfully making up wild stories about the people inside. Some were secret assassins, others were dragon tamers, a few were noblemen seeking anonymity for an evening, and still others were common folk who snuck into parties professionally. After a particularly amusing scenario of Darius' design, she tipped her head back and laughed in earnest.

Turning to take in the view, she leaned over the railing. "The mountains make me miss Orford," she murmured longingly. Darius came up beside her and took in every inch of her as she looked up at the crescent moon and continued, "I adore the moon when it's just a sliver like that."

He didn't so much as glance at the moon. Instead, he took

her by the waist and pulled her against him.

"I am thoroughly in love with you, Luvenia Rousseau. Heart and soul, beginning and end." He gave her no chance to respond, he didn't need her to. He pulled her tighter and kissed her with tender passion, his fingers digging into the small of her back.

Something deep within her fell into place. Something she didn't know she'd been searching for. Something she was only beginning to find. Something that felt immensely like a weary traveler finding their way home at last.

Darius pulled back before he crossed a line he knew he wouldn't have the strength to uncross and kissed her once more, gently. He held her close for a moment, both of them embedding the moment deep within their hearts.

"We should go back inside," he breathed at last, resting his forehead on hers. He took her hand and led her back into the ballroom where the revelry remained in full force.

Only a few paces within the room, Veni's bliss was abruptly replaced with alarm and a dreadful stone dropped into her stomach. She gripped her general's hand tightly, "Darius...something is wrong."

He turned to her, worried she'd gone ill or she regretted their kiss. "What? What is it?"

"I don't know. Something is wrong. I—I can *feel* it," she told him.

Just then, a sudden, strange hush and a taste of dread ushered through the room like an invisible fog. The calm before the storm.

Within seconds, all the doors burst open, and Collectors rushed in. The sounds of breaking glass and screams filled the air as guests scrambled every which way to escape. In the midst of the boisterous festivities, none of the guests had heard the bloodshed taking place outside of the ballroom. No guards or warriors followed the Collectors in, Veni noted, her mind spinning to assess the situation. She assumed they must have paralyzed them with the Venom or killed them. She knew there was no possible way they could have gotten to them all...

They must have managed to blockade us in.

They were indeed trapped, causing more panic as most of the guests huddled in corners, under tables, and on the balconies. Darius wrapped one arm around Veni and withdrew his borrowed sword. Veni hiked up her dress to retrieve the borrowed throwing knives strapped to her thigh and together they ran against the fleeing crowd toward the source of the panic. Emperor Nakamura, Thera, and Khyan did the same.

Thera stood like a cat ready to pounce, her dagger at the ready. The emperor had drawn his long blade and assumed a protective position slightly in front of Thera. Khyan seethed violence that sent a chill through the air. The four guards within the ballroom faced the threat as well, though it was apparent they had never encountered a Collector and the sight of the unknown had shaken them.

An Orford Warmonger Mouthpiece strolled in amongst the standoff, whistling— footprints of blood and Venom trailing behind him. Darius snarled at the audacity.

"Good evening, citizens of Anjali," the Orford Warmonger announced in the mother tongue of the people. Darius translated to Veni under his breath the best he could manage. "We mean you no harm. Most of your warriors remain alive. We have merely come for the princess. Her presence is in direct violation of Her Majesty Queen Lilith Pietro's new alliance with Emperor Nakamura."

"How is that?" the emperor growled in the Orford common tongue. "And killing my men is not? I fear you could have just begun a war, you filthy manservant."

The Warmonger turned to Thera, ignoring the emperor— nothing more than a petty distraction to him. "Theralin Revencloud. Come with me. This is not a Collection unless you make it so."

Thera batted her eyelashes and smiled at him, utterly feline. "I'm flattered, little Mouthpiece," she purred. "But you are mistaken if you believe I shall go *anywhere* with you." She turned from feline to savage in an instant. She lunged toward the nearest Collector—the spark that set the room on fire.

Thera jumped and launched herself off of one Collector, sending him to the floor, catapulting herself onto another's shoulders. She twisted his neck with a sickening snap and jumped off as he slumped to the ground, kicking and slicing at any Collector near her. She dislodged the Venom pack from the fallen Collector and wielded it alongside her knife. She managed to fight more off and use the Venom to paralyze three other Collectors, while Darius slashed two more within seconds and ran for the Anjalian guards—two already fallen.

Adrenaline pumping, Veni threw her first knife at a Collector charging her. His uniform was too thick, and the knife merely bounced off, hitting the floor with a clang. She froze in fear. Khyan spun away from the Collector he'd just stabbed, a second one crumpled at his feet, and plunged his knife into the neck of the one charging Veni.

"Neck!" Khyan shouted, telling her their weakest point. They hadn't fully discussed the killing part of her training, but he knew she could handle this—she had to—and they would work through it when they survived. *They would all survive*, he told himself.

Darius thrust his sword straight through the Collector attacking the guards—one paralyzed and one left fighting. He looked into the eyes of the guard, who nodded with understanding. There was no language barrier between warriors with a common enemy. They turned and stood back-to-back, moving together in almost inhuman unity as they slashed through several more Collectors, blood and Venom spraying far and wide. Darius' arm had been gashed open by the knife of his first kill, allowing some of the spraying

Venom to seep into his wound—just enough to make his head swim and his arm go numb. He roared—the hindrance propelling him forward instead of back—and took his sword with his opposite hand, fighting on.

The rest of them had cleared a perimeter around Veni and she knew she would most likely survive by staying put, her back against the wall and her friends waging war before her. But when she heard Darius roar in pain and fury, her fear bowed its knee to outrage. The clanging of weapons and the screams of Anjali citizens as her ballad, she ran to where her knife lay upon the floor, swooping down to retrieve it. She spun and threw the knife deep into the throat of the Collector in front of Darius. Another was approaching her on the right, too close for a throwing knife.

Forever grateful she hadn't worn the other monstrous dress, she kicked her opponent square in the chest with enough force to hold him at bay long enough for her to punch him in his throat. Enraged, the Collector lunged at the girl with his Venomous needle. She used one of her knives to slice the tube, spilling the sickening green liquid onto the marble floor, mingling with the abundant blood already there. His greatest weapon debilitated, he wielded a dagger. Veni knew he was much stronger, and she would not stand a chance against the dagger. She threw herself back and over, flipping away—a little trick Smithwick had taught her—putting enough distance between them to throw her knife. She did, with delightful precision, resulting in a successful kill—a horrible and triumphant feeling that ripped through her.

"Where have you *been* all my life?" Thera shouted at Veni, impressed, as she cut open another Collector.

The emperor, also a very skilled warrior, had gone back-to-back with Thera, having seen Darius and his man's success. There were only a few Collectors left, two of them being dealt with by Khyan. Nakamura broke off from Thera, remembering the Orford Mouthpiece that suddenly seemed vacant. Looking for the man, Nakamura failed to see the Collector approaching from behind. Veni screamed a warning, but she was too late. The Collector thrust his Venom needle into the side of Akio's throat, paralyzing him within seconds. Thera spun around at Veni's scream, her knife still lodged in the stomach of the Collector she'd just stabbed. Seeing Nakamura on the floor, Thera ran to him, barely missing the knife Veni threw into the enemy standing over the emperor. Thera slid to a stop on her knees and took Nakamura in her arms.

"It will wear off, just hold on," she told him gently.

The Collectors taken care of and the Mouthpiece forgotten, Darius and the Anjalian guard picked up the emperor and carried him to the doors, the others trailing behind. The frantic citizens would have to wait until their emperor was safe.

They should not have forgotten the Orford Mouthpiece, for he had not fled in fear.

The group rounded a corner to meet five more Collectors and the Warmonger Mouthpiece blocking their way, Venom at the ready. None of them had time to react properly before they were subdued and injected, every last one of them. Darius and the Anjalian guard dropped Emperor Nakamura as all three of them crashed to the floor at once. Thera clawed and screeched at the Collector holding her down, to no avail. He injected her successfully and she went limp in his arms. He handed her to the Mouthpiece who began dragging her away, shouting for his men to retreat.

Veni lay on the warm marble floor smoldering with pain, pushing past it with enough sense to lie still. They couldn't know she was the immune girl, or they would take her too. Khyan's Keeper blood pushed some of the Venom aside, though he only had enough movement left in him to throw a few shards of ice at the Collector and Mouthpiece dragging Thera away, not caring about the consequences. This drew enough attention from the men for them to turn when a shard stabbed into the Mouthpiece's shoulder. Veni could tell they were torn between curiosity at what kind of man could draw ice from his hands and accomplishment of their queen's mission.

The mission won.

As they ran out of the castle with her friend, Veni knew that Mouthpiece would be back for Khyan someday.

Veni rose, fighting the burning in her veins, and pulled each of her companions back into the ballroom. Khyan came to first and tied the stirring paralyzed Collectors as she calmed the guests and shielded the emperor until he too regained movement.

They fled that very night and flew back to Orford, the emperor left behind to gather his men.

Chapter Twenty-Three

They'd planned endlessly for days how to infiltrate Pietro's castle and get Thera back. None of them had slept and Khyan was completely exhausted from flying to meet Emperor Nakamura each day. They had settled that the best plan of action was to join their forces with Nakamura's and wait until Sebastian confirmed Thera's location before they went in. Khyan had deterred the emperor from declaring a full out war, at least until they had Thera back. The alliance may be off, but Anjali wouldn't survive such a war.

In between the chaos, Khyan and Darius had also attempted to address the rift in Luvenia caused by her first kill. The girl couldn't reconcile all her emotions—guilt, wickedness, confidence, and a knowing she'd done what she had to do. They helped her understand the difference between slaughter and the burden of a righteous kill. They also explained that in Aureland, murder was accompanied by a permanent marking that appeared of its own accord upon the skin in harsh black ink—called the Bloodguilt.

"You have no Bloodguilt. Look at your arms," Darius told her. "It never gets easier, Luvi, but if a man's life was taken solely for the immediate protection of another's, you can lay your head down at night knowing you are not a murderer. Do you understand?"

They'd told her as much, and she knew she'd had to protect Thera and the other citizens. She knew she may have to kill another to protect Ester, but she still thrashed each and every night, awakening to survey her arms countless times, waiting in terror for the Bloodguilt to appear.

Everyone else occupied and her training complete for the day, Veni was exhausted yet unwilling to be alone. She wandered the garden looking for Queen Nuria, thinking possibly they could have lunch early. She knew neither of them could really eat. They were worried to the point of illness about Thera, but the queen's presence was calming.

She found her swaying in the snow, to music Veni couldn't hear. Softly she sang, yet the purity of power infused within her song held Veni transfixed in her place.

In pursuit of us, majesty overflows.
Light crushes the darkness. O, the fury it holds;
Calling in precious ones, their shelter from the storm.
Illuminating the night, bringing them safely home.

Somewhere deep within the caverns of Luvenia's soul, drums pounded in time with the queen's words as the song turned fierce.

May the tempest of love shake the ground,
Bringing freedom to the captive.
May all the earth hear the sound,
As furious love defeats the grave.
In pursuit of us, majesty overflows.
Light crushes the darkness. O, the fury it holds.

The silence following her final, soul-wrenching note left Veni raw. She stood for several moments just watching her queen stare at her frosted roses, tears on her cheeks.

"Hello, Veni," she spoke softly without turning. Of course,

she'd known she wasn't alone.

"Hello," Veni squeaked. "I thought perhaps you would like to have lunch already. Though, I don't think I'm hungry..."

"Nor am I. I would love the company, however," she said, turning to meet the girl's eyes. "We'll have some tea, shall we?"

They walked silently to Nuria's study. A gloom woven with threads of peace hovering over them. Tea in hand, they sat in armchairs across from the hearth for a long while without speaking, Veni twirling her hair, lost in thought.

"Will the storm ever cease?" Veni finally asked, all her loss swirling within her mind. "I don't know how much longer I can endure losing everyone I love. Who is next? Darius?" The queen looked intently into her protégé's eyes with such sorrow it made Luvenia stir in her seat.

"Oh, Luvenia," she mused, shaking her head. "The things you have seen...endured. So very much..." She trailed off as she stood and walked from her chair to look into the fire.

The queen's silence began to seep into Veni's nerves, and she set to picking at her nails to distract herself from the slow fade into the ever-beckoning abyss.

Mercifully, Nuria finally ended the silence, the flames dancing in her eyes, "Those sorrows in your heart, the turmoil in your very *bones*..." She turned to face Veni. "Will you let them break you, or will you let them forge you into a mighty weapon? The time has come to decide, dearheart. What will it be?"

How could anyone look so fierce, yet be kind as a dove? Luvenia wondered as she pondered her answer.

"A weapon for whom? What is there left to even fight for?" Veni finally said.

Nuria knew deep in Luvenia's shredded heart there lived a warrior. They'd all seen the remnants of her. She stormed across the room, her elegant dress gliding swiftly along the floor behind her. She leaned over the girl's chair. Stopping inches from Veni's face she burst out, "Still you only think of *your* battles? Can't you see?"

"See *what*?" she spat back. "I see death and despair and the travesty that is our *reality*."

"So, your decision is to surrender?" the queen questioned. "To give up? You are willing to lose Ester for good and Darius as well? That is where all of this is headed if we do not fight. *We need you*. You are not selfish, Luvenia, you are *afraid*."

Not caring what royalty Nuria might be, Veni knocked the queen's hand off the arm of her chair to stand. She suddenly felt very claustrophobic and needed to get out of the room. She stormed to the door. "I have to go." A quick glance over her shoulder before she slammed the door revealed deep emotion written on the queen's face. Sadness? Pity? Disgust? Luvenia didn't care.

With a sigh, Nuria made her way to the comfort of her favorite ornate, red velvet and gold chair across the study. Picking up the book splayed across the arm of the chair she spoke out, "Do you plan to remain hidden in my armoire the entirety of the afternoon, Darius?"

The doors of the armoire opened slowly and a sheepish general bowed. "My apologies, Your Majesty. I came to retrieve the map of Morrec you spoke of and when I heard you and Luvi coming, well, I..." he trailed off and found a book on the shelf that seemed interesting.

"My dear general, you are so fearsome on the battlefield and yet your heart is as soft as down feathers. Not to mention you are an atrocious liar," she said with a smirk.

The general blushed. "I wasn't exactly lying—"

"Quite right," Nuria interrupted. "No need to dig yourself in further. The map is there, in the desk. Top left drawer."

"Thank you." Darius picked up the map, bowed, and made to walk out, but stopped, one hand on the doorknob. "Nuria, may I ask you a question?"

The queen looked up from her book with a raised brow, "Dispensing with the formalities finally? Your embarrassment has ceased, I see. Certainly, you know you may ask me anything."

The general strode over and took a seat on his chair. "It's about Luvi."

One of Nuria's brows rose again. "Is that so? Who would have ever guessed?" She tried to hide her amusement.

"Yes. How can she be so callous? So afraid. So..." He struggled to find the right word.

"So daunted?" Nuria finished for him.

"Yes, so daunted. I know she's stronger than she seems. I know she can win any battle she may face. I've *watched* her turn into a formidable opponent. Yet she's still so... I just don't understand. One moment the curtains draw back to reveal such *life* within her and then she snatches them closed again. She means the world to me. I simply cannot understand why she has encased herself in fear and doubt like it can protect her."

The queen set down her book on the end table between them and leaned forward to grasp her general's hand. "Have you not known heartache, my beloved Darius?"

His brows furrowed and he shook his head. "Of course, I have, you know that. Grief is my oldest friend."

"Grief gave way to the hope that forged you into a leader. Grief gave way to the hope that made you a fierce warrior and a loyal friend. Grief in and of itself *builds* nothing of value," she explained, "but it is necessary, and it can give way to hope. And hope builds everything."

"Grief breaks before hope can be built. I was broken too. So very broken for a time," he said.

"Exactly. Grief has broken our sweet Luvenia. But the warrior within lives, the warrior of hope, just as it did in you. I can see it in her eyes, and you can see it in the formidable opponent. We must teach her to hone that grief, anger, and fear into a weapon for good. To let it be forged into hope. I have said it before, and I shall say it again...*treasure* awaits within those scars. We shall see that wild-hearted spirit yet. Mark my words." Nuria squeezed her general's hand and returned to her book.

Darius left without another word, hoping with all his might that Nuria was right. He'd seen it all along, treasure hidden deep within her. He just didn't know how to make her see it.

Once in the cool hallway, Veni all but ran to the stables to retrieve Vesper and ride to her tree. But Khyan found her there, crying as she saddled her horse.

"Veni? What's the matter? Are you alright?" He rushed over.

"I'm fine. Just leave me alone." But she wasn't and she crumpled to the ground sobbing.

Khyan knelt down to her and lifted her head by her chin, gently. "Luvenia Rousseau, look at me. Tell me what's happened. Is it Thera?"

Veni shook her head yes...then no, then shrugged. She took a deep breath and regained her composure. "Nuria all but called me a coward. She said the time has come for me to let all the horrors of my life forge me into a weapon instead of letting them break me. I told her I don't see anything left to fight for and she told me I'm merely afraid." She started to cry again. "She's right."

Khyan held her in his arms among the straw and mud until her tears ceased.

"Veni, would you like to know a secret?"

"Alright," she whispered.

"We're all afraid. Every one of us. The reason we are afraid is because we *all* have something left to fight for. We have each other and we have freedom. Freedom has always been, and will always be worth fighting for," he told her.

She sniffled. "You're all afraid? Even you?"

"Even me. But Veni, I fight anyway. There is far too much at stake to let fear debilitate me. I look fear in the face every single day, and I keep fighting. *Do it afraid*, Luvenia. True defeat comes only when you let fear stop you completely. We can continue fighting in the face of fear if we have hope."

They sat huddled on the ground for a few moments longer as he let the words sink deep into her heart. She missed her family fiercely, but she would be forever grateful for the owl that stepped in to be the best replacement he knew how to be.

Finally, Khyan stood and pulled her out of the mire. "Come, I have something to show you."

He led her to a section of the castle she'd only seen in passing during the tour Darius took her on months ago. He'd said it was where many of the weapons were made, but they hadn't entered.

Khyan held the door open for her and they went inside of a dark, suffocatingly hot room made of stone with many hearths and kilns filling the space. "I want you to see how a sword is forged," he said.

She watched in awe as the blacksmiths forged swords in various stages. Some pounded hot steel or copper violently with heavy hammers, folding it over and pounding it again and again. Others were immersing their makings of a blade in molten fire. One man was cracking some sort of hard, white substance off a mold for a hilt and pouring the molten liquid into it. Still others sharpened their blades, honing them into mighty weapons.

After watching the smiths work for a while, Veni requested that Khyan walk her to her chambers. There she fell asleep and dreamt of embers and steel.

Her father stood before her. He was dressed in the purest white, like the sails of the ship he'd captained in her other dreams. He stood poised to attack, but she wasn't afraid. She knew he would never hurt her, not this version of him—the true version. He was nothing like the ghoul. Her very bones cried out to him, like they knew him too, like there was more to him than she could see. She wanted to see his face. She knew it was her father's face, though it never cleared.

He came to her, extending a hand. With it, he reached inside of her chest and grasped her heart as she watched, all her insides visible. Suddenly, golden, perfect, beautiful molten fire poured from the heart in his hand, filling every part of her. When it filled her completely, she burst open in a crescendo of light. In her place stood a woman in glowing armor of fire.

Side by side she stood with her father, their armor of light as bright as the sun. “Keep coming," he said to her. Her father's strong, yet tender voice. "We have so much we're going to do together. Keep coming."

The dream went black as a redbird sang and Luvenia Rousseau opened her eyes a warrior.

Chapter Twenty-Four

Queen Lilith Pietro dug her sharp nails into the cheeks of a bound and gagged Princess of Vilora as she held the girl's face in her hand. Thera's gift hadn't worked on the Orford Queen, and she'd let no one else near the princess' cell since the Venom had worn off the last time.

"No one is coming for you, *Keeper*," she hissed, "or they would have weeks ago. They don't want to reveal their move just yet." She slapped the girl hard across her face, "Oh, but they will. Nuria can't protect the Liberator forever."

Darius and Luvi hadn't discussed what changed in her over the past several days, but he saw it. Nearly overnight she had begun to step confidently into the woman she was meant to be. She walked alongside him wild and untamed—unabashedly herself. He'd long felt that person was far more than any of them yet realized.

Together they trekked through the dunes on the other side of the Monarbre Forest toward the Papien Village. The air was so stifling hot it burned their lungs and sand covered every inch of them, still managing to find its way into their mouths regardless of being covered in scarves that concealed all but their eyes.

Darius looked over at his Little Bird and couldn't help but smile. All they'd been through and all they faced couldn't dampen his joy that she was finally ready to take flight. Not a potion-aided flight, but free flight. It hadn't happened yet, but it was on the horizon. He could feel it in the air. The dry, hot air.

"This is my least favorite part of Aureland," he told her. "I'm not fond of hot weather, and no matter how many times I bathe, the sand still remains for days. I do, however, find the Papiens immensely interesting. Especially Hugo. The brilliant mind he possesses astonishes me. I think you will find him intriguing."

She smiled at him behind her scarf. "Perhaps he can teach me a thing or two."

"Oh, he will. Generally, I find my head is aching when I leave Hugo's presence. I once stayed with him for a good stretch of time, simply out of sheer thirst to learn. Learn I did, and thirst I did. Thirst is insatiable in this place."

Just the thought of it made him indeed parched. He took a long pull from his water skin as Veni did the same.

"It isn't much farther, just over that dune there." He took her by the hand and led her on.

The pair climbed the sand dune, laughing far too intensely when Luvenia continued to slide backwards in the shifting sand. Finally, they made it over and a sand covered village rose before them. As they approached, Veni was amazed by the people. They were all immense in size and looked as if they were made of parchment and sandstone. They had the texture of stone, yet their faces were contorted like parchment crumpled and folded into unique creatures of varying ardor. They didn't appear to have eyes or real mouths, though she knew they must, for they all gave her broad, papery smiles as they passed.

They reached a massive structure with a door thrice Darius' height and he promptly banged upon it before they both removed the scarves from their mouths. A middle-sized Papien answered their knocking, wearing a monocle over his one, seemingly invisible eye.

"General Cremeux!" he burst out. "How are you faring old

friend?"

Darius clasped arms with the sandstone man. "We've seen better days, Hugo, but we will triumph."

Hugo issued an acknowledging rumble from his chest. "Indeed, my friend. And who is this flower blooming in the Papien Desert, hm?"

"This is Luvenia. The one you made the flycatcher potion for."

Hugo adjusted his monocle. "Ah, the flycatcher." His deep voice rolled through them like thunder. "I am pleased to make your acquaintance, Luvenia. Come, the both of you. I've just put on a pot of tea."

They followed Hugo into his home filled with the evidence of a brilliant man ever in search of more wisdom. His entire home was essentially a vast library. Shelves upon shelves lined with books. Parchments and scrolls littered every visible surface that wasn't already covered with liquid-filled vases and tubes. One section—the section the teapot was singing in—had bubbling amber liquid coming from a glass container and steaming pink smoke flooded out of another.

Hugo ignored the strange potions and went for the screaming pot to pour them some tea. He pointed an empty glass in the direction of a stack of papers behind Darius. "Beck's notes are there. Intelligent boy, he is."

He handed them each a hot alchemical glass full of tea—something Veni found strangely humorous.

"The happenings in Pietro's alchemy laboratory are strange and fascinating indeed. It appears that she has discovered how to draw from her gift, the Touch of Death, and synthesize it. If one is well versed in the matters of alchemy, this is but a rudimentary subject and not incredibly difficult to accomplish. However, she has learned how to synthesize it into aer fixus. Were she not our enemy, I should certainly enjoy sitting under her teaching and learning more about her discoveries. She is not a dense woman by any means."

Darius interrupted, "Aer fixus? Her Kiss of Death?"

"Correct. Though I find Beck's term to be lacking original thought, we may call it that for comprehension purposes. In the synthesizing of her gift into aer fixus…the Kiss of Death, which is a vapor issued when she releases her breath, she has decreased its potency enough to illicit the breaking down of mortal fibers, replacing them with a destructive incarnation of death without the actual demise of the body. I fear the mind of these Collectors is trapped somewhere beneath the impending beast. However, the pleasant news is Pietro still, currently, needs a touch of immortal power to achieve the final demise of the human and the release of her demon. Therefore, the beast beneath the Collector in the Aureland dungeons broke through. I do fear she is close to achieving the same results in the mortal realms, though she is not there quite yet."

"Why is the aer fixus visible, as Beck mentioned? Does her gift make it so? She loses her strength with each batch, does she not? What about the fear toxin that seeped out of the beast, sending us into visions of terror?" Veni asked.

Hugo smiled at the girl. "I must say, I like you, little flycatcher. I believe the answers to all your many questions go hand in hand. The aer fixus, the Kiss of Death, is visible to the naked eye because it is laced with the fear toxin. I have concluded she has phlebotomized her own Keeper blood and used it to concoct said toxin. The potent fear toxin is most likely what holds the human mind at bay when a Collector has been given the memory inhibitor and the injection that allows her control over them. All her toxins and injections are working in concordance with one another to create a ghastly monster indeed.

When the beast within is successfully uninhibited, the toxin is released into the air as a vapor. It is so potent that it debilitates anyone who breathes it in or soaks it in through the pores of their skin. Interestingly enough, somehow, the injecting of herself with the fear toxin causes Pietro to be immune to its effects as well as replenishing a semblance of her gifts, though it would seem to me in a diluted way. In addition, I am willing to assume that the further she injects herself, the further away her Touch of Life drifts. She cannot continue mass production of any toxin much longer—any that stem from her own chemicals, that is. Not without discovering a way to replenish herself truly and extend the reach of her gifts further.

I am still researching this interesting bit of information, though I believe if she takes another Keeper's blood and injects herself with it, she can become immune to their gifts as well. I fear she might have such a terrible thing in mind for our dear Theralin. Such a task would be quite an experiment and one that I'm certain would fail countless times, so I conclude she would test on someone else before herself. I have heard talk of blood experiments in her laboratories, however, and I believe she may be well on her way."

Ester.

"Let me ensure I understand this properly. You're saying she would use the blood of a Keeper to experiment on a mortal in order to test the efficiency of her toxins?" Veni asked, dreading the answer.

"She would," he answered forlornly.

Veni's heart lodged in her throat. "Would she have more success on a child, considering they heal more swiftly and need less toxin?"

The Papien's paper brow furrowed. "I hadn't considered that possibility, but I'm afraid you could be correct."

Sebastian Olliander bolted through the Rellum Forest toward the portal into Aureland. Upon reaching it, he smacked his horse on the rear so it wouldn't loiter near the Gate, and he entered. There hadn't been time to send for Darius, so no one met him on the other side.

"Smithwick!" he bellowed from the cave, hoping the Porter would hear. "Tell Darius I'm here! *Quickly*!" He shouted it over and over while pacing, deciding how long to wait. Maybe if he ran now, he would make it to the castle or ...

A Bluestreak Rapidflyer hovered in front of him, a note in her beak.

He's coming.
-S

A short while later, a large black lion raced into the cave, morphing into his general.

"What is it?" Darius asked him urgently.

"I've found Thera. And Lilith is sending her men into Anjali in the morning. They're already stationed outside the border. She's going to destroy them. We have to warn Nakamura, but we can get Thera out while they're occupied, Lilith is going with them." He continued to pace frantically.

Darius ran a hand through his beard. "We can send Nuria to Nakamura. She has much to discuss with him already. I will assemble a troop immediately and meet you at sunrise in the forest."

Sebastian nodded and ran back through the Portal as Darius drained his second vile of potion and bounded off as a lion.

Darius led his small band of warriors through the woods to the home in which he was born. The home in which a leader was forged.

Sebastian met them at the cottage and quickly ran over the details. Thera was in solitary confinement deep within a hidden fortress outside of Taule. Guards were stationed outside, but none within range of her gifts unless Pietro was present. She'd discovered the distance they must keep from the girl during the first few days when Thera almost escaped on multiple occasions.

"The quickest route is to cut through Alban," Darius told them. "Leave your horses here, we travel on foot. Don your hoods, we mustn't be recognized. Draw as little attention as possible going through Alban. In fact, we go in pairs until we're through. Luvi, you and I. Khy, you and Felix. Olliander, you and Rovak. Veni and I will lead the front, the rest of you leave ten minutes apart. We'll meet behind Lydigen and Sillow's safe house. Maker be with you."

Veni and Darius ran through the sludge of mud and melting snow, their cloaks whipping in the wind, for as long as they could. Near Alban, they slowed and adjusted their hoods, appearing to merely be two cold Market patrons. As they slowed further to a forced stroll through the alleyways, they noticed a crowd gathering in the square.

The same dread and knowing she felt at the ball filtered into Veni again. "It's for us. Something is there for us," she said cryptically as she pulled Darius toward the crowd.

They wove their way through the frightened and whispering crowd little by little until they saw it. Indeed, something for them. Mariah and Beck hung lifeless, impaled on sharp posts. A piece of parchment was held onto Beck's chest with a dagger:

Who shall Liberate the Watchdog?

It was all a game. She *wanted* them to rescue Thera. She knew what they were. And she thought the Liberator was one of them.

Darius gripped Veni's hand and pulled her as quickly as possible through the dense crowd, several of whom had vomited at the sight upon the platform. Neither one of them spoke the entire way to the safe house. They had some time until the others made it there and Darius wanted to ensure Lydigen and Sillow were safe. He scaled the back wall of the building, entering in through the window. Deeming it safe, he leaned out to motion for Veni to climb up—he didn't want her down there alone—but she was already almost to the window. He frowned at her independent stubbornness and helped her inside.

Everything seemed to be in order, but he checked all possible hiding places and ventured to the bottom floor of the building just to be certain. With no signs his men had been harmed or found out, he quickly jotted a coded note on a scrap of parchment and left it in Lydigen's coffee container. They shimmied back down the wall, landing on the ground just as Sebastian and Rovak arrived. Khyan and Felix were already there, leaning against the wall.

"Did you know?" Darius immediately growled at Sebastian, closing the distance between them.

"Know *what*?" He backed up defensively.

"*General*," Khyan warned him sharply, holding a hand to the man's broad chest. He could see the rare, rash anger building. Things did not end well when it did.

Darius ignored his prince and shoved his hand away, livid. "Beck and Mariah. They're *dead*!" he spat. "Impaled in the town square for the world to see." Sebastian looked like he was going to be sick, but Darius continued, "Did. You. *Know*?"

"No," Sebastian said quietly. "*Maker*... That's what that crowd was about? No, I didn't know, Darius." He ran a hand through his hair, obviously shaken. The others all looked at their feet, feeling the loss as well.

Darius looked long and hard at Sebastian but decided to believe his friend. He breathed heavily in an attempt to cool his anger. "It's a trap," he finally said

Khyan, Felix, and Rovak all snapped their heads up to look at their general. Sebastian looked like someone had slapped him. "Beck had a note stabbed into his chest, *'Who shall Liberate the Watchdog'*—she knows. She's waiting for us."

"She believes the Liberator to be one of our own, General? A Keeper?" Rovak piped up.

"It appears so. Do you know anything, Sebastian? Anything at all?"

The informant shook his head. "No. Lilith has been seeking the counsel of her other courtiers and advisors more than mine in recent days."

"Does she suspect you? Could she have told you Thera's location to test you?" Darius asked.

"I don't believe so. She is more playing a game of cat and mouse. She doesn't understand why I... cut things off with her. She deems it some sort of challenge to win and it's distracting her from matters of importance in conversations with me. I'm merely a toy to her currently." This made both Darius and Veni's hearts ache for the man that stood before them. "She didn't give me Thera's location. I followed her there the last time she went."

Darius put a hand on his friend's shoulder, immensely glad his earlier anger had been unfounded. "We're getting you out of there as quickly as possible, Sebastian."

He simply nodded. "We better be going."

Taule was almost a full day's ride from Alban. It would take them significantly longer on foot, but they would stay less visible off the main trails, especially as a band of six. They walked briskly for the entirety of the day, running when they had the energy and only stopping briefly to eat some bread and cheese. When the sun began to set, they headed deeper into the woods to build a small fire and camp for the night.

As the rest of them slept like the dead, snoring on their bedrolls around the fire, Veni and Darius sat up watching the flames. Veni's nightmares had stopped for the most part, though she still had trouble sleeping, and as long as she was awake, Darius was too.

"What is the first thing you're going to do when you have Ester back, Little Bird?" Darius asked quietly, crickets chirping all around. The snow had mostly melted, and spring would soon be upon them—the wildlife could hardly contain their excitement.

"Always the optimist," she said simply.

"I just know the woman who sits next to me will accomplish what she's set out to do. If that's being an optimist, then so be it."

She smiled and made swirls in the dirt with a stick. "You have always seen the best in me. You all have."

"Here, let me see that," he said, taking the stick. She answered his question as he sat in front of her in dirt, making an intricate drawing.

"I shall first take her directly to Aureland, to Viridian Bay to see the mermaids. Aside from my tree, that is my favorite place. Then I, of course, want her to meet Smithwick—she will find him hysterical. Then I think a nice dinner with our new family would be divine." She paused for a moment. "I think we will visit Mother's grave, as well. She'll need to see it." Veni looked at her fingers. "I fear she will be a broken version of herself when I get her back."

Darius ceased the drawing of his scissor-tailed flycatcher and sat again next to her. He took her hand, and looked into her eyes, their little flecks of amber glowing in the light of the fire. "There is beauty in brokenness too, Luvi. The brokenness itself is tragic and bleak, but the person beneath it remains and awaits to be made whole. The road may be long and winding, but Ester will be herself again, regardless of what that monster has done to her. Hope may wane, but it never burns out. It can always be fanned into flame again."

His words gave her enough comfort to rest her head on his shoulder and fall fast asleep. When she woke, she found she was on her bedroll and Sebastian hovered over her with a tin cup.

"Coffee?" he grunted, clearly not a morning person.

Once they'd practically inhaled their coffee and cinnamon bread, they ventured on to save Thera—the six of them.

When Sebastian declared they were nearing the abandoned fortress Thera was contained within, Darius stopped them all to go over the plan—for the fiftieth time.

They huddled together in the woods as he forcefully whispered, "Khy, you go in first. We don't know what to expect, so assess the situation and use your gift only if *absolutely* necessary. She knows we belong to the Aureland Horde, but we still don't want to give away our specific identities, and we want everyone out of this alive. All of you, *do not take lives* if at all possible. We take some of them captive back to Aureland and the rest we leave disabled for Pietro to find. Sebastian says there were eight Warmongers and four Collectors on duty when he followed Pietro. We can easily handle those numbers.

Felix and Sebastian, your job is to disable the Venom packs—paralyze them if possible. Rovak and Khy, you two and I will take out the Warmongers. Luvi," he turned to her, suddenly wishing she hadn't come at all, but knowing she could handle her task. "*Get Thera.*"

She nodded, feeling the full responsibility of those words.

One by one they donned their hoods and concealed their faces, no more than wraiths prepared to swoop in and take back what was stolen from them—their friend. The prince nodded to his fellow warriors before sprinting toward the fortress. Minutes felt like hours while they waited for the signal call that finally came.

Darius unhooked the flap concealing the lower half of his face and pulled Veni's down. He kissed her hard and said, "You can do this." He re-hooked his mask as Veni did the same. The general raised Nahaliel and they all sprinted to join

Khyan.

The fortress rose before them in haunting disrepair. The stones were broken and rotted, ivy invaded entire walls, and there was a distinct reek of death hovering in the air. The prince had the Collector at the front gate already paralyzed and his pack cut open, Venom spilling on the ground. In unison, they ran through the gate. Sebastian and Felix stopped to disable the Collectors at the front door, though a warning had already been raised. Khy, Rovak, Veni, and Darius pushed past the scuffle and into the dank fortress, the stench growing more potent. Warmongers and Collectors rushed in on them, responding to the raised signal. Khyan and Rovak stood back-to-back, fighting them off until they could subdue them. Darius and Veni sprinted down sets of stairs deeper and deeper into the fortress, debilitating anyone in their way.

The farther they went the safer they would be—none of Pietro's men could go within a certain distance of Thera. The pair of them reached a locked, steel door that Veni swiftly picked the lock of—another skill she'd perfected.

"*Go*," Darius whispered. "I love you."

He shut the door behind her before she could respond and she raced down the steps, heart pounding. Not out of fear for what she would face, she knew no one could be near Thera without her being able to escape, but for her friends that were fighting upstairs. She pushed the fear away. She had to get to Thera.

The staircase wound downward, so deep her ears popped and the smell made her gag. Eventually, she made it around a turn and saw dim candlelight. Clutching her knife, just in case, she snuck quietly toward the light. Rounding another corner Veni saw a cell. Thera lay inside of it, bound and bleeding, still in the almost unrecognizable gown from her ball. Veni sheathed her knife and ran for the cell.

Upon seeing her approach, Thera's eyes went wide, and she

croaked, "*Wait*—"

Before she could warn her to stay back, a half-masked Collector stepped into view. Veni's heart pounded in her chest, and she had her dagger back in her hand in an instant.

How can he be in here?

"He's immune to my gift," Thera warned her.

"Shut your mouth, Keeper," he roared, his voice familiar.

The Collector raised his gloved hand and removed the goggled mask. Luvenia gasped. Her brother stood before her—evil incarnate.

"*You*," she snarled, gripping her knife tighter and ripping off her own cloth mask.

Thera watched the standoff in confusion until the Collector spoke, his voice dripping venom. "Hello, Sister."

Veni's eyes went dark—pure hatred and violence pooling behind them until all she could see was rage.

Thera crawled to the bars of the cell as fast as she could. Gripping them frantically, recognizing the look in her friend's eyes. "Veni, *no*."

"Where is my sister?" she growled, twirling her knife.

"Exactly where she belongs. Lending her life to the service of her queen." His voice was not his own.

He's not Jacob.

She softened. "Jake, I know you're in there. Somewhere. *Tell me where Ester is*."

Jacob let out a bone chilling laugh. "You think I'm trapped beneath a beast, hm?" He inched close to her face as her mind flew between stabbing him and the hope she'd been wrong about him. "I'm not," he breathed. "I am the beast I've always been. I've waited ten years to make you pay for what you did to our father." He stood straight and the fury within her came like a torrential downpour.

"It wasn't my fault," she growled.

"Oh, but it was. You were always the treasured one. The

treasured one that ruined *everything*."

Veni gripped her knife until her knuckles turned white, eyeing him with malice. She held onto that waning hope she had that his words weren't true. But it was slipping from her grasp.

Thera called to her again, "He's lying to you. You know who you are. Don't do this, Veni. It cannot be undone…"

Veni couldn't hear her over the roaring in her head and the slithering whisper of the ghoul who visited her dreams.

Darkness is what feeds you and makes you stronger. You are evil through and through. Avenge Ester. It's the only way to pay for what you've done. Be a warrior for the dark.

She bellowed and launched herself onto Jacob, the force of her weight and a jab to his throat sending them both to the ground in a heap. Having the upper hand, she twisted him over and sliced open the Venom tube on his pack. He was far stronger than her and soon had her on her back, knocking the breath out of her.

He gritted his teeth, his hands around her neck. As he choked her, she let out a stifled, sickening laugh. She curled her arms in at her chin and threw them out wide, causing him to lose his grip and balance before she sent the heel of her palm into his chin. With her brother stunned, she kicked the side of his head, knocking him unconscious.

Veni took his keys and ran to the lock of the cell. She opened it and untied Thera as quickly as possible before taking the ropes and using them to tie Jacob and drag him into the cell. Just as she deposited him inside and began to lock the cell door, Jacob came to.

"That's all you've got?" he groaned, catching her attention. She froze with the key still inside the lock.

Thera doubled over in pain near the entrance to the room and urged her friend not to let him torment her. "Veni," she breathed heavily, cradling her side, "Don't. He's not worth it.

Let's *go*. Let Pietro deal with her own worm."

Veni remained eerily still, her hand on the keys. Warrior for the dark. Every man is wooed by both darkness and light. Keep coming. Revenge. It's the only way to pay for what you've done.

The whispers of truth and the ghoul's twisted lies warred violently within her, permeating her soul.

"Veni. *Please...*" Thera begged. "Let's just *go*."

Luvenia looked at her with the eyes of vengeance they'd all fought to extinguish. "I'm sorry," she whispered to her friend, flinging the cell door open and stalking in to her brother.

He simply stared at her, a wicked smile upon his lips.

"*No*!" Thera screamed and lunged for the cell, hindered by her injuries.

Veni merely smiled venomously back at her brother and made to plunge her dagger up and into his heart. Jacob froze in shock as an owl swooped in and threw himself under the knife. Searing pain immobilized his gift and Khyan fell to the ground, shifting back into human form, clutching his bloody abdomen. Thera's mouth hung open in horror at what her friend had just attempted to do and what her prince had sacrificed.

Khan rose unsteadily and used the last of his remaining strength to slam his elbow into Jacob's temple to knock him out. Veni's knife clattered to the ground as realization struck her. She began to tremble uncontrollably as a scrawling mark began to etch itself upon her forearm.

She screamed.

"*Theralin*," Khyan shouted over her. "Get her out of here." And with that, he slumped to the floor unconscious.

Luvenia was near hysterics. The injured Keeper threw every ounce of her gift at the girl, sending her into a deep sleep. Thera then ripped her already tattered and filthy ball gown and ran as fast as her injuries would allow to clot the dying prince's wound. She left Veni and her Collector brother both on the fortress floor and hauled Khyan up as best she could. She dragged him up and up the stairs, needing to stop several times.

Huffing and covered in blood, she reached the top of the stairs and banged on the jammed door. Darius opened it and his eyes went wide as he beheld the groaning Keeper Prince and his disheveled friend. He looked in Thera's distraught eyes, assuming the worst.

"*Luvi...*" he questioned, petrified.

"Alive. I put her to sleep. She—her brother is down there. She tried to kill him, Darius. And Khyan stopped her."

Luvenia awoke in a cell. The same cell that had held the beast within the Collector prisoner. She knew two things. She was in Aureland, with no recollection of returning. And she had killed Khyan.

She looked down in terror as she had so many times before—but this time it was there. A grotesque, grey imprint upon the inside of her forearm.

The Bloodguilt.

She vomited violently and her body trembled without ceasing.

How could I have done such a thing?

Veni sat numbly for many hours, contemplating all the ways she could kill herself, deciding it was the only thing that made sense. She discarded her tunic and ripped it to make a noose. She was fitting it around her neck when she heard footsteps. Queen Nuria came around the corner, her eyes red and swollen. She unlocked the cell and ripped the tunic from her hands. Nuria commanded that Veni undress and wear a thin, brown frock. She took the girl's other clothing and left the cell.

Nuria locked it again before she spoke, her voice shaking.

"You defied your general's direct orders. You attempted to take a man's life with *hatred*, not for protection. He was subdued, Luvenia, *defenseless*. Theralin has attested to this.

You, Luvenia Rousseau, took vengeance knowing it was wrong. You have been trained here, fed here, clothed here, and taught the difference between battle for freedom and vengeance. *Months* we spent teaching you the value of human life and the value of choosing what is right over what you *feel*."

Veni had never seen the queen so livid.

Nuria sighed. "My brother is alive, Luvenia. As is yours. Thanks to Theralin and Darius. They took Jacob to a healer you all knew in your village and left him there, his injuries were minor. Khyan, however, suffered greatly and is only alive because Theralin and Darius got him to our own healers quickly enough.

This does not, however, ease your punishment. You have been imprisoned here to await sentencing." Without another word, the Queen of Aureland turned, tears in her eyes, and strode away, instructing a guard to not let the prisoner harm herself.

Veni shook uncontrollably in numb shock, utterly sickened by what she'd done. The fact that Khyan still lived—though she was eternally grateful for it—eased none of her shame.

She knew not how much time passed, but no one else visited her.

Chapter Twenty-Five

Days later, two Aureland Hordemen led Luvenia—blindfolded and hands bound behind her back—to her sentencing. She'd ridden in a prison cart for most of the day, horribly ill and numb, and she had vomited bile several times. She deserved whatever punishment they issued.

She felt sand beneath her bare feet—they had taken her boots when she tried to beat herself with them—and she heard waves crashing. She stood on the shore of Viridian Bay. The pain of what she'd done sliced somehow deeper with this fact. She would be sentenced by her greatest friends, in her most beloved place aside from her tree. The tree she would never see again. She wondered for the thousandth time how she could have managed to cause her greatest fear to come to fruition. The loss of everyone she held dear destroyed her own hand.

One of the Hordemen placed her where she was to stand and removed her blindfold. The sun had set, but she blinked against the bright light of an enormous fire in front of her. She wondered numbly if they were going to burn her.

They should.

It was then that she noticed their faces. All around the fire—encircled around *her*—stood everyone in Aureland that she loved. Every last one. The somber faces they wore shattered what was left of her broken heart. She couldn't believe they would all be there to witness her demise. She then noticed with great terror what each of them held in their hands.

Stones. They're going to stone me.

Trembling, it took all of her waning strength to remain standing. The other Hordemen untied her hands—to her great surprise—as Khyan stepped forward, fully alive and well, stone in hand. Sparks danced around his hair, the same color as the flames. She'd never seen his face look as it did in that moment, riddled with despair, almost as if she were already dead. She supposed that to him, she already was. These white souls had no room for the murderous heart of a blackened one.

Khyan did not lift his stone. He merely held it at his side and looked at her. She stared at him with dread and confusion until he finally spoke. "Luvenia Jane Rousseau. *Remember who you are.*" Tears welled in his eyes, spilling down his cheeks. "Remember your heart. The heart that beats for others. The heart that loves with an unmatched ferocity."

Tears flowed from Luvenia's own eyes as she listened, not understanding why he would say such things.

His voice faltered but he continued. "Remember giving up everything for Ester. Remember everything you've done to rescue her. Remember comforting your weeping mother when you were a mere child. Remember how hard you've worked to become the woman you are. Not the one you *think* you are, but the real you. The lover of humanity. The warrior. Remember your worth, my kind and utterly irreplaceable friend. *Remember who you are.*"

Khyan walked forward with his stone. Luvenia flinched, but he simply set the stone next to her feet and returned to his place in the circle, wiping his tears.

Thera stepped forward with her stone, her beautiful face darkened with anguish. "Luvenia Jane Rousseau. *Remember who you are.*" Her bottom lip wobbled at the sight of Veni's face twisted in a mask of confusion and shame. "Remember defeating obstacles you never thought you could. Remember the joy you bring every time you smile." Thera's tears began to flow freely. "Remember fighting for what is right. Remember rescuing my *life*. Remember your purpose. Remember the hope that lives within you. *Remember who you are*."

Thera set her stone next to Khyan's and returned to her place as Darius came forward with his stone, face already soaked with tears, his cheeks gaunt as if he hadn't eaten or slept in days. Luvenia looked in his tortured eyes and wept uncontrollably

"What is this?" she choked out through a sob. Darius came closer, staring deep into her eyes as the sparks of the raging fire continued to dance in the night air.

"Luvenia Jane Rousseau. *Remember who you are*." He could barely speak. The words came out in choked whispers, but she understood. "Remember you have *my heart*," he croaked. With those words, Veni hit her knees in the sand and wept bitterly, but he continued. "Remember you taught me to love again. *You hold my heart in your very hands*. Remember I love you, heart and soul. Remember I am by your side in brokenness and in wholeness. Remember your soul is *not* black, Luvi, regardless of what you think. Remember you are my Little Bird. *Remember who you are.*"

Darius set his stone next to Thera's and returned to his place in the circle, Veni still on her knees in the sand.

Smithwick stepped forward, hardly visible. He reminded her of how tenderly she cared for the animals. How lovingly she cared for Darius and her sister. How free she felt when she swam in the bay. He told her she did not hate her brother. He told her several times that she did not hate him, until Veni finally understood the truth in it. He placed his tiny stone next to Darius' and made his way back to the circle.

The woman she'd clothed in the woods all those months ago stepped forward to remind her how selfless she'd been. How she had given the clothing off her very back, not caring about shame or danger, to aid someone in need. She, too, placed her stone among the others.

Sebastian, Felix, Lydigen, Rovak, Sillow, Corbin, Imogene, Helga, Chester… They had all come. For her. Not to stone her, but to *restore* her. One by one, every last person in the circle stepped forward to remind her who she was and place their stone by her feet.

Finally, Nurianta Romaniloff Karra—Keeper, Queen of Aureland—approached and knelt before her protégé, her prisoner, her friend.

"Luvenia Jane Rousseau." The drums from that day in the garden began pounding within Veni again as her queen spoke. "You are *light*. You are not darkness. Both war within you, as they do for us all. It is time to choose between them. You are remorseful regarding your actions?" the queen asked fiercely. Veni nodded, tears continuing to fall into the sand. Nuria spoke on, "You chose to be made a weapon, though you must now choose to be a weapon for *good*, not evil." Nuria held out a hand, gesturing around the circle. "In front of all these witnesses, do you wish to declare yourself as such?"

Luvenia's heart surged. Her memory flashed with the image of her father in her dreams.

Keep coming.

She felt him call to her. It was he who beckoned to her now, not the queen, not her friends, not even Darius. He'd been showing her something. The source of all good. All power. The source of *freedom*. Accepting one's own darkness and reconciling oneself to be light.

"I do..." she choked out, sobbing.

There was a beat of tortuous silence.

Nuria smiled with utter joy. "Very well." Veni was confused by the sudden change in emotion, but Nuria explained. "You are *forgiven*. Though your actions still warrant consequences. You will wake early to be at the training mercy of Prince Khyan. You will meet with me for counsel every day after lunch. You will be on kitchen duty until further notice. And you are *not* to enter Orford alone. Thus concludes your sentencing. You are free to go."

Everyone in the circle shouted, loud enough to shake the mountains, and rushed toward her.

Forgiven.

They all danced and sang until the wee hours of the morning. Luvenia did not join in. Not until Khyan found her amidst the revelry and whispered in her ear that he still believed in her. That he knew she hated what she'd done and that she needed to forgive herself. He showed her that each stone around the fire had a word carved into it, chosen by the person who placed it there, to describe Luvenia. He told her the stones would remain where they were until they became dust and sand—a continual reminder to her of who she is.

Brave. Kind. Selfless. New. Precious. Friend. Loved. Wise. Protector. Warrior. Forgiven. The list went on and on.

Veni turned to Khyan to beg his forgiveness, but he merely held up a hand to silence her. “You’ve had my forgiveness all along.”

“Thank you. For saving my brother,” she managed past the lump in her throat.

Khyan took in her face—this girl he’d watched grow up and protected in every way he possibly could for so long. “I didn’t do it for him, Veni.” The prince shoved his hands in his pockets and strode away.

The weeks following her sentencing—Remembrance Ceremony, Nuria had called it—were some of the most difficult of Luvenia's life.

She had been forgiven by the people of Aureland for her greatest failure, yet she still had to learn how to live with herself. Not only that, to her, the punishments were far worse than being imprisoned in solitude to torture herself. She had to *face* herself.

Every morning, she was required to train with Khyan—who was, in fact, merciless. He reminded her endlessly that he believed in her, but that a warrior must be punished for defiance, and she was to be no exception. Most days she could barely walk after he was through with her. Her body became immensely stronger, though, and somehow it made her heart stronger, too.

The Bloodguilt remained upon her arm, despite Khyan's recovery. The prince explained that it would continue to fade from grey to hardly visible, but it would indeed be with her until her demise.

She met with Nuria every day, no longer over carefree lunches, but in her study for long, extremely raw conversations. The queen dug bitter roots up and out of the girl. Ones that Luvenia never knew were there. Self-destruction, depression, fear, horrific thought patterns, trauma she had never dealt with... The process ripped Luvenia apart, but it knit her back together, as well.

Darius met her at her tree every afternoon for tea. He simply loved her. He loved her in her mess. He loved her in her brokenness. He loved her as she grew. He loved her when she succeeded. He loved her when she failed. He listened to her and cheered her on. He taught her to paint and made her laugh. He even snuck in every night during her kitchen cleaning duty and helped her. Sometimes Thera would come too.

Thera also came into her rooms most nights when the castle had gone to sleep, just to keep her company. She told her of her wild adventures as a nomad and of her own many failures. She reminded her that she was not alone and that they had all failed. Her beautiful friend would drag a chair into her bedroom and sing until Veni finally fell asleep. The princess spent countless nights with an armchair as her bed. She always sang her the same song, peace flooding the room. Peace that did not come from Thera's gift.

Love sings louder than my failures,
It sings of mercy raging wild.
Love sings louder than my failures,
It sings of freedom like a child.
Love is my redemption song,
The sweetest refrain upon my lips.
Love is my redemption song,
All else stands eclipsed.
Love sings louder than my failures,
No longer mine alone to hold.
Love sings louder than my failures,
A hope, an anchor for my soul.

Each time the song was sung, Veni dreamt of her father's whispers upon mists of purest white and the peaceful hymns of redbirds.

Keep coming… Keep coming...

Together, her chosen family waged war against Luvenia's walls. They tore them down stone by stone. And in their place, they built her battlements of precious rubies. They themselves locked within, forever by her side.

Though Aureland remained peaceful, much had taken place in Orford and Anjali since the rescue of Thera. For a time, they all successfully kept Veni out of it, but after weeks of improvement, Darius—acting only as her general, according to him—informed his queen and prince that she should be deemed fit to return to the front lines with the rest of them. They needed her. Nuria had agreed, allowing Veni into their next council meeting.

"Anjali has almost fallen," Queen Nuria announced severely. Khyan put a comforting arm around Thera, who closed her eyes against the news. "Emperor Nakamura has refused aid and sanctuary until now," Nuria continued. "General, assemble the Hordemen and remaining relief factions. They shall leave Aureland at dawn. Rovak will lead them in. You shall receive the emperor at the Gate and accompany him to our castle, handing him off to Linden. He does not know what we are, and this could potentially be a horrendous mistake, but it is important that Akio Nakamura survive in order to rebuild his empire."

Darius nodded and Nuria addressed the room as a whole once more. "Orford appears to the public to be unchanged, with no move yet on the part of the Zealots or the Liberator's Rebels. However, Pietro has administered the weaponized fear toxin into a large band of higher-ranking Collectors. We are not certain how, but she has increased the production substantially, and we fear she shall administer it to all Collectors within a short while. We are also uncertain if the Collectors can split into savage beasts, as did the one beneath our castle last winter, or not, unless they are in Aureland.

Regardless..." She held up a graceful hand and continued with vigor. "Do *not* panic when I say what I am about to tell you." A hush permeated the room as if every one of them had ceased drawing breath. "The man Thera and Luvenia disabled in the forest last autumn has finally broken."

Most of them had forgotten about the man. Little did they know, Darius and his men had been pulling information out of the filthy mongrel for months.

"Pietro gave him a Portal Key. She knows how to come within our borders." They all sucked in a collective breath, looking petrified. "Do *not* panic!" the queen roared. "I will not have my court and my kingdom fall after all we have been through. *Forget not who you are.* We are the warriors of light, the mighty Aureland Horde. And we will stop that wretched villain if it is the last thing I do. You have my word."

Each person in her council chamber sat a little straighter. "Until they break through our Gates, we fight as if they are unable to do so and prepare as if they already have. Am I clear?" This was met with nods and murmurs of agreement. "Very well. Our second order of business… Pietro has revealed her hand at last concerning the shipments of children." Veni could hardly breathe in anticipation. "She knows Sebastian is my informant and has decided to lead us into a trap. She believes the Liberator is one of us in this room." That was certainly not what they were expecting. "We shall be entering into this trap, for we *will* intercept that shipment.

Darius, Sebastian, Khyan, Thera, Veni and myself..." She held up a hand to silence Darius, who had opened his mouth to undoubtedly object. "We shall lead a small troop of Hordemen into Orford. Pietro claims the shipment is leaving Morrec at sunrise three days from now, for a two-day trek through the Arichan Mountains to board a ship set sail for another continent." She paused, bleak. "I do not know what we shall face. I do not claim to believe it will be easy, or that all of us shall make it home. But those innocent lives will."

Chapter Twenty-Six

The band of warriors had led their small, divided troops deep into the Orford woodlands, skirting Morrec, two days prior. The Aureland Hordemen awaited orders at their camp—hidden in the mountain caves—while Queen Nuria and Prince Khyan soared high above, merely two unsuspecting owls. The four others slunk through the trees near Morrec, following the Orford Warmonger travel party into the mountains.

Hundreds of children were packed into prison carts. Most of them were utterly broken. Others continued to find it within themselves to wail. Veni couldn't help but hope that Ester was among them, yet also desperately hope that she was not.

Upon locating the precious cargo, Veni and Thera had been instantly reduced to tears, Darius had gone rigid with fury, and Sebastian… Sebastian had become deathly still and tortured—most likely remembering things of unimaginable horror. It occurred to Luvenia in that moment that Sebastian's eyes looked very much like those of the Anjalian people and that possibly the poor soul had also been transported in such a manner as a small child.

They all swallowed the bile that threatened to rise, and ran on alongside the carts, hidden in the trees. They were to meet the troops when the shipment made it to the Lamort Valley. Half of the Hordemen would enter from the north, near their camp, and half would enter from the south, effectively blocking Pietro's men in the valley with no way out. As they were approaching an area not far from the valley, Veni glanced up to see Khyan veer off from Nuria and head back toward their camp. Something was wrong. The strong sense of dread she'd begun to understand as warning flooded her and she signaled the others to stop.

"Something is wrong. Khy just flew off back toward the camp," she whispered.

Darius glanced up to see Nuria between the trees, still heading for the south side of the valley. He knew her senses were typically dead on, but they'd come too far to halt. "We keep moving. Nuria hasn't stopped."

They continued for a long while, the dread in Veni's stomach thickening with each passing step. They had learned along the way that the traveling party would be stopping at another abandoned fortress, where hundreds more children were being kept. There had been no time to alert the troops, or even Nuria above them. Therefore, they would have to worry about the fortress children after the current battle was all over. Nearing the valley, Darius signaled silently toward the direction of their troop. Once the shipment made it all the way past them, the six warriors would enter the valley and disable the drivers and guards, rescuing the children, while the troops at the north and south fought off the Warmongers and Collectors stationed there in the mountains.

They had hoped Pietro would not surround the shipment with troops, though they all knew she planned to trap them, and there was no guarantee she would not use massive amounts of force or some other means of disabling them. As they waited, huddled behind a large boulder, Nuria swooped down to perch atop it. Darius whispered the plan one final time. He also informed them of the other half of the shipment and added that as soon as they had succeeded—because they would—they must head to the fortress.

Nuria shifted long enough to kiss them all and transformed once more. She soared high above the valley, ready to give the signal. As the last cart rattled into the valley, Nuria let out two short hoots. It was time to advance.

The four of them sprinted toward the carts, their troop already waging war outside the valley. Metal scraped as swords crashed, arrows whistled as they shot through the sky, and hundreds of children screamed in terror. Just as they reached the mouth of the Lamort Valley, a piercing screech sounded overhead. Still running, cutting down anyone in their way, they looked up to see Khyan coming in fast for a landing. He shifted midair and landed next to Darius in a crashing heap, an arrow protruding from his chest.

"They found our camp," he groaned, clutching the arrow as Darius knelt beside him. "The north side has been at battle with a troop thrice our size since just after dawn. There is commotion at a nearby fortress as well." He winced, having to shout over the battle noise.

Darius waved Sebastian and Thera on toward the carts. "Get those carts to safety!" he roared and they reluctantly obeyed.

Darius and Veni quickly pulled Khyan into an alcove within the mountain. Darius reached for his coat, but Veni stopped him. He needed to remain protected from the Venom—she did not. She discarded hers and placed it on the fallen prince. Darius held him upright. "Stay with me, Khy. The rest of the shipment is there at the fortress you saw, we heard talk of it among the Warmongers. What sort of commotion?"

"A battle. I don't know. I couldn't tell who was who. Collector on Collector and Warmonger on Warmonger." He winced, clutching his chest. "Some were servants... It looked like a revolt," he explained, beginning to fall in and out of consciousness.

"Khy, stay with me!" Darius commanded, shaking the Keeper's head gently. "You can't sleep, Khy, stay awake." Veni hovered over them, panicked. "Khy!" Darius shouted again.

The Keeper Prince ceased responding.

Veni knelt down close to his ear and spoke gently, "Khy… you can't sleep now. Wake up. I *need* you to wake up." He began to stir at the sound of her voice, his eyes opening ever so slightly.

"Luvi, stay with him. I've got to find Healer Collins *now*, or he's not going to make it." With that, the general took up Nahaliel and began fighting his way toward the Hordeman healer.

Veni took her injured friend's bloody hand. "Khy…wake up. Don't you leave me here without you. *Wake up*." Tears and fear were building rapidly, but he stirred once more, giving her hope. "That's it. Wake up, Khy." A thought struck her. "Tell me about Mai."

"Mai?" He groaned, waking up further. "Is she here? Oh, I miss her." He smiled, but he was beginning to tremble. "Beautiful Mai…"

Darius rushed back into the alcove with Collins on his heels. Collins knelt before the prince and gave Veni a reassuring nod. He placed one hand on his chest, and the other on the arrow.

"This is going to hurt, Prince." He yanked the arrow out and Khyan howled in pain, arching his back. Collins placed his hand over the raw wound. Veni watched in bewildered astonishment as muscle and tissue knit itself back together, war still raging behind them.

"Good as new…again," Collins told the prince, who promptly fell asleep. He turned to Darius and Veni. "His body will still require sleep. He can't stay here, General."

"Get him to safety. Whatever you have to do," Darius ordered the healer before waking Khyan up one last time.

"Khy, Collins is going to get you to safety. You have to rest." The delirious prince tried to rise, and Darius pushed him back down. "No. *Rest*. Stay with Collins. Luvi and I will go to the other fortress."

The two men clasped arms before Khyan pointed them in the right direction and slumped back over. Collins hoisted the prince up and dragged him further into the mountains.

Battle raging, Darius and Veni fought their way through, slicing and disabling. At any possible opportunity, they used Venom packs on the opposing force and helped any Aureland Hordemen they could. Blood and Venom covered them all. Thankfully, the Hordemen had prepared for such a case and remained completely covered, allowing no Venom to penetrate their uniforms. Veni had left her coat with Khyan, though she remained well enough covered and the Venom that did find her skin left less and less effect on her.

Slowly, they made their way through the gore and broken bodies to a trail leading deeper into the mountains. They ran as fast as their legs would carry them up the winding trail.

"How did you get Khyan to stay awake?" Darius huffed as they ran.

"I had him tell me about Mai."

"How did you know that would work?"

"Something my father said once. He told me a dying man needs hope and if he can look upon something beautiful, he will regain hope. She was what I thought he would find most beautiful."

Before making it to the mouth of another valley, they were halted by the sounds of petrified screaming coming from the battleground they'd left behind. They scrambled up the rocks for a better view, only to find the waging of war had given way to nightmare and sheer terror. Roiling black fog seeped into the air as several Collectors ripped open—suit and skin—to reveal the horrifying beasts within. The beasts tore through the panic-stricken Hordemen with little effort. There were only a few carts of children left. The others' mission was succeeding.

But the Hordemen…

"*Maker...*" Darius breathed, watching as his men were torn to bits and still others bellowed in terror as they beheld phantoms of their greatest fears within their minds. "We have to keep going. They'll come here next. We have to get to the children."

Sprinting on, loathing the choice they'd had to make, they finally reached the abandoned fortress—much different than the one where Thera had been imprisoned. This fortress was built into the side of a mountain, much like the Orford Castle, and overlooked a beautiful valley meadow, alive with blooming flowers. The sight was so utterly wrong in the current circumstances. Their friends were being shredded to ribbons behind them, children were imprisoned before them, and bloodied bodies lay sprawled out in the flowers. Khyan had been right. All the bodies in the meadow were dressed as Collectors, Orford Warmongers, or Orford servants. Aside from the very distant sound of crashing waves, the scene was eerily silent and twisted.

Quietly, Darius and Luvenia made their way past the bodies and into the open door of the mountain fortress. They were met with continued silence as they slunk through the halls, until Veni heard a small commotion coming from above as they passed a set of stairs. Pausing to listen before rushing up, they heard the cry of a child. Without thinking, they both launched themselves up the stairs as quickly as possible, jumping over the deceased. The stairs continued up, and the sound continued to come from above. Higher they climbed, never seeming to come closer to the cries.

As they ascended the final steps to the top floor of the fortress, they slowed their pace realizing the halls were empty and the noise had vanished, leaving the building again eerily silent. A servant woman—a nursemaid—lay broken and contorted on the floor, but alive. Checking both directions,

Luvenia took valuable seconds to bend down and reassure the dying woman.

"Hold on, it's going to be okay," she whispered, squeezing her gory hand, unsure if she were telling her the truth. "Help is coming. Just hold on. Where are the children?"

"They're…gone..." she choked out. Veni's heart sank to her toes. She made to stand, but the woman reached for her arm with unexpected strength. She was smiling. Luvenia met her eyes, with both empathy and disgust.

How can she smile at this?

The nursemaid gasped out, "Help has already come. He saved them all."

"Who? Who saved them all?" Darius asked, rushing forward.

Breathing her last, she whispered, "The Liberator. He came for us." With that, she closed her eyes and gave up the ghost. The two warrior lovers looked at each other in disbelief and shock.

Darius checked her pulse just to be certain and shook his head. "Ravings of a dying woman?" he asked as he stood, too afraid to hope.

"What if she's right? Something is clearly awry. A battle among Pietro's men? Maybe that's why we couldn't find the opposition. They were among her men, successfully infiltrated like we'd hoped. But I thought that noise was coming from up here..." she trailed off, following the grim hallway as silent as shadow.

Most of the candles had blown out amidst servants, guards, Collectors, and Orford Warmongers running past. Blood streaked the walls and the ground remained cluttered with more bodies and Venom. Every step felt more and more like a nightmare, but the knowing dread she'd come to rely on as her signal for something horrid was distinctly absent. Veni reached massive wooden doors of what appears to be an old, unused council chamber. One door stood slightly ajar, enough for Luvenia to peer inside as Darius stood protectively at her hip keeping a lookout.

The scent of death sank into her senses for the first time as she slowed. She reminded herself this was reality.

Blood and gore everywhere. She reminded herself it had all been done to protect the innocent. *Utter silence*. She reminded herself she could do this afraid. *Not even a whisper of sound. No sign of life.*

But she could sense it.

She turned her back to the door and raised her sword to the ready, giving Darius a curt nod to alert him they were going in. Slowly, Veni opened the door enough for them to slip in silently.

A lone man stood in the far corner, his back foolishly to the passageway out. He had one hand folded behind him as he peered out of a window carved into the rocks toward the grotesque valley below—littered with bodies.

Luvenia froze.

Her sword clattered to the cracked marble floor—the sound deafening in the silent hall. The man did not so much as flinch. A single tear threatened to spill over onto his cheek. Darius remained poised for battle, Nahaliel at the ready, but something was very, very wrong. Why had she dropped her weapon? Ready to leap in front of her, he was halted by the look of trepidation upon her features.

The man shifted his feet and turned to face the two intruders, the lone tear leaving a clean line down his bloody, dirty face. Luvenia trembled, sucking in half a breath, and put a shaking hand to her throat as she uttered one cracked, petrified word.

"Father?"

The man smiled painfully and held out a bloody rose, dry and crumbling. "Hello, Love." He turned to Darius like an old friend and nodded. “Lionheart.”

Luvenia sank to her knees and her general choked back a

sob.

Part Three

Late Autumn

Genevieve stood alone in her candlelit room, brushing her long chestnut hair, when a voice whispered tenderly from just inside the window behind her.

"Hey..."

She closed her eyes and savored the peace and familiarity of that voice before turning around. "Hey yourself," she whispered back as she faced him.

The old chiffon curtains fluttered in the chilly midnight breeze as she smirked at him. He bound, silent as a phantom, across the room and crushed her mouth with his. He held her face fervently between his hands as he kissed her, trying to commit to memory the taste of his wife. He picked her up and took her to their bed for what they both knew would be the last time.

Genevieve lay on Henry's chest, wrapped in the tangled bed sheets. He ran a gentle finger up and down her bare arm and breathed in the scent of her, his cheek pressed against her hair. He inhaled deeply the aroma of roses and clean soap. Nothing in all the world could smell as pure to him as the woman in his arms.

"She has the amulet?" he whispered and kissed the top of her head.

"Yes. I sewed it into the lining of her riding jacket after she went to bed." The cadence of her voice was softer than usual.

"Are you afraid?"

Genevieve's eyes were closed, but she was far from drowsy. They both knew what she would face the following morning.

"No. I'm not."

Henry let out a shuddering breath against his wife's hair. "I'm terrified." Genevieve sat up on one elbow, looking in Henry's grey eyes with concern. "I've loved you for thirty-two years, Gen," he explained. "I don't know how to do this without you."

She sat up fully and took her husband's face in her hands. "Henry, it's only for a short while and we'll be together again. This must be done. For our children. For humanity."

Henry reached up to take one of her cold hands. He kissed her palm and got up to close the open window, the autumn night chilly. "Luvenia won't understand," he breathed as he sat down on the side of the bed, his head bowed.

Genevieve crawled across the bed to wrap her arms around him and lay her head on his shoulder. "Not right away. But she will. Sometimes something must die to bring new life, remember?"

"But does it have to be you?" Henry couldn't stop the emotion from sounding in his voice.

"Yes, my love. It does."

Chapter Twenty-Seven

The wisp of a girl twitched.

She didn't even bother opening her eyes as the bug men came in. As they thrust needles into her ripped arms—again. As the healer came in to revive her after foam leaked from her mouth and death whispered warm pleasantries. As the witch came in to survey her prey and tell her she was a good little girl.

That was how she'd remembered what she was—a girl.

Her insides burned. Her arms itched and stung. Her stomach roiled. Her mind sat vacant.

A girl.

A good little girl.

The beautiful witch meant something by those words.

A girl.

A good little girl.

She couldn't remember what good could be, but she thought it had something to do with the voice she heard, always murmuring the same thing.

Sunshine.

Henry Rousseau walked along a rushing river in the Amethyst Woodlands of Aureland next to his little girl. His little girl he'd not been able to talk with since she was seven years old. His little girl who was now a woman.

The battle against Pietro's men in the Lamort Valley had ended two days prior in a venomous, bloody mess. The fear toxin released by the Collector beasts hung in the air long enough to result in a devastating loss of Aureland Hordemen.

Queen Nuria had managed to soar above the cloud of fear toxin and remain unscathed. As an opening presented itself, she swooped down and lit the beasts with her Keeper gift of fire magic. As the shrieks of burning Collector beasts grew, the terror-filled screams of her Hordemen fell silent. Panic subsided.

Queen Nuria—along with the other Keepers in the Horde—had no option but to wield their powers instead of weapons in order to defeat the Queen of Orford's men and save the rest of the Hordemen. Prince Khyan had refused to return to Aureland once the shrieking of his people ensued. Despite his injuries, the prince rained down ice while Nuria shot forth infernos. Other Keepers in the Horde cloaked the injured from the Orford Warmongers' vision, shape-shifted into ferocious creatures of their own to rip apart the enemy, grew to giant size, created sandstorms, brought swarms of insects, and many other wonders that confounded and eventually defeated the Orford force.

In the midst of the chaos, Thera and Sebastian successfully made haste with the prison carts full of children just before the Collectors split open, though Orford Warmongers had set fire to the last cart out of the valley. Thera sent them fleeing with her gift and managed to pull most of the children out with little damage, though she herself and a few of the children sustained severe burns and remained under the care of the Hordemen Healer, Collins, in the Aureland castle.

While Luvenia's closest friends battled for their lives and the lives of the innocent, she found herself face to face with the leader of a Rebel force, dubbed the Liberator, who happened to also be the father she'd believed to be dead for the last ten years. Khyan had brought her father through the portal into Aureland where she now faced him again, battle over and safety present for the time being.

"The children you rescued from the fortress," Veni finally spoke. "Are they alright?"

Henry nodded. "My men took them deep into the mountains."

A plethora of emotions still raged through her, even days later, and Veni couldn't hold it off any longer. "I simply don't understand all of this," she told him.

They'd discussed that he was indeed the Liberator and also the Zealot that Darius met in the market years earlier. They'd caught up briefly in between meetings with the Queen of Aureland. But they had not yet approached the difficult subjects. Luvenia kept him firmly at arm's length, and for good reason.

Henry Rousseau's heart had never been so shattered, and he'd never missed his wife so fiercely as he did in that moment, looking in his daughter's pained eyes. Veni ceased walking and discarded her boots. She sat along the edge of the river and let her feet dangle into the cool water. Spring in Orford was in full swing and the Amethyst Woodlands—already stunning in autumn and winter—had come out to play in the warm sunshine.

She sighed and Henry sat next to her. "Why couldn't someone else do it? Lead the Rebels. Why did it have to be you?"

Henry ran a thumb gently across Veni's cheek as he held her chin for a moment, grateful she didn't flinch away. "There was no one else to do this, Love."

Every time he said his loving name for her she thought her heart might burst. Just the sound of his voice outside of her dreams and nightmares made her feel that way, but she wasn't ready to trust this person. She didn't even know him. Not really.

"How did you get the rose?" she asked him, torn by despair at what she'd missed of him and painfully thankful he was there now. "You were there in the forest, weren't you? When I dropped it the day Mother was killed?" She looked at him sitting next to her and he nodded.

"I was. I trailed you that entire day, up until when you went through the portal into Aureland—where I knew you'd be safe."

Veni closed her eyes and took a deep breath to calm the growing fury building within her chest. "You watched my mother…your *wife* die? And you watched them take Ester? You watched Jacob betray us all? And you did *nothing*?"

"Yes." Henry found excuses to be lacking honor and he would not lower himself to that level. If she hated him for what happened, she had every right to.

Luvenia failed to stifle the sob that bubbled up out of her. All the images of her chivalrous father were melting away, though she knew deep down that they shouldn't. A thought that made her even angrier. "I have to go. Thera and I are taking the children to the inn."

"Right." They both stood. "I forgot that was today. I'm relieved they're ready to be moved." He ran his hands down the sides of his trousers. "Please consider my proposal on your journey."

Veni nodded once and left her father standing alone in the forest.

Queen Lilith Pietro stood before her gold filigree looking glass, preparing to paint her face with cosmetics. The Queen of Orford steeled herself to look at the reflection she would find staring back at her.

She lined up her brushes—each a glimmering onyx and

pixie hair work of art—for the fifth time.

She would not flinch. She would not shy away from the woman in the mirror.

Her eyes lifted so far as to view the bodice of her gown—its crow feather lines accentuating her curves and offering enviable décolletage—before she looked back to her brushes and reached to fuss with them once more.

"*Coward*," the looking glass whispered. "Paint your face up something elegant. Cover the rot. Perhaps they'll truly never know. Go on, then," the mirror mocked.

Pietro's lip curled and she snapped a brush in her hands, lifting her gaze to meet her eyes' reflection.

The decay had worsened.

Almost the entirety of her left profile was consumed by decomposed, charred flesh. She reached up to gingerly touch her cheek, only to find flecks of alabaster skin coming away onto her fingertips.

She inhaled a deep, shaky breath, and dipped one of her brushes into the paint.

"Do you think she'll choose to come with me?" Henry Rousseau spoke from the doorway of Queen Nuria's study.

Henry did not sit. He strode to the window overlooking the blooming gardens. He'd faked his own death ten years prior. How could he ever expect his daughter to forgive that? That wasn't exactly the truth, though, either. Things had gotten too risky in Alban. King Alestair had died—presumably by the hand of his adopted daughter, Lilith—and Henry's small band of Rebels against the new queen had caught her attention. When Schrute met him halfway to Alban that night and said their comrade's family had been killed—their newborn daughter taken—he knew he couldn't go home.

Because of that choice, his wife was dead, his son mentally

fractured, his daughter contemptuous, and the little girl who began it all was imprisoned. All because of him.

"It was," he breathed, his breath fogging the glass.

The gleam of Nuria's gown caught the sunlight, sending stars dancing across the window as she came to stand next to Veni's father. "I know all too well the tortured leader's soul, blackened by the decisions we have had to make." She squeezed his hand briefly. "Fret not, my old friend, Luvenia is a strong one."

Henry squeezed her hand in return and nodded, gaze still locked on the gardens below.

"Give her a while longer to process all that has happened. I think once she has, she will be inclined to take on this journey with you."

"I have to leave in a weeks' time at the latest. I cannot wait much longer." He turned to face Nuria. "But I have another reason for barging in on you—"

Together they turned toward the sound of footsteps. Khyan made it to them in three strides of his long legs, his fiery hair uncharacteristically untamed.

"Am I interrupting?" the prince inquired, his jaw flexing as he looked at Henry.

"Not at all," Henry answered for them both. "I was just beginning to request that your presence be allowed on my quest, along with Veni, should she choose to come. I'm under the impression you know the way quite well."

Khyan eyed his sister. "I've not been briefed on the details of your journey." He pinned Henry with a stare before biting out, "But if Veni chooses to accompany you, I will as well. Otherwise, you're on your own."

"*Khyan*," Nuria censured.

Henry met Khyan's challenging stare. "I believe the choice is that of your queen's, *Prince*."

Khyan snarled, but Nuria silenced him. "Henry is a guest in our castle, and you will not instigate a quarrel over matters you know little about, Brother."

"He's a liar and a fraud, Nuria," Khyan shot back.

The queen opened her mouth but the Liberator advanced to stand toe-to-toe with the prince, peering into Khyan's soul until he made him squirm. "I do not fear being misunderstood by you, Prince. Think of me what you wish, it matters not to me. But the safety of my daughter does. I know you don't care for me right now, but I know you *do* care for Veni. I also know you're her best shot of making it out of Marche de Blanc unscathed."

Though surprised, Khyan did not back down, he only grew more livid. "*Marche de Blanc*?" He chuckled, low and humorless. "Not only did you deceive her for ten years, but you mean to take your *daughter* into the White Market? The underbelly, *the vilest corner*, of the Underground?"

Henry inched closer with a touch of a smirk. "Was her training under your tutelage insufficient, then?"

The prince ground his teeth, his hands balled into icy fists, but the Liberator stepped back and addressed Queen Nuria, "I'll be taking my leave about now." He bowed his head to the queen and prince and strode out with his hand on the pommel of his sword.

Nuria waited a beat before turning to her brother, stirring her tea idly.

"*Old friend?*" Khyan whirled on her once the Liberator vanished. "You knew him prior to all of this? Did you know he was alive and well this entire time and you let Luvenia think otherwise?"

"First of all, *Brother*, you will not intrude upon my private meetings. *Or* listen in."

Khyan rolled his eyes. "The door was open, Nuria."

The queen held up a finger. "Silence. Second, you will not accuse me of things you know nothing of. What I wish to keep private is none of your concern. And *third...*" Nuria smoothed her dress. "No. I dreamed—I dare say I *hoped*—he was still alive, but no, I did not *know*. It wasn't until Sebastian brought word of the Liberator and his Rebels that I truly entertained the possibility. It sounded like Henry, but the likelihood was slim."

"You know him well, then? Why have you never told me this?" Khyan's heart panged at the truth that his sister had hidden such a thing from him.

Nuria took a seat and fluffed her gown. "Again, I had no reason to truly believe past hope that Henry Rousseau and the Liberator were one and the same, or I would have told you. You never questioned why I sent you to keep watch over the Rousseau farm, and I never felt inclined to give a reason. Nor do I particularly feel inclined to do so now."

The prince poured a cup of tea and bit into a biscuit as he sat. "Frankly, I assumed my watch of the farm was due to its escape from Pietro's eye. We still don't know why that was the case until Jacob gave them up."

Nuria took a teacup her brother offered her and sipped, thinking. "No, that is still a mystery. Precisely why I need you to cease this loathing for Henry. We have much to discuss, the three of us, without the two of you having a battle of wills."

"I don't trust him, Nuria. No matter how long you've known him or what importance he held to you. You're truly going to just let him take Veni into the White Market?"

Nuria smirked. "She is her own woman, Khy, and you may not trust Henry, but I do. Bear in mind that I could have sent any of my men to watch over Henry's estate, but I sent my own brother. That should tell you enough." The Queen of Aureland tapped her nails on the arm of her chair. "However, it *is* Marche de Blanc. A terrifying place indeed. That is why you will, in fact, accompany them."

"If she even chooses to go," Khyan muttered.

Nuria set her teacup on the side table and rose. "Yes, well, that remains to be seen. Now, run along." She shooed him out. "I have things to do."

"Good morning, General."

Darius continued his training regime without pause. "Morning."

Thera scrunched her face and threw a hand to her hip. "You look awful."

Darius glared at her. "Thanks, Thera. How kind of you to notice."

"Oh, don't be so sensitive." She took up a practice sword and gestured for the general to spar with her.

They practiced long enough to be a bit winded before Thera inquired over the clang of steel, "Are you sleeping at all?"

"No." His sword scraped hers. "They just keep coming."

"They?"

Darius threw his sword down and ran a hand through his hair. "The messengers. With more dead accounted for."

"Darius. There was nothing more you could have done." She set her sword against the wall."We got the children out. That was our first priority."

The bench groaned as the general dropped his bulk onto it. "I could have been more prepared."

Thera crossed her arms and sighed. "How? You had absolutely no way of knowing those Collectors would rip open and monsters would wreak havoc against our men."

"I knew it was a possibility. I knew Pietro was capable of it. I should have expected it."

"You're being ridiculous."

Darius frowned. "Ridiculous? I failed my men. I failed my *people*," he ground out. "*Maker's teeth*, Theralin, have some decency."

She rolled her eyes and stalked forward, taking a seat next to him. "I'm not being insensitive, you oaf. You may lead the

Horde, but you're not solely responsible for what happens to them, or Aureland, or Orford."

"That's exactly what being a leader means. If anyone below me fails, *I* have failed. If a Hordeman dies in battle, it's by my hand as much as the enemy's. That's how it works."

"I hate to break it to you, but you're not a deity. You're not even a Keeper. If you'd like to be precise, *Keepers* are the ones meant to do the protecting and leading. So, if it's anyone's fault, it's ours."

"I was still in charge, and I still made the ignorant call that got my men killed."

"You were put in charge by a Keeper," she countered. "You see? Stop being a walking martyr and realize we're all in this together. The failures belong to us all just as much as the successes."

Darius nodded but his jaw remained set as stone.

"What else is bothering you?"

He glanced at his friend. "That's not enough?"

"Oh, that's plenty." Thera clapped him on the back. "But you forget I've known you a very long time. You've seen war and you've led many men on missions that never made it back. This shouldn't have been that different—terrifying beasts aside. So, out with it." She moved her hand impatiently.

The general absentmindedly touched a finger to his self-branded Mark of the Zealots. "Luvi has been behaving strangely since her father asked her to go with him to Maaraveor. I told myself she's grappling with ghosts and facing a difficult choice, but I don't think that's the whole truth of it."

"Perhaps it is, though," Thera considered with a shrug. "The girl has gone through no small amount of tragedy as of late and I'm fairly certain her father essentially rising from the dead after a decade tops the list of strange happenings.

It's a lot to deal with."

"Perhaps you're right. She's asked me to go with her to Dakterra tomorrow. Surely I'll know more then."

Henry made his way through the Aureland castle halls toward his daughter's chambers. He vaguely found himself marveling at the familiarity of such an act, regardless of how long she'd thought him dead and the difference between such a grand castle and the modest cottage he'd last walked through to get to her room so long ago.

Dodging looks of suspicion from some and nodding politely in exchange for others' words of reverence, he finally approached Luvenia's door. It appeared many in the castle didn't know what to make of him any more than his daughter did. Their relationship had been tenuous and strained in the days since she'd found him in the abandoned mountain fortress overlooking the battlefield. He saw the torrent behind her eyes of conflicting emotions every time she looked at him. A child always wishes to believe the best of their parents, he supposed, but that didn't lessen the betrayal or ease her hurt. He knew they had a long road ahead of them. He merely hoped she would agree to begin wandering down it.

Henry tapped on his daughter's door in the rhythm he'd used to let her know it was him when she was a small girl.

Veni grunted by way of greeting as she opened the door and shuffled back to her chair by the fire without an intelligible word. Henry chuckled at her disheveled hair and the bleary-eyed glance of annoyance she shot at him as she sipped from her coffee.

"Did I wake you?"

"No. I haven't been to bed yet, actually. Thera and I just got all the children settled into the inn late last night. Thera had to be back this morning, so we rode through the night. Granger's daughters came with him to help. We thought it best to keep the little ones' associations of a...*human* nature for a while. Aureland is the safest place for them at present, but it's not the easiest to comprehend."

"I suppose you're right about that." Henry stood awkwardly just inside the door.

She eyed him and left pleasantries behind. "I haven't made my decision yet—about accompanying you to Maaraveor."

"That isn't why I came. I wanted to make sure you returned safely."

Veni rose. "Clearly I have, and I'll be on my way back there after breakfast, so if you'll excuse me—"

"Would you like some company? I could join you. I'd like to see the children as well."

Henry knew she wanted to say no, but he appreciated the decency she had to at least pretend to consider it. When she didn't answer, he pressed on, "Those questions burning a hole in you need to be answered whether you travel with me to Maaraveor or not. Simply put, there are some things that need to be out in the open between us." He studied her sullen face and sighed. "It's not half a day's ride, Love. If you regret allowing me to go, I'll ride right back to the castle without objection."

Veni hated that she still trusted him—that his relentless efforts warmed her heart.

"Fine. But I choose what we discuss and when we discuss it."

Henry gave his daughter a slight bow. "Certainly. I would expect no lesser stipulation."

Luvenia led her father to the royal stables. He'd arrived in Aureland after her and had not yet seen Vesper. Despite her simmering fury with him, she was anxious for him to see his old steed alive and well.

The reunion turned out to be tearful and mutual. Vesper

whinnied, stomped, huffed, and nudged Henry for several moments before they calmed him down enough to ride out.

They rode in silence for nearly half the journey before Henry finally spoke. "Are you willing to burst or are you going to ask the question that's boiling within you?"

Veni pursed her lips, twirling the end of her braid. "How could you leave us?" she finally asked after a long moment.

He'd known that would be her first question, in some form, but it still felt like a punch to his gut. Before he could respond, Veni spoke again. "How could you think so little of us to assume we couldn't keep your secret? That we couldn't help you with your purpose? I suppose I understand that Jacob and I were too young to comprehend it all, but Mother? How could you leave her all alone? How could you leave your children without a father?"

Henry sifted through all his daughter had said, trying to identify the question she most needed answered right away, but hadn't asked outright. "Are you asking if I chose my mission over my family?"

"No." She pulled her horse's reins to a stop and looked at her father for the first time since they'd left the stables. "Not *if*. You *did*. And I want to know why. Did you ever stop to consider that your duty was to your own family, not to save the damned world?"

Vesper snorted anxiously at the growing tension.

"Yes." Henry searched her face. "That duty to my family is precisely why I did what I did and precisely why I couldn't let you know I was alive."

Veni gritted her teeth. "That is *not* an answer. I don't want riddles. I want honest answers. I know fighting for the freedom of those children and for the freedom of this land from Pietro's clutches is honorable—of *course* I do—but it came at the cost of your own family."

She ran a hand down her face and lowered her voice. "Your son is a monster now." She watched as her father's eyes turned glassy. "I spent over half my life convinced your death was my fault—I carried the weight of it for *years*." She paused for a heartbeat. "Your wife is *dead*. She spent ten years mourning you and now she's dead. We," she put a hand to her heart, "*we*—your family—are the casualties of your choices. *We* were the very ones you were supposed to protect."

Veni let silence fall, but only briefly. "This was a mistake. I think you should ride back to the castle." She wilted atop her horse and kicked his sides, urging him onward and away from her father—away from the conversation.

But she only made it a few strides away.

"Six days," Henry called out after her, his voice gravelly and thick.

Veni pulled the horse's reins and turned to look at her father. "What?"

"Six days." Henry swallowed the lump in his throat. "That's how long I let your mother mourn me before I couldn't take it anymore and I went to see her."

The words felt like a blow and a relief. "What are you saying?"

Henry slid off his horse and walked to his daughter. He looked up at her upon her horse, tears leaking. "I'm saying I told her everything." He took Veni's hand, and she didn't pull away. "I'm saying I didn't plan for any of this to go the way it has—"

Veni snatched her hand back. "But it did. And what you're telling me is my mother lied to us as well? She let me go on believing your death was my fault, too."

"Absolutely not. Love, everything we decided, everything we've done, has been with you in mind." He shook his head. "I know that doesn't make sense to you right now and they weren't perfect decisions, but it is the truth. We had no inclination you considered yourself responsible for my death. That should have never crossed your mind." The fiery love of a father shone in his eyes. "Ever," he reiterated.

She stared down at him. "I know that my mother loved me—lies or no. But I also think *you* should have known me well enough to realize I would blame myself. You both should have known me well enough to realize I wouldn't just receive you with open arms and view your betrayal as a blessed resurrection. You left me here," she gestured around them, "in this horrible world—alone. Then you try to tell me it was all out of love for me?" She shook her head. "I can't just accept that. No matter how much I do believe you mean it."

"Love, there is so much you don't yet understand—"

"Then explain it to me!" Birds rushed from the trees, startled to flight by her outburst.

"That's exactly what I intend to do." He took her hand once more. She glowered at him but did not pull away. "Come with me," he implored. "The journey to Maaraveor will have many trials for you and me, but we'll face them together this time and we'll mend our broken places."

Veni opened her mouth to respond, but Henry spoke first. "For now, I will return to the castle. I know you prefer solitude in order to think. I will await your return." He gave her hand three gentle squeezes and returned to his horse, leaving only dust and much to consider in his wake.

Chapter Twenty-Eight

"This isn't exactly what I envisioned when you said you'd planned for us to get away for a while." Darius stoked the fire outside their simple canvas tent and sent Luvenia a wry smile.

She looked up from her book, slowly processing what he'd said as the words from her page flitted away. She shrugged. "We each have a quaint cabin to run off to and a castle with all the amenities we could ever dream of. That leaves a secluded tent in the mountains."

Darius smirked. "Right. Because we don't have enough time spent in tents during our travels."

"For our *duties*, not for leisure."

"Very leisurely this is indeed. Riding horses, smelling of filth, hunting our own food... As opposed to those laborious charmed baths and meals fit for a king back in Aureland." Luvi kicked a cloud of dust in his direction, and he chuckled. "Tell me, Little Bird, why Dakterra, anyway? What are we truly doing all the way out here?"

Luvenia set her book down but didn't respond.

"Luvi. Come on, tell me what we're doing here. I know it isn't because of some mountain getaway." He rose to take a seat next to her. "Are we trying to forget your father's proposal to go with him to Maaraveor?" He nuzzled her neck. "Because I'm more than willing to help you forget it." He kissed a trail down to her collarbone. "I just need to know that's what we're doing way out here."

She pushed Darius playfully, blushing. "I'm not trying to forget it, I'm *mulling*." She ignored his eye roll and continued with defiance. "And whilst I mull, I need to *do* something."

Darius pressed his lips to her neck again. "I can certainly help with that…"

Luvenia pushed him away once more. "I didn't mean *that*." If she wasn't careful, she would most assuredly let him distract her for far too long.

He chuckled and kissed her cheek. "Ah, this is about what you overheard in the Alban Market, then?"

She picked at her nails. "He said there was a monster terrorizing a village. I can't just ignore that."

Darius sighed. "Luvi, you know we have an entire army whose job it is to hunt these creatures, right? I sent four men out when you told me of what you overheard. *You* don't have to be the one to do it."

"I have to, Darius." She pulled away and stood. "Ever since those…*things* burst open in the battle and ripped our Horde apart—" She shook her head. "I've not been able to stop thinking of them."

"I know. Nor have I but hunting down a *possible* monster isn't going to stop that. What if it's nothing?"

Luvi paced. "What if it's not? The least I can do is give a few village children peaceful woods to play in again; allow a lonely widow the relief of no dead chickens in the morning." She halted and crossed her arms. "Until I can slay *our* monsters, the ones bent on destroying *our* lives, I have to at least rid the world of *some*."

Darius ran a hand through his unkempt curls. "Alright, my huntress. We'll rid the world of monsters together, then."

She gave him a small smile. "Together, then."

"How's this?" Darius held up an atrocious hat and Veni laughed.

"You're supposed to be listening for intel, General, not

playing dress up."

They'd left their camp in the mountains of Dakterra to venture closer toward the village supposedly being haunted by a monster. Veni had to admit a night in a normal inn on the outskirts of a small town had been a nice change of pace. One could get too used to court life in a palace. It was revitalizing to eat stew that was more broth than sustenance, to drink ale that was a bit too sour, and sleep on a mattress more lumps than anything else. Not that there had been a great deal of sleeping… It was also revitalizing to not have to sneak Darius in and out of her room.

The whole ordeal reminded her of her little farmhouse and the family she missed greatly. Veni already knew a large portion of her search for this rumored monster was just to distract herself from dealing with her father—now if Darius would just cease saying as much, over and over and over. Regardless, if the monster was real, they needed to know. It could mean Pietro had headquarters in Dakterra. It could mean she had made moves to take the country as she had Anjali. It could mean there was an entirely different problem at hand. It could mean a lot of things.

Darius had indeed sent four men to the little town of Cretch, Dakterra, but they'd returned too early for Luvenia's liking. It was a two-day ride into the town from the Aureland Gate through Vilora and that meant they'd only been in Cretch for three days total.

Darius frowned. "I can watch and listen whilst entertaining myself, considering you are absolutely no fun on this little getaway of ours." He wrapped his hands around her waist and pulled her close. "We've been wandering around this minuscule market since dawn, and we've not heard an inkling of anything awry. I think we would have heard about a monster by now."

He pulled her into a shadowed alcove just inside an alleyway and reclined against the wall, bringing her with him until she was pressed up against his chest. "Let's take a break."

She looked up into his eyes. "I can feel it, Darius. Something isn't right here."

Luvenia's strange sense of the foreboding nature had saved their skin multiple times. Darius was not about to discredit it now. "You didn't mention that part, Little Bird."

She pulled back and began pacing the dim alley. "I get nervous that it's all just in my head when that feeling sets in."

Darius tilted his head to the side, considering. "I don't think so, Luvi. I don't know where that comes from or how you have such incomprehensible intuition, but we've already learned it's spot on." He pushed himself off the wall. "If you feel like something is wrong here, we need to stop listening and start digging." He took her hand, headed for the bright, cold air of the town, when a voice sounded behind them.

It came from the other end of the alleyway—harsh and gravelly. Darius held a finger to his lips and slunk forward, staying in the darkest of the shadows. Luvenia followed close at his heels, both straining to hear.

"*Find it*," the voice ground out. The two men were no more than silhouettes against the bright sun spilling onto the street behind them, but Luvenia would know that voice anywhere.

She yanked on Darius' sleeve, and he halted. "It's Shiv," she whispered.

"I advise you not return to Orford at all if you don't locate it within the next three days and bring it to heel."

Veni's heart slammed against her ribs. It certainly sounded like an animal or beast of some sort, but was it Pietro's? Or she merely wanted it as her pet?

"He doesn't have a mask on." Darius' voice was so low she almost missed it. "I'm going to get closer and try to see his face. Go back toward the street."

The other man grunted a response to Shiv as Darius slunk forward. It was all Veni could do to make her feet go in the opposite direction of Darius, but she managed a few steps back toward the market. She risked a look over her shoulder and saw a large shadow was creeping along the wall silent as a wraith. Darius reached out to grab her wrist just as she could hear the scuffle of footsteps beyond him.

"He's headed this way," Darius whispered in her ear.

There wasn't time to make it completely out of the alley before Shiv would be upon them, so Darius did the only thing he could think of. He shoved Veni against the brick wall, pressing himself into her, and kissed her like their lives depended on it. It was very likely they did. She resisted for a split second before melting into him and slipping her fingers into his hair.

The Chief Collector reached them and made a disgusted snort. "Find a room, you filthy mongrels," he muttered.

But it was exactly what Darius needed him to do. He pulled back from Luvenia with haste. "Apologies, sir." He ran his hands down his pants nervously as Luvenia fussed with the buttons of her blouse. "We didn't know anyone was in the alley, sir."

Shiv eyed them, the sunlight from the street bleeding in to illuminate half of his face, just long enough for Darius to commit it to memory. The unmasked Collector made another disgruntled noise and strode away.

As soon as he was out of earshot, Darius took Luvenia's hand. "Come on, we have to follow the other one."

They raced down the alley, skidding to a stop on the back street. The man was already gone, and they hadn't seen what he looked like. Darius cursed but Veni pointed to a trial in the dirt.

"He drags his left foot," she said.

Darius wanted to kiss her again. "Remind me to make you an official Horedman one day."

"Horde*woman*," she corrected, and he laughed.

"Come on, Little Bird."

They followed the trail until it stopped at a nearby tavern. Luvenia grumbled that none of them had time for him to go into a tavern, but Darius thought it the perfect place to sit back and watch him for a while. Upon entering, they were relieved to find only a handful of patrons. It was only midday, after all.

"Can you tell which one it is?" Veni asked, hovering over her untouched ale.

Darius tipped his back and drained the dregs of it. "My best estimation is the one in the corner."

Luvenia frowned. "But he already has three empty glasses in front of him and we've only been in here a few moments. He couldn't have beaten us by *that* much."

Darius lifted his empty glass. "Doesn't take long." He took Luvenia's glass and drank some, slamming it down onto the old, damp table as he stood. "He also spoke in the Orford tongue."

"What are you doing?" she whispered, but Darius just winked and strolled to the man's table.

"You from around here?" The man simply stared, unreadable. "I don't mean to intrude. I thought I heard you speak to the serving girl in the common tongue of Orford and, well—" Darius licked his lips. "As you can probably guess, I'm from Orford and I just needed to know if you've been staying somewhere pleasant. You see," he pointed at Luvenia, "my wife and I have had the worst luck with vermin in our room while we stay here, and we need a good recommendation." The man blinked at him, and Darius leaned in closer, resting his hands on the table. "It's our honeymoon, see—"

The man's face broke into a nasty grin. "Can't have vermin interrupting your...activities." He nodded in understanding and straightened. "I prefer to camp, myself, but I heard the place just outside the town line to the east is a nice place."

Darius put a hand to his chest. "Thank you kindly, sir."

The man gave him a knowing smile that Darius wanted to slap off his face. He'd gotten what he wanted, but he wasn't sure it was worth the images that disgusting louse would have of him and Luvi.

Darius slid back into his chair opposite her. It took no small amount of effort for her to wipe the ire off her face. She was well aware Darius knew what he was doing, but she preferred to be in the know about such things.

He sipped a fresh ale the serving girl had brought in his absence. "He's camping somewhere on the outskirts of town."

Veni's face fell. "That's not helpful. This place is surrounded by wilderness. How will we find his camp?"

"We're going to follow him, Little Bird." He dipped his chin to the man as he walked toward the door. Darius threw far too much coin onto the scarred table. "Come on." The glint in his eye made her pulse quicken. "If he happens to catch us, I told him you're my wife."

He pulled her toward the door and Luvenia blushed.

"We've been following him around the woods for over a day, Darius." Luvenia lay sprawled in the tall spring grass just west of the man's camp.

Darius trailed a downy cattail across her bare stomach. It had taken a little convincing for her to leave their mission momentarily, but they hadn't found a beast any more than Pietro's man had, and eventually Luvenia craved Darius just enough to walk away for a while.

"I don't know if he's going to find this thing. We need to lure it in ourselves."

Darius' chest rumbled in agreement, and he kissed a line

from her belly button all the way up to her lips. To his immense delight, she returned the kiss hungrily. They did not, however, have time for more distraction, so he pulled back. The sun was going down and, though he might like to continue their trajectory, he'd pieced together the beast hunted just after dusk.

"Whatever you're thinking with that look upon your face, Little Bird, please don't forget it, but we have to get clothes on and head into the woods."

Her face slipped from sultry to intrigued. "What do you know?"

He explained while they dressed. "Our friend over there has not moved his camp. If he didn't know where the beast frequented, he would have moved around to get a better idea, especially with only a day left to find the thing. Therefore, we're pretty close. Also, the old chap slept a good portion of the day today. Anyone fearing their life was on the line for failing would not sleep during a prime opportunity to catch such a thing. Thus—"

"The beast only comes out at night. That's also how it isn't spotted."

"It comes out at dusk. Our friend was back at his camp by the time the moon shone high last night. My best guess is the beast feeds at dusk and crawls back into whatever hole it came out from."

"The caves."

Darius beamed. "Precisely."

Luvenia eyed him, hands on her hips. "How long have you known this?"

He bit his lip. "Long enough to know it was fine to use up our afternoon the way we did." Luvenia scoffed and smacked his arm as he chuckled.

When they were armed to the teeth, Darius kissed her forehead, and they made their way to the caves.

He glanced up to the bruised sky from where they sat

crouched behind a massive boulder. “Are you ready?”

Veni nodded once. There were several caves near the area, but only two with enough space for something large to reside in without being seen. Granted, they didn’t know how large the creature was, but the story Luvenia overheard led them to believe it was at least the size of a large man. They were also riding on the fact that Pietro probably wouldn’t select a daft man to go hunting for it, so it had to be hidden enough that he hadn’t been able to locate it. So far, it appeared the man hadn’t quite figured out the cave part yet, though, and that made Luvenia question his intelligence after all.

No sooner had she thought it, did a rustling sound on the other side of the boulder. She looked at Darius with alarm, and he rested a finger against his lips, his sword—Nahaliel—at the ready. He made to peek around the boulder, but a horrifying growl sounded from the cave mouth, permeating the air until the ground shook.

They’d found it.

Darius and Luvenia locked eyes, waiting. She expected an outright roar, or ground-trembling footsteps...at the very least the grass rustling, but it was eerily silent. Even the crickets had gone silent and the trees hardly whispered. It didn’t make sense.

There was a rough curse from the other side of their boulder and Darius jumped up. He rounded the rock to see Pietro’s man slinking toward something. With Luvenia close on his heels, they stalked through the waning light with no visual on the beast and only a vague outline of the man to follow. Veni was certain he saw it or he wouldn’t have had cause to curse and go off into the tree line. Her stomach was twisting uncomfortably, and she knew it wasn’t her nerves or mere trepidation.

She made to say something terrible was coming, but Darius flung an arm out and roughly pushed her back just as a form crashed through the trees toward them. Luvenia swallowed her scream and caught her balance, steadying her sword and drawing a dagger. But the creature only landed in a crouch and sniffed the air before sneaking forward on two eerily nimble feet. It had found its prey. And it wasn't them.

Darius reached back to check on Luvenia and waved her forward. There was no way a creature so stealthy didn't know they were there, but it had its sights locked on something else. At the same moment a terrible realization hit Luvenia, a man screamed—gut-wrenching and terrible. Darius sprinted through the trees and Veni followed. The screams grew guttural and pained, accompanied by a sickening wet, tearing sound. Luvenia tried to prepare herself before they rounded the tree that she knew the beast was behind, but there was no way she could have.

What used to be a human, nude and deformed, sat on its haunches, bent over the mutilated body of Pietro's man, his intestines in its fists. The grotesque creature froze. Its twisted and hunched spine became rigid as it turned its head, sniffing the air like a wolf, entrails hanging out of its mouth. Luvenia put a hand to her mouth so as no to cry out, and Darius put a hand on her arm. He locked eyes with her and nodded once. He was going to advance.

He moved on nearly silent feet, but the creature sat alert, ready. Darius stood still behind a tree until the creature snarled and went back to its meal. The general raised Nahaliel high and snuck up behind the beast. With its back turned, Darius slammed the tip of his sword between its ribs and into the creature's lung. It shrieked and clawed at the sword, too quick for Darius to retrieve it. It flung a preternaturally strong arm back and knocked Darius to the ground, turning to attack.

Luvenia surged forward and threw her dagger straight into the creature's forehead. It clawed at the dagger with nails as long as Veni's fingers. It managed to get her dagger out with an unnerving sucking sound and reared back to launch itself at her. Darius was up and pouncing before she could blink.

The two landed in a heap of growls, Darius slicing at its flesh with his knife and the creature clawing through his clothing.

The thing was so much stronger than Darius, he wouldn't last long, but Veni couldn't stab the beast without the chance of harming Darius. Indecision was costing them precious seconds and Darius bellowed for her to run. But that was not a choice she was willing to make. Veni rushed forward, sword poised to strike, as an arrow whizzed past her head and landed straight in the creature's heart. It instantly went limp, right over Darius' face. Luvenia scanned the trees for the archer, but there was no time. She rushed to help Darius lift the beast off of himself and check his wounds. He gently pushed her hands away and made to stand, his attention darting every which way to find the archer.

A weathered woman with dark hair and shrewd features stepped through the tree line, bow in hand. "*Varulv*," she spoke, pointing her bow at the dead creature.

Darus shifted in front of Luvenia, blood soaking every inch of him. She had no way of knowing how much was his and they had no way of knowing if this woman was friend or foe.

"Thank you," Darius spoke in the common tongue of Dakterra. She must have noted his accent, for she slipped into a heavy-tongued Orfordian dialect.

"He has ravaged my caravan for a fortnight, once he tired of the village chickens. He grew stronger and stronger. Never could I catch him. Full of that," she pointed carelessly to Pietro's dead man, "and distracted by you, I kill him." She put a gnarled hand to her chest. "Runa. Leader of the Vanir clan."

"Thank you," Darius repeated, stepping forward to shake her hand. Luvenia caught a stiffening in his shoulders at the mention of her name, but he kept his face smooth. "Roland. This is my wife. What do you know of this creature?"

"Little. It came out of nowhere, ravaged the village, came

after my troupe. I kill him."

"You have no idea where it might have come from? You said *varulv*. They are a myth, yes? Men bitten by rabid wolves and turned feral?"

Runa nodded curtly. "It seems correct, does it not?"

Luvenia had to agree it did. But it didn't make *sense*. "Could he have been a man from Cretch or a nearby village?" she piped up.

Runa took her in with narrowed eyes. "No. We have been near Cretch for long time. It's a small village and no one has gone missing. Someone bring him here, let him loose."

Darius offered a small bow. "Thank you again, Matron Runa." She cocked her head at him, her brow furrowed. "I owe you a life debt. We must be going."

Runa smiled cunningly. "You know my customs, Roland. Tell me how that is."

"I have done my share of traveling, Matron. That is all."

Runa did not believe it for a moment, if the look on her face were any indication. However, she simply smiled and waved a hand of dismissal and walked back into the trees.

"How did you know her?" Veni asked as she cleaned and bandaged Darius' many wounds back at the inn.

"Thera lived in her gypsy caravan for a while several years ago. She made quite an enemy out of that woman. Thera has always lived a bit like a ghost outside of Aureland, so I doubt she mentioned me, but I had to be safe."

Veni thought for quite some time about Thera's wild adventures as a gypsy nomad. The Keeper had told her once that she'd been dubbed the Ghost Raven in more than one country and spent over a decade of her life trading secrets and dealing fortunes.

Chapter Twenty-Nine

Luvi shifted in her saddle as they neared the Aureland castle. "What do you make of my father's offer? What do you think I should do?"

"Oh, we're speaking of his offer now, are we?" Darius gave her a teasing smirk. She rolled her eyes and he shrugged, holding his horse's reins gently. "I don't know."

Luvenia let out a sharp laugh. "You, Darius Cremeux, the one who has something to say about *everything*, has no opinion on this very important matter?"

"I didn't say I had no opinion," he said around a laugh. "Of course I have an opinion. However, as you said, this is a very important decision with a lot at stake. For that reason, I don't think you should consult with anyone concerning what to do. This is your decision to make, no one else, and their opinions, as well meaning as they might be, are only a hindrance to your decision."

"I suppose. But what if someone else has thought of something I haven't."

"Perhaps they have. Or perhaps the things they've thought of will only get in the way of what you already know about the situation. Consult others if you'd like, but you still won't hear my opinion on it. I know you are more than capable of making the decision on your own. In fact, I think you already know what you'd like to do."

"And what is that?" she prodded.

Darius' laugh rumbled. "That, I truly *don't* know. What I do know is that I will support you fully either way. If you choose to go with him, I will help you pack. If you choose to stay, or shun him forever, I will saddle his horse and kick him out on his arse."

Luvenia gave him a small smile and he reached his hand across the space between their horses to take hers.

She did already know, deep down. She knew going on this journey with her father was a second chance she could never pass up. She knew whatever awaited them in Marche de Blanc could get her one step closer to rescuing her sister. She knew, despite how angry she was with her father, that her mother would want her to learn their story—to get to know the real Henry Rousseau. Veni knew the questions burning holes in her every waking moment were not going to be answered if she didn't go with him. She knew this journey would change the course of her life—again. But she had to do it. Alone.

There lay the problem. Luvenia wasn't certain she was willing to give up her newfound life. The one thrust upon her when she fell through a portal in the woods outrunning Collectors. The one with Darius.

There were plenty of difficulties in this new life as well. There was Queen Pietro to defeat, monsters to slay, her sister to rescue from the queen's clutches, Anjali to rebuild, Aureland to protect… The list was endless. But...*Darius*. Not to mention the others she'd grown to love impossibly fast upon stumbling into Aureland all those months ago. This new journey with her father would mean saying goodbye to all of it—saying goodbye to Darius. At least for a time.she wouldn't be the same when she returned. She already knew it.

Darius would insist that wasn't true. He would insist on going with her. He would insist on many things. But Luvenia knew the truth. She needed to take the journey with her father alone, and she needed to forge her path from there.

Thump.

Thump.

Thump.

The Toulonan sentinels froze, mid-bite, and looked at one another.

Thump.

Thump.

Thump.

Osiris took up his spear.

THUMP.

THUMP.

Rrrrrreeeeee.

Silence.

Net took down a torch from the wall.

Sand stirred within the tomb.

The men advanced, the glow of the torch illuminating a few paces ahead of them.

Shk.

Shk.

Shk.

Osiris and Net halted.

A strip of ancient linen spilled out of the sarcophagus onto the floor.

The two men looked at each other again and gripped their weapons.

Net slowly raised the torch.

Two sharp intakes of breath faced a jagged, dusty wheeze.

"She's done it." Osriris trembled.

"Theralin." The Queen of Aureland glided into Thera's

chambers where the young Keeper had just fallen asleep.

Thera groaned and put a pillow over her face. She'd spent every possible moment with the children at the inn. Granger and his daughters—Veni's Orford neighbors—were doing a marvelous job of caring for the young ones, but after seeing their frightened faces and their malnourished bodies, Thera had difficulty leaving them for even a moment.

She was supposed to be helping Akio acclimate to Aureland. She was supposed to be aiding in the relief of the other Anjalian citizens, but she just couldn't bring herself to leave the little ones. The Anjalian Emperor had taken personal offense and hadn't spoken to her in days. Thera wondered if Nuria was there to talk her into shifting her focus back to Anjali.

"I've only just fallen asleep, Nuria," she said, her voice muffled by the pillow on her face.

"It appears sleep will evade you for a while longer, dear. You are needed elsewhere." The queen sat on the edge of Thera's bed and lifted the pillow.

Thera stared daggers at her. "I don't want to go to Anjali. Not yet."

Nuria's lips turned down at the corners. "Is this because Akio has been keeping his distance?"

"Partially, but he's keeping distance because I don't want to focus on Anjali until I know the children are healing."

Nuria put a hand on Thera's head, stroking her dark hair. "Oh, darling, that healing is a long way off. You do not have to be there every second and neglect your own well-being for them to know you have their best interest at heart."

Thera nodded mutely.

"However, I am not here because of the children or Anjali, or even Akio." Thera raised an eyebrow at her motherly queen and Nuria sighed heavily. "Smithwick has informed me that a Toulonan man has entered Aureland through the Gate this night. I sent Khyan to speak with him and he has requested to see you before he tells us who he is or why he is here."

Dax. Thera's heartbeat grew loud in her ears. She hadn't seen him since their brief escapade in Anjali as they tormented poor Akio. "How could anyone I know from Toulona possibly know of Aureland and how to get here?"

Nuria lifted one graceful shoulder and folded her hands in her lap. "If this man is Dax, as I assume by the look on your face it is… My best estimation is the two of you have kept many secrets from one another. Find out all you can, darling, but do not let your guard down simply because you have a history." A history she could only half-remember.

Thera launched herself out of bed as quickly as possible and dressed in a rush.

She was not prepared to see his face in her home. Seeing Dax within the walls of her precious sanctuary—within the mystical land of Aureland—was jarring in the most heart-wrenching way. It was one thing seeing him briefly in Anjali to catch up. To see him when she was well-rested and had the eye of another man. It was an entirely different thing to see him with all her defenses down.

That day in Toulona flared in her memory. The moment they both forgot their love for one another by unnatural means. She'd expected it to feel like nothing, to forget *them*. Instead, it often felt like a missing piece. Thera wondered for the thousandth time if it felt like that for Dax, too, or if it was her Keeper gift that left the impact cavernous.

"Theralin." Dax rushed forward and embraced her. "I heard what happened after I left Anjali. I got here as quickly as I could."

Thera kissed him on the cheek and pulled back. "Nuria, this is Dax Abayomi." She gestured between them. "Dax, this is Queen Nuria of Aureland."

Dax dropped into a low bow. "Apologies, Your Majesty."

"It is no matter, Dax. How were you to know who I am? I

am not your queen, after all."

Thera's brows furrowed at Nuria. It was a strange thing to say and it felt...probing.

"That is not entirely true, Majesty." Thera's attention snapped to Dax as he spoke. "But if it is alright with you, I would still like a word alone with Theralin, and then I will answer anything you ask."

Nuria's smile was a knowing one. "Of course."

Dax bowed low once more. When Nuria had gone and Dax stood straight, he laughed outright at Thera's scrunched up face.

"You have some explaining to do, I'm afraid." She crossed her arms. Dax smirked, but she felt his nerves.

"No more than you, Keeper."

Thera clenched her jaw. "How did you get into Aureland?"

Dax held up an old thimble. "My Portal Key."

"You mean to tell me you're truly one of us?"

"I am. And I believe we have a very dear mutual friend in Eshe-Femi Anippa."

Thera's heart panged. She hadn't seen Femi in a long time and only brief correspondences had passed between them after she'd left her in the care and training of another dear friend, Naiheeli. "Femi would never reveal my secrets." She hoped it was true.

"She did not. That's not in Femi's nature. She did, however, mention meeting you on the road once and that was when…" Dax ran a hand through his hair and shoved his fists into his pockets. His nerves were accompanied by hope and something that seemed almost precious, but she couldn't quite identify it. "That was when the dreams came back."

Thera blinked. "Dreams?"

He fidgeted. "My gift is dreaming. They're not all...reliable, though. I have a dream and then I must sift through it and dig into things to know if it's my gift or just a dream. It's a process."

"And what does this have to do with me?"

Dax frowned at her. She knew her self-preservation often showed itself in nasty ways. Dax knew it, too. But how was she supposed to believe this?

"The fact is I know you did something to me, Theralin. To *us*. You and I." Her stomach dropped to her toes. "I dreamt every night of you and I, things that felt so real. At first, I thought they were certainly just dreams. They eventually faded and I moved on.

But then Femi mentioned meeting you on the road and I had just seen you in Anjali and learned your true name and… The dreams came back. This time they were stronger. It was as if…" He rocked his head back and forth. "They were *memories*, Theralin. I knew it was my gift and not mere dreams. I could *feel* your hand in mine. Taste your skin. Hear you say things my *friend* would not say…"

Thera's heart slammed against her ribs. She couldn't remember any of those things, not after what she'd done, but in her bones she still knew it was real. Dax's gaze bore into her, and she took a step back.

Hurt flashed through him. "Tell me it wasn't real and I'll leave. I'll speak with Queen Nuria about the information I came with, and I will go." He stepped closer and Thera had a hard time breathing. "Tell me it wasn't real or undo what you did to me."

"What I did to us." Her voice was hardly a whisper. "It was real, but I don't remember anything past friendship."

Dax's hope swirled with unease. The tempest sluiced through Thera and left her feeling bereft.

"Why did you do this?" Anger flashed within him as well.

"Dax…" She took a steadying breath. "I wanted you to grow old with someone. And I knew it couldn't be me."

He looked deep within her eyes until she couldn't stand the silence any longer. Thera felt so many emotions that her legs nearly gave out. She felt his want, his need. His utter relief and hope founded in learning the truth. She felt his desire and his worry. His anxiety that perhaps he was just making a fool of himself.

And Theralin felt her own desperation to know him again, the way she erased.

"You were wrong." He stepped toward her and took her face sweetly in both his hands, resting his forehead on hers. "Undo this, Theralin. *Please*."

"I don't know if I can," she whispered.

"Will you try?"

Thera nodded as a tear slid down her cheek. That hollow space begged her to be mended.

Dax pulled back and smiled down at her. "As immensely happy as this makes me...I'm afraid I also came here to deliver some unfortunate news to our Queen of Keepers."

Dread pooled in Thera's stomach at the same moment she felt Dax's own trepidation.

Darius wiped the sweat from his brow and planted a kiss on Luvi's cheek, huffing. "What are you doing awake, Little Bird?"

"What are you doing training in the middle of the night?"

"Fair enough. How did you know I'd be here?"

Luvenia pursed her lips. "You aren't as mysterious as you might think. You always come here when you can't sleep."

"So do you," he teased.

"And there you have it." She smiled but it failed to touch her eyes.

"What is it?" Darius unwound the wrapping on his hands and took a swig of water, watching and wondering at her discomfort.

"I've made my decision." The words were quiet. Too quiet.

"That's great, let's hear it."

"I've decided to go with my father," she let out.

"Well then, we're in for some packing. Your bag first, or mine?" He tried to look in her eyes when she didn't respond, but she kept her gaze firmly locked on the floor in front of his feet. "Luvi, what's the matter? Do you not want to go?"

"I do."

He could hardly hear what she said. Darius took a step toward her, his hand outstretched, but she stepped back. His stomach turned over. "What's going on here?"

"I need to go alone, Darius."

"Alright." He tried to keep the surprise from his voice. "Well, then I will be here waiting for you when you return." He ignored the growing dread in his stomach.

Luvi shook her head, biting her lip.

Darius crossed his arms. "Dammit, Luvenia. Stop making me guess what you're thinking and just tell me. What are you hinting at? Are you trying to end things with me?"

She finally met his stare. "No." She shook her head to clear it. "It's simply that I need to do this on my own."

"Then I won't go with you, I'm needed here, anyway. It's a journey, Luvi, it's not the end of the world or a death sentence."

Luvenia nodded mutely. Darius reached out to take her hand, the lump in his stomach growing thicker. He knew she wouldn't be the same when she returned, but surely she wasn't planning to be done with him over this journey. Surely, she didn't have some ulterior motive.

"Just tell me this doesn't have anything to do with hunting more beasts like the one in Dakterra. Tell me you're not going to throw all of this away, throw *us* away over some damnable thing that *may* lend a clue to where Ester is?"

Luvenia shook her head sharply. "No. I do hope this

journey could somehow lead to Ester, I think it's why my father is going at all, but I don't mean to throw us away." She squeezed his hand and let go to place it on his cheek. His whiskers tickled her palm, and she committed the feel of his face to memory—just in case. "I love you, Darius. I simply need to do this on my own."

He searched her eyes for a long moment before bending down to kiss her gently. "You have my full support, Little Bird. Come on, I'll help you pack."

"You asked to see me?"

Queen Nuria said nothing. She merely gestured for Darius to sit. With a heavy sigh, the queen closed her book, resting it on her lap. Her very soul was *tired.* "So Luvenia has decided to accompany her father, then?"

Darius nodded, dropping into his favorite chair within Nuria's study. "She has. I just left her rooms and she's all packed. And she's decided it's a journey she wishes to take alone."

"It is not altogether a poor choice, though I am certain it wounds you."

The general shrugged nonchalantly, but she could see the pain in his eyes.

Oh, to be so very young. Everything felt exponentially more final and immensely stronger at such a young age. "Darling, the journey will only take a fortnight and they'll not be there many days. She will be home before you know it."

"But it's Marche de Blanc… What if something happens to her."

Nuria reached over and rested a hand on Darius' arm. "Khyan will never let that happen."

Darius swallowed. "I know. But I still prefer it to be *me* protecting her."

Nuria squeezed his arm and let go. "Of course, darling."

The queen took a deep breath and Darius frowned.

"That isn't why you called me in here, is it?"

Nuria shook her head, her snowy hair shining in the candlelight. "No, it is not. I am afraid we've received very grave news from Toulona this night."

Darius leaned forward, resting his elbows on his knees.

"Do you recall Theralin mentioning a Dax Ab?"

"Of course. The poor chap she erased from her life with Forgetful Cakes."

Nuria grimaced. "The very same. He is, to everyone's shock, one of us. A Keeper."

Darius reared back. "How did we miss that?"

"Oh, it is not so very difficult, dear. Not all Keepers want to be in Aureland and not all Keepers wish to be known. When he showed up here tonight with a Portal Key and Thera's name upon his lips, I suspected. He confirmed as much to me himself. However, that is not the most interesting of the information he possessed."

"Why do I get the sinking feeling the rest of his information isn't quite so welcomed."

"That is because it is not. This young Keeper is the Toulonan Ambassador to Anjali. He returned home to report to the Roah just before the madness in Anjali ensued. Do you recall the empty pyramids we learned of after Theralin met the Heiress Apparent a couple of years ago?" Darius nodded. "Dax had some...concerning news. He states the men patrolling the pyramids have begun to whisper of an army of creatures."

"Like the one Luvi and I encountered in Dakterra?"

Nuria's lips turned down. "No. Dax did not understand all of the information he repeated, but there was mention of Pietro's gift being used to raise the creatures."

Darius balked. "Her Kiss of Death?" Realization struck and Darius stood, cursing. "Are you alluding to an army of the undead?"

Nuria nodded. "It's the only thing that makes sense."

"Hugo was certain using her aer fixus so widely with just the Collectors would cause her demise. She's either found a way around that or she's putting herself in the grave for us."

"We can't count on that. I need you to accompany Theralin and Dax to Toulona."

"I'll take a troop of Hordmen just in case. We can be rid of this army of undead before it becomes anything."

"No, Darius. I want you to gather information and that is all. I find myself worried this could turn out to be a trap."

Darius' brow crumpled. "You don't trust this Dax character?"

"I do not trust that Lilith's men are letting important information simply fall out of their mouths unbidden."

Darius murmured his agreement.

Chapter Thirty

Veni threw her bundle of sticks down next to the fire with too much force. Khyan looked up at her from where he sat perched, sharpening his knife against a whetstone. He raised one fiery eyebrow and slid his knife along the stone.

"Are you ever going to tell me why we're really headed to Marche de Blanc?" She threw a hand to her hip and Khyan almost snorted.

"I'm not exactly an admirer of your father, but I'm not going to sow division into this plan. We need it to work."

Veni glowered. "Division was sown the moment you two decided to keep me in the dark about all of this. Since when are you so protective of my father and his precious plan?"

The prince regarded her incredulously. "I'm not protective of your father, I'm protective of *you*."

"You're insufferable."

Khyan gave a dismissive shrug. "You've called me much worse."

"How can you call dragging me on a mysterious quest with no information protecting me?" Veni growled. "I agreed to come on this little excursion to learn more and the both of you have remained tight-lipped about everything. We've been on the road for days and we'll enter Maaraveor in only a handful more. Yet, I still have no idea what we're even doing and none of my questions have been answered!"

Henry appeared then in the tree line. "Is there a problem here?" He approached the fire and set down his fresh kill of rabbits.

"No," Khyan chirped.

Veni shot him a look and turned to her father. "*Yes*. I want to know why we're going to Marche de Blanc. And no more ridiculous answers about my ignorance keeping me safe."

Henry remained silent, contemplating his daughter and her ire for many moments before speaking. "There is information we seek regarding a prophecy of sorts."

"Henry," Khyan warned.

The Liberator dismissed Khyan. "She's right. She deserves to know. This...*prophecy* has come to both me and your mother over many, many years. Some of it has become clear, and some of it is still shrouded in mystery."

"You and mother? A prophecy?" She shook her head and sat hard next to Khyan. "I don't understand."

Henry sighed. "It's becoming clear that the Great War we've all feared has begun to come upon us."

"Pietro."

Henry nodded. "Her Enenra have been loose for years and there is talk of other great beasts in her employ. There is vital information to be learned and Marche locations are the greatest places to glean it. However, the epicenter of the White Market is where I believe the children were headed and I want to know why. And what it has to do with the impending War."

"If this prophecy is the reason that you left us, then I want to know it. I want to understand it, and Mother's involvement."

Henry ran a hand down his face. "You choose this night to know?"

Veni nodded. "I do."

"Love…" Henry took a deep breath. "You cannot unsee what I am to show you."

Veni wondered at his choice of the word *see*, but merely

nodded resolutely. "I'm ready."

Her father considered her for a long moment. "Do you have your Portal Key?"

"Of course." She fished in her pocket and handed him her mother's amulet, worried he would somehow find a way to use it to send her back to Aureland and lock her away for safekeeping.

"I'll need your necklace as well."

Veni reached up and unclasped it, then let it drop into his outstretched hand with a *tink*.

Henry ran a gentle finger over both amulets, his expression pained and wistful. After a moment of silent reverie, he fiddled with them until both released their purple stones into his hand. Veni gasped.

"They'll go back in. Here." He handed her the empty necklaces, devoid of their glory. He placed the two stones side by side and a little flash of light ran between them. "Prince," he addressed Khyan. "Listen carefully and you should be able to hear some of what she sees."

Khyan nodded and Veni's heart rate kicked up.

"Are you ready, Love?"

There was no way to tell what she was about to see—or learn. She worried, somewhere within the confines of her soul, that what she was about to learn would make her unable to trust her father ever again, for how many secrets he'd kept. Alas, a much larger portion of her soul already knew the tiny stones he held within his fingers were going to reveal the why of it all. Why he'd left her. Why he and her mother had kept so very much from her. And that realization was far more frightening. For what could lead a man that loved his family with unmatched ferocity to do all Henry had without a terrifying reason?

She reached out and took Khyan's hand. He squeezed it and Veni gave one sharp nod, her mouth set in determination.

Henry joined the two halves of the orb together and the

forest erupted in violet.

A young man stood skipping rocks in a serene river. His hair was pitch black and unruly. He was still lanky with youth, but Veni could tell he was on the cusp of it giving way to the less awkward build of young adulthood.

She inched forward, wondering if he would speak to her—if he would know she was there. Her boot kicked up a flurry of tiny pebbles, but the boy never turned. Content to believe she was merely an observer in this strange vision, she walked slowly forward to view his profile. It was her father. Her heart ached and swelled simultaneously to see him in a way wholly impossible in the natural world. Veni took a step forward, halting when she heard a whisper of sound behind them. She turned with young Henry at the sound.

An ancient woman walked toward him in the wilderness, bent over her cane. Veni looked at her father, but his face was just as crumpled in confusion as her own.

"Hello, Henry," the old woman spoke.

Henry's brow furrowed further. "Good afternoon, madam. Do I know you?"

"You do not." She halted a few steps away, studying him intently.

"Then how do you know my name?"

One corner of her mouth twitched up in the way unique to those wizened by time. "I'm afraid it is you who does not know your name."

Veni and her father frowned in unison at the woman.

Henry huffed an awkward, breathy laugh. "Could I accompany you back to the village?" He smiled gently at the woman and Veni's heart constricted. She knew the kindness of her father better than anything. She wondered how she could have ever questioned his motives.

"Dear boy, it is you who needs some guidance." She hobbled forward, her wooden cane clunking on the dirt. "The man and woman you call Father and Mother are not your parents."

Veni looked frantically between them as her father's brows drew together and his face reddened. He was shaking his head and backing up from her, nearly toppling himself backwards into the lake.

"Y—You're wrong. I'm not certain who you think you are, but—"

"Your name is Matthias. Your true parents were instructed to name you and ensure no one ever knew whose child you were. When they learned of your purpose, they elected to bring you here, to the Rousseau farm, to be raised by a couple they trusted who could not have children of their own."

Veni was beginning to feel dizzy and as if she might vomit. A glance at her father revealed young Henry—Matthias—was feeling quite the same way.

"This cannot be." His words were hardly audible, and he continued shaking his head. This time, instead of backing away, he started pacing. "Who are you? Why should I believe you?"

"I am an oracle, Matthias."

"My name is Henry," he ground out.

The woman held her ground. "Listen to me carefully, boy." Henry stopped pacing and looked at her, his chest heaving with barely controlled emotions. "There is a great evil awakening. You will soon meet a young woman. You are one half of the answer that will vanquish this evil. The young lady is the other." She hobbled the last distance to Henry. "Hold out your hand."

Henry eyed her momentarily before reaching out. She gently rested a stone into his upturned palm. Banking on her invisibility within the vision, Veni surged forward for a better look as her father narrowed his eyes at the stone. Veni's breath caught. It was violet and beginning to glow. Half of the orb her father had held in front of her to show her that very vision.

"What is this?"

"This will show you all you need to know in due time, Matthias."

The woman vanished and Henry whirled around every which way looking for her. Veni watched as her father marveled at the half-stone and tucked it into his pocket. As he walked back toward the village, the air turned purple with fog that cleared to reveal another scene.

Henry appeared slightly older, the beginnings of stubble lining his jaw. He sat under a tree, mindlessly flipping a purple half-stone up into the air and catching it. Veni's grandmother—or, she supposed, not her grandmother—set a basket of apples next to him and teased that he would survive one afternoon without Genevieve.

Unbidden, a sob choked from Veni's throat. She closed her eyes and hoped the vision would not end before she could see her mother again.

Henry's mother walked away, and the tree rustled above his head. He looked up and his face broke into a joyous grin.

Veni watched as her father stood and reached a hand high up over his head and a figure jumped out of the tree without taking his offered assistance. It was all Veni could do not to rush forward and crush her mother with a hug. She was nearly a mirror image of how Veni looked standing invisibly before her parents, if not a little bit younger. Tears streamed down Veni's cheeks as she watched her father take her mother's face gently in his hands and kiss her sweetly. It was an image she saw so many times as a child that it ached of home.

Henry finally pulled back. "I thought you weren't coming today."

Genevieve smirked. "I couldn't stay away."

"Someday you won't have to." Henry pulled her to himself and wrapped his arms around her waist. "One day you'll be my wife and we'll never have to part."

Genevieve's face fell.

"What's wrong, Gen?"

She stepped back and twirled the end of her braid around and around. "The oracle came to see me again today."

"What happened?"

"Henry, she said a great war is coming."

"Gen, since the first time she visited each of us, we've both known there would be a great evil."

"Yes, but this isn't just a great evil, this is a war. This isn't just about us anymore. This isn't the two of us fighting it, when it arrives. This is other people fighting and dying."

Henry rushed forward and gently took her shoulders, looking intently into her face until she finally met his eyes. "Gen. We will figure this out. She told me it is still many years away, and we've already begun preparing."

Genevieve's brow furrowed. "Meeting with a few men like Schrute that actually believe in this foretelling isn't going to accomplish anything, Henry."

He only smiled at her. "Of course, it will. There will come a day when we need support. When we need a reminder that we've not gone mad. There will come a day when our family needs protection."

"You haven't told them, have you? Please tell me you haven't."

"You are the only one alive that knows who I am aside from the oracle. But there will also come a day when they need to know who they are following."

Genevieve pulled out of his grasp and sat hard under the tree. "And you're certain you want me to be your queen?"

Veni's lips parted as a surreal understanding landed in her mind. She watched in awe as her father knelt before her young mother, a tender smile playing at his lips.

"I have never been more certain of anything in my life."

Genevieve started to cry, and Henry took her in his arms.

"Did you know the oracle isn't as old as she appears?"

Veni looked on, still processing the incomprehensible truth her mother had just revealed. Her mother sniffled.

"She's not?"

Henry chuckled. "She doesn't even need the cane. She told me people tend to trust an ancient oracle more than one that is...less weathered."

The precious scene fell in on itself and unfurled into yet another.

Veni's tears began anew as she beheld her mother in a flowing white gown. A tapping sound came from the window and Veni looked with her mother as a snowy owl flew in and transformed into the regal Queen of Aureland.

Genevieve beamed. "Nuria," she breathed, rushing forward to crush the queen in a hug."

"Oh, my darling." Nuria rested her cheek on Genevieve's head before pulling her back. "Let me look at you." Tears shone in the queen's eyes. "You are a ravishing bride. Your mother would be so very proud."

Genevieve swallowed, a ghost of a smile on her painted lips. "I'm sorry she could not be here, but I'm so very pleased you came."

"I would not miss it for the world, my dear." She kissed the top of her head. "Now, is this man good to you?"

Genevieve huffed a tearful laugh. "Better than anyone."

"Could I meet him?"

"Please. Come with me, we'll meet him now."

Genevieve pulled Nuria out into a hallway. "Just a moment," she said and barged into a room two doors down.

"Gen!" Henry exclaimed, covering his eyes. "I'm not supposed to see you yet!"

"Oh, pish." Genevieve pulled Henry's hands down and he drank her in. "I'd rather you see me without prying eyes."

Veni couldn't control her sobs. She did not deserve to look

in on this moment. It would rest in her heart as a valued treasure until long after she drew her last breath. She watched as her speechless father blinked away tears of his own and kissed her mother tenderly.

"I have someone I want you to meet," Geneviève spoke, pulling back. She took Henry's hand and pulled him toward the door. The Queen of Aureland strode in, the perfect picture of elegance and grace.

Henry's eyes went wide and he dipped into a low bow. "Queen Nuria, it is an honor."

Nuria beamed, glancing sidelong at Genevieve. "You must be Henry."

He righted himself and nodded. He placed a hand on his chest, just beginning to broaden with all the hard labor of maintaining a farm after the man he knew as his father had passed. "I want to thank you for loving my Genevieve and ensuring she was cared for. It is no small act for a queen to do such a thing."

A tear slipped down Nuria's cheek and she looked from Henry to Genevieve with pride that made Veni's soul ache as she watched. "Oh, her mother was not just any Keeper." Nuria rested a tender hand on Genevieve's cheek. "Viola was my life's greatest friend."

The scene began to blur and fold in on itself until Veni heard a clamor of voices all speaking at once.

"Enough." Henry's firm voice was hardly audible compared to the others', but they silenced themselves immediately.

They were all quite young, not much older than Darius. One she recognized as the butcher, Schrute, who had come to tell them of her father's supposed death—the very same man Darius had set eyes on months ago as a member of the Rebel group. Veni watched as her father rose from his seat next to her mother and addressed the cramped room of individuals.

"We don't know where the threat is going to come from. Just because the queen has perished suspiciously does not mean the Great Evil will come from within the castle. Alestair is a good man. At this point, until we know more, we do not grow our numbers, but prepare to do so as soon as necessar—"

Henry was abruptly cut off by a man barging in with a young, squawking child covered in blood. "I—I'm so sorry, Henry. I didn't know where else to bring him."

Another man rushed forward and took the child. It wasn't until Veni saw him begin to examine the little boy that she realized he was a very young Healer Merric.

"What happened?" Henry demanded.

"The father. He—the mother is dead. But I took the boy. It's not his blood, Merric. I don't think he sustained injuries." The young man turned back to Henry as everyone else watched on. "I don't know what to do with him."

A chair slid across the floor, and they all turned. Veni watched as her mother stood, her belly swollen. "We'll take him."

Henry's eyes widened but he only nodded once.

Realization of who that little boy was hit Veni like a battering ram at the same moment the room began to spin. It stilled to reveal her father, older and irate.

Henry thrust a finger out toward an older woman. It took Veni a moment to realize it was the oracle without all the embellishments that made her appear much older. Genevieve stood bouncing a toddling babe as she wailed.

"This Great Evil never would have had a throne if you hadn't told my parents to conceal me!" Veni had never once heard her father shout at anyone. It was not in his nature. It struck her then that she must have heard him shout because that toddling babe crying in her mother's arms must be her.

"That woman would have killed you to claim the throne, Matthias." The oracle stood straight. "It is not my place to decide what I see and do not see. Just because it doesn't make sense to us does not mean it is unfurling incorrectly."

"This is madness, Naiheeli! None of this would have happened if I had been raised as who I rightly am."

"You would not be who you are if you'd been raised with a silver spoon, Matthias."

He shoved a finger back in her face. "You did this. And now you want me to simply accept that you've Seen that my wife has to die for this cause?"

Veni gasped and looked at her mother. She was pale and clearly anxious, but her face was resolute.

"How am I to be half the relinquishing force of this Great Evil and Gen the other if she's dead?" Henry snapped.

The Oracle said nothing, she merely looked at the crying baby—Luvenia. Henry, Genevieve, and Veni all gasped in unison.

Geneivieve's eyes welled, and Henry came near to her. She kissed baby Luvi on the head. "I will do it, Henry."

"No!" Henry roared before turning back to the oracle. "Fight your own damn war. My family will remain safe."

The scene exploded into one that smelled of rot and charred flesh.

Veni blinked at the dim room before her, a shadowed man at the center. It was Shiv. He wore no mask and only the plain clothes of an Orford soldier, before they became Lilith Pietro's sinister Warmongers and eventually Collectors. She couldn't quite make out his face, but he was standing over something in an old abandoned smithy. When he took up a branding iron from the fire, its tip burning bright with heat, Veni realized what Shiv stood over was a person. He shifted on his feet, and Veni saw her mother filthy and on her knees.

Her lip was bleeding, and her dress was ripped, hanging half off her shoulder.

Veni watched in horror as Shiv leaned in close. Her mother snarled and he slapped her. "I will find out who you are one day Zealot, and you will pay for what you and your disgusting band of false prophets have started." He inched closer, holding the branding iron close enough for Genevieve to feel the heat on the hollow of her shoulder. "No one believes your lies, little Zealot."

With one swift jolt of his arm, the iron was against Genevieve's skin, singing and branding her. She did not even flinch. Her eyes filled with moisture, but Genevieve Rousseau remained still, her teeth bared at the vicious man in front of her, as he marked her for life.

"Thanks to you, all your followers will be gifted with such a mark."

Everything began to twist, revealing snippets of moments in time. Pietro hanging one of the Zealots. Naiheeli arguing with her father. Her mother forging Family Records to include Jacob and sending them with a man to trade them out for the real ones. Schrute meeting her father in the woods on the eve of Veni's eight birthday. Bleeding and dead bodies littering the ground in a battle during the Purge War. Her father breaking into the castle…

The swift rotation of scenes left her nauseous, but they finally slowed into one set in her own home.

Henry Rousseau nimbly climbed through the second story window of his wife's bedroom and slipped silently into bed next to her.

"You really should lock that window, Gen," he whispered in her ear.

Genevieve didn't so much as flinch. She barely opened one eye as she murmured, "You really should know anyone else sneaking through that window would be dead already." She turned over to face him. "I didn't know you were coming tonight." The look in her husband's eyes sent panic through her blood and she sat up. "Henry, what's the matter?"

"Are the children asleep?"

"Yes, of course. For hours. What's happened?"

"The baby—"

Gen's pulse quickened, petrified of what Henry would say. "What did Lilith do to her?"

Henry ran a hand along his beard. It was thicker than he'd ever worn it before. Veni supposed he hadn't had much opportunity to shave while battling men and setting up a revolution in the mountains.

"I got the baby out of the castle."

Genevieve's eyes went wide. "You what?"

"I had to, Gen. She's been there for weeks, and I don't know what Lilith would have done to her."

"You could have been caught, Henry."

He sat up and slid his hand to the nape of her neck. "But I wasn't."

His wife studied him for a long moment. "Bring the baby here." Henry balked in response. "I'll raise her as ours."

"You cannot be serious. What about Family Records? We can't forge them twice, Gen. What if someone comes here to inspect the farm and finds her?"

She held a hand to her husband's cheek. "I'll take care of it."

"Henry opened his mouth to object, but a quiet knock sounded at the door.

Luvenia's voice came softly through the wood. "Mummy? Are you awake?"

"Yes, Luvi. One moment..."

Henry swiftly kissed his wife, eyes full of unspoken words, and climbed back through the window. Once it was shut, he deftly held onto the stones of the house and watched with no small amount of pride and heartache as his beloved daughter walked into the room.

"Are you alright? I thought I heard voices."

"I'm perfectly fine, dear. What are you doing awake so late?"

"I had a nightmare."

Everything turned violet and fell away to reveal the woodlands of Maaraveor.

Henry rushed forward to catch Veni just before she collapsed. She slumped against him, and he lowered to the ground, cradling her.

"Y—you're…" She began to sob as all she'd witnessed sunk in.

Henry held her, gently rocking back and forth like he had when she was a little girl. Khyan made himself busy roasting the rabbits and making tea.

Even for Khyan it was an incredible amount to process. He couldn't see what Veni saw, but his bird-like sense of hearing had indeed revealed most of what was said. He'd known Henry was important. He'd even entertained the possibility that Jacob was not Veni's real brother. But Khyan had not known who Henry truly was and he'd not known the little girl that Nuria's closest friend gave birth to was Genevieve. Nuria had told him she did not know Henry was the Liberator, but had she known the rest? He handed Veni some tea and she finally spoke after a few shaky sips.

She pulled back from her father and rose to sit on a stone. "You're the rightful King of Orford, then?"

Henry nodded, almost imperceptibly. "Alestair was my father. Though I never met him."

Her lip wobbled. "And Jacob?"

Henry let out a long, low breath. "He is not my blood. But he is still my son."

It was all too much. Veni let her full cup fall to the ground and retired to her bedroll for the evening.

When Luvenia ceased her squirming and surrendered to peaceful sleep, Henry turned to Prince Khyan. "Thank you, Prince."

Khyan raised an eyebrow with intrigue. "For?"

The Liberator cleared his throat. "For loving my daughter. For stepping in where I failed, and for taking her in. For giving her the amulet…" He trailed off, worried things were getting a bit too personal.

"She is very special to me. And I would do it all over again in a heartbeat." Khyan snorted. "She did stab me once."

Henry's attention snapped from the fire to Khyan. "Did she now? And here I heard it told that you saved my son's life and my daughter's heart."

Khyan looked at his feet. "She is very special to me." He fiddled with his cup, debating the need to continue speaking or to let the moment simply pass. "I—" He sighed. "It's difficult, to grow ancient and yet stay perpetually young. It makes it difficult to find true comrades. Darius and Theralin have always been like young siblings or even my own children. Luvenia, however, has a soul as old as mine in many ways. She has become an irreplaceable friend to me."

Henry considered the prince's candor for a long moment. "You know, Luvenia has always been like that—an old soul." He smiled wistfully and Khyan finally looked at him. "From the time she was able to toddle and speak, she never asked common questions. She wanted to know the *deeper* things. She wanted to know the *how* and the *why* of things. She's always known what truly matters and has held wisdom far beyond her years. While the other children ran wild and socialized, my Luvenia would be found huddled in solitude with a book." Henry chuckled.

Khyan's lips turned up at the corners. "That does sound like her."

Henry heaved a great sigh. "What do you think she'll do

when she rises?"

"Mmm," Khyan muttered behind a mouthful of tea. "She will become the Princess of Orford and the woman we've all known her to be from the start."

Chapter Thirty-One

"Can we get on with this?" Darius set one of Hugo's many books back on the shelf and crossed his arms. "We need to be in Toulona in a matter of hours."

"Don't rush me, Darius," Thera snapped.

"He's not rushing you, dear, he's rushing me." Hugo adjusted his monocle over one papery eye. "It should be ready in 3...2...ah, there it is." The beaker in his parchment hand flashed blue and a plume of smoke shot forth. Hugo waved it away and poured it into two empty beakers.

When Hugo handed one to Dax, his face scrunched. "Has this previously held anything...poisonous?"

"Most assuredly." Hugo handed the other beaker to Thera. "Do not question my sanitation methods, dear boy."

"Are you sure this will work, Hugo?" Thera inspected her beaker of blue elixir while Dax shifted his from hand to hand, avoiding—with failure—the heat of it.

"Certainty is never a good bargain to make. Is it probable? Most likely. Though, memory is a fickle thing to predict. You could both remember it all, or none of it. You could one remember all and the other none—a true tragedy indeed. Or you could remember bits and pieces. My best estimation is that the stronger the moment and emotion, the more likely it is you'll remember."

Dax smirked. "If my dreams are a good indication, we're in luck. Quite a few of those moments were rather...intense."

"*Dax*," Thera censured, shooting him a glare while Darius

hid a snort.

"Drink up," Hugo instructed.

"Cheers." Dax clinked his glass with hers and downed it in one gulp.

Thera did the same, the liquid burning her throat and all the way down to her stomach. That was when the rush hit her. Dax staggered backwards as if he'd just taken a blow and both their eyes filled with tears. Memories flooded them—passionate, adoring, deeply connected moments. It was the *emotions* Thera was not prepared for, though. She felt them from every direction and in the depths of her soul, both the ones she'd erased with the Forgetful Cakes those years ago, and the ones shooting like sparks from Dax's own flood of remembrance. When it was over, Thera let out a whimper and Darius took one step forward, just in case she needed him.

"Dax—" Her voice broke. "I'm so sorr—"

She had no chance to finish, for Dax rushed forward. One hand found the nape of her neck and the other her waist. His lips crashed into hers and Thera couldn't believe she'd ever given him up. *Ever*, for even a moment. When he finally pulled back from their passionate kiss, Dax beamed from ear to ear.

"I've missed you so."

Darius and Hugo had busied themselves elsewhere during the kiss, but the general cleared his throat. "We've a long journey ahead of us. The perfect time to catch up." He turned to Hugo. "My friend, until we meet again."

Thera grumbled about the sand in her...*everywhere* for the thousandth time. "Isn't your father the captain of the Roah's guard or something?" she asked Dax as she fumbled with her headdress and the scarf over her mouth.

Dax chuckled. "I thought you loved Toulona, *Princess*."

"It was you I loved, you oaf. Now, why can't we stay in that darling little oasis you broke us into. I take it you actually have a *key*, considering it's your father's home?"

Dax shrugged. They were trailing behind Darius at a far too leisurely pace for the general, who was already in a foul mood about traveling with two love birds. Especially while he missed Luvi.

"We can't stay with the captain, Thera. We're supposed to arrive quietly and gather our information quietly."

Thera snarled at Darius' back. "Pray tell how we can be *concealed* along these blasted sand dunes, General."

Darius stopped and turned to her, his face set in hard lines beneath his own head covering. They did little to keep the sand out, but the sun was unrelenting without them. "Have you forgotten Julian again?"

A short burst of laughter escaped Dax. "How could we not forget him, General."

"That's very rude." Julian made himself visible, alarmingly close to Dax—who jumped.

"It's rude to stand so close to me."

Thera rolled her eyes. "Julian, are you concealing us all or just yourself."

"Dammit, Theralin," Darius interrupted. "Why must you never listen to a word I say? I've told you three times that if Julian is invisible, *so are we.* Abayomi, the proximity in which Julian stands to us directly affects how concealed we are." Darius turned and began walking up the next dune.

"Thank you, General," Julian spoke meekly and went invisible once more.

"Why can we see each other, though?"

"I thought you'd find it strange to not see one another. I, however, have no choice. For you to be invisible to outsiders,

I must be totally unseen."

"But can we talk?" Thera asked. "Will people hear us?"

Darius growled and picked up the pace.

"It's best to keep fairly quiet, Princess Theralin."

"Thank you, Julian."

"Yes. Thank you, Julian," Darius spoke over his shoulder. "I can't take another moment of her prattling."

Dax snickered and she smacked him. "You're supposed to be on my side."

When they'd set up three shoddy tents whipped every which way by wind and sand, Thera ventured out in search of water. All three men had protested, and she had left them with several choice words and a couple crude hand gestures. They all knew she could handle herself.

To her great shock, Thera indeed found a minuscule patch of water not incredibly far off. Judging by the slight drop in temperature and the bit of wet sand here and there, it must have uncharacteristically rained in the area just after nightfall. She might have been angry with those sodding men when she left camp, but she didn't wish for them to die of thirst in the deserts of Toulona, so she'd snatched up their water skins as well as her own.

When the last one was filled and tied to her waist, Thera stretched her neck up to look at the blanket of stars. It reminded her why Toulona had stolen her heart just before Dax did. When she looked down at the sprawling sand, she swore a sprinkle of starlight was sliding over the dunes. She took a step closer and then she felt it. The strange, vibrant Kaleidoscope of emotion unique to— But it couldn't be. That was when she felt another set of emotions, distinctly mortal and following the turquoise lights bouncing toward Thera. She squinted in the dark, but nothing more was visible.

"You wretched creature," she heard the mortal set of emotions cloaked in darkness mutter. "Where are you leading me in the middle of the night." The voice spoke in crystal clear Toulonan and Thera would know that haughty voice anywhere.

The starlight bounded closer, turning into a blur of light and fluff. A creature unlike any other in the mortal realm or even Aureland jumped into Thera's arms and purred loudly. "Nahara," Thera cooed. "How did you find me, my sweet flifna." The creature's long rabbit ears tickled her chin as she nuzzled her. The little flifna's misty white light between those long ears winked out and she looked up at Thera with her feline eyes.

"You filthy mongrel—" The voice cut off abruptly when she realized she was not alone in the dark.

Nahara's whiskers turned bright white, illuminating Thera and her new guest.

"Theralin!" she gasped.

"Femi." Nahara jumped down and Thera enveloped Femi in a hug, the cat-rabbit encircling her two mistresses, purring loudly.

"What are you doing out in the middle of nowhere with no supplies?" Thera chastised. "Surely between Naiheeli and myself we have taught you to better care for yourself."

The Heiress Apparent of Toulona scoffed. "And I should think Naiheeli and your Keeper Queen would have taught you better than to camp in the middle of *nowhere* without checking the perimeter first." Femi pointed in the direction she and Nahara had come from. "My father has a small oasis home just there. I've been residing there for some time now."

Thera's face brightened. "Are you, by any chance, in the mood to welcome a few visitors?"

Femi rolled her eyes but agreed. She walked with Thera through the abominably sand-filled night, Nahara's whisker light guiding them. She refused to leave Thera's arms and Femi made several comments concerning the flifna's ungrateful—but much appreciated—behavior.

"She's stayed with you since that night in the woods when

I left you with the druids, then?"

Femi scoffed. "Relentlessly. I thought when I traveled back home that she would find you or stay with Naiheeli, but she has stayed ever by my side."

"And everyone else merely sees a cat, yes?"

Femi nodded. "One of my father's advisors looks at her in a peculiar fashion, though."

Thera smirked in the dark. "It's come to my attention that Toulonan Roahs have employed Keepers since...the dawn of time, really." Femi halted. "I think that is why your tutor knew of them and how she found the book you showed me."

"Where did you learn this?" Femi's voice was soft with the cadence of learning a great secret to something pondered for an entire lifetime.

Thera did not get to answer, because Dax was upon them in an instant. "How far did you go? You've been gone for ages. Darius wouldn't allow me to come look for you."

Darius strolled up with a lantern, his face cross. "Who's this?"

"Dax?" Femi squinted at him in the lantern light.

"Femi?" She cleared her throat and he frowned. "My dearest *Heir Apparent*," Dax mocked.

Thera looked between them, gauging everyone's emotions. Darius was perturbed, but frankly he'd been perturbed since the second Veni's horse had ridden away to Maaraveor. Dax was...confused, but excited. It seemed a friendly enough joy. Femi was… Thera snorted. Femi was simply her snobbish self, though Thera could detect a bit of joy from her as well.

"Darius, this is Eshe-Femi Anippe, the Heir Apparent of Toulona." To his credit, he dipped into a slight bow and muttered *Your Grace*. "Femi, this is General Darius Cremeux. He is the leader of our Aureland Horde."

The Heiress' eyebrow ticked up at that. "The mighty

Keeper army?"

Darius nodded once.

"And Dax, of course. You two know each other."

"Unfortunately," Femi whispered.

"She's just angry I'm sent out and she's not. That's all."

"You're just an errand boy. I am to be the Roah one day and he's just the son of the Captain of the Guard."

"Right. Meaning your life is a tick more valuable than mine," Dax shot back.

"But I have been trained by the mystic *druids*."

Thera's mouth fell open. "You *tell* people that? Femi!"

The heiress waved a hand at Thera, numerous gold bracelets tinkling. "It was that or let them kill whomever they thought had kept me for a year." She turned back to Dax, gesturing toward Thera. "Is this the girl you wouldn't stop yammering about and then she fell out of your life?"

"This has been lovely," Darius broke in, "but could we please get the heiress and her...cat? back to where she came from. We need sleep."

"Femi has so graciously invited us to stay with her at her oasis home." Thera preened. Darius grunted.

In a matter of moments, their meager camp was packed, and they were headed for an enchanting slice of Toulonan desert comfort.

"Femi, this place is divine." Thera reclined on a mat next to a sprawling palm and a peach tree.

The group had gone inside the small mud brick structure Femi lived in, but after so long out of doors, it felt stifling hot, no matter how many shuwts the guards fanned them with. Alas, they'd drifted outside to dip their toes in the water and feel the night breeze on their skin.

"I do enjoy it here immensely." Femi spoke in the common tongue of Orford for the benefit of those less familiar with Toulonan—namely Darius and Julian. "My father has insisted I stay here for months, though. I'm growing rather bored."

Darius sat up on an elbow from where he was laying on a mat looking at the stars. "The Roah has you all the way out here on purpose? This is not a holiday?"

Femi shook her head, dark, silken hair and golden jewelry catching the moonlight. "It began as a holiday, but when I prepared to return to the city, my father insisted I stay. That was weeks and weeks ago."

Thera and Darius sat all the way up in unison. "The Roah knows, then?" Thera questioned the general, his brows knit tightly together.

"My father knows what?"

Darius ignored the heiress. "Abayomi, you obtained your information outside the palace, yes?"

"Correct. I wasn't aware anyone within the palace knew what was happening, but if I could hear it, so could the Roah's informants."

Femi stood and stamped her foot. "If the lot of you do not tell me what's going on this instant and what you're doing here, I will kick you all out into the harsh desert on your own again." She crossed her arms and Thera smirked at her friend.

"Your father gave Queen Lilith a row of pyramid tombs—"

"I know that much, General."

Darius frowned. "Where does your knowledge end then, Heiress? We can save some valuable time." His dry tone only ruffled Femi more.

"The pyramids were supposed to be housing valuable food to be shipped to Orford. Grains and vegetables, that sort of thing."

"Vegetables? Were they somehow turned into greenhouses of sorts?"

Femi nodded. "That was the rumor. This piqued my curiosity, because if the Orford Queen could achieve something like that, my people would benefit from doing the same. When I went to investigate myself, all I found were empty tombs and those horrible Collectors your queen employs."

"She is not our queen," Darius ground out. "Didn't Thera mention Enenra following you to the border of Vilora?"

"Yes. I've not seen any since Thera vanquished them that night we met."

Darius stood and ran a hand along his jaw. "They've been spotted a few places since then, but with minimal damage that we know of." He chewed his lip and walked along the water.

"I wonder," Thera spoke, standing, "If the Enenra are sentries of a sort. That's what I gathered when they chased Femi. They wanted to scare her away from pursuing the information she'd gathered. What if that is their purpose?"

"Wouldn't that mean they're following Abayomi?"

All five of them fell silent, glancing around the oasis with suspicion.

"The Enenra are smoke creatures. They can spy using small flames like candlelight or lamplight, but they can't come forth unless there is a larger fire."

"I haven't used more than a lantern," Dax held up the one in their midst and promptly snuffed it out, "since I left for Aureland. I had no need of a campfire."

"Julian." Darius startled the Keeper by looking directly at him. "You haven't been invisible since we entered the oasis, remember?"

Julian blushed. "Right, General."

"Could your invisibility hide us from Enenra?"

"I've not had a great deal of experience with Enenra, but I would venture to say we remain somewhat hidden, though if there is a large enough amount of smoke, or it gets close enough, one could wrap around our forms, and we would be somewhat visible."

Darius swore. "We keep flames to a minimum and far from

Abayomi. What else do you know, Heiress?"

"That is all."

"Aboyami, fill her in and spare no detail. I've not heard the account from your mouth, either."

Dax adjusted his position on his mat as Thera sat next to him. He wrapped an arm around her and pulled her closer. "I hadn't been to Pietro's line of pyramids in ages. I was stationed in Anjali for some time and before that I was sent to Dakterra for a time. Femi had mentioned once in passing how odd she thought the pyramids were, so I made a mental note to check in on them periodically. I found no more than what she spoke of until the last time I went, days ago.

When I arrived, the Collectors were stoic, but a few of the Warmongers were off duty playing cards. I snuck behind their tent to have a listen. They spoke of nothing important, and I made to leave, but two Toulonan guards came into their tent and told them *she's done it.* They didn't say what, or who, but they were so shaken that their voices trembled.

I followed one of the Warmongers and he led me to a tavern in the city where he let slip to another man, a Toulonan, that Pietro had created some sort of monster in the tombs using her Keeper gift. I kept up with him the rest of the evening, but he said nothing else. I entered Aureland that night."

Darius ran a hand through his hair. "Why would one of Pietro's men offer any information freely to anyone? You have no idea who this man was that he told?"

"No. I assume he was a Marche de Blanc informant."

"She would never allow her men to divulge any information without intent, and they're so controlled there is no way they offered it freely with their own agenda."

"Agreed," Thera said.

Femi chewed her thumbnail. "What kind of monster?"

Dax shrugged. "I don't know. He didn't mention any more details."

"After the Enenra, the Collectors ripping apart, and the

beast Luvi and I saw in Dakterra, it can't be good."

Femi's eyes were wide. "Collectors ripping apart and a beast you saw?"

The group spent the rest of the night explaining all they knew and filling in the heiress, the moon as their only source of light, until sleep claimed them one at a time.

Henry halted his horse, sliding out of the saddle as his companions brought their own mounts to a stop. "I believe you and my daughter have something to discuss before we venture through the Nameless Caves and into Maaraveor tomorrow, Prince." He tied his horse to a tree and took up his bow.

Khyan eyed him warily. "You're in the business of meddling now?"

Henry slung his quiver across his back. "You wished for her to know." He flourished a hand. "Tell her and she shall know."

"Says the king of secrets," Khyan muttered.

A low laugh rumbled in Henry's chest. "This is as good an area to camp as any. Find shelter and talk. I'll return with dinner."

The prince turned to Veni, finding her expression difficult to decipher. "Intrigue or trepidation?" he asked carefully.

"Fair bit of both, I suppose." She pointed ahead. "There is a rock face just ahead. We'll set up there."

"You Rouseeaus are demanding this evening."

The two of them set to pitching their tents, laying out bedrolls, and starting the fire. Veni fought nerves and a wild imagination as she went.

After learning the insane identity of her father—and she supposed herself—and learning that her very own parents were the original Zealots...that her brother was not even her brother… It was all too much. She'd held her head high and let her father in after witnessing the full truth. Admitting to herself that she was any sort of royalty was not going to happen, though. She refused. It was pure madness.

She sighed. And now Khyan wanted to add to the secrets being revealed.

"Did you know Nuria knew my mother?" She'd been a bit cold with the prince since learning that fact herself. It wasn't his secret to tell, but it still stung.

Khyan set another log on the fire. "I did not."

Veni's brown crumpled. "You didn't know?" That seemed implausible.

"I did not," he repeated as he dusted his hands on his trousers with little to show for it. "I knew your grandmother, Viola, but she left Aureland many years ago. I was informed she had a child, but that was all I knew. I did know she perished, but there was no way for me to have made that connection. It seems my sister kept all the dealings with your family secret from me as well."

"Yet she sent you to watch over our farm."

"She did. And I did not question her."

Veni made a noncommittal sound. "Well, let's have it then. Your big secret."

Khyan sighed and sat, patting the log next to him. When Veni remained standing, arms crossed, he finally spoke. "You won't like the man you see me become within those caves."

Veni rolled her eyes. "I'm well aware of the plan, Khy, and if things go awry, I've seen you kill people before."

"I'm not referring to the plan." Her brow furrowed and he trudged on with another sigh. "The best place to hide is often in plain sight, yes?"

Veni gave him a curt nod.

"I am well known in Marche de Blanc."

"For?"

A smirk touched the prince's lips and he shrugged. "Sales?"

Veni's eyes narrowed, unamused by his attempt at lightening the mood. "*Of*?" she demanded.

Khyan scrubbed at his chin. "Information."

Veni let out a breath and dropped her arms. "Is that all? You made it sound so sinister."

The prince shook his fiery head. "It's not that simple. In order to keep my reputation there intact, the information I deal in must be true. That, I'm afraid, can be quite costly at times." He stilled, waiting for her to judge him. Think less of him. Fear him.

Veni looked him over, his nerves growing ever thinner. Finally, she asked, "Have people died?"

The truth. "Yes."

"Have many been saved?"

Again, the truth. "Yes."

Veni nodded, face stern. "I trust your judgement, Khyan."

"I don't always make the right call."

"No one does."

"I don't relish the thought of you seeing me act in such darkness. It's not the real me, I assure you."

Veni sat next to him. "Khy, if I've learned anything, it's that every person has darkness and light. It's which we choose to follow that matters. Nuria taught me that when I first arrived." She took Khyan's hand, watching his face illuminated by the fire. "I don't care if that *is* part of you—that sinister dealer of secrets. I know you wield it for the greater good and I know your heart."

"You are too good for us, Princess." Khyan smirked and Veni yanked her hand away.

"Don't even start with me."

"These pyramids are incredible!"

"*Julian*," Darius censured. "*Quiet*."

The Keeper wasn't wrong, though. Darius had not seen the pyramids up close, and they were no small wonder. Sand whispered under their boots as they slunk through the guards' camp, invisible with Julian's gift, save for the footprints they left behind. They needed to be careful of those.

Darius cursed himself for the fifth time for allowing the heiress to come with them. They'd had to sneak past her guards which meant they would be looking for her at any moment. Not to mention the horrifying possibility of them getting caught and the Heiress Apparent of Toulona being captured—on his watch.

He held up a fist and they all halted behind him. "Abayomi," he whispered. "Take the heiress back to the oasis."

"He will not, General. Need I remind you these are my lands?"

Darius ground his teeth together. "Thera, please talk some sense into her."

"If we're caught, she is the only one with the right to be here." Thera crossed her arms and Darius' jaw clenched at the heiress' equally haughty expression.

"I'm very certain Pietro's men don't care who the hell she is."

"We stick together." Darius' face darkened and Dax relented. "That is my opinion, anyway."

The general grumbled but motioned them forward.

"This is it," Dax whispered.

The group slipped past the guards one at a time and into the dark tombs of the pyramid. Remaining silent within the narrow inner passageways proved difficult, but there appeared to be no one guarding them. There were, however, many lanterns.

"Is that enough combined smoke for Enenra?" Darius questioned Thera.

"No, though it wouldn't take much more and if they have

their sights on Dax, they're certainly watching right now."

"Heiress."

She pushed forward.

"Is there not a hidden chamber deep within the ground?" Femi nodded. "I think the Roah burial chamber is less likely for Pietro to hide her monsters in. We need to turn around and go down."

It didn't take long for their ears to pop and the sense of unimaginable weight on top of their heads to prove nauseating. It quickly became crippling for Julian. After a great deal of argument and much dry heaving from Julian, Femi led him up and out of the pyramid.

They were on their own and visible.

"I have a bad feeling about this," Thera whispered when they'd nearly descended to the bottom.

"Can you sense anything?"

Thera tucked her bottom lip between her teeth and focused. "Two guards. They're rather bored." Her brow furrowed and then her eyes went wide. "I sense...something. Many somethings… I—I wouldn't call them human, but they're not inhuman. They're not asleep, but they're not awake…"

"The Undead."

Thera's attention snapped to Darius.

"Pietro's Kiss of Death. It's what Nuria and I suspected. She's found a way to reanimate dead bodies within the hearts of these pyramids. I wanted to be certain before I mentioned it. Now we know."

Thera scowled. "What do we do now? Just go in and snatch one?"

"Just a look. But we don't have Julian's cover anymore. We'll have to knock the guards out."

Thera nodded resolutely and sauntered off ahead of them.

"*Thera*," Darisu whispered harshly.

By the time he and Dax caught up to her, both guards were slumped on the ground, and she shrugged. "They're lonely guards. I was lost."

Dax smiled wickedly at her and Darius thought he'd be sick. Surely, he and Luvi weren't so nauseating.

They slipped past the unconscious guards and into a tomb the size of a bed chamber. Darius took a torch off the wall and slowly took in the space. At the back, an unlit antechamber beckoned him forward.

Thump.

Thump.

Thump.

"What is that?" Dax spun in a small circle, looking for the sound.

THUMP.

THUMP.

"Darius?"

"I don't *know*, Thera. It's coming from that dark antechamber."

Rrrrrreeeeee.

All three of them froze.

Sand stirred ahead of them.

Darius motioned for them to stay back. He withdrew Nahaliel and inched forward toward the beckoning dark and what lurked within it.

Shk.

Shk.

Shk.

The sound grew closer and closer, still Darius inched forward, his torch lighting a few paces ahead of him but beginning to smoke too much.

"Darius, we need that torch blown out."

He risked another step forward.

Shk.

Shk.

Shk.

Darius sucked in a breath. His torch illuminated a gnarled,

skeletal face wrapped in filthy linens. The undead creature moved toward him, moaning, its arms reaching. Darius threw the torch down and took a swipe at the creature with his sword. Its arm hit the ground with a plume of sand and the general coughed against the lungful of dust, blacking up, sword at the ready. He snatched up the arm from where it had fallen and still the creature stalked toward him, arm outstretched and reeking of death.

From behind, Thera threw a knife and it landed with a hollow *thunk* in the creature's linen-wrapped chest. Still, it advanced.

"Get out of here!" Darius commanded, and they shot through the tunnels as quickly as they could.

They stumbled up to the entrance of the pyramid, hoping against all hope that Julian had gotten himself together. Nearing the blinding light of the entrance, an invisible hand touched Darius' arm and their presence vanished. They snuck past the entry guards and crouched behind the pyramid, catching their breath.

"Femi," Darius breathed. "Can you get back to your oasis from here on your own?" The heiress nodded curtly. "Julian, go with her. Keep her safe." He reached into his pocket and handed Thera and Dax each a vial, keeping one for himself. "Compliments of Hugo. Drink up."

They downed their vials and Femi gasped. A massive black lion pawed at the sand. A lithe leopard preened. And a sandy wolf sniffed the hot air.

"Come, Heiress." Julian led her away.

Darius took up the pyramid creature's lost limb in his teeth—a horrible choice indeed—and the lionheart bounded off into the sand dunes, leopard and wolf in tow.

Just before the Gate into Aureland, something sharp stung the lion's flank as a wolf growled and a leopard shrieked. Everything went dark.

When the lion finally managed to open his eyes, a form

stood before him, a sickening smile adorning her painted face.

"Hello, General."

Chapter Thirty-Two

"Here we are."

Veni blinked. "This is just a regular market."

Henry nodded. Khyan smirked.

"There are no caves. You said we were going through the Nameless Caves. We never went through caves."

"It's a fair bit more inconspicuous to simply stop by and pick up a new coat at the same time as a few stolen jewels, rather than a banker walking into a random cave, don't you think?" Khyan smiled.

"It's not what I expected."

"Precisely." Henry put his daughter's arm through his. "Lead the way, Gabriel."

Khyan scoffed. "I am Gabriel here," he explained to Veni. "The tea house is just over there. I'll go in and take my usual table. The two of you come in just after me for a nice tea."

"We know the plan, Prince."

Khyan grunted and strode across the bustling street to a quaint confectioner and tea house. If it weren't for the circumstances or the shock to her system, Veni might have been incredibly excited to take tea at a foreign tea house with her father and great friend. She had wondered why they all dressed in finery before they left the inn that morning. And why, upon arriving, they'd checked into an inn at all. It made a lot more sense now.

"Are you sure about this, Love?" Henry turned her by the shoulders to look into her eyes. "This might look pretty, but it will, in fact, be quite dark. The setting somehow makes it all the more disturbing."

Alas, she was not meant to enjoy a lovely tea.

"I'm ready. It makes me feel better than you're here with me, I must admit."

Henry swallowed hard at her sudden warmth. They'd certainly been on better terms than when they left, but the distance remained in many ways. One couldn't erase abandoning their child, not for any reason.

"We're in this together, Love. From here on out." Luvenia squeezed her father's arm, and he placed his hand over hers. "Shall we?"

Veni nodded and they followed the path Khyan—Gabriel—had traversed into the confectioner, her indigo skirts whispering along the cobblestones.

Seated at their table adjacent to Khyan's, Henry told Luvenia to order whatever she would like. It was such a simple, yet fatherly thing to say and her heart constricted. She was beyond grateful for this second chance at life with him, even if she had a hard time grappling with some of his choices. They sipped their tea, talking of trivial things so they could hear Khyan and any other conversations around them. In a matter of moments, the confectioner himself came out and clapped Khyan on the back.

"Gabriel!" He sat down across from him. "Haven't seen you in these parts in too long, old friend."

Henry leaned in and spoke under his breath. "They're going to speak in a code of sorts."

"It's been a long time since I craved your confections, Sal."

The old confectioner leaned back, his chair groaning. "What are we in the mood for?"

"What have you got?"

Sal's lip twitched. "That will depend on how much you're willing to spend, my friend."

Khyan set his elbows on the table, his face stern. "Say, isn't your daughter of age now and looking for work?" Sal stiffened, almost imperceptibly. "I could certainly clear that up for her."

Sal eyed him, jaw tight.

"What's happening?" Veni whispered.

Henry hid his words behind his teacup. "It sounds like Sal's daughter is obtaining wages in an unsavory way. Khyan knows about it. He's blackmailing him."

"It sounded like he was offering her a better job."

"He'll do that, too, I'm sure."

Sal's sullen demeanor shifted back to an amiable host in an instant. "I've a lovely Viloran tart—"

Khyan waved a dismissive hand. "No tarts."

"Ah yes, apologies, Gabriel. I forgot who I was speaking to for a moment."

Veni didn't have to ask what a tart was.

"I've also a load of truffles."

"*Bits of gossip*," Henry whispered.

"Three cakes."

"Jewelry or other fine goods."

"Several soups."

Khyan's brow rose. "You dabble in soups now?"

"*Forged papers*," Henry clarified.

"I do indeed," Sal announced proudly, then he leaned in. "Also have a fresh pan of baklava."

"There it is."

Veni looked at her father. This tête-à-tête concerning baked goods was giving her a headache.

"Fresh baklava, you say?" Khyan leaned back, his fingers laced behind his head. "What recipe?"

"Orfordian. The very best baklava."

Orford did not specialize in baklava.

"An entire fresh pan?"

Sal nodded.

Veni's heart was beginning to race. She had a sinking feeling they were speaking of a person. She'd known one of their first missions was to discover where Pietro had been taking the children, but it had been weeks since they intercepted that shipment. Could there have been another?

"Are they talking about—"

"People."

Veni groaned.

"How fresh?" Khyan asked.

"Just pulled it out of the oven this morning."

"I'm not sure what that means," Henry whispered. "It's after midday so it depends on the timestamps of their code."

Khyan's shoulders lost some of their tension and Veni would wager it meant the people this *baklava* was referring to were not children.

"You don't have anything a bit fresher?"

Veni was going to be sick. Khyan had been right that she would not like this side of him, but she knew the truth of what he was doing. He wanted to know just as much as she did if there were any little souls in danger.

Sal leaned in, his voice hardly carrying. "I've heard tell of a strawberry tart straight out of the oven. For the right price, I'm willing to locate it for you."

"*Ester*," Henry breathed.

Veni's attention snapped to her father's eyes. She glanced at Khyan, and he was clenching his fist underneath the table, his face unreadable.

"Name your price."

Sal smiled. "This tart is delicate. The kind favored by the Queen of Orford herself."

"Is this particular delicacy difficult to get to?"

"Not for me. And, you know, you're quite right. My daughter *is* in need of some new dresses and if you hear tell of a lovely governess position, I would be most grateful." Khyan nodded once and Sal grinned. "I hear you're quite the connoisseur of truffles yourself."

"I know a good one when I taste one."

Sal nodded and stood. He came around to clap Khyan on the back. "How does tomorrow sound, Gabriel?"

"Brilliant."

Sal strode away and Khyan sipped his tea. Veni was anxious to follow the lead. To get Sal's whoring daughter a better job and some new clothes so she could find her sister. But Khyan just...sat there.

"Come, Love. We're done here." Her father paid and they strode out into the windy spring air of Maaraveor.

"We have to find her," Veni demanded.

"Slow down. Khyan has to make good on his end of the bargain or we're less likely to find her than if we've never gone in there." He steered her toward a row of dress shops. "Khyan will sit there the rest of the afternoon. He is well-known here. As soon as Sal tells someone Gabriel is here, he will have a line of people waiting to make deals with him. It is how he will discover the information valuable enough to offer Sal in exchange for the girl's whereabouts."

They strode toward a shop with frilly items Luvenia wouldn't be caught dead in. She frowned when it was the very shop they approached and entered.

"Bear in mind," Henry said under his breath as he dipped his head to the shopkeeper, "this child might not be Ester."

But he'd said strawberry, as in strawberry hair, and he'd said the tart was a favorite of the queen's and well-guarded. It had to be her. It simply had to be.

"What are we doing here?"

"I have someone I'd like for you to meet."

"In this dreadful shop?"

Henry chuckled. "No. She has a smoke room in the back."

"It has been a long time, dear boy," the elderly shopkeeper

spoke. "How are you?"

"I'm well, Marta. Is she here, by chance?"

The woman smiled kindly, if not a bit shrewdly. "You're in luck. She hasn't left her druids in many months, until this very morning." Her eyes crinkled at the edges. "I've a feeling she knew you'd come."

"Thank you, Marta."

He took Veni's hand and led her through a door in the back, behind a curtain. Smoke filled the small room they stepped into, rendering the plain space ethereal. It was, however, no comparison to the ethereal creature that stepped forth, clad in the colorless garb of the druids.

"Matthias," she murmured, coming forward to rest her weathered hands on his cheeks.

"Naiheeli. It has been too long."

The oracle. Veni's lips parted, and she hardly contained her gasp. Part of her wanted to loathe this woman. She'd kept her father from his rightful home. From his parents. She'd told him things that led him to leave their family. That led her mother to forfeit her life when she could've run. But looking at this woman, she could *feel* her wisdom and knowledge. She heard her words from the vision, "*It is not my place to decide what I see and do not see.*"

Naiheeli released Henry and stepped in front of Luvenia. To her great dismay, the old oracle dipped into a low bow before rising and taking her hands. Veni blushed and tried not to squirm.

"Luvenia. I've not seen you since you were but a toddling babe. My, how lovely you have grown. You are the exact likeness of your mother."

Veni pulled her hands out of the woman's grasp. She nodded knowingly and addressed Henry again.

"The Great War is upon us, Matthias. Are you prepared?"

Henry nodded. "We're here gathering as much intel as we

possibly can. Do you have anyone you can direct us to?"

Naiheeli tapped a finger to her chin. "I believe your owl prince is doing quite well in that department."

"The general of the mighty Aureland Horde," the Queen of Orford mused.

Darius had never seen Pietro up close. He found himself itching to sink his lion's teeth into her throat and rip her pretty head from her shoulders.

Lilith Pietro prowled around him, Darius straining at his chains and falling limply back to the ground on legs still numb. He snarled and roared at her as she circled him with a mocking smile.

"You, Darius Cremeux, are the crux of it all."

He eyed her intently. Memorizing every word, every movement she made. As he did, the general noticed that pretty face appeared to have something already strangely wrong with it. Sensing his scrutiny, she turned the other way.

"You and your Keeper mongrels have a new little pet." Pietro's lips turned up in a vicious smile. "The *immune girl.*" She tipped her head back and a bone chilling laugh escaped her. "It was her immunity that set it all in motion, dear general." She adjusted her obsidian crown and crossed her arms. Her elegant gown dipped in black gemstones was a ridiculous sight in a dank dungeon smelling of refuse.

"I used to think it was the strawberry-haired girl." She drummed her razor-sharp nails on one arm, bored. "I thought I'd secured my place as queen the moment I killed that baby's family in the caves and took her to be my own. Then, she was taken right out from under my nose. That was when I realized my error."

Pietro inched forward, just out of Darius' snarling reach. "You see, dear general, only one bloodline can be immune to my Venom. The one I used to create it." She stepped back and tisked. "I realize my folly now, but that's the thing about the past." She shrugged. "You can't change it. Oh, it took me a decade to find that baby, but I found her. Imagine my surprise when she wasn't immune at all. But her sister on the other hand…"

Darius roared and pulled against his chains once more as the queen laughed.

"And then she fell for *you*, General, and you both led me straight to the Liberator. The true bane of my existence." She cackled a mad, hysterical laugh. "After all this time!" The queen clapped gleefully. "But I cannot very well kill him without eliminating his heir as well, now can I?"

Darius' growl came out in a low rumble that shook the ground.

Pietro leaned in to look within his lion eyes. "Your Little Bird will come for you, General. They'll all come for you. And I *will* be ready."

Darius snarled as she turned on her heels and strode out. His head swam with the effects of whatever she'd tranquilized him with, but he did his best to piece together the information she'd given him. There was a gnawing in the back of his mind that knew she wouldn't divulge any information at all if she intended for him to live.

He worked through why Pietro would have used Luvi's bloodline to concoct the Venom if she didn't even know who the family was… The realization struck home with a sickening sense at the same moment a Collector strolled into his cage and tore itself apart.

Darius stood chained against a wall, hardly able to move a handbreadth. Instinctually, he struggled against the restraints, the recesses of his mind warning him to be prepared for the horror soon to come.

It's not real. It's not real.

The words he chanted made no difference as his Little Bird was dragged in by her hair, kicking and clawing. Darius lunged, only to feel the bite of metal against his skin. The Collectors strapped her to a table, and she screamed his name. He roared and struggled against the chains, effectively ripping his wrists.

It's not real. It's not real.

This was his fault. This is what they would do to his Luvi because he'd failed to protect her. Because he'd been foolish and gone into a pyramid he knew held treachery.

The Collectors tore open her dress and Darius roared again. He watched in horror as they shoved needles into every inch of her skin until she sobbed and writhed in pain, foaming at the mouth. Still, she said his name. Over and over.

"I'm here. This isn't real, Little Bird. It will be over soon." He said the words through tears countless times until the Collectors left the dungeon and the queen walked in.

"No."

She stalked forward, a grotesque smile playing at her lips, and fit a rag in between Luvi's teeth. "So no one will hear you sing, Little Bird." Bending over Luvenia, she watched with satisfaction as the girl growled through her gag at the queen, snot and tears mingling. Even trembling in fear Luvi held herself with strength.

Pietro bared her teeth, raising her hand. Her nails came down across Luvi's face, tearing through flesh and down to the bone. Painstakingly, the queen tore the flesh off piece by piece to reveal her exposed skull as Luvenia writhed and screamed. Darius' knees buckled and he slumped to the filthy floor. Blood dripped from his wrists, but he continued to struggle.

It's not real. It's not real.

But it would be if he didn't wake up soon.

Chapter Thirty-Three

As soon as Khyan walked into their room at the inn both Veni and her father jumped up to hear his news.

"She's here. Just outside the city."

Veni immediately burst into tears. "You're certain it's Ester."

Khyan shrugged. He looked bone tired. "I'm fairly certain, but we need to be prepared."

"Right. She'll be heavily guarded." Henry moved for his weapons, but Khyan cleared his throat, halting him in his tracks.

"There...might not be much humanity left in her. We all need to prepare for that possibility."

Veni sunk onto the bed, grappling with what the prince had just said. "Did they tell you this?"

Khyan sat on her left and her father on her right. "Not exactly. But I did gather that she has been horribly mistreated. She's malnourished and she has been the subject of many of Pietro's blood tests, as we feared."

Veni began to tremble. Henry put his arm around her and rested his chin on the top of her head. "Hope is not lost, Love. She is alive and we are going to get her." He looked over Luvenia's head at Khyan. "Tonight."

Khyan nodded. "I did also learn the name of the man that owns Greer's Orphan House. Mr. and Mrs. Greer died many years ago, far before even Sebastian lived there, and the place has gone through several owners since. The man that owns it now is someone from Pietro's days prior to her mother marrying King Alestair."

Veni thought fleetingly how strange it was to know that man was her grandfather. That Pietro was her aunt.

"Their endeavor was not to bring the children to Marche de Blanc, it was to bring them to her fortress here, where Ester is. She grows weak and won't be able to withstand procedures much longer. Lilith wanted more children. She was meant to take several and let the rest be sold off as slaves."

Veni's stomach roiled, and Henry cursed colorfully, followed by a mumbled *sorry, Love.*

"That's why we're taking her out of there," Khyan said. "At nightfall."

"Happy Birthday, my queen."

Nuria looked up from her book to find Smithwick on a Bluestreak Rapidflyer hovering just in front of her face. She attempted to smile at the little ruffian, but it did not reach her eyes.

"Are you pouting because everyone is away for your birthday?"

She huffed a laugh. It was truly a lovely spring night in her gardens, and she simply couldn't enjoy it. "It is the middle of the night. And when you are as old as I, Smithwick, you quite forget when your birthday is. I am saddened because I miss my family and I worry for their safety and the safety of Aureland every moment."

"I suppose I will have to do, then, as far as birthday companions go. Come along, then."

There was really no point in arguing with Smithwick. Nuria tucked her small book away and followed the creature upon his bird. "Where are we going?"

The Sean'an Porter beamed. "I have the greatest gift I have

ever given anyone, and it is for you, Majesty."

"Schmoozer," she coughed, and Smithwick laughed.

Schmoozer he might be, but he had not been wrong.

Nuria gaped openly. Something she had not done in nearly five decades at least. "Smith...you cannot...this cannot be…"

Smithwick smiled with pride as his very dignified queen talked herself in circle with gibberish.

"Smith, it is a *dragon*." Nuria stepped forward gingerly, her hand outstretched. The enormous beast sniffed the air, blowing Nuria's hair back from her face. "Hello, lovely," she cooed. "What is your name?" The creature closed her eyelids and leaned into Nuria's hand. "Does she have a name?" she asked Smithwick over her shoulder.

"She is yours to bestow a name upon."

"Hmm." Nuria looked over her, stroking her forehead. "Let me see your fire, dear one."

The dragon's eyes sparked. She lifted her great head and spewed fire the color of blue ice into the night sky. She turned to Nuria proudly and pushed her head up against the queen's hand once more.

"*Impressive*. I shall name you Bleu."

The dragon shot another spray of blue fire into the air, letting it shoot like fireworks. When Nuria laughed—truly laughed—Bleu threw her head back and blew a great frame nearly as large as a small cottage. A massive plume of smoke hung in the air as Nuria and Smithwick praised the great beast. So enamored were they by the dragon's tricks, they missed the tendrils of smoke as they formed haunting shapes of soot and nightmares.

Somewhere nearby a child screamed. Nuria didn't even spare a thought. She climbed atop Bleu's back and urged her high into the air. Never mind that she had never ridden a dragon in all her years. Bleu felt like home. "Let us find the danger, Bleu."

The dragon huffed and flew in the direction of the scream.

Nuria bit back her own exclamation. "*Enenra*," she breathed. They were everywhere. Terror ensued on the streets, fires grew to enormous, overtaking homes. Chaos fell upon that peaceful corner of Aureland. She needed to put a stop to it.

"*Smith*!" the queen bellowed as she reached within the bodice of her gold dress for her Portal Key. Enenra could only be expelled by purest light. The only source of that in all the realms aside from the sun was the magic that lay within Portal Keys.

"Yes, Majesty." Smithwick was wild-eyed when he appeared next to her on his bird. Bleu's wings pumped so hard that the bird struggled against the wind.

"Get to Sebastian. He should be headed back from Orford. Tell him what's happened. And spread the word to anyone with a Portal Key that the light within them will protect them."

"Majesty, the Portal Keys will no longer work, then."

"I fear that is why they were sent here, Smith. Go. *Hurry*."

Nuria breathed a prayer to whomever was listening and urged Bleu toward the nearest Enenra. She took the dagger from her thigh and stabbed her Portal Key until blinding light burst forth. She held it high in the air as Bleu instinctively flew erratically and gained her access to several Enenra before her light winked out. Nuria instructed Bleu to land amidst the chaos until she could locate another Portal Key.

To her surprise, light burst forth just ahead of her and she saw Theralin screaming at the Enenra and wielding her own Portal Key's light. She turned to see Dax doing the same behind her. In a few moments that felt like hours, Keepers of all races joined together to destroy their Portal Keys yet vanquish the Enenra. Peace, fragile and disheveled, at last descended upon Aureland once more.

Nuria tucked away the travesty of losing so many Portal Keys in one fell swoop the moment she locked eyes with Theralin. Her sweet Thera's lip wobbled and Nuria's stomach fell to her toes. *Darius*.

Thera ran to Nuria, slamming into her so hard it was a struggle to keep upright. "They took him. We barely made it out. They took Darius."

The smell reached Veni first.

Refuse. Vomit. Mold. Rotten food. Blood.

The stark realization that her precious little sister had lived—no, *survived*—this way for the last half a year made Luvenia's stomach contents curdle. They were all clad in black from head to toe, appearing every inch as thieves in the night, and she supposed they were. Thieves stealing back an innocent girl.

Henry disabled the last guard on impressively silent feet, and they descended the steps toward the horrifying smell. Toward Ester. They had not anticipated the three Collectors stationed at the bottom of the stairwell.

Khyan took out the first with no issue. The second charged Henry and the third had Veni by her hair in seconds. Khyan sliced across the belly of the one holding her, reaching behind him with the other hand to take the Venom tube and stab his neck with it. He dropped to the ground with a thud. Henry held a hand to his own neck where he had been injected with the Venom, and Veni threw her knife into the Collector's shoulder just as Henry thrust his sword into his abdomen. Henry cursed under his breath, but the Venom did little harm.

"You're immune too?" Veni asked in awe.

Henry grunted. "Yes, but it still burns like hell." She'd never considered the other immune person the Collectors spoke of could be her father.

When it all went quiet after the scuffle, Veni heard the whimper. She lunged the last few steps to the cell, terrified of what she'd see. Terrified it wouldn't be her Sunshine. She took one look at the unruly mop of red curls atop the prone girl lying on the floor and her breath caught in her throat

"Sunshine," she spoke through tears. "Sunshine, it's me. It's Veni. I've come to take you away from this place."

Henry approached with the keys and unlocked the cell. Veni rushed forward and stooped next to her sister. "We have to go now. You're safe, Sunshine."

Sunshine.

She heard it. She heard the voice. It was closer than before. Almost like she could touch it. Just reach out and touch it.

We must go now.

This was it, then. She'd hung on as long as she could, and it was time to leave this world. She hoped it would be better there. Less pain.

You're safe, Sunshine.

It was all she needed to hear.

Ester went limp.

"Father, hurry. She's lost consciousness."

"We need to get her out of here. Now, Prince."

"I'll send a messenger bird to Healer Collins to meet us at the inn immediately."

Henry nodded and took Ester's eerily thin form in his arms. "Love, you have to watch our backs.

They made it to the inn with no small amount of effort and got Ester into bed. She was still unconscious, and Henry paced the room while Veni washed and changed her sister. The fact that she was in the same dress as the last time she saw her in a prison cart, their dead mother in the house behind them, left Veni bereft. That one simple fact sent her into near hysterics, but she needed to hang on. For Ester. For her father who was slowly losing his wits, too.

Khyan strode back in and the look on his face nearly pushed her over the edge. "What is it?"

"Aureland has been attacked. Nuria and Thera have handled it, but Healer Collins is occupied with the few injured."

It wasn't as bad as she'd feared, then. *Wait.* "Thera is in Aureland? Where is Darius?"

Khyan's Adam's apple bobbed as he swallowed. "He's been taken hostage."

Darius could hear heels clicking on stones, headed toward him. He sat slumped against a filthy wall, returned to his human form and he was covered in a sheen of sweat. The chains bit against his wrists, ankles, and neck. His mouth was dry, sweat was dripping into his eyes, and he was in no mood to speak with Pietro again.

"Hello, General," she purred as a Collector opened the cell door.

"Hello, Lilith." His voice was raspy from roaring in his lion form and disuse since he'd shifted back.

The queen merely laughed at his disrespect. "I would like to play a bit of a game, General."

"No."

"Oh, now don't go and get all sullen on me. They'll come for you eventually. Your Little Bird, your Liberator, and your dear *mother*." Her lips slid up on one side.

Darius huffed a humorless laugh. "My mother is dead, wench."

Pietro stooped down to his eye level. From that proximity, Darius could confirm there was something very wrong with the queen's face. Even in the low light it appeared as if her very skin was cracking.

She cocked her head to the side. "Is she?" Something disturbed and twisted passed behind her eyes. "Hm. I could have *sworn* I heard an owl in the rafters."

She looked up and Darius stopped breathing. It took every ounce of self-control he possessed to not look, to not give her the satisfaction. She was playing him. Trying to confuse him. Trying to get him to question Nuria.

Lilith put a hand to her chest and laughed, shrill and menacing. It echoed off the walls as her face smoothed back into the viper, poised to strike. "Now would be a good time for that little game of ours, don't you think? A trade of information, perhaps?"

He knew she would only offer information if she planned to kill him along with Luvi and Henry. Yet, if she failed to doing so, he would potentially have ammunition against her. It wasn't a risk he was willing to take, with the truth, anyway.

"No."

The Queen tisked. "That is unfortunate. I suppose we'll have to do this in a more interesting fashion, then."

She waved a hand and a Collector stepped in. The last thing Darius saw was her wicked sneer before he was enveloped by nightmares.

When he came to, gasping, from watching Luvi and Nuria be burned alive, Pietro was standing over him.

"Shall we try this again?"

Darius caught sight of the beast behind her, the one that had sat dormant under the Collector's human skin. It stood perfectly still, idle and vacant. Waiting.

"No," he barked through heaving breaths.

Pietro snapped and the beast launched toward him. This time, instead of creating nightmares with its fear toxin, the creature wrapped its gnarled hands around his shoulders and squeezed until it's dagger-sharp claws punctured his skin. Darius cried out as it slammed him against the wall and pressed with all its might.

"How about now, General?" Pietro cooed.

"No," Darius ground out through gritted teeth.

The queen sighed and the beast dropped him, its nails making a foul tearing sound as they pulled free of his flesh. Despite the pain, all Darius could think as he dropped to the ground was *how*. How was she controlling these things with a snap, a sigh, a breath?

"Do you know how your father went mad, General?"

Darius couldn't keep his eyes from ticking up to her at that.

"Because I do."

Damn her, she knew she had his attention. Pietro came forward and dipped one of her long fingernails into the wound on his shoulder. He bit back a sharp intake of breath. He watched in disgust as she lifted her fingernail, dripping with his blood, to her tongue. Her eyes closed as if she'd just tasted the sweetest of morsels and she all but moaned.

Darius prepared himself for the mental combat. She would lie, she would cheat, but he would arise triumphant in this. His head was still foggy from lack of nutrition and sleep, and now the loss of blood, but he had endured worse—so far.

"So very much she has kept from you." The queen shook her head. "You see, dear general, when I found out your mother and queen had a weakness in the form of a lover..." She looked from her nails to Darius' eyes, her head tipped to the side. "I tried to kill him."

Darius strained against his chains. His mind was muddled with fury and disbelief. There was no way. He remembered his mother.

"Your father was once a mighty man of valor. Quite like yourself. Nuria moved him into Aureland to keep him safe from yours truly and he began commanding the Horde." She stalked back and forth against one wall. "I was not privy to the information of where Aureland was. Not since my own mother refused to send me with Nuria to train as a child.

Then, one day, your father was living in a cottage within the woods of Orford, caring for a newborn son." Her smile was demented. "I knew you were hers. My spies would see her enter his home under the cover of darkness. Eventually, an argument broke out and Nuria left, only to return with a woman. A woman who was with child, that could care for you in Nuria's place."

Darius was shaking. He couldn't control the tremors wracking his body. It had to be a lie. All of it.

"Nuria thought she'd tricked me. That I would believe this picture of a happy family and think her lover had moved on. I'm certain she did it all as some ploy to protect you both." Pietro rolled her eyes. "But she was wrong. Oh, I let it play out for a while. I wanted to be certain you were her child.

You were stronger, faster than any other child. Your mind was sharper. You were most assuredly the seed of a Keeper." Lilith's eyes narrowed. "So, I killed your new mummy. Poison." She shrugged.

Darius' breaths were coming out in short bursts through his nose. He forced himself to calm. To listen. It was all a lie. And if it was not, he needed every bit of information.

"Nuria came to comfort him. She revealed her hand at last. However, she sealed your father's fate that night when she returned to Aureland without you. I tried to take you." Pietro shrugged again. "It was a good enough plan, really. But your father caught me. He put a dagger in my shoulder, to tell it truthfully." The queen stopped pacing and licked her lips, leaning close to Darius' face. "*So, I drove him mad.*"

Lilith laughed as Darius futilely pulled against his restraints again.

"That's when she brought him back to Aureland. You and your sister, too. And I learned, at long last, where the Keeper Realm was located. I've bided my time. I've waited. I've built my army. But the time has come, General. I will do away with all the royalty *and* all their heirs." She leaned in close enough for their breath to mingle and Darius snarled. "There will be no one left to stand in my way."

She stood straight and clasped her hands behind her back. "Now, it is your turn."

"No," the general growled.

The queen sighed. "Very well."

This time three Collectors came in, and it was a long time before Darius stopped bellowing in pain.

Chapter Thirty-Four

"I'm going after Darius." Veni stormed for the door, but Khyan blocked her exit.

"We cannot be rash. We need to get Ester help immediately. And one of us has to go with you." He looked at Henry.

"I'll go with her. Get Ester to safety, Prince." They nodded at one another and Veni pushed past them. "Love." Henry grabbed her arm. "We need provisions. It's a long trek and I'm certain Nuria is already on her way. Get Ester ready and I'll acquire what we need. We'll leave in an hour."

An hour was far longer than she was willing to wait, but her father was right. Nuria was probably on her way, and Ester needed medical help. At least they'd agreed to leave before dawn.

They sat huddled behind the inn, not wanting to draw attention with an unconscious child. They'd told the few people they did come across that she was sleeping, but it was clear she was unwell.

"I'll purchase a horse in the next village. We should be in Aureland by late afternoon. I'll send a messenger bird to you as soon as we arri—"

Khyan's words were abruptly cut off by a scream that sounded from in front of the inn. Henry put a finger to his lips and slunk to the front to discover what was going on. When he returned, his face was grim. "Pietro's men have found our trail. This is where we part ways. *Now*."

Henry and Khyan clasped arms. "Maker be with you."

Veni kissed her sister on the forehead. "Be strong,

Sunshine. You're safe now." She hoped with all her might that it was true.

She and her father sprinted into the woods, using the cover of darkness to their advantage. When they broke through the treeline toward the Toulonan border, the wind whipped at their cheeks, making their eyes water.

"I think we can slow for a moment, Love," Henry huffed.

Veni did not want to slow down, but she couldn't see. It wasn't until the sun was beginning to set the following day that the temperature turned more tepid and Veni could almost smell the sand and spices of Toulona.

"Do you know where we're going?"

Henry's brow knit together. "I think so."

Darius was certain he heard the hoot of an owl. He tried with all of his might to open his eyes, but they were swollen nearly shut. He managed to get his finger to move a fraction and he felt something soft. There was a small scraping sound and the softness pressed against his hand. One eye opened enough for him to make out a blurry white shape.

Nuria.

His mother.

He tried to speak but nothing came out. She nuzzled his cheek and there was a slight flash of light. Darius heard a *whoosh* and a thud, then he smelled charred flesh.

"Darius."

Her voice sounded miles away.

"Darius. Darling you must wake. We have only moments, and I can't carry you, my sweet."

The general groaned.

"Darling, I sent word to Luvenia, and she is on her way.

You do not want her to make it all the way here to Pietro."

Darius growled and managed to make it up onto an elbow.

"Your injuries are grievous, but not fatal." Nuria did what she could by way of cleaning and stitching with what they'd been able to procure.

Nuria had disabled three more Collectors, all while hauling a half-conscious general out of the fortress. They'd trekked slowly through the unforgiving sand under the cover of night until they came upon a small village. An inn was too dangerous, so Nuria opted for hiding them in a stable full of camels.

"That was too easy," Darius remarked as she stitched the cut over his eye. "Shouldn't they be after us by now?"

"Yes. It is alarming that we evaded them so easily."

He studied his queen. In truth, he was entirely unsure how to feel about her. "It's all true then?"

Nuria ceased her stitching and let her hands fall to her lap. To her credit, she looked him straight in the eyes. "It is."

Darius' heart sank. Part of him hoped Pietro had been lying. Not because he didn't want Nuria to be his mother, but because he didn't want Nuria to have kept so much from him. "How could you not tell me?"

"I thought keeping you in the dark would keep you safer. I did not know she was aware you are my son."

Darius' traitorous heart warmed at her calling him her son.

"I see that I was so very wrong, Darius."

A memory flashed in his mind, of Luvi's birthday. "I took Luvi to meet Father on her birthday. When we were there, he kept insisting a bird was coming to pay him a visit." Nuria nodded. "You went, then?"

"Yes. After Luvenia's dinner. I visit him as often as I can."

"You truly loved him?"

"I still love him, Darius. With all my heart." She shook her head and looked off in the distance. "I knew the risks of loving a mortal, but we held onto hope. We thought perhaps Hugo could come up with something to make him age more slowly, or some other foolishness."

She sniffed. "But we held onto that ridiculous hope until you were born. I knew then that it was all lost. I would have to lose not only my love, but my son. I sent you both away, with great protest from your father. I set him up with a good life—a good woman—but he hated me for it.

When Pietro killed your mum and drove your father mad, I knew I had to bring you all to Aureland. I thought—I thought she did it to torture me by harming your father. I did not know she knew you were my son. I thought we had been so careful. But we were fools. Blinded by love. Blinded by our perfect little boy."

Darius watched her for a long moment, his heart breaking. Finally, he reached out and took her hand.

"I have not always made the right choices, Darius. But I have always loved you fiercely."

He knew it to be true. "Did Khyan know?"

She nodded, a tear slipping from her eye. "Do not fault my brother. It was my secret and he kept it out of duty and my own wishes. He told me on numerous occasions to tell you."

Darius squeezed her hand. "Pietro isn't after Orford or Anjali, or any mortal place. She's after Aureland. And knows where it is."

Nuria nodded, setting her shoulders. "I was indeed in the

rafters for that conversation."

"What do we do?"

"We prepare for war, my son."

"Darius." Nuria gently shook his shoulder. "Darling, we have to get going. Luvenia and Henry are near."

The general roused at that, but his muscles were stiff, and his entire body screamed with pain.

"They are headed to Pietro. They do not know you are no longer there. We cannot let them get near her."

Darius sat up, gritting his teeth. His vision swam, but he righted himself and stood. "Let's go."

It was slow progress with his injuries and Darius growled regularly, pushing against the pain.

"You need to rest."

"No," he bit out. "We need to intercept Luvi."

Nuria's mouth formed a thin line, but she relented. The sun was unforgiving and the heat suffocating, but they trudged on.

"How did you know where they were?"

"I sent messenger birds to scout for them. They should be close. When we get to that village up ahead, you will rest, and I will fly out to find them and bring them to you."

Darius groaned but he didn't argue. He could see the sandstone buildings on the shifting horizon. As much as he loathed the idea of sitting and waiting, he knew it was to his detriment to keep going. They could miss Luvi or he could succumb to his injuries and not make the trek back to Aureland. "Fine."

Settled in the shade against a blissfully cool wall, Darius sipped from a water skin with great effort and fell in and out of consciousness. After what felt like years, he heard far off voices and a small intake of breath. When he peeled one eye open, his Little Bird was crouched in front of him, one hand on his forehead and the other on his chest.

"Hey, you." His voice came out gravelly.

"Shh. You're burning up, Darius." Luvi turned to Nuria. "He's too hot."

Nuria strode forward and touched his cheek. "He did not have a fever when I left him. We need to hurry." She turned to Henry. "Wait with them here. I will fly into Aureland and bring back…transportation." In an instant Nuria was gone, flying off into the hot sun.

"How did things go in Marche de Blanc?" He expected Luvenia to shush him, but she sat down and took his hand.

"I'll go retrieve some food and water," Henry mumbled and walked away.

Luvenia sighed.

"That good, then?" Darius tried to laugh but it hurt his ribs and turned into a cough.

"You should rest." She put one of her hands in his and stroked his hair with the other. "And you need a bath." Her smile felt like the most potent medicine. He instantly felt better, but also as if he could sleep for ages. "When my father returns, we'll get a room here."

"I don't think that's safe."

"Neither is it safe for you to be sitting here out in the open and in the heat."

She scowled at him, and he chuckled painfully. "Alright."

Once they had him cleaned and in a relatively cool bed, they all took turns explaining the events of the last fortnight.

Henry rubbed his jaw. "An army of *Undead*?"

Darius nodded, propped up on pillows. "Undead. But Ester is safe, that is a massive triumph." He squeezed Luvenia's hand where she sat on the edge of his bed.

"Khyan rushed her to Aureland." She swallowed. "There's one more thing." Luvenia looked at Henry and he nodded once.

"Best to let him know what he's gotten himself into now."

Darius' brow crumpled as he looked between them. "What is it?"

"I—" She fiddled with a loose thread on the bed sheets. "Well, my father is—"

"We are the rightful heirs to the throne of Orford," Henry finished for her.

"Yes. That."

Darius smiled wide. "You're not serious." Luvenia nodded with a grimace. "I can think of no family more perfect for—" Darius' face contorted. "Wait a moment. Pietro mentioned the immune girl...you...that your bloodline was immune because she used it to create the Venom."

Henry came closer. "She used King Alestair's blood to make the Venom?" He blew out a breath and ran a hand through his hair. "I did wonder why we were both immune. What else did she tell you?"

"She's after Aureland. The terrorizing of the other countries has all been a ploy to gather an army to storm Aureland."

"She said this?" Henry pressed.

"Not exactly, but it was heavily inferred. Nuria was in the rafters in her owl form for that *conversation* as well. I don't think we have long until she finds a way in."

"It worries me she volunteered all this information…"

Veni and Darius both nodded their agreement.

"I don't think she expected me to live. What bothers me now is the fact that no one has come after us."

"It's almost as if we're playing right into her hand, isn't it?" Veni spoke up.

Darius sighed heavily. "There is...uh...one more piece of information Pietro told me." Henry and Luvenia looked at him. "Nuria is my mother."

Luvenia gaped and Henry's eyes went wide.

"Everything she's done makes so much more sense now,"

Luvenia mused. "How strange to both have such hidden families."

Darius nodded and squeezed her hand.

A sound came from the window in their room and all of its occupants readied for a fight. They were met with a snowy owl eyeing them incredulously and they breathed a sigh of relief.

Henry let her in and she shifted into the queen. "You look so much better already, darling. We need to get going. I am afraid I had to choose between healer or anonymity, and I selected the latter."

Luvenia had no idea what the queen was talking about, but she was correct. They needed to get out of Toulona and back to Aureland as quickly as possible. There was much at stake and a distinct pit was forming low in her stomach.

"Meet me behind the inn." Nuria shifted back into an owl and flew out the window.

Luvenia helped Darius up, with Henry's assistance, and they exited the inn with as much stealth as they could muster as three foreigners, one bleeding and limping.

"I thought you were bringing transportation," Veni remarked when they stood behind the inn, only endless dunes as far as the eye could see.

Nuria smirked. "Walk forward, Dearheart, hand outstretched."

Veni's heart kicked up the pace, but she obeyed. After a few steps her hand pressed against something invisible. And scaly. She drew back her hand quickly, with a sharp intake of breath. Her eyes were the size of saucers, but a smile slid across her face. "Tell me this isn't Smithwick's dragon."

"It is not." Veni's face fell and Nuria chuckled. "She is mine now." The queen had been walking back and forth, monitoring if they were truly alone. Satisfied that they were, she nodded once to the open space and said, "All, meet Bleu."

The air rippled with an iridescence before revealing a

massive dragon lying in the sand. They all gasped. She was magnificent. Luvenia hadn't seen her since she was a tiny thing, small enough for Smithwick to ride her.

They spent a moment marveling at her grandness before Darius spoke. "*Julian*?"

Luvenia turned to see a man had appeared with the dragon that she didn't know, and Darius was looking at him, confused.

"I am Jasper, General. Julian is still with the heiress north of here."

"Apologies, Jasper. I can't believe I still confuse the two of you."

"You can cloak things." Henry marveled at the Keeper just as much as he had the dragon.

"I can, Your Highness," Jasper answered.

Henry flinched at the title he'd never truly born. "Henry will do, Jasper."

Jasper nodded and disappeared, Bleu with him.

"Climb on, loves," Nuria commanded. "There is no time to waste."

Henry helped Veni and Darius on before clambering on himself. Veni had thought the journey she took to Vilora as a flycatcher had been marvelous but flying high in the clouds as herself was unreal. The beautiful beast was so large, she had them to the portal into Aureland in astounding time.

Upon their arrival, there was a great fuss over them all from Khyan, Sebastian, Thera, and even Dax. The greatest fuss was from Helga, though. The sweet Elfe had two Healers ready for Darius and within two days he was much improved.

As soon as Darius was settled, Veni ran to Ester with Thera.

"I've given her something to soothe her mind. I've not

blocked things out, but it's softening the edges."

"Lionheart," Henry addressed Darius from the doorway of the general's rooms. "You look much improved."

Darius smirked. "It's a wonder what Keeper magic can do. I've promised Luvi I'll stay in this bed until tomorrow and then I will be free to assist in the preparations hands on."

Henry's lips twitched up in a wistful way. "Genevieve always called her that—Luvi."

Darius dipped his chin. "I know. It was my way of honoring your wife."

Henry swallowed. "I appreciate that."

"You know, I never would have thought you'd remember me after we met."

"That was not just any meeting, son."

"You knew who I was then?" Part of his respect for the man sunk. It was one thing to have a life-changing moment with a stranger. It was quite another to hear pretty words from someone that knew all about you and pretended he didn't.

"I did not, no. I meant every word I said, and that day changed me as well, Darius. Meeting you, I could see your potential, your heart, just in a simple conversation. But the things I said to you, they were wholly true, and they reminded me who I was. Who I'm supposed to be.

I lost a lot of that when I turned my back on my family. I knew it was to keep them safe, but surely there had been another way." Henry ran a hand through his hair. "I'm not sure if there was or not, but I had to find a way to remember who I was and what I was fighting for. You did that for me."

Darius cleared his throat, fidgeting in the bed. "I see who you are. Luvi will see it too, in time."

Henry's eyes crinkled at the edges. "We're getting there." He came forward and handed a stack of papers to the general. "I have to leave and ensure my men in Orford are prepared and assembled. Sebastian thinks we have mere days."

"Does he have more information?"

"It's all there. I will return in two days. Take care of my daughter, Lionheart."

"Of course, sir."

They'd made an agreement that they would not refer to one another as *prince* of anything. Not until they saw Pietro defeated once and for all. Henry left and Darius woefully looked over Sebastian's notes, as well as all the others from his Hordemen. Pietro had no intention of hiding her imminent strike, but the how of it was a mystery. There were Collectors and creatures aplenty, but there was no stir. Still, Sebastian insisted the verbiage he heard from her inclined him to believe it was very soon.

She had to have known Darius escaped relatively quickly, but she hadn't sent anyone after him. Or had she? Thera had said the Enenra followed the heiress and that led them to believe they might be following Dax. But he hadn't used a flame big enough for them to emerge. Though, they'd come forth in Aureland just after Dax left. And they'd attempted to attack Nuria first. Enenra—spirit creatures unseen by most and able to move from flame to flame… They were watching. And they did Pietro's bidding.

Darius shot out of bed, papers flying and ran into the hallway. He nearly bowled Luvenia over, barely catching her by the shoulders before they both would have tumbled to the ground.

She laughed. "Where's the fire?"

"That's the problem." He grabbed her hand and pulled her down the hallway. "We need to get to Nuria."

"What's happened? What's wrong?"

Darius cursed, looking around wildly. He halted in his tracks and pulled Luvi to a stop next to him. "I need you to find Smithwick. Tell him to check the Gates with a Seer. It's the Enenra. They've been watching us and they're in

Aureland. Tell him to get a message to your father, too."

His words sent fear coursing through Luvenia and the dread she'd been mulling over for days settled surely in her gut. They ran in opposite directions, Veni shouting Smithwick's name, and Darius sprinting toward his mother's council chambers.

Chapter Thirty-Five

The room was stiff with the unknown. Clouded with apprehension.

"They've assembled," Smithwick went on from the middle of the table.

Luvenia looked into the faces of almost everyone she held dear. Nuria at the head of the table, her father at the other end. Khyan and Thera—his hand came to rest on her shoulder at Smithwick's words. Dax to Thera's right and Sebastian next to him. Lydigen, Sillow, and Emperor Nakamura. She knew in her bones it was the last time they would all sit around the same table. A tremor went through her and Darius took her hand under the table.

"This is Lucy." Smithwick gestured to a lovely woman the color of a summer sky. "She is the best Seer of the unseen in Aureland. Lucy, dear, please inform them of what you saw."

Lucy rose and blinked her violet eyes, obviously ill at ease, but her voice was clear when she spoke. "In Toulona, outside the Aureland Gate, there are thousands of Undead creatures wrapped in tattered linens." The air in the room stilled. "In Orford there are Collectors as well as terrifying beasts with horns and claws—black as night." She swallowed hard. "In Anjali there are Warmongers and Collectors. "And Vilora—" Dax took Thera's hand as Lucy went on. "The king's army is assembled."

A collective murmur spread through the room. "*Silence*," Nuria commanded.

"But there are also terrible beasts. They look li—like they

used to be men."

Like the one Veni and Darius fought in Dakterra. Akio said something in Anjalian, but it didn't take a translator to know it was a colorful swear.

"I don't think the king's army can see them," Lucy finished.

"General." Darius straightened as Nuria addressed him. "Why would the king's army be assembled? Are they friend or foe?"

"Lucy," Darius spoke to her instead. "They can't see the beasts, but are they cloaked in invisibility like the other forces?"

Lucy shook her head. "No. Smithwick could see them as well."

"Friend," Henry announced. "My men have been spreading. Anjali was torn apart, so many had plans to make it to Vilora. It sounds as if they have."

Thera breathed an audible sigh of relief. Luvenia wondered if the king and queen had sent their army to protect their daughter. The look upon Thera's face led Veni to believe she also wondered if they were capable of such a thing.

Nuria rose and Lucy sat. "The time has come to stand our guard. We believe the Enenra will be the first line of attack. We must ensure every available Portal Key is at the ready and send a mandate that fires are not to be used, nor torches. Candles and small lanterns will have to suffice until this is over."

Darius looked at Lydigen and he nodded, understanding the mandate was his duty.

"General, I defer to you on where you would like our men placed."

Darius squeezed Veni's hand and rose. "Theralin, you and Dax will lead a troop of men to Viridian." They both nodded. "Emperor Nakamura, you and Sillow will take men to stand at the Anjalian Gate. Khyan and Sebastian, you take the Orford Gate." He looked at Henry. "Liberator, your men are ready in Orford?"

He nodded. "They're in the mountains near the Gate."

"Good. You and I will hold the castle." Darius looked at Luvenia. "You're with me."

Nuria sat with one eyebrow cocked. "And what about me?"

"Jasper will keep you hidden."

"Like hell he will." Everyone's eyes widened at Nuria's words. "I will not have my home ransacked without a fight. I will take to the skies with Bleu."

Nearly everyone opened their mouths to object, but she silenced them.

"What of Toulona, General?" Lydigen spoke up. "I will take it."

"So will I." They all turned to the opening door across the council chamber.

"*Naiheeli*," Henry, Thera, and Nuria all whispered at once.

"As will I." Femi strode into the room next to the druid oracle.

"Why can't I have a fire? It's cold in here. Could I have some more of that delicious soup?"

Veni's eyes filled at the ceaseless prattling of her sister that she never thought she'd hear again. "You can't have a fire because there are dangerous things that can come through the fire right now, but we are going to take care of it. It's not that cold in here." She unfolded another blanket and covered Ester. "And yes, I'll send someone for soup for you."

"Could you send Helga? I just love her."

Veni chuckled. "Of course I will."

Ester smiled and snuggled into her blankets. The Aureland Healers had done wonders for her wounds, but her mind was another matter. For now, Thera and Hugo had worked together to charm a lavender locket that Ester wore. Luvenia had slowly begun to tell her sister the truth of things in a way fitting for a child. The problem was the horrors she endured were fitting for no one, the least of all a child. It would be a long, long road. For the time being, Ester was simply content to enjoy being with Luvenia again and the lavender locket's magic was strong.

"It's time, Love." Henry stood in the doorway. When he noticed Ester was awake, he came and planted a kiss on her head. "You look well, beautiful girl." Ester beamed. She didn't know who exactly Henry was, but she'd taken to him instantly.

Veni kissed Ester on her forehead and handed her a few books. "I think you'll like these." She ruffled her hair. "I'll send for your soup and Helga will keep you company. Stay in this room no matter what. Okay, Sunshine?"

She nodded and took up a book, humming in the worry-free way of a child with nothing to fear. Luvenia hoped with all her might it was true.

"If no one starts a fire, the Enenra won't be able to come and Pietro's forces won't get in, right?" Veni asked her father as they walked.

"Someone will start a fire. There's always at least one fool."

"And in defeating the Enenra, all the Portal Keys will manage to open the Gates?"

"That's how I understand it, yes."

Darius met them in the courtyard and kissed Luvenia's cheek. "Ready to stand watch?"

They both nodded, sullen. Henry took front and center, standing in the middle of the bridge leading to the front of the castle. Veni and Darius stood with a dozen or so Hordeman—all that could be spared—within the castle's outer wall.

Nuria patrolled the skies on Bleu and Khyan routinely flew overhead to berate her for it. When the sun dipped behind the skyline, the prince returned to his post and hoped his sister would leave the skies.

Sure enough, a fool lit a fire.

Screams pierced the night and Thera took a dagger in one hand and her Portal Key in another. Dax drew his sword and reached in his pocket for his own Key.

"Keys ready!" Theralin shouted to the Hordemen behind them.

Keys ready, they advanced toward the sound. Thera's mouth fell open and Dax cursed when they broke from the tree line and saw the Viridian village engulfed in flames. Corbin and many other Viridian residents stood in the rows of Hordemen, watching their homes burn.

"Open your Keys," Thera screamed. They took off at a run, the sounds of crushing glass, breaking metal, and ripping leather as their ballad. Blinding light shot forth and as they neared, the Enenra hissed and screeched. Their smoke and fury forms twisted and clawed at their sightless, hollow eyes until they dispersed with shrieks.

But they were too late. The light of their Keys had opened the Gate.

Dax cursed and Thera looked to where his gaze was fixed on the coast of Viridian Bay. Thousands of creatures, man-like in their essence but twisted and bent, clawed their way out of the water and onto dry land. There were Viloran soldiers, too, sputtering and grappling with the creatures in the water and on the sand.

Even the Merpeople had come to drag under all they could, but it was not enough.

"Hold your ground!" Thera shouted.

She could feel the troop's fear. Feel their confusion and desire to flee.

"Hold your ground!" she shouted again. "This is your

home, and no one is taking it from you!"

Maker, she hoped that was true.

Thud. Thud. Thud.

"What is that?" Sebastian looked at Khyan.

"They can't break through the Gate by brute force."

"Why can we hear them pushing against it, then?"

"Lucy." The Keeper came forward. "What do you see?"

Lucy closed her eyes. "I—I can't tell. They look like they're coalescing around a Portal Key."

"Can they strengthen the power of a single Key to let more than a few people in?" Sebastian asked.

Khyan ran a hand through his hair. "It's unlikely. Perhaps if they have a few Keys and a powerful Keeper…"

"Lilith is extremely powerful."

Fire flared behind Khyan's eyes. "Then if they make it through, she's with them." And he would immensely enjoy killing her.

"Can you See anything, Naiheeli?" Femi whispered in the night.

"Not a whit. It's dark."

Femi scoffed. This was no time for the ornery druid matron's dry wit. "I meant as Oracle."

"Oh. No."

"What if they don't come through?"

"They will."

"Did you See something?"

"Stop asking me that. No. Pietro no doubt has a secondary plan. This is the Great War after all."

Just then, a scream sounded from the front lines. Then

another, and another. An acrid smell filled the air up ahead and Femi inched forward until Naiheeli threw her back with surprising force. The Oracle lit a small lantern and surged forward into the screams. The men were writhing on the ground in some unseen nightmare, but several walked forward mindlessly toward the Gate, hands outstretched with Portal Keys.

"No," she whispered. But Naiheeli was too late.

A line of Collectors stepped forward, chained beasts of terror in tow. From them emanated the horrible smelling toxin. Every Hordeman and Keeper the fumes neared fell down in terror.

There had to be a way to stop it. Naiheeli blocked out sight and sound to reach into the far recesses of her mind. Of her training in Caim Undara—the realm of healing. A distant proverb landed in her memory. *Come face to face with your fears and no more power will they hold.*

Naiheeli turned back to where Femi was stationed behind a tree, eyes wide and looking past the druid.

Creatures wrapped in linen and devoid of true life came forth through the Gate.

"Femi," she took the heiress by her shoulders. "Look at me." The girl was in shock. Naiheeli slapped her hard across the face, finally gaining her attention. "We need to force the cloud of toxin back toward them. We need to light as many fires as we can."

"But the Enenra. The general said no fires."

"I know that. I think the Enenra will mingle with the smoke of the beasts and turn their fear on them."

Femi needed no more instruction. She ran to the closest Hordeman and told him the plan. It spread like wildfire, and they began breaking down branches to build a gargantuan fire and several smaller ones. Femi and Naiheeli set a group of people to constructing as many fans as quickly as they possibly could with anything available.

The Enenra came forth within moments, set intently on the Hordemen, until one lonely, makeshift fan sent the Enenra's smoke mingling with the fear toxin. A few of the beasts screeched, writhing in agony and terror until they hit the ground.

Femi yelped, but too many Hordemen were still going down. A Keeper rushed forward to Naiheeli. "My gifting is wind."

Naiheeli's eyes widened. "My child you have found your great calling."

The man nodded and blew with all his might. The fires sputtered but remained alight, and the Enenra slammed into the smoke of the fear toxin, driving Collectors and beasts mad.

The Undead staggered against the wind but kept coming. The fear toxin had no effect on them.

The Anjalian Gate held. Until it didn't.

There was a scratching sound on the other side of the trees, in mid-air.

"I can't blasted see in this dark," the emperor snarled. "I need to *see*."

He reached for his lantern, and Lydigen lunged. "No!"

But it was too late. Akio had turned the lantern up and just enough smoke curled out the top before Lydigen snuffed it out. An Enenra whorled along the tendrils of smoke and hissed. It grew larger and larger, clawing with unseen talons into the Hordemen until several opened their Portal Keys, blinding the smog creature with their light.

There was a beat of silence before the pounding of boots

shook the ground.

"Hordemen!" Lydigen shouted. "Stand your ground! Keepers! Give them hell!"

Darius stood absolutely still. Armed to the teeth and lethal in his stance. Henry rocked back and forth on the bridge, flexing and unflexing his hands around the hilts of his twin blades. Veni paced. She couldn't hold still. Not with the gnawing, looming travesty close at hand.

They were in. Pietro's men and beasts were within the sacred Gates of Aureland. She could feel it.

When Nuria swooped down upon her dragon and landed in the courtyard, Veni knew she was right.

"They are here. They are within our Gates. Nakamura fares the worst. I will go help them. Guard the castle, my darlings."

"Nuria, no." Darius rushed forward. "I don't think that's wise. You need to stay here. Protect the castle."

"I will return, my son." She kissed Darius on the cheek and ran a tender hand down Luvenia's face. "Fear not."

She hopped back onto Bleu and flew toward Anjali.

"I can't sit here and wait," Darius growled.

Henry came forward. "This land is yours to rule one day whether you like it or not. There will be a lot of waiting and there will be a lot of strategic maneuvering. Remain steady."

Darius' jaw clenched and unclenched. He wasn't a Keeper. Nuria would far outlive him. He would never have to rule Aureland. But the man was right. Just because peace had reigned for so long within their realm, and just because he hadn't had to lead a true battle as general, didn't mean he needn't learn how to do so correctly. It was now or never. He

resumed his position.

Thera bellowed, sending her knife into the skull of a half-man beast. She sliced the stomach of another, rotting innards falling at her feet as she pivoted away from yet another.

Dax grappled with two of the beasts not far away. He managed to slice the head off of one as a Viloran soldier gutted the other.

Two Vilorans came up behind Thera, turning their backs to her and each other, forming a tri-horned adversary. They advanced, cutting down the beasts, until they reached the waterline and Collectors swam forth, their obsidian uniforms slick with the sea. Thera's beautiful sea. She let out a guttural cry and surged forward, slicing, parrying, and kicking. She cut through three Collectors' tubes before using her sword to decapitate another.

There were too many, even for the Raven, and she knew she had to fall back. They needed another plan.

The Gate opened and Khyan let out a piercing war cry.

The Hordemen and Keepers launched forward with no need for further instruction. The Collectors readied their Venom tubes, piercing anyone within their vicinity as they stalked forward. Khyan dodged and hacked, eyes searching for Pietro.

Sebastian thundered past him, vengeance contorting his features, and Khyan knew she'd been spotted. The man howled and ran forward, his dagger poised to strike. Khyan slowed, sending his sword into a Collector and pulling it out, only to send it into the chest of a Warmonger. The man was hardly even of age and Khyan's stomach roiled.

He tore his eyes from the fallen boy and searched frantically for Sebastian in the chaos. When he finally saw him, he was prowling around Lilith, a sick smile on both their faces.

"Well, well, well," she crowed. "My toy has betrayed me."

Sebastian snarled, baring his teeth. "I've plotted your murder since the day you took me out of Greer's." He stalked forward. "Now I will have my vengeance."

Khyan watched as the area around them cleared. Something wasn't right.

"Sebastian!" he called out, but his friend couldn't hear him.

Lilith tipped her head back, her black crown slipping to the side, and laughed. Sebastian inched closer, his knife ready, but the queen snapped. A wicked little grin adorned her lips just before a Collector ripped open and Sebastian hit the ground, screaming. Khyan lunged for him before rearing back. He couldn't intake the fear toxin.

Nuria hid in the clouds. Her cover of night was no longer an option now that half of Aureland was in flames and torches were lit everywhere to better view their attackers.

Below, Enenra clawed unseen at the lay people, Collectors released fear toxin to torment her people, beasts prowled, the Undead consumed Keepers, and somewhere, in all the chaos, Lilith Pietro was attempting to take Nuria's land.

The queen ground her teeth together and urged Bleu lower. "Light them up, my darling."

Bleu needed no more instructions. She flew dangerously low to the trees and torched Collectors, beasts, and Undead alike. The magnificent dragon knew precisely who to burn and who to leave alive. She was extraordinary. The Keepers broke their Portal Keys, sending blinding light to expel the Enenra that rose from the fires, and the residents of Aureland began to see a fighting chance yet.

When numbers of the enemies became manageable in some areas, Nuria returned to the castle, for she knew Pietro would not fall back so easily. She wanted Nuria's throne, and she would stop at nothing to get it.

Bleu landed in the courtyard with a ground-shaking thud and Darius rushed forward. "Are you alright?"

"I am fine, darling. Bleu here has done us an astounding bit of good. We might triumph after all." She smiled and Darius' shoulders lost a fraction of their tension.

"I will go and assist my brother now. I merely wanted you to know I was alright."

"No," Darius protested. "Please, stay here with us. Let Jasper hide you."

"Darius—"

"Mother, please."

Nuria's heart cracked, but she was shaking her head. Veni knew one way to make the queen stay, though.

"Protect Ester," she said. "She is alone in her room with Helga. Please, protect Ester."

Nuria nodded once. She took Darius' face in her hands and pulled him down until she could kiss his forehead. She did the same to Luvenia and dipped her chin in respect to Henry.

"To Ester." The queen strode into the castle.

There were too many. And Lilith had vanished. Fear gripped Khyan's very soul. There was no way the Orford Queen would battle out there. She wanted the throne.

Khyan looked amongst the bloody chaos for her, but she was nowhere to be seen. He shifted into owl form and took to the skies. He searched for too many precious moments and almost gave up before he spotted her. There was a circle of Collectors around her, and she was nearing the castle.

Quickly. Too quickly.

"Keepers!" Thera roared, her voice raw. "Do your worst!"

Men and women rushed forward from the fray, some with hands splayed, others with weapons. Boils broke out on one beast, as another burst into flame. A Warmonger covered his ears and another vomited. The impact of the Keepers' gifts gave her an idea. A brilliant, risky, potentially terrible idea.

"Dax!" She ran about, shouting his name until he approached, bloody and panting. "Dax." She took precious seconds to kiss him, ignoring the rank stench of the beast blood on his face. "I need your help."

"Anything." The gleam in his eyes made her knees inappropriately weak.

"I'm going to find a Keeper gifted with sleep. And then I need you to make these beasts dream."

Dax's returning smile was manic and villainous. "Yes."

Thera asked everyone in sight if they knew of a Keeper with the gift to make others sleep. After too many moments, a young girl stepped forward. "I can do it."

Thera's heart constricted. "How old are you?"

"Thirteen."

"I cannot ask you to do this."

"Then don't. I'm doing it anyway."

Thera watched as the girl stepped onto a rock jutting out of the sea and sang. It was gut-wrenching and horribly beautiful. Even the Aureland residents were swaying on their feet by the time she was done, but the beasts and Collectors were snoring on the beach.

"Dax," Thera whispered. "Make them dream."

Khyan soared through the clouds, surpassing Pietro and landing in the castle courtyard on human feet.

"She's near," he panted. "She's coming."

Veni turned to take up her position, but Darius grabbed her wrist, pulling her to him. He kissed her hard, everything they'd faced, and everything to come unsaid within that moment. He pulled back and looked fiercely into her eyes. "Just in case."

Tears crowded her throat, but there was no time for emotion. They had a queen to kill. They took up their stations just as the sound of heels clicking on stone sounded across the bridge.

"Oh, dearest darling," Nuria murmured. "Luvenia will be back shortly."

"Could you read it again?" Ester's eyes were nearly closed, but still she resisted sleep. Nuria worried the monsters behind her eyes were too much for even Thera's magical amulet.

"Of course, my sweet."

"You remind me of my mummy."

Nuria's heart cracked, and she could not stop the tear that escaped her eye. Her entire world was fighting beyond the walls of the castle, and she was not there to help them. She could, however, comfort this precious broken soul. "Lie down, sweetheart. Let me tell you a new story."

Nuria told her of a fierce woman with a love for her children that knew no bounds. A woman that gave everything to see her loves safe and happy. She told Ester of a man that lost it all, just to give his children freedom. She told her of a girl who faced horrors to bring her sister home. Of a sister who would face anything to let her Sunshine *live*.

Ester's eyes fluttered shut at last and Nuria tucked her in.

She kissed her forehead just as she had with Darius and Luvenia, and she rose to look out the window at her burning land.

"I believe you've taken something from me."

Nuria whirled around to find Shiv standing in the doorway, his Venomous needle in hand dripping. Nuria hadn't even heard a cry of alarm.

"And what would that be, Collector?"

"*Chief* Collector," he corrected. "And *that*." He pointed to Ester.

"I am afraid no being belongs to another, *Chief*."

His mouth twisted. "Everyone belongs to my queen." He stalked forward and all Nuria could think was how much she pitied the man. He took another step toward Ester and Nuria shot fire at his half-masked face.

"Matthias, Matthias, Matthias." Pietro tisked. "Hello, Brother."

"I am not your brother." Henry raised his sword to her eye level. "And you will not leave here alive."

The queen inspected her fingernails briefly before waving her men forward. But they were ready. Henry took down four Collectors on his own before Veni could blink. The rest surged past him and Darius was on them in an instant, Khyan at his side disabling Venom packs. The Hordemen battled the remaining few and Pietro slipped right past them, stalking toward Luvenia.

"You are a sight to behold." She reached out to touch the end of her braid and Luvenia sliced her arm with her dagger. Lilith only laughed. "The immune girl. The heir to my throne." She held up her dagger-sharp nails to Luvenia's cheek. "Now, we can't have that."

Veni thrust a fist out toward the queen's face and connected with her jaw. She balked as bits of charred alabaster skin drifted off in the breeze. Pietro snarled and launched for her again, but Veni kicked her in the chest, hard enough to knock the breath out of her. The queen withdrew a thin dagger, lethally pointed end poised to strike Veni, but she whirled away just in time. The dagger came down on the stones with a piercing clang. Pietro's eyes were wild when she lunged again. Despite all her powers, despite her madness and insanity, she was not a trained fighter like Luvenia.

She came forward, fist raised, and landed a blow that knocked the queen back. Veni watched in horror as her face broke apart at the jaw like porcelain. A gaping hole was left behind, but Pietro kept coming, her sneer all the more disturbing.

Veni bounced on the balls of her feet, prepared to land another blow to her fragile face, when the queen's hand shot forth at inhuman speed. She grabbed Veni's braid and yanked until she had the girl in her clutches.

Veni kicked behind her and spun away, but the hold on her braid was tight and she did not expect the knife that surged for her abdomen. But her father had.

Henry Rousseau threw himself in between his daughter and the killing blow. The dagger landed deeply, too deeply, in his chest and he slumped to the ground.

Lilith cackled as Henry bled out onto the stones and Luvenia screamed. She slid across the ground and took her father's hand in hers. "No. No, no, no. Please. Please."

The Orford Queen bent down and rested her hand on Henry's forehead, using up the last of her Touch of Death before scurrying back, a crack sliding down the right side of her face.

"It's alright, Love. Finish this." Henry breathed his last and Luvenia rose with a fury she'd never known she could possess.

She stalked toward the mocking queen, prepared to do

whatever it took to see the demise of this woman. Luvenia threw fist after fist, cracking Lilith's body. Blood spilled from her lip and eyebrow, but still she laughed and still Veni attacked.

Nails sliced across Veni's cheek and down her arm, but she felt nothing. Nothing but the loss of the father she'd just gained back.

The courtyard grew eerily silent as Veni locked eyes with the queen. The source of all their horrors. The killer of her mother. Her father. Her grandfather. The source of Darius' father's madness and the reason Nuria had to hide her son. The reason Ester was broken. Luvenia withdrew her last jeweled throwing knife.

When Pietro smirked, she ran for her, jumping in the air and kicking her square in the chest until she fell backwards, her skull cracking on the stones. Luvenia stepped over her, landing one boot squarely on her chest. The queen groaned and coughed a bit of blood, yet still she smiled. Luvenia crouched down and put the tip of her knife to the hollow of her neck. Lilith Pietro's eyes sparkled and Luvenia knew it would only take one motion. One thrust of her hand, and it would all be over. This queen that hid behind her dark, twisted creations would finally be dead.

Luvenia heard Darius' footsteps. She would not be like this monster. Never again.

"Bind her."

"Are you certain?" Darius' voice held no censure, nor judgement.

"I'm certain."

Darius and Khyan bound the Queen of Orford as Veni wept over her father's lifeless body. They tied Lilith to a post and sent men to watch over her while they surveyed the castle and the battles that were still raging.

When Luvenia looked up from her father's lifeless face, she locked eyes with the queen across the courtyard once more.

She blinked and Lilith Pietro's gaze never left hers as her body broke apart like pottery crashing to the floor, and the pieces floated off in the wind like ash.

Veni's mouth fell open and a hush permeated the whole of Aureland. There was a heartbeat, and then a cry of triumph that shook the very realm pierced the sky. She closed her eyes against the tears of relief, until she remembered her sister.

"Ester."

She ordered a Hordeman to guard her father's body until she returned. Veni shot through the castle, her heart in her throat as she witnessed Keeper and Hordeman alike slumped on the floor. Some were unconscious and others were hacked to pieces. She ran as quickly as she could, up and up until she reached Ester's hallway.

Bodies littered the hallway in pools of Venom and there were burn marks on the doorframe. "No. No…"

Veni rounded the corner to see Darius slumped over a body. A sob threatened to escape her throat and she hit the ground next to him.

"Nuria," she breathed.

"Oh, Dearheart."

Blood was oozing from her mouth and a terrible gash on her abdomen. Darius sat bowed over his mother. She tried to lift her hand to his face, but she was too weak. Veni leaned forward and took her hand gently. She placed it in Darius' hand and Veni took the other. They both cradled each of her hands against their cheek.

"My son. You will rule Aureland with an unmatched ferocity."

"I'm not a Keeper. I can't rule." Tears slid down his cheeks.

"You carry Keeper blood." She shifted her eyes to Veni.

"And so do you. You have nothing to fear."

"Please don't go," Darius choked out.

"Tell your father I love him."

Khyan rushed in then and fell to his knees. "Sister."

"Oh, my precious Brother. You have all been my greatest treasure. Please, tell Theralin and Sebastian my love outweighs the sun."

Khyan leaned down to kiss her cheek and Darius did the same. Nuria's eyes fluttered shut and it was a long time before they all ceased weeping.

"Veni?" Ester spoke groggily from the bed.

Veni jumped up, swiping at her tears. "Hey, Sunshine. It's not quite morning yet, you should lie back down."

It was then that she saw the lifeless body of Shiv on the other side of Ester's bed. The little girl rested back on her pillows and closed her eyes. A fresh wave of tears came to Luvenia. "She died protecting my sister."

Khan's lips parted and Darius leaned over his mother and wept.

Alban, Orford, Three Days Later

Luvenia Rousseau stood behind a curtained platform, knees weak and hands trembling. Darius murmured comforts in her ear, but she didn't hear them, not over the beating of her own heart.

"Veni." Khyan appeared through the curtain. "Everyone is assembled." He took one look at her green face and smiled kindly. "You can do this."

She nodded and stepped forward beyond the curtain. The sea of faces made her stomach roil, but Darius stood to her left and Khyan to her right. She cleared her throat and spoke.

"People of Orford." Darius smiled with pride and her courage swelled. "Your tyrant queen is dead." A bone chilling hush spread through the crowd. "So has your rightful king." She let the words hang for a moment, allowing herself to feel them as she wished the people to. "Lilith Pietro was a fraud. Matthias Cornwall, whom many of you know as Henry Rousseau, or the Liberator and Leader of the Zealots—"

Veni was cut off by gasps and whispers. She rose her voice over the din. "He was the rightful heir of Alestair and Millicent Cornwall. He was struck down in the pursuit to overthrow your wicked queen—his wretched step-sister." Remembering that fateful moment filled her with boldness and she stepped forward, her voice growing louder. "I am Matthias Cornwall's only heir." A collective gasp permeated the air and Veni wondered if she'd made a grave mistake.

Then, a thud sounded as knees hit the packed dirt. The crowd knelt before her. Her lips parted and Veni began to step backward at the sight of the first rows of people kneeling, but Darius put a strong hand to her back, and she stood straight, lifting her chin.

Thousands of people knelt in fealty to her. "All hail the queen!" someone in the crowd shouted, and it was echoed by everyone in attendance.

Three Years Later

"Luvi I cannot believe you've given us twins." Darius huffed a laugh in disbelief.

Khyan ran a finger down the cheek of one babe. "They're Keepers, too. The both of them." Darius and Veni looked at him in shock and he smirked.

Thera walked in with Sebastian and screeched. Everyone shushed her and she apologized. "Wait. There are two of them? How marvelous!" Her face fell. "I only brought one set of throwing knives, though. Now they'll have to share." Thera pouted and Veni laughed.

"You brought throwing knives for our infant children, Theralin?" She shrugged at Darius.

"Twins," Sebastian marveled. "You were awfully round."

Veni punched him in the arm.

"Have you thought of names?" Ester beamed, peering over Darius' shoulder.

Darius looked at Luvenia. "Well, Luvi?"

"Henry Darius for this one." Luvenia planted a kiss on the boy's tuft of hair.

Jacob came forward, peering at the babes. "He does look a bit like Father, doesn't he?"

Luvenia smiled up at her brother and reached out to squeeze his hand. His detox from Pietro's control had been tumultuous, but their reconciliation as siblings had been easy. "He does."

Darius kissed his daughter sweetly on her head. "I say Nurianta Genevieve for this one."

My Dearest Reader,

I hope with all of my heart that you enjoyed this book. It is one of my greatest dreams realized to publish a novel, and this—the first of many—was such a beautiful, life-giving journey for me to pen.

I am of the persuasion that many don't know how they feel until they begin to speak it, or in my case—begin to write. Therefore, much of my heart and soul is in ink upon these pages and I desire for the words to ignite something in you.

Something that lets you know you are loved, treasured, and valuable. Something that causes you to realize you are not just a bag of bones. You are an unstoppable force of life with a lion heart. YOU are amethyst within the broken out bits of a tree. YOU are the gem of unimaginable price, simply because of *who you are.*

I would adore hearing from you. Be it a review on Amazon—which basically feeds my family, by the way—an email, an Instagam direct message or photo tag, a stop by my shop, Wicked Whimsy, a visit to my blog…wheresoever you wish. I cannot wait to continue this magical journey with you all.

Much love and fairy dust,

JL

Instagram: wickedvampa
Email: vampajl@gmail.com
Blog/Website:www.jlvampa.com www.wickedwhimsyboutique.com

Acknowledgments

Jac- I am so thankful for you. For your endless love and support in the pursuit of my dreams. For all your sacrifice to see them come to pass, no matter how crazy. For all the munchkin wrangling, meals cooked, and shopping done so mommy can write. For your creative genius and silly jokes. For all the tears and fears calmed. For giving me our sweet babies. For leading our Night Court. For fearlessly serving our family and taking us on crazy adventures we'll never forget. Let's get divorced so I can marry you again and when I die you better get in the coffin with me.

Bram & Wren-There are not enough words in all the languages of the universe to express my love for you, and to remind you how proud I am to be your mommy. You interrupted my writing, added gibberish words to this book, inspired much of it, and there is no one else I wish to make proud than the two of you and your daddy.

Mama- You've endured with grace and poise what would have easily crumpled others. You taught me strength, mercy, and the importance of placing others before myself. You've been Jesus to the least of these, especially me and mine. There simply is nothing more valuable in all the world than that.

KayleighAnne- You've never given up on me. Even when I deserved it. You, my dearest friend, have seen my darkness and loved me despite it. Your beauty is truly and deeply unmatched. No one in all the world compares. No one. HLM forever.

Amy-Thank you for seeing this book in its original form and then sending me that first DM. You went from a first reader to a great friend to a writer buddy to the best CP and one of my most treasured companions on this planet. Cheers!

Katelyn Sybella- Thank you for the endless emotional support of your resident Enneagram 4. For our shared hatred of almost everything, and for being the best thing I've ever found on the internet, stalked, and became BFF with.

To my first readers- YOU guys are the real MVP. You're the reason I finished this story. You're the reason I kept going and wrote the second, third, fourth, and now fifth book in my arsenal. I'm deeply indebted to you .

Made in the USA
Coppell, TX
18 September 2021